A PERFECTLY PARANORMAL HALLOWEEN

A PERFECTLY PARANORMAL ANTHOLOGY VOLUME 2

LEISL LEIGHTON   MARNIE ST CLAIR

SAMANTHA MARSHALL   HELLUCY HOWE

LOVE PNR? JOIN OUR PERFECTLY PARANORMAL PARAMOURS FACEBOOK GROUP

If you want to get to know the Perfectly Paranormal Anthology authors a bit more, get sneak peeks of what's coming up as well as giveaways, special offers and just some PNR fun, then join our Perfectly Paranormal Paramours Facebook Group.

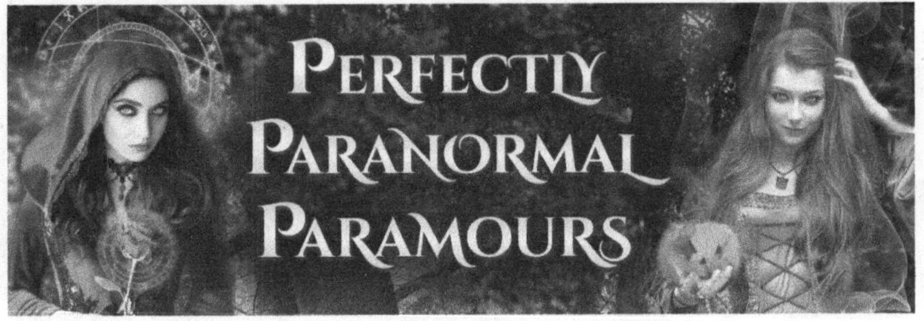

Find us here:

https://www.facebook.com/groups/251663560162131

CONTENTS

SOUL CURSED

LEISL LEIGHTON

SOUL CURSED

A Gods Cursed Novella
Book 2

Leisl Leighton

Published by Leisl Leighton as Permien Press. For more information, email: leisl@leislleighton.com

First published 2021 in the A Perfectly Paranormal Halloween Anthology. Republished 2022 as a single title novella by Permien Press.

Cover design – Samantha Marshall; Editor – Marnie St Clair

❀ Created with Vellum

ABOUT SOUL CURSED

A soul cursed, a love discovered, an evil unbound ...

Immortal witch Korinna Soteira has spent almost 2,000 years trying to save the souls lost when she failed to stop Mt Vesuvius from exploding. Except, what she needs is a spell and a magical gem, both forgotten in time.

When Tamuel, the betraying cupid she once loved, turns up in the Underworld with the very items she needs to set things right, she thinks the Fates are having a good laugh. Especially given he's on a quest to win his mother and father their happy ever after – something he's been cursed never to have for himself. But she won't let the meddling Fates get the best of her. She can work with the annoyingly attractive cupid if she has to.

However, the Fates aren't finished playing with Korinna and Tamuel, and if they are to complete their quests, they must face up to one of the most dangerous witches of all time – a witch who will play their fears against them and make them sacrifice everything, even their love.

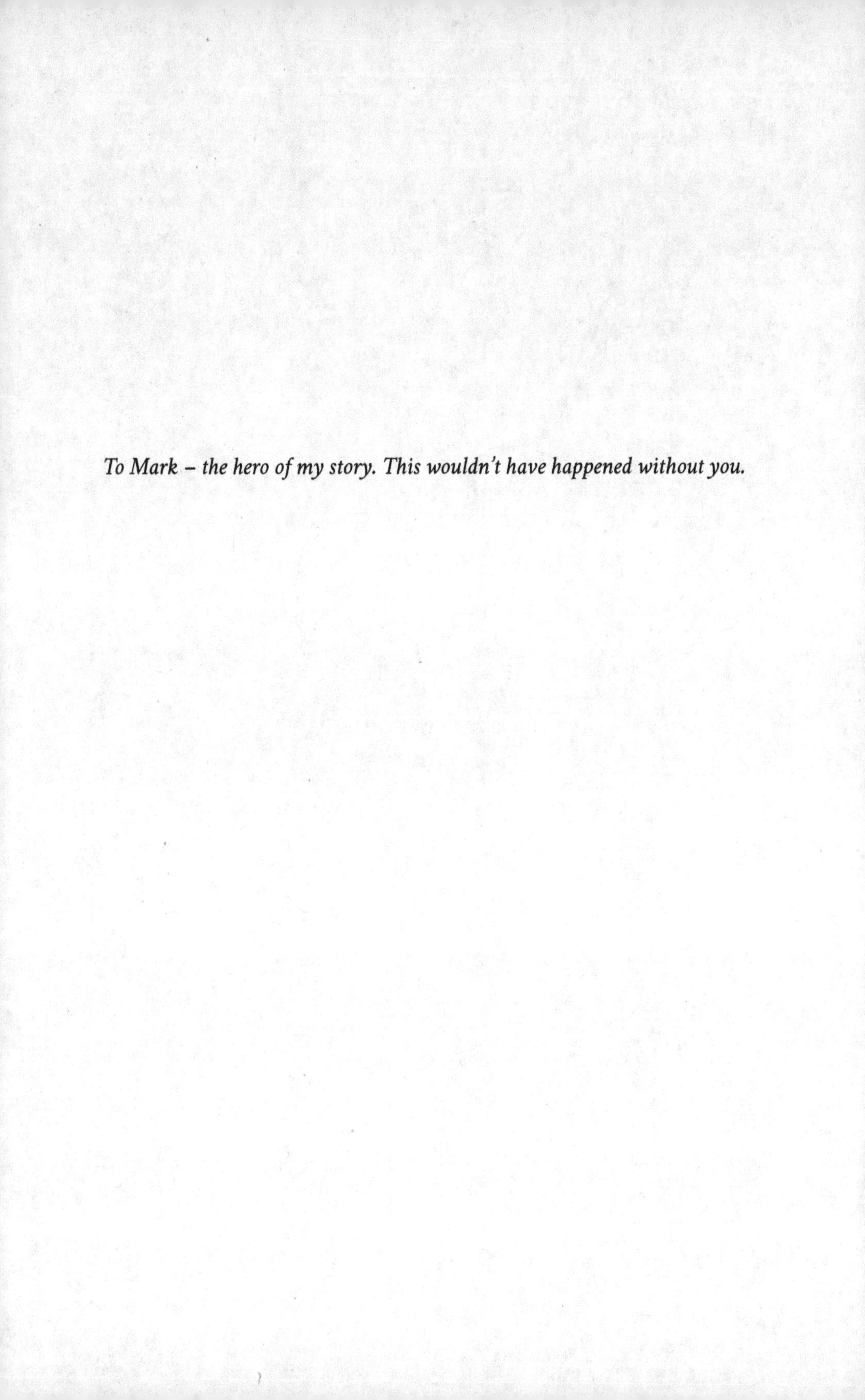

To Mark – the hero of my story. This wouldn't have happened without you.

TAMUEL'S CURSE

"You cannot kill this child, witch, for he belongs to me. Of my flesh, I am the only one with the authority to take his life. But as you point out, the Gods' laws dictate that the son will pay for the hubris of the father. I will curse this child's soul, not for your purposes, Clodia, but for mine!
Hear me this day: I bind this child to my service, to be bound more tightly than any other cupid by his cupid powers. He will find love for others in his service, but is never to seek it for himself. Only the cracked piece of his soul's mirror, cursed both equal and opposite, will make him whole and set him free."
Eros to Vestal Priestess-Witch Clodia: as etched into the holy Keeper of the Curses, Revenant of the Eternal Well.

CHAPTER 1

amuel stumbled on the smooth black floor as the portal closed with a little whoosh behind him. He quickly steadied himself, blinked then glanced down at the chronometer on his wrist. The ancient clockwork dial glowed as it whirred silently. Not too bad. The time difference between the Underworld and the Earthly Realm hadn't shrunk too much as the veil thinned for All Hallows' Eve. He took a breath – time to get on with his quest. It wouldn't do to get caught here.

He looked around, orienting himself. This wasn't quite what he expected the tunnels of the Underworld to look like, but then again, what would he know? It wasn't like there were tourist brochures. Perhaps there should be though. The veins of red, purple and green that ran chaotically along the glossy black rock walls, lighting the space, were quite pretty.

But why was it so warm? He didn't think this part of the Underworld was supposed to have the Fires of Hell – that was a particular quirk only found in the Morningstar's kingdom. Damn – had the portal dumped him in the wrong part of the Hell Realms?

He turned then stilled. He wasn't in tunnels – he stood in what looked like a large lounge room complete with spring-green rug, red upholstered furniture and flowers on every buffet, side table and antique drawers scattered around the room.

Standing in front of a fireplace that looked like it had been hewn by giant teeth, limned by the flickering firelight, were a couple in a lover's embrace.

Not just any couple. Hades and Persephone.

Shit-fuck-damn! What in all the hells were they doing here? They were supposed to be at Persephone's All Hallows' Eve party.

He must have done something wrong. His spell was supposed to have dropped him right outside Varagustus' cell. It sure as damnation wasn't supposed to drop him into Hades' private lounge room.

This was not at all going to plan.

Thank all the Gods neither Hades nor Persephone noticed him portal in uninvited. Famous for their displays of PDA, they were currently too wrapped up in their kiss – and in a state of half-undress – to notice him standing near the door. Actually, only Hades was partly undressed. Persephone was obviously in costume for her Halloween party. A quick glance at the broken horns, trident and torn cape that lay on the green rug in front of Hades' throne-like armchair had Tamuel guessing it was the reason they were still here. Hades famously hated dressing up.

What a bloody cock-up! He hadn't taken Hades' mood into consideration when planning this. The Fates must be meddling again – they loved pulling on unexpected threads and watching the chaos that unfolded. He was certain they did it for shits and giggles. He wished there was a way to show them just how not funny their meddling was.

He glanced at his bloody right wrist where the sigil for the portal spell was carved into his skin. Hades and Persephone still being here could ruin everything. He had to find Clodia and get her to tell him what she'd done with his mother's powers. He'd made a vow and it was either succeed or die trying.

He'd prefer the dying part didn't happen now though.

He backed up, hoping to reach the open door behind him before they finished kissing. This could still work as long as he could get out of here before they noticed him.

He was almost at the door when Persephone muttered, "Please, my hell beast. I'll let you suck on my toes if you put on the Luther costume."

"But you don't like it when I do that, honey-flower."

"But you like it, my sexy-wexy-lover-boy. And while you do that, I'll suck your c—"

"'Ew -ew.' TMI even for a cupid. Tamuel skittered backwards, desperate to get out of the room before he saw something he'd never be able to forget. He turned ... and bounced off Hades' naked chest.

Damn you Fates. He'd obviously made enough noise to catch the God of the Underworld's attention. Rallying – and trying to ignore the God's raging hard-on that tented his jeans – he smiled up at Hades. "Happy All Hallows' Eve, Uncle."

Hades didn't smile. "I don't remember receiving notice from Eros that one of his cupids was coming down for a visit," he said smoothly, turning back to look at his wife. "Do you remember asking Eros to send one of his cupids down here, my passion flower?"

Persephone crossed her arms, shaking her head a little. "No, I did not, pooky-wooky. What are you doing here, Tamuel?"

"Well, I—"

"I smell blood." Hades' gaze snapped to the blood dripping on the floor then at its source – the sigil carved into Tamuel's skin.

He made to back away, but Hades grabbed Tamuel by the wrist, lifting it to his nose. He sniffed at the bloody sigil then, black eyes flaring red as they met Tamuel's, he snarled, "You're corporeal. Who showed you that magic, boy?"

Shit. Shit. This so wasn't going how he'd planned – slip in, find Varagustus, get the information he wanted, steal a Hells-Key, travel to Tartarus and question Clodia, then back out before Hades even knew he'd come here. But there was no point lying to the angry God standing before him. Hiding his wince of pain as the God of the Underworld's fingers tightened around his wrist, he said, "Nobody, Uncle. I found it."

Hades growled, fingers tightening further – pain slashed through Tamuel as something snapped in his wrist. Hades' grip tightened as he barked out, "I don't believe you. Zeus and I made Persephone and Demeter rid the world of this heresy many centuries past." He leaned in closer, a growl in his throat, black eyes flashing orange then red. "Tell me who told you of this spell."

The God jerked his hand; something else snapped. Lights sparked before Tamuel's eyes and he almost went to his knees.

"Well?" Hades shook him.

Tears stinging his eyes, Tamuel managed to say, "I've always been ... interested in ... the Eleusinian Mysteries. I found ... writings on them."

"Impossible," Persephone said, coming forward to stand beside Hades. She might be pixie-like to her husband's towering brute, but in that moment, she was the far more frightening. "Who betrayed us?"

"I—" His mind whirled, trying to come up with something, anything, but the pain as Hades crushed his wrist made that impossible. Darkness whirled around him and he ...

Shaking brought him back to consciousness; pain spiked through him, the warmth of blood running down his arm – his suit was going to be ruined, he thought groggily. Someone was yelling something. More shaking and pain brought his attention back to the God still holding him up by his mangled wrist. "Wha?" he slurred.

"Tell us, cupid, or your body and your spirit won't leave the Underworld this All Hallows' Eve – or ever again."

Despite the danger and threat, Hades' beautiful voice coiled around Tamuel, drawing him in, making it impossible to deny him what he wanted, no matter how he'd promised not to tell on ... "Demeter."

"My mother?" Persephone said.

He nodded, then cried out again as Hades squeezed and broken bones ground together. Darkness threatened to take him down once more. "Please, my lord," he gasped. "My wrist. You're crushing ... it."

"Ease up, pumpkin pie. You don't want him to pass out before he tells you what we want to know."

"Whatever you say, honey bunny." He let go.

Tamuel dropped to the floor. He knew he shouldn't take his eyes off Hades, but couldn't help looking down at his shattered wrist. He almost fainted at the sight. But it wasn't so much the bones that poked through his skin that made him break into a cold sweat: the sigil was destroyed. He hadn't memorised it; had hoped to copy it from one wrist to the other for his return but now ...

"Oh Hades, look what you've done."

"It's no more than he deserves for using that spell."

Hades tapped his foot. Tamuel looked up at him, mind whirring, his thoughts clearer now that Hades had stopped inflicting pain. Eros had spent hours lecturing him when he was younger about the importance of dealing with what came next rather than what came after. He really wished he'd listened because if he didn't find some way of getting Hades and Persephone to understand, then there was no point in worrying if he could remember the sigil or not: he wasn't making it out of this room alive.

Trying to ignore the sick throbbing pain in his wrist and arm – and the fear he maybe had finally bitten off more than he could chew – he pushed to his feet, straightened his shoulders and met the God of the Underworld's angry gaze. He'd already broken his promise, so ... "Demeter gave it into my keeping centuries ago."

"She wouldn't do that," Persephone said, delicate features filled with hurt and anger.

"She did."

"But we destroyed all the words together. Wiped all the followers' minds."

"Not all. She couldn't do that to her favourite priestess, Carianthe. She hid her from you and let her keep her memories. Carianthe wrote her life's work all over again in the last years of her life. After she died, Demeter couldn't bring herself to destroy it, so she gave it to me to hide with the other treasures I had in my keeping."

"Your mother," Hades snarled at Persephone. "I should have known she'd find some way of screwing this up. I just never thought she hated me so much that she'd risk this. Wait until I get my hands on her ... I'll—"

"You'll do nothing to my mother," Persephone said, grabbing her husband's hands as they made a wringing motion. "I will take her to task over this. But first, we must find out why Mum gave Tamuel a copy of the Eleusinian Mysteries Grimoire. Did she want you to use this spell?"

Hades turned to him, fire in his eyes. "Did she?" He grabbed Tamuel's wrist, pulling him up by it. "Did she?"

He clamped down on the scream, forcing himself to hold onto consciousness – he'd never seen his uncle this angry before. Didn't want to think what might happen if he passed out. "No," he ground out through clenched teeth, pain a writhing thing inside him. "She just wanted me ... to keep it safe ... in memory of her ... beloved priestess."

"Why did you look at it then?"

"Your mother said ... I might have use of ... certain spells one day ... when I was desperate. She said I was only to ... look at it then ... I would know when. Please, Uncle. My wrist."

Hades pulled him closer. "Did you tell anyone of it?"

"No!" Well, except for the ghost who had helped him realise what the spell was. But Hades didn't need to know about that. He met the God's angry gaze as he said earnestly, "I would never ... give this spell to anyone else. Never."

Hades stared him down for long moments, eyes sparking.

Gods, was he going to kill him? His uncle had always been kind to him. Much kinder than all the other Gods. Probably helped by the fact that Persephone had taken him under her wing for a while when he'd been a youth, allowing him to be trained alongside her Soteira at the Amazonian and Gargarean warrior training camp; something no other cupid before or since had been allowed to do.

"Silly boy," Persephone tutted. "What did you think was going to happen when you were caught with this spell on your arm? You have to know it not only allows someone in and out of the Underworld in corporeal form, but allows a spirit to gain a body and use it to escape?"

"You weren't supposed ... to be here."

She shook her head at him. "My fondness for you may not be enough to get you out of trouble this time." She brushed her hand down the side of his face, frowning. "I really was hoping to get to my party on time this year."

He looked at her, desperately. "I had no choice. I made a vow."

"The Eternal Well accepted?"

"Yes," Tamuel grated.

She gasped, glancing at Hades. "This is what made you break one of our most sacred laws?"

"I need to speak to … one of your guests," Tamuel panted, spots still sparking in front of his eyes. "I just need … information … to get my mother's power back."

A look flashed between Hades and Persephone before she said, "Enough, Hades. We need to hear what the boy has to say." The Goddess put her arm around Tamuel. "He doesn't deserve to be punished for what is obviously one of my mother's meddling visions."

"But that spell—"

"I'm sorry I … used it … I just … want to get my mother's … powers back to her. Without them, she'll only have … a human life. I can't lose her … or my father … again. I just can't." He swallowed hard against pain of a different sort that thickened his throat. "Besides … they deserve … a true happy ever after. Like you have."

Hades shared a look with Persephone that made something in Tamuel's chest tighten, then suddenly let go his grip. Tamuel almost wept in relief as he clutched his broken arm to his chest, thankful Persephone was there to hold him up – despite her diminutive size, she was very strong.

"I wish I could help you with your parents' plight," Hades said quietly. "But I do not have your mother's powers, boy."

Tamuel took a few long, deep breaths, finally managing to push the pain aside as he'd been taught to do – at least enough for him to say steadily, "I know. But that witch-bitch Clodia does. And I know she's here. I know that you and Zeus tracked her down in the Void and imprisoned her in Tartarus for her hubris in stealing my mother's Goddess-given powers."

"I shoved her in a cell myself and set her punishment. But the power you say she stole is no longer in her."

He'd heard that too. "I want to ask her what happened to it," he said as Persephone began to shepherd him towards the couch.

"Given the fact she didn't tell me, no matter how much I tortured her, what makes you think she will tell you?"

"Because I have this." He pulled on the chain that hung around his neck, lifting it until the HeartsBlood Gem popped out from his shirt to swing in front of him. "Clodia tied her soul to this. With the right spell, I can compel her to answer my questions using the power the gem has over her."

Persephone lowered him to the couch. "This is the reason you decided to use that spell?"

"The only way to bring it here was if I was in corporeal form. It's the only thing that will get Clodia to talk. But ... It won't work for me. I was hoping to speak to Varagustus first – the spell was supposed to take me to his cell."

"Varagustus?" Persephone shared another look with Hades. "Why Varagustus?"

"His knowledge of magical gems is greater than any before or after him. But I think he held a lot of knowledge back from his writings. I'm certain he will know what I need to do to use the gem."

Persephone looked up at her husband. "Hades ..."

"No good will come of it."

"It's what we've been waiting for," Persephone said, her hand on Hades' arm as she looked up into his eyes. "She's only gotten worse. She's not been anywhere for centuries. I had no idea when I agreed ..."

"Don't blame yourself for that, my blooming rose."

Persephone shook her head. "What matters blame if she's intrigued enough by this? Especially with the HeartsBlood Gem in play. What if this is the true reason my mother sent him down here? She has always felt guilty about what happened. About the choices we all made. Please, honey-bee."

"But you know how our guest feels. I wouldn't want to force her, my spring's delight."

"It isn't your choice, bunny-wunny."

"Her who?" Tamuel asked.

They didn't answer, just had a staring match.

Finally, Hades threw his hands up, sighing gustily as he turned back to Tamuel. "Fine. Say I do agree to you travelling to Tartarus—"

"You will," Persephone said, beaming at him. He glared at her but she waved her hand at him as she took a seat next to Tamuel. "If for no other reason than you and your siblings do not wish that power to stay wherever it is. It unbalances things. It should be with the witch it was intended for – Tamuel's mother."

"So, you'll help me?" He couldn't believe his luck in this turn-around. He had no idea giving up Demeter would lead to this – he'd deal with her anger later. Right now, he wasn't going to look a gift horse in the mouth. Not even what could be a Trojan one.

Hades nodded begrudgingly. "I will. But there are three issues. The first being, I will not let you anywhere in my kingdom with that spell etched on your arm for anyone to see. Persephone can heal your wrist, but that sigil will not be left intact. You will need to remember it, only carving its mirror into your other wrist just before you wish to travel back."

Tamuel swallowed hard. "Not a problem." He hoped. He just needed a moment to sit down and go into his memory vault and retrieve it.

Hades nodded. "The second is the matter of the ticking clock. If you don't mirror that spell work and get back through the portal by the time the clock strikes twelve in the Earthly Realm on All Hallows' Eve, your soul *will* be cursed to stay trapped down here forever."

He opened his mouth to say it wouldn't be a problem, but Persephone raised her hand, her voice echoing strangely as she said, "The veil is thinning and time is constantly changing. This year more than any others. The current alignment of the stars heralds dark portents that place a shadow over all the Realms." She blinked and swallowed hard. "It is not a good time to travel through the Underworld, especially for a corporeal being."

He didn't like the sound of that. Not that it mattered – it was now or never. "Lucky I'm wearing this then." He gestured to the chronometer. If it worked as it should, it would tell him how the time shifted and warn him of changes in relation to the Earthly Realm – no matter what the stars heralded with their eerie portents. "I should be out of here well in time, even if the weeks I currently have turn to days. As long as I can have a Hells-Key?"

Hades' brow lowered. Persephone coughed. They glared at each other, making Tamuel wish he could read minds because he was certain there was quite the conversation going on.

Finally, Hades rolled his eyes. "I will give you a Hells-Key to move around the Underworld with more ease. But there is one last sticking point, one I have no say over."

"And what is that?"

"Varagustus didn't write those treatises on gems. The woman who did is not one of my prisoners."

"What? But if I can't find out how to use the gem, then my trip here is pointless."

Hades raised his hand. "She is not a prisoner. She is a valued member of my household. And she has refused to see anyone for centuries – aside from us, the servants and those she wants to inter-view of course."

"I will do whatever it takes to make her agree to help me."

"She may want the HeartsBlood Gem in payment," Persephone said.

He glanced down at the gem hanging around his neck. It wasn't his to give but … "Fine. I cannot go home empty-handed."

Hades and Persephone shared a look again before she said, "Then I will take you to her. But first, I will heal your arm – Korinna doesn't like the sight of blood."

"Korinna?" His mouth dried. "You don't mean Korinna Soteira?"

"The very one." Persephone shot him a brief, sad smile as she began the healing.

Korinna Soteira. The name rang in his head, his thoughts too lost to the past to truly feel the pain of the healing as it burned through his skin and bones.

Korinna had not only broken his heart but had crushed it under her dainty foot almost two thousand years ago. The rejection had left him bleeding and wishing for death.

But none of that mattered now. All that mattered was his vow. "Take me to her. I'm sure she will speak to me." She owed him that at least.

$\mathcal{K}$orinna stared at the screen before her, the words hazing. She pressed her fingers against the bridge of her nose, squeezing her eyes shut. Tired. She was just tired. If her Aunty Seph was here rather than on earth celebrating spring with her mother and sisters, she'd insist that she eat and rest.

But how could she when she still hadn't saved those who had been under her care – even if the only way to save them now was to find their lost souls and send them to Elysium?

All those people. Their screams. Their cries for help as the volcano dust choked them, encasing them where they stood, still rang in her mind. Men, women, children. The entire beautiful city of Pompeii. All dead.

Her fault. All her fault.

If anyone needed to pay for their sins, it was her.

She only wished Seph would stop trying to make her feel better. How was a person supposed to get over something like that? Hades was far more understanding of the need driving her. She couldn't feel better. Wouldn't feel better. She deserved to live in darkness for eternity.

Countless centuries of research and study and she'd come up with nothing ... until now.

The Eleusinian Mysteries. She was certain the key she needed was held in the ancient grimoire. It was thought destroyed, but she knew differently. The last lost soul she'd interviewed in their Underworld cell had told her what Demeter had done. Now she just had to figure out some way of asking Demeter to give the grimoire to her without Seph or Hades finding out. Not so easy when Demeter never came down here, hating Hades as she did. And it wasn't like she could go to Demeter – she was bound to this place by her vow; an unfortunate wording issue making her unable to travel. And of course, she couldn't use her magic to help send a message. And she couldn't send a message via one of the other Soteira – they might be her friends and sisters, but their loyalties lay with Seph.

She rubbed her eyes again. The problem was, she wasn't devious enough. A dreadful fault for someone who lived among the Gods, whose deviousness was legend. The only time in her life that she'd ever got away with anything was with Tam—

She brutally cut the thought off before it could truly form and concentrated on the screen in front of her again.

She didn't need him or anyone else to help her figure out how to do this. Seph was forever saying Korinna was one of the smartest people she'd ever known. Those smarts had led her to discovering how to save the souls she'd sent spiralling into the Void and convey them to Elysium where they would live in peace and happiness forever more; to knowledge of the spell that would allow her to do it.

All that was standing between her and it was her ability to contact Demeter *and* get the Goddess to give her the grimoire without tipping off Hades or Seph. They'd destroy the ancient book of spells before she could use it if they so much as got whisper of its existence. She couldn't allow that to happen.

She rubbed her temples, eyes closed, but nothing came to her.

Perhaps she should take a walk, clear her head.

She stood, made it half-way across the room before dizziness hit.

The room swayed around her. She staggered to the couch Seph had placed in front of the fireplace when she'd last decorated Korinna's room and fell into it. How long had she been staring at the computer screen?

Her stomach chose that moment to growl.

Oh. When was the last time she'd eaten?

She couldn't remember. Food was brought for her and placed at her elbow every day, morning, noon and night, but if she was deep in her work, she often forgot it was there. They would take away her untouched tray and replace it with another, so it was impossible to tell when she'd last eaten by looking at the tray currently on her desk – a plate of her favourite lasagne, now cold, the cheese congealed on top with no obvious signs she'd touched it.

Way too long, going by how dizzy and weak she was. Damn it. How stupid could she be? It would do no one any good if she passed out. She sniffed, catching a whiff of herself for the first time. She couldn't remember the last time she'd showered and changed either. She raked her hand through her hair, fingers getting caught in the knots she'd ignored when she'd piled the mass of greasy curls on top of her head this morning. Or was it yesterday morning?

Damn it. Hades would give her a lecture if he found her in this condition. And then tell Seph. And Seph would worry.

She wasn't sure why he hadn't come in already. He wasn't as much of a worry-wart as Aunty Seph – only checking on her a few times a week – but he would normally have been in by now. She glanced at the large chronometer – her own design – on her wall. Its hands showed her the shifting of time due to the thinning of the veil. All Hallows' Eve. Of course.

Seph's Halloween party. It explained why he'd been such a grump the last time he'd come in to check on her. She'd thought it was because it was spring in the southern parts of the Earthly Realm so it was Seph's turn to go there. Hades was always a grump for the months – years down here – that his wife was away from him thanks to the bargain between him and his mother-in-law. It was why Seph had always made such a thing out of celebrating Halloween – it allowed them to see each other in this time of separation with the veil thinning as it did. Although Hades had never liked having to dress up in whatever couples-inspired outfit Seph decided upon in any given year.

Thank the Gods Seph had given up requesting Korinna's presence at those events many centuries ago. It was one guilt trip she certainly hadn't needed.

So, shower or food first? The room still swayed around her when she stood, giving her the answer. She pushed away from the couch, heading to her desk and the cold lasagne. Dizziness surged. She staggered, tripped over the rug, hurtling across the floor, arms wheeling.

"Rinna," a voice called out. Then hands caught her, steadying her. She looked up into achingly familiar indigo eyes.

"Tam."

He smiled at her. Actually smiled at her. "I'm here. Are you okay?"

She tore herself from his grasp, all signs of dizziness gone as fury overwhelmed her. With a growl, she punched him square in the mouth.

Tamuel staggered back, touched his bleeding lip, eyes wide. "What the hell, Rinna? What was that for?"

"As if you don't know."

"I don't."

She hit him again.

The look on his face was comical as he staggered again. She would have laughed except she was too mad.

Mad? No, that didn't express what she was. She was furious. Betrayed. Hurt.

He'd promised to stay by her side and help her with her first assignment – to keep Vesuvius asleep and ensure the people of Pompeii remained safe. He had known how nervous she'd been; how much she'd doubted her ability to take on her dead mother's post and do it justice.

Then he'd left without a word the day before she was due to leave.

After all they'd shared, he'd treated her as if she was nothing.

And she'd never forgiven him.

She'd spent months looking for him, waiting to hear something, anything, every day of silence increasing her anger, her despair, her hurt. Enough that she missed the signs a true guardian wouldn't have missed. Enough that she had acted erroneously and made everything so much worse.

His fault for leaving. His fault for not being there to help her see what she missed. And worse, his fault for not being there in the weeks and months after to help her, with the balancing warmth of his powers and his friendship, to help her cope with what had happened. She'd failed as Guardian of Pompeii. She'd needed her best friend, had cried out for him. After promising her he would always come when she needed him, there had only been silence and grief and an endless loneliness that had never abated.

If not for him – for his lies, for his leaving, for all his betrayals – she would never have tried the impossible; would never have been forced into making a vow that, one way or another, would bring her death.

She'd long wanted to make him pay, but he was beyond her reach, in Eros' service. Sharing his love around like a typical cupid no doubt – why she thought he'd be any different she didn't know. Their friendship – it had all been in her head. He'd obviously never felt the same, no matter that he'd made her think he did, because he'd left without a word, hadn't replied to any of her letters, had ignored her entirely. Everything they'd shared was a lie.

She punched him again.

"Oh dear," Hades drawled as he caught Tamuel and set him back on his feet. "I don't think she's going to help you like you thought she would."

"Korinna dear. Are you okay?"

Hades had a shit-eating grin on his face, Seph a frown of concern on hers. "I'm fine," she snapped, wanting them all to just go away and take the betraying arsehole with them.

"Is *she* okay?" Tam asked, touching his split lip. "What about me? I'm the one whose been sucker-punched for no good reason."

She glared at him. "No good reason?" She lifted her fist, ignoring the throb in her knuckles – it had been a long time since she'd sparred and her body wasn't used to the pain.

He raised his hand in self-defence. "Whatever I did, I'm sorry."

"Whatever you did? Whatever you did!" Hell, she sounded like a shrieking banshee. Nobody had ever made her lose her cool like he could. How was it that he could still do it all these centuries later? "You left. Without a word. After you promised to stay. When you knew I needed you the most!"

"Hang on. That wasn't my fault. Eros just came and took me. Besides, you never really needed me. I got that message loud and clear when you ignored the letters I sent to you. I might not have been able to come with you like I promised, but *you* were the one who abandoned our friendship."

She jerked. "I never abandoned ... I never got any ... Don't turn this around on me. You ignored my letters!"

"What?" He looked insulted – and hurt. "But that's not possible. I wrote every day, then when you didn't reply, once a week. I thought maybe you were just busy with your duties. I begged Eros to let me go to you – but it took months of bargaining every privilege I had to make him agree. As soon as he did, I went looking for you but Pompeii was gone. I went to the training camp but you weren't there and nobody would tell me what had happened or where you had gone. It was like you'd disappeared off the face of the earth. I thought maybe you died." He glanced around him, his face paling. "You're not dead, are you?"

She snorted. "No. Did my fist in your face feel incorporeal to you?"

He rubbed his chin. "Then why are you here? *How* are you here?"

"I'm a Soteira. Hades allows us to reside here with Persephone as her handmaidens."

"Right. But that doesn't answer why I couldn't find you or why you abandoned your post."

"I don't owe you an explanation." Her gaze bore into him as she tried to let fury burn away the hurt his words caused.

"Surely you've not been here since I left?"

She pressed her lips against all the words she wanted to shout at him and just said. "Pretty much."

"But what about your plans? You wanted to travel the world after your contracted years as Guardian of Pompeii were up. To keep helping people."

She shrugged. "Plans change."

"Not this much."

She glanced at Hades and Seph. They watched her carefully, as they always did, as she wished they wouldn't. She wasn't breakable – you couldn't break what was already broken. But they obviously hadn't told him anything. Good. Not that she thought they would. They'd kept her secrets all these years. They were hardly about to spill them to one too-handsome auburn-haired cupid.

"Rinna, what happened?" he asked more softly.

She hated that his voice could still get inside her like that; curling around her heart, making her want to soften, to confide. She straightened her back. "I decided research was my forte. And Hades has been kind enough to let me live in his palace where I can do my research undisturbed." She turned back, glowering at him. "So, if you don't mind, I would like to get back to what I was doing before you interrupted."

"I ..." His fingers grazed her arm before she could turn away. "Rinna, please. You have to believe me. I did send you letters. I did try to find you."

"I don't believe you." She bit back on the sob in her voice, too aware of the others watching.

"I wasn't allowed to leave Eros' side for an entire year. I was bound to him. I couldn't break free until I had permission."

"And it took *you* a whole year to get permission?"

Tam lifted his hands and let them drop. "Eros was intractable. A fact you would have known if you had got my letters."

"Well, I didn't get any letters."

His gaze raked over her face. "And I didn't get any from you, yet you say you sent them."

"I did. Are you saying somebody kept them from us? Why would they do that?"

"I have no idea. But the real question is, why won't you believe me? Why would you think I would leave without a word? You obviously think very little of me."

"I ..." She clenched her fists at her side, trying to stop the tremors shaking through her body from showing. "You. Left. Me."

Tam took a step closer, his violet eyes ablaze with indignation that seemed so real. "Not. By. Choice!"

He stood so close now, his breath brushed over her face. She stepped closer. "So. You. Say."

His jaw clenched. "It seems to me like you were just annoyed that I didn't deign to get your permission before I left."

"Deign to get my permission?" Her fingers curled into fists.

"Oh-oh. That was a mistake," Hades said, snickering.

"Hades, you need to do something," Persephone whispered.

"Why? This is fun," Hades whispered back.

She ignored them, attention boring into the annoying cupid in front of her. "Deign. To. Get. My. Permission?" She poked him in the chest with each word, her finger bouncing off firm, defined muscle.

He grabbed her finger, holding it firmly in his warm grasp. Fire zapped through her veins at the contact. Ah hells. He'd always been cute, but now ... He'd grown into his demi-God-hood in the almost two thousand years since she'd seen him. And how! She took a gulping breath and forced herself to stare unblinking into his beautiful eyes. "How can you say that to me? After all we shared?"

His full mouth thinned as her question struck him. Then, jaw clenched, eyes blazing, he asked, "How is that different from you accusing me of betrayal after all we shared?"

"I ... I ... Get out." She tore her hand from his and pointed at the door, her powers fizzing inside her, sparking on her fingertips. She mercilessly pushed them back. She couldn't trust them. Not after ... "Get out before I do something I can't take back."

"My pleasure, my Queen." Tam bowed, waving his hand, an obvious mocking of the gesture he used to make to her; one that had always made her laugh. It should have made her angrier, but the anger died the moment she saw the mark on his wrist.

Gasping, she grasped a hold of his arm. "What is this?" The marking, marred by an obvious attempt to heal it, was damaged by a nasty scar running through its middle but it was unmistakably from the lost Eleusinian Mysteries Grimoire. Every reference she'd managed to get her hands on had spoken about the unmistakable difference in the spell work and sigils – and this was different. Even damaged, it made her skin both crawl and shiver in excitement. "This spell. Where did you get it?"

"Persephone! I thought you'd healed him," Hades said, moving as if to stand between them.

"I did," she answered, appearing at Hades side, reaching for Tam's hand. "But I can't make a spell like that disappear. It's damaged though. Nobody will be able to copy and use it." She turned her gaze on Korinna. "What I want to know is how my darling Soteira knows what it is."

Korinna's heart pounded faster as she glanced between her mentor and Hades, their expressions harder than she'd ever seen, and aimed at her. "It's the answer," she whispered. "Not this spell particularly, but where it comes from."

A light of understanding lit Persephone's eyes. "You should have come to me. Told me you were looking for the grimoire."

"Why? You wouldn't have been able to help. You and Demeter never took any notice of what your worshippers did until they created their spells, until a grieving lover created and used this one." She gestured at Tamuel's wrist. "Then you destroyed everything they'd created, just so nobody could use any death or soul translocation spells again. Not only could you not tell me what I needed to know, I knew you would never let me have it."

Seph drew closer, touched her cheek. "My darling girl. Of course I would. If it is what you need to help get over your self-imposed exile and stop grieving, I would have searched the Realms to find someone who remembered it."

She blinked rapidly. Of course, Seph had no idea what the consequences would be if she used the grimoire ... but she couldn't let herself think of that guilt and grief now. Not when the answers were so close to being in her grasp. She looked back at Tam. "This is how you got here in corporeal form?"

He nodded.

She wanted to demand why he would do such a risky thing, but too many other questions vied for attention and came spilling out. "But how do you come to have that spell? Did you find someone who remembered it? Do you only have this spell? Do you know the location of the Eleusinian Mysteries Grimoire?"

"Not just the location. I have the entire grimoire," he said.

"You've got a copy of the entire grimoire?"

"I do." He smiled. A smile she used to love; a smile that had encouraged her into one mischievous scheme after another, overriding her more cautious nature; a smile that had got her through so much; a smile she had missed like no other when it was gone from her life.

She steeled herself against it and said, jaw tight, "You're not lying?"

"I would never lie to you, Rinna. Not about the letters I sent or trying to find you. And certainly not about this."

Her breath a shallow pant as she looked deep in his eyes – he'd never been able to lie to her. At least, she hadn't thought he could until he'd left and she'd realised she'd been fooled. But what she saw in his eyes now, openness and a need for her trust, it made her nod. Even though she still didn't quite believe him about the rest, she believed him about this. She held out her hand. "Then show me."

He snorted. "I don't have it on me. Do you think I would carry such a thing around, especially down here?"

"Of course not."

"But I am happy to give it to you after I'm finished here."

Korinna trembled, her breath a rough gasp in her throat. "You will give it to me?" The very thing she'd been looking for to right her past wrongs? It seemed too good to be true. "Why would you do that? It's priceless."

He flicked his hand. "Its only value to me was in getting me to and from this place in corporeal form. But now, its value is far beyond anything I had thought it."

"How is that?"

"Because I will give it to you only after you help me."

CHAPTER 3

The wonder in Korinna's eyes evaporated, to be replaced by bitterness. Tamuel swore deep inside. He hated seeing that bitterness in his best friend's eyes – ex-best friend according to her. Her fury was more welcome than the rancour and disappointment currently dulling the golden-topaz of her large eyes.

"You wish to hold my services to ransom?"

The way she said it – it cut him to the core. That she would think so little of him ... but then again, she already had thought so little of him given she believed he'd left without a word; without trying to find her. And he'd thought so little of her for the same reason.

Someone had got between them, of that he was certain, even if he had no idea why. But now wasn't the time to get into that. Now he had to make her agree to help him – the rest could wait. He gentled his smile. "No, of course not. But I cannot give you the grimoire until I return to the surface to retrieve it, and I cannot do that until I have finished my quest here."

"Quest?"

"To find and retrieve my mother's powers, stolen from her by the ancient Vestal High Priestess, Clodia."

Her gaze flickered in interest and she turned an accusing gaze on Hades and Persephone. "Clodia is here? Why didn't you tell me?"

The Goddess of Spring waved a hand at the desk. "You have been rather busy with your research, dear. I'm certain nobody wanted to disturb you with such insignificant news."

"Insignificant news? The fact that Hades has finally captured the outlaw Vestal High Priestess who tried to steal Goddess-given power – and who was last seen with the HeartsBlood Gem – isn't insignificant news?" She spun around, pacing to her desk as she mumbled, "It's like you don't know me at all."

"I don't know why you're getting upset about it now, especially given our little cupid here has the HeartsBlood Gem with him."

"What?" She spun around to face him, her hand out as if to reach for the gem. "Why didn't you start with that? How did you get it? Let me see."

Tamuel couldn't help chuckling in appreciation of the fire of interest in her eyes. It reminded him so much of the past when she'd become fascinated by some topic and wouldn't let up until she knew everything. "To answer your questions, a) I was getting to telling you about it, but you punched me; b) my mother gave it to me after she took it from Clodia in our showdown with her on Valentine's Eve; and c) here it is." Slowly, he pulled the gem out from where he wore it under his shirt.

The red glow of it reflected in her eyes as she drew near. "It's beautiful." She reached for it, stumbled.

He dropped the gem, the weight of it banging against his chest, and caught her. She trembled, but he didn't think it had anything to do with excitement. She was almost skin and bone. He'd not noticed it when they'd walked in and she'd punched him. But now he had his hands on her shoulders, steadying her, he couldn't help but feel how fragile she was. Or notice how the mass of her curly black hair – that she'd always kept scrupulously clean even though she always raked it into a tight ponytail or bun – was matted and oily. Or that the lemon and spice scent of her he'd always loved was overtaken with the distinct pungency of someone who'd not had a shower in days, possibly longer.

What had she been doing to herself? And why the hell had Hades and Persephone let her get like this? Was she being punished?

In a blaze of anger, he turned to them, but stilled as her hand landed on his chest, fingers flexing.

Fire zapped over him, through him, almost as if she'd used her power on him. But she hadn't.

Her gaze flew to his, eyes flaring with awareness. Of him? That seemed impossible. While he'd loved her with a passion that went well beyond friendship when they'd trained together, she had never shown any romantic interest. Their friendship had been close – the closest he'd ever had – but nothing more than that. Not that he'd had expectation for more – the curse placed on him by Eros at his birth made certain of that. The curse had been the only way Eros had of saving him from Clodia; the only way he could take him as one of his own, given Tamuel's father was only a demi-God and his mother a human witch – not the ideal combination for a cupid; the only way he could stop him from giving into the human weakness of falling in love. A cupid couldn't get tangled in his customers' needs and desires. He had to stay separate if he was to help lead the lovers in the direction the Fates desired for them.

Love was for others, not for them.

So, he'd bound Tamuel to him in the only way he could, cursing him to find love for others but never for himself. He had woven a cryptic 'out' clause into the curse, but nobody had ever been able to figure out the bit about the broken mirror, equal and opposite. It made no sense – but that was Eros for you. And the God wouldn't talk about it; he said Tamuel would need to work it out for himself. That was how curses worked.

That was all very well for Eros to say, but it was particularly painful when the way this curse worked didn't stop him from falling in love – a fact he'd discovered when he'd met Rinna, fallen in love with her, but could never act on it. He could never declare his love while the curse made certain nobody would ever fall in love with him.

And given he couldn't make sense out of the cryptic mirror crap in the curse, he was doomed.

Except ... Rinna's eyes were lit with something he'd never expected to see there: passion. Desire.

Although, those emotions, while often tied to love, didn't mean there was love. Perhaps ...

No, he was wrong. He was just projecting what he wanted to see – because the truth was, he still loved her as much as he ever had. He'd thought he'd hardened himself enough to no longer feel it, but he'd been wrong.

Even as she'd punched him, he knew he'd been wrong. And now, her fingers flexing against him while she looked up at him like that ... it was doing things to him he didn't want. Certainly not here, under Hades' and Persephone's eagle eyes.

He quickly set Rinna away from him, letting go of her as soon as he knew she was steady, the gem swinging against his chest.

Her gaze finally broke from his and went to the stone. She reached for it.

He stepped back, holding the gem out of reach. "Ah-ah. Not yet."

Aggravation flickered over her lovely but too-thin features – her chin and cheekbones more pointed, her eyes larger in her heart-shaped face. Her gaze went from the stone to him. "Don't be a tease. Let me see it."

"I will, but ..." He raised a finger. "Only after you have eaten and showered."

"You sound like Seph and Hades."

"And you sound grumpy. Like you do when you need to sleep."

"I don't need to sleep."

She wavered on her feet.

He turned to Hades and Persephone. "Why is she being tortured like this?"

Persephone's perfectly manicured brows shot up. "Tortured? She is beloved, not tortured."

"She's not being tortured," Hades boomed at the same time. "What makes you think I would do that to someone as beloved to my wife as Korinna? She is looked after as an honoured guest."

"Really?" Tamuel asked, gesturing at Rinna. "Then why is she skin and bone and wavering on her feet as if she hasn't had a proper meal or a good sleep for weeks?"

Persephone's eyes widened as she took a good look at her favourite Soteira and then turned to hit Hades in the chest. "You promised you wouldn't let her get like she did last time she got lost in her research. How could you have let her do this to herself again?"

Hades stepped away from his wife, rubbing his chest. "I didn't. I made certain she had three meals a day and came in every few days to make certain she showered and slept."

"Did she eat the meals? Did you stay to make certain she actually got in the shower? That she actually climbed into bed and went to sleep?"

Hades looked sheepish. "I didn't think to check."

"Hello? I'm standing right here." Rinna waved at them, her motions jerky – possibly due to annoyance, but Tamuel thought it was more likely due to exhaustion and undernourishment. "Stop talking about me as if I'm a baby unable to care for myself."

"Well," Persephone said, hands on her hips as she glared at her protégé. "If you managed to actually look after yourself without supervision, I would. How could you have let yourself get like this again? Hades wasn't the only one who gave me promises."

Rinna's gaze dipped. "I didn't exactly break my promise. I ate and showered ... sometimes."

"And when was the last time you slept?" Persephone guided Rinna to the lounge in front of the fire – this one carved out of the black rock like the one in Hades' lounge room, but rather than a jagged bite, its mantel was carved with depictions of spring – obviously Persephone's work, as were the tapestries on the walls and the colours of spring within the rugs and furnishings.

Rinna rubbed her brow as she sat. "Umm, a week ago?" Persephone angled her a look. "Maybe more," she admitted softly.

"Hmm. That is hardly keeping your promise."

"I did better than last time. I did remember to eat. And shower."

"Not enough. Tamuel is right, you are skin and bone and ready to collapse."

"I was going to eat when you came in with Tam." She gestured at the unappealing lump of lasagne on the desk.

Persephone gave her a withering look. "You can't eat that now. Hades, please call for more food and ask Dianna to prepare a lovely hot bath for our girl – she needs a good soak. And some relaxing herbs in the water to help her sleep."

"Don't fuss. You've got a party to get to. I don't want you to be late."

Hades waved his hand and disappeared in a whirl of black and fire-red smoke.

Rinna moved forward on the couch as if she was about to stand, but Persephone's grip on her tightened. "Where are you off to?"

"Umm, to have a bath?"

"And?"

"To eat?"

"And?"

Rinna glared at her mentor for a long moment. "Oh, don't be like that, Seph. I don't need to sleep. Not now." Her gaze went to Tamuel and the gem lying against his chest. "There's too much to do. Besides, Tamuel still hasn't told me why he needs my help. And given the spell he's used and the fact he's using what looks like my chronometer design—"

"You created this?" he asked, looking down at the steam-punk looking watch on his wrist. He'd had no idea she was the creator of the book of magical contraptions he loved to potter with.

She waved her hand as if it was nothing. "It was a phase. Given you're wearing the chronometer, I gather you have a time restriction."

"I do. This spell could only be cast at the end of sunset on All Hallows' Eve and lasts until midnight. It was just before eight o'clock in the Earth Realm when I cast it and crossed through the portal. By the chronometer's calculations when I landed here, four hours Earth Realm time gives me at least a month down here—"

"Only if the thinning of the veil doesn't make our time closer to Earth Realm time."

"Don't forget what—"

He shot a warning glance at Persephone as she went to blurt out the worrisome information she'd dropped on them earlier about this All Hallows' Eve Realm-alignment being even trickier than usual. He didn't want Rinna to worry – she needed to rest. "I won't forget."

"Forget what?" Rinna asked, gazing suspiciously between them.

"To set the alarm. You don't have to keep reminding me, Persephone. I'm no longer a child. I am capable of looking after myself."

She snorted. "Your actions today would seem to indicate otherwise."

"I think it's turned out all right." Tamuel shot her cheeky smile, thankfully making her chuckle. "Don't worry. I don't plan to get stuck here. I won't be able to help my mother if I do. But even with the trickiness of the spell and everything …" He turned to Rinna. "There's still plenty of time for you to rest before helping me."

"Tamuel is right." Persephone said, smiling beneficently at him before returning her attention to her Soteira. "So, no arguing. And no more punishing yourself for something that was truly not your fault."

Rinna's gaze shadowed just before she turned away so he could no longer see her expression. But he could tell something wasn't right – she held her shoulders so stiffly it looked like her spine would snap with the effort. "I ... umm ... I'm not punishing myself."

Persephone grasped Rinna's hands, held them even when it looked like her Soteira wanted to pull away. "Remember who you are lying to, my darling one," she said softly, brushing another stray lock of hair behind Rinna's ear. "It is time it stopped." She glanced over at Tamuel. "Maybe my mother knows what she is about. Maybe now is the right time to forgive yourself."

<h1 style="text-align:center">CHAPTER 4</h1>

"**F**orgive myself? I can never do that," Rinna whispered harshly. "Never."

She glanced at him briefly, and for the first time since he'd walked in, the first time since he'd known her, Tamuel saw something he'd never thought to see in her: vulnerability. And a hurt so deep, it ached inside him.

What had happened to make her like this?

Did it have something to do with what happened to Pompeii? Nobody had ever been able to tell him exactly what had occurred, let alone why she'd left her post, but he'd never believed the disaster her fault. Ultimately, if the Fates had decided Pompeii was to end like it had, then it would happen. No amount of magic could stop a fixed Fate from occurring. Surely, she knew that. Didn't she?

Looking at her, at how broken she seemed by whatever Persephone referred to, by the very fact she'd hidden here in Hades' Palace for two thousand years by the sound of things, he couldn't help thinking perhaps she didn't.

For a perfectionist like Korinna Soteira, what happened to Pompeii would have been the ultimate in failure. Especially after she'd dreamed for years of taking up her dead mother's post and doing her proud.

Why had he never thought of this before? Perhaps she was right about him. He was a shit friend.

He stepped forward, wanting to add his words to Persephone's, to try to make Rinna see what the rest of them did, but a servant – a Soteira like Rinna – appeared next to Persephone. "The bath is ready," she said. "And cook says the food will be sent up in ten minutes or so."

"Is Lord Hades getting into his costume yet, Dianna?" Persephone asked.

Dianna grimaced. "I saw him throwing it in the fire, my Lady."

"Aggravating man. I better go deal with him while you take care of Korinna."

"I can take care of myself," Rinna said grumpily.

Persephone just patted her hand. "Please, let Dianna take care of you. For me."

Rinna glowered at her mentor and grumbled, "Fine." She glanced at Tamuel, the look on her face questioning.

"I'll go eat too. I'll come back later."

She nodded briskly and disappeared into her bedroom with Dianna, leaving Tamuel to follow Persephone out the carved ebony door.

As it closed behind him, he asked, "What happened to her? Why is she down here? Why did you say she was punishing herself? It's not because she thinks what happened is her fault, right? You wouldn't let her think that, would you?"

"You better than anyone should know things are never that simple."

"What happened? I have to know."

Persephone glanced back at the door, biting her lip for a moment before turning back to him. "That is not my story to tell, young cupid. But if you play your cards right, you might just get her to tell you herself."

"Play my cards right?"

She touched his cheek, the gesture as intimate as ones he'd received from his mother, Jules. "There is a loophole to every curse, my dear boy. I think Korinna is the one to help you find it. Now," she clapped her hands together and stepped back before he could do more than gape at her. "Go eat. There'll be something set up in the dining hall for you. Then once you've had your meal, you can come back and settle into your room and get some rest. I instructed Dianna to give Korinna one of Hypnos' sleeping potions, so she should sleep for hours."

"Are you heading off to your party?"

"Yes – after I've got my costume-hating husband in hand. We won't be back until after your deadline has passed – I hope not to see you down here then. I trust you to look after our girl."

"Of course," Tamuel said. Although he doubted very much she'd let him. He touched his aching jaw – the warrior-witch still had a mean right hook.

"Good." She touched his shoulder. "I hope I'm correct and you're the exact man for the job. And don't forget what I said about the portents. Don't expect things to go to plan."

"I never do," he said, tapping the chronometer. "I wasn't joking about the alarm. It will tell me the moment anything changes."

"Very well. Good luck, my dearest boy." She spun around and disappeared from his sight, a brush of warm, flower-scented air the only sign she'd been there.

Tamuel stared at the carvings of flora and fauna on the door, his mind a-whirl.

He'd not expected any of this when he'd set out on his quest, and while he wanted to help Rinna, he couldn't forget what had brought him here.

He had to get his mother's powers back. Without them, she would eventually die a human death. And when she did, her soulmate, his father, would find some way to follow her into death and be with her in Elysium. And then Tamuel would be all alone. Again.

He'd sacrificed so much to break the curse that had destroyed his family and bring his parents back together, bring them *all* back together, as a family. And he'd succeeded. They were together, but only for one human lifetime. He couldn't lose them again. It was why he'd made his vow to the Eternal Well, tying his lifeforce into his promise: do or die. He couldn't allow their love to be destroyed by something as simple as death. Nothing would stop him. Certainly not the fact that being with Korinna Soteira was going to hurt.

He knew she would never love him, but he never imagined she would hate him.

At least he could change that. He had to make her believe he *had* been devastated when Eros took him from the camp in the Ceraunian Mountains where they'd been trained by Amazonian and Gargarean warriors, witches and warlocks. If only he could share his memories with her of that time, then maybe she would believe him. Because if he knew one thing about his friend it was this: she would never let him help her if she didn't trust him.

He paused in his pacing. Perhaps he could let her see his memories. There was something he'd read in one of the Stevens' grimoires that touched on memory sharing. He could find a quiet spot and enter the trance to retrieve the exact wording of the spell from his memory vault. Although he really needed to use the energy required for that kind of trance-work to extract the precise design for the sigil from there first. And it would take days, possibly weeks, to power up enough to extract both memories to the degree he would need to succeed with either of those tasks. And he'd have to be very careful not to tap into the tenuous link between him and the magical ark or power he'd used to get here – the link to that power secured his way home. He would need all the power there to get back to the Earthly Realm in his current form.

He sighed. Any other time this wouldn't be so difficult, but down here in the Underworld, with the power fluctuations that were bound to occur due to the Realms realigning, not to mention the death magic all around that was a constant drag on his cupid power, making him rely more on his warlock power, nothing was going to be easy.

So, prioritise. To get out of here, he needed that sigil. Helping Rinna could happen after. *Would* happen after.

However, none of that could happen until he'd refuelled. Opening that portal and stepping through had taken a lot more out of him than he'd bargained on even with using the power stored in the ark. Probably not helped by the pain of having his arm pulverised and then his face used as a punching bag. He touched his chin and winced. He wished he'd asked Persephone to heal his bruises and split lip before she went. It was times like this he wished he'd got more of a share of his father's powers – Bastien had healed all of them after the fight with Clodia without breaking a sweat. At least being a cupid meant he'd heal faster than most others would. He should be perfectly fine in twelve hours or so. It was going to be fun eating until then. Maybe he'd ask for soup.

Sighing, he headed down the hall to the dining room.

An hour later when he returned to Rinna's rooms, he was shushed by Dianna, who was just coming out of the bedroom. "She's sound asleep," she whispered.

"Did she eat?"

She nodded. "And had a much-needed shower – I couldn't talk her into the bath." She walked closer, her chin lowering so she looked up at him through her lashes in a sultry move that would normally have had his hormones sitting up and taking notice – but not a twitch.

"Hades created a room on the other side of her quarters," she continued, her every move seductive – she was a handmaiden of a fertility Goddess after all. She gestured at the door in the curved wall to the left of the entryway, her wheat-coloured hair swishing against the upper curve of her bottom. "The Lady Persephone wanted you to be close by in case Korinna needs you. She sometimes has ... nightmares."

"I'll keep an ear out."

She bit her lip as her gaze raked over him. "I've put some more appropriate clothing for you to wear in the wardrobe and made up your bed." He glanced down at his crumpled suit, blood spattering his pants leg.

"If you need anything," she said, touching Tamuel's chest with a blood-red fingernail. "Just ring this bell." She snapped her fingers and a bell appeared in her hand.

Tamuel edged a step back. In the past he would have happily taken up her not-so-subtle offer, but now that he'd seen Rinna again ... "Aren't you expected at Lady Persephone's party?"

Dianna smiled slowly. "I have time. I'm not part of the set-up team." She edged closer again. "I've not been with a cupid before. I've heard you are all very ... talented. So ..."

"So ..." He edged back, glanced at Rinna's bedroom door. "Thank you for your help. I'm sure I will be fine."

Dianna gave a little pout, her gaze darting from him to the bedroom door and back. Then she smiled slowly. "Lucky girl. But if you change your mind ..."

"I'll be sure to ring the bell."

Her lips twitched as she placed the bell on the table by the door, bowed and left.

He should get some rest as well. Then go into his mind vault to find the spell. Actually, he'd do that first then rest.

He was just settling on the plush green rug in front of the fire when a sound from the bedroom caught his attention. He rose and rushed to the bedroom door, pressing his ear against it. Korinna was making little noises of distress.

He opened the door to peek in.

The room was stark with barely any furnishings aside from the huge canopied bed she lay in. His gaze arrowed in on her, noting how she twitched, her lips pulled back in a grimace. Sweat glistened on her furrowed brow, her curly hair a spill of black on the white pillow.

A nightmare. Should he wake her? He flicked on the bedside lamp, hoping the light might wake her. It didn't. It just seemed to distress her further. "Wake up, Rinna. You're having a nightmare." He shook her shoulder gingerly.

She grasped his hand – fire shot through him at the point of contact, but he shoved the sensation aside. "Rinna. It's okay. It's only a nightmare. Wake up."

Her eyes fluttered open, gaze sliding around until it landed on him. "Tam. My Tam. Where did you go? Where did you go?"

"I'm sorry, Rinna. I didn't want to go. But I'm here now. I'm right here."

She tossed her head, her gaze roving around, unseeing. Was she still asleep? "I'm so sorry. I didn't mean to do it. But you weren't here. You weren't here and I hurt so much I missed the signs … I shouldn't have done it. I shouldn't have done it." She was sobbing now, her body jerking harder with her distress.

He sat on the edge of the bed, pulled her into his arms, stroked her hair. She gripped him hard, burying her head in his chest, sobs racking her body. "Shh, shh. Rinna. It's okay. It's not your fault. I know it's not your fault. Everything's going to be okay. I'm here. I'm here."

"You're here," she said, her sobs abating a little.

"I'm here. I'm always here."

"But you weren't. And now I can never be forgiven." She looked up at him, her eyes a vibrant glowing gold in the semi-dark room – the gold that only showed when she was using her power. But as far as he could tell, she wasn't using it at all. In fact, her power felt … like there was something horribly wrong with it.

What the hell was going on here?

He didn't have the chance to ask as she buried her head in his chest, mumbling, "Don't leave me. Please don't leave me."

"I won't," he said, his voice a harsh blade in his throat. "I promise I will never leave you if you need me."

She rubbed her head against him, gripping him more tightly. His arms firmed around her as he shifted his legs onto the bed and laid them both back against the pillows.

As soon as he did, she went completely lax, losing herself to sleep once more – if she'd ever truly woken from it in the first place. He doubted she had.

Hells.

It seemed she did truly blame herself. But still, the depth of her grief, of her guilt, didn't make sense. Not after all this time. Not when she must know – and Persephone and others must have tried to make her see – that a disaster like Pompeii was something nobody could have prevented, no matter how talented or strong.

Fuck. What exactly had happened to make her punish herself like this?

One thing was certain though: he wasn't going to go anywhere tonight. He'd have to get into his mind vault in the morning after she woke and he could think clearly again. With her in his arms like this, he could think of nothing but her.

Damn, he'd hoped when he couldn't find her that she was happy, safe and fulfilled – even in the depths of his heartbreak, when he'd thought she had dismissed their friendship and forgotten him, he'd wished that. To find out her life was so far from that …

Residing in the Underworld, a permanent treasured guest of Hades and Persephone, didn't even come close to meeting his idea of the life she deserved. He would fulfill his vow to get his mother's powers back and somehow, some way, while he did, he would find a way to make his Rinna happy.

A rumble of thunder followed by a loud knock in the distance told him he'd tied himself to another vow.

He didn't care. He would fulfill them both or die trying. It was the least he owed to the people he loved most in all the Realms.

CHAPTER 5

Korinna woke the next morning warmth blazing along her back, a heavy arm over her waist, the forearm and hand of which she clutched against her breasts. Had she taken someone to bed? She couldn't remember doing so. Hadn't felt any kind of inclination for a sexual partner for a very long time. Perhaps she dreamed. She pinched herself.

"Ow."

The man behind her moved, muttering a little, something hard and jagged poking into her back. But not his cock – although that had firmed a little against her bottom when she moved – but something that lay between her shoulder blades.

It was uncomfortable. She shifted around to see what it was, not caring too much if she woke her bed companion.

"Morning," said a deep, sleep-roughened voice. A voice she knew too well.

"Tam! What are you doing in my bed?" She sat bolt upright, completely dislodging his hold on her, memories of yesterday flooding her mind.

Ah hells! She'd yelled at him, hit him, argued with him then struck a bargain to help him so she could get the Eleusinian Mysteries

Grimoire and a closer look at the HeartsBlood Gem – which still hung around his neck. It had been the hard thing poking her in the middle of the back.

She wanted to see the gem, to feel its weight and warmth in her hand, to poke at the magic that lay at its core with the help of Dianna, to uncover its secrets, but right now, her mind kept spiralling to the fact he sat on her bed. And the fact she'd woken up, clutching his arm, spooned against him.

How the hell had that happened? What the hells had happened?

She glanced down, almost sighing in relief when she saw she had her Yummy Sushi pyjamas on – a present from Persephone and Hades on her last birthday in a nod to her Buffy obsession – the TV show the only thing for centuries that Persephone had got her to engage with from the Earthly Realm.

If she was wearing her pyjamas, it meant nothing had happened between them. And he still had his suit on – she couldn't believe Tam wore suits! – although the jacket was missing and the white shirt, looking a little less crisp than it had yesterday, was rolled up at the sleeves to his elbows, showing off the tattoo of an owl on his right forearm.

He still had that? After all this time, it should have worn off, but it looked as fresh as the day she'd put it on him. She touched the matching one hidden under her sleeve, her gaze darting up to his, questioning.

His lips curled in *that* smile again as he gestured at her. "Nice jim-jams."

She pulled the sheet up in front of her. It seemed to amuse him more, his lips twitching as he edged up onto his elbows.

"They look better on you than they did on Buffy."

"You watch Buffy?"

"Of course." He cocked his brow. "I'm a little surprised you do."

"Why? Why wouldn't I like a show where the kick-arse heroine fights evil and wins the day?"

"Well, when you put it like that ..." He smiled at her, the curve of his lips having a similar effect on her as a caress.

She clutched the sheet tighter. "Why are you in my bed?"

He rubbed one hand over his dark auburn hair, the movement giving her a glimpse of his tanned chest – he'd undone the top buttons on his shirt – and the chain that held the HeartsBlood Gem. Her mouth dried. He looked deliciously dishevelled sitting on her bed, his hair spiked up now in a sexy just-awake kind of way, his jaw covered with a red-tinted five o'clock shadow – a far cry from the suave, suited stranger she'd been so angry with yesterday. She tried to ignore the way his dishevelment made him even more handsome and raised her brows – a look he used to call 'haughty Rinna'. "Well? Why are you here?"

"You asked me to stay. You were having a nightmare."

Oh hells. She hoped she hadn't talked in her sleep. She looked more closely at him. He didn't look like he was appalled, or pitied her. He looked his usual self. Well, not quite his usual self. He'd been a young cupid of fifty when they first met and had left her just as he'd entered his manhood at one-hundred years old. His face was even handsomer now than it had been back then, his unruly auburn hair cut short at the back and sides with just enough at the top to sit up without the help of product – not flop all over his forehead like it once had. His indigo eyes were even more vivid than she remembered – probably something to do with the increase in power emanating from his every pore. And he'd filled out. Her fingers tingled as she remembered the sensation of the wiry muscles of the forearm she'd clutched in sleep, the taut strength of the chest and stomach muscles she'd nestled against last night. She had a vague memory of doing that, of holding him tight and not letting go.

How embarrassing! What must he think of her? She swung away from him, intending to get off the bed, make an excuse about needing to get dressed. She needed to find her anger again: it was her only armour against him.

But he touched her arm before she could get off the bed and she froze as a tsunami of sensation flooded through her – ye Gods! How could he still make her feel like this?

"Rinna. Are you okay?"

She glanced back over her shoulder. He blinked, his gaze roving over her in a way that made her tingle low in her belly, a sensation that heralded an earthquake of trembling deep in her core.

She leaped to her feet. "Fine. I'm fine. Very rested. Thanks for helping with the ..." She waved at the bed. "Nightmares."

"My pleasure." He smiled, that slow curl of lips on one side that made a dimple pop out.

The tremors went up a notch on the Richter scale. How could this be happening? She was angry with him. Wasn't she?

"Are you sure you're okay?"

"Fine." Had she just squeaked? She cleared her throat, spoke deeply. "Fine."

His lips twitched. "Good. I'm glad." He swung his legs around and over the side of the bed. As he moved, a darkly red shadow under the crumpled white of his shirt caught her attention. The HeartsBlood Gem. How could she have forgotten about it?

She wanted to see it again.

Her fingers brushed against the hot skin at his collar as she reached for the chain.

He stilled. She stilled.

Slowly, their gazes met.

He swallowed hard. "Rinna."

"Yes," she breathed. She stood in between his legs, the warmth of him wrapping around her. Ye Gods. The trembling tightened, tightened: an eight on the Richter scale; a nine ...

He leaned up. She leaned down.

The door opened with a loud squeak.

Korinna jumped away from Tam as Dianna walked in, a tray in her hands. "Breakfast is prepared at Lady Persephone's request – Oh, sorry, did I interrupt something?"

"No." She couldn't even look at him. "Tam was just showing me his gem."

Dianna's lips twitched as she walked closer, her gaze roving over him salaciously. "I bet he was."

"Not like that!" Korinna blustered, her face hotter than Satan's fires. "The HeartsBlood Gem. Show her, Tam."

He grinned as he pulled it out slowly from beneath his shirt, playing up to Dianna, who had put the tray down to say, "Oh my," while she fanned her face, her gaze not on the gem, but lower. Embarrassment gave way to a spark of anger, which quickly devolved into self-pity. Dianna made flirting look so easy. As a Soteira should. As she'd somehow never been able to do.

Not that she wanted to know how to flirt with Tam. That would be completely inappropriate. Particularly as she hated him. Was mad at him. Furious really. No amount of Richter-scale trembling could make her forget that. So no need to want to flirt or anything like it. And definitely no need to keep thinking about the way his gaze had dipped to her lips as he'd leaned towards her before Dianna had barged in. Or the way she'd woken. Warm and ruffled from sleeping. In his arms. All night.

Or how she'd almost orgasmed standing between his legs as they'd looked at each other.

Oh hells. She wanted to fan herself, but then, that would give away too much. Wouldn't it?

Yes, yes, it would. Not to mention, she wouldn't look sexy like Dianna did – eyes sparking flirtatiously, her entire body screaming she'd be up for sex if it was on offer.

Was it?

Her gaze darted to Tam.

He no longer looked at Dianna as he held the HeartsBlood Gem out of his shirt. His gaze was fixed firmly on her.

Her face flamed to volcanic levels in less than a second. Why now? Why Tam?

She reached for the glass on her bedside stand, desperate to have an excuse to look away and hide herself for a moment – suddenly horribly aware of the fact she was in pyjamas, her dark hair a wild mess of curls falling everywhere. Dianna, with her sweep of long, glossy blonde hair and slinky black party dress and heals, looked far sexier without trying than Korinna had ever managed.

She gulped down the cooling water. It helped, but not as much as if she could tip it over her head, or bury her face in it.

Satan and all his devils be damned. This morning was not going like she meant it to. Not that it was entirely her fault. *I mean, I didn't ask Tam to come to my bed. Well, I did. But not like that. And I certainly never intended to sleep with him.*

An image of rolling around naked in the bed with him imprinted itself in her mind. A little gasp escaped her mouth.

"Rinna – are you okay?"

He was there in front of her again suddenly, the gem she should be concentrating on glittering as it swung against his chest. But she couldn't seem to focus on it. Only on his brilliant indigo eyes and their framing of long dark lashes. Those eyes glowed as he touched her, as he looked down at her. His voice buzzed in her ear. She looked at his lips as they moved over words of concern. All she wanted to do was put her thumb in the divot right in the middle of his bottom lip. Then she'd like to follow up with her tongue.

"Ye Gods!" she muttered. This was insane. Why was this happening to her? It never had before. Maybe it had something to do with the gem. Yes. That must be it. It was said to be a piece of the Goddess Vesta's heart – she was the Goddess of home and hearth but also fecundity. Maybe there was a little something sexy, a little something naughty, locked inside the depths of the gem that spoke to her; made her feel like this. Maybe it had unlocked the sensuality that was supposed to be part of her Soteira nature.

It made more sense than the alternative. That she wasn't furious at Tam. That she ...

She groaned again, not wanting to put words to the feelings inside her. It would make them too real – whether they were influenced by the gem or not.

His hands tightened on her shoulders at her groan. She wished he'd let go.

"You don't feel dizzy again, do you? Perhaps you should rest some more? Or eat? Dianna – bring that tray over here."

"No, no, I'm fine. It's not that," she managed to say, her voice so dry, as if she'd swallowed salt and sand rather than water only moments ago. "I'm rested enough." Her entire body sang with energy in a way it never had before. Ye Gods. Was this desire? It felt nothing like what she'd felt the times she'd taken a bed mate – primarily to get Persephone and Hades off her back about not living a full life. And also, because the scholar side of her wanted to see what she'd been missing. All the other Soteira made such a fuss over how great sex was. But after trying a dozen bed mates over a few centuries – she'd needed a reasonable selection to gather the relevant data – she'd come to the conclusion that, despite having been brought up as one of them, she wasn't a true Soteira. Not surprising given she'd been taken in by Demeter as a kindness when her mother had died not long after her birth, her mother having been friends with the Goddess. Nobody knew who her father was – her mother took that secret to the grave. She'd been quite content to believe she just wasn't that into sex … until now. So why had she made such a massive mistake?

Maybe the problem was her sample group hadn't been big enough. Or maybe they just hadn't been good enough. They certainly had never made her feel like this just by gripping her shoulders and staring solemnly down at her. And none of them had ever smelled like Tam; like lemons and sandalwood and the wildness of the sea – how that could be a scent, she wasn't sure, but it was the perfect description for the elusive aroma that teased her and made her ache.

He was staring at her. He'd asked her a question. What was it? Ah yes … was she rested. "Plenty rested," she choked out.

"But you're trembling."

"Ah … hungry. Need food."

"Yes. Of course. Dianna?" He helped her sit on the bed as Dianna went to place the tray next to her.

Korinna popped up before the tray hit the mattress. "Ah, not here." She couldn't sit in bed and eat with Tam watching her. Remembering all over again how she'd woken. "I don't like eating in bed."

"It's hardly in bed …" Tam began, but she was already out the door, heading towards the table – where she could sit at one end and he could sit way down the other end as far from her as possible.

CHAPTER 6

Korinna fell into her seat and gestured to the one at the other end of the table for Tam. He glanced at it, brow cocked, but then headed towards it.

"Don't sit down there." Dianna – the traitor! – put the tray down in front of Korinna and pulled the chair out catty-corner to her. "It's much easier for everyone – namely me," she said, pursing her lips and touching her hair, "if you sit down here. Then I won't have to wear out my pretties traipsing between you both." She waved at her hot pink strappy stilettos.

Korinna eyed her friend's outfit. "I thought you were supposed to go in a costume to the party."

"I am in costume. I'm Samantha from Sex in the City." She rolled her eyes at Korinna when she just stared. "You know – sex on legs, wears LBDs and stilettos." She cocked her brow at Tam. "I was hoping I could sell it."

"You certainly do that," Tam said as he took his seat.

"LBD?" Korinna asked, jaw tight.

"Little Black Dress," Tam answered, reaching for the coffee pot.

Of course he would know that. She glanced down at her friend's feet again. "They look like little torture machines. Why would you wear them at all?"

"I love my Louboutins – they're so pretty. And they do such great things for my calf muscles." She did a little turn to show off her legs.

Korinna shook her head and chuckled. "Maybe you should give them over to Hades to use on his worst offenders. A couple of centuries wearing them would be the best punishment ever."

Dianna took a step back, hand to her chest. "Sacrilege! You will not even suggest such a thing to our lord. He might just do it and then I'd be without my pretties."

"You are ridiculous, you know," Korinna said to her friend.

"At least I'm ridiculous with pretty shoes. Right, Tamuel? I see from your suit you're a man who enjoys fashion."

He nodded. "I am. And your shoes are lovely. And certainly shouldn't be wasted serving us. You should go to the party now."

Her pale blue eyes glowed. "Really? If you're sure? I could always stay a little longer to see to your every need." She winked as she stepped back from the table.

He didn't respond. In fact, his gaze was on Korinna, not Dianna. Strange. Not only would most men be begging at Dianna's feet about now, he was a cupid. Playful flirting was his thing. Pity she'd realised that too late when they were younger. Frowning, she said, "We'll call if we need anything." She didn't need Dianna to help her investigate the gem's magic. At least, not while Tam was here. "Have fun at the party."

"Thank you. You're the best, Kor." Dianna kissed her on the cheek before turning to Tam. "Ring if you need anything." She draped her hand on his shoulder. "Anything at all." Then she spun in a circle and disappeared in a cloud of pink and lavender.

He waved his hand, coughing a little. "Someone should tell your friend she needs to work on her exit magic."

Korinna snorted. "Oh, I think it worked exactly as she wanted it to." There were now pink and lavender sparkles shining in Tam's auburn hair. Korinna's fingers tingled with the need to brush them off. Her friend couldn't lay claim to him! He was hers first.

She blinked, pulling her hand back into her lap, fingers curling in so hard, her fingernails bit into her palm.

Tam wasn't hers. He'd never been hers. It was best she remember that.

She glared at him as he brushed the sparkles off his shirt. He glanced up, a rueful smile on his face. She quickly looked at the tray, grabbing the first thing that came to hand.

"Umm, since when do you like bacon?" Tam asked.

"Since forever." Instead of putting it on her plate, she bit into it and chewed, swallowed.

"Do you want some more?" he asked, lips twitching as he watched her.

She forced herself to swallow the last bit, managing not to dry retch at the salty-fatty taste left in her mouth. She couldn't let him know she'd been so distracted as to pick it up in the first place. He'd want to know why and that was a question she did not want to answer. No way, no how. She smiled brightly at him and waved away the plate. "No, it's fine. You take the rest. I know how much you love it."

"Who doesn't love bacon, right?"

"Absolutely." Her smile slipped as he tucked in. She grabbed the cranberry juice, pouring herself a large glass and swallowed it down in one go. The tartness helped rid her of the taste of bacon. Blech. Horrid stuff.

Tam had always teased her about her hatred of bacon – he'd said it was unnatural. Perhaps it was. But then, many things about her had never been quite right, had they? This was just one more thing.

She turned her attention to the rest of the tray. Eggs, scrambled as she liked them; sourdough toast, lightly golden; a bowl of fresh berries – strawberries, blackberries and blueberries, her favourites; and a couple of croissants and jam. She frowned a little as she spooned some eggs onto toast. There was way too much food here for one person.

Oh! Dianna's surprise when she'd caught Tam in Korinna's room this morning had been fake. But how had she known he was there?

That was when she spied the door, slightly ajar, on the opposite side of her room. Where had that come from? Her suite comprised of this living and study area, her bedroom and an ensuite. There wasn't another room off it. Why would Hades have added a room—

Persephone! She'd obviously asked Hades to create a room for Tam to stay in as part of her suite. Why on earth would they do that? They had never situated any other interview subjects near her suite, let alone created another room that led right off her living area.

What in all hells was Seph up to? And was Tam in on it?

She gave him the side-eye. He didn't notice, too taken with his breakfast to do more than stop to breathe. A smile flickered, unbidden, on her lips. He had always loved breakfast the most of any meal, even when the fare had been minimal through various parts of their training. Perhaps he'd been hungriest then. She'd never asked. But it had always been enjoyable watching how he tucked into the food they were given to break their fast. He always ate like there was no tomorrow. But then again, he'd kind of lived like that too. At least, he had when she'd known him. A cupid version of a mid-teen terror when he'd first moved to the mountain camp, he'd been turning into the grown-up version before he'd disappeared.

Her smile faded.

Anger returned. And a terrible sadness along with it.

She pushed at the sadness, grabbing at the anger, wanting it to fill her. But the sadness remained. She had to get over it though. She needed to go with him to visit Clodia, especially given they had the gem. The ancient witch was rumoured to know things about the ancient Gods and even more ancient magics that lay at the heart of the very spell she wanted to use from the Eleusinian Mysteries Grimoire. Talking to the Vestal High Priestess would bring her one step closer to completing her vow. She would have to spend up to a week with him. She could rope in these wayward emotions and desires to get what she wanted. She would rope them in. It wasn't like he could return her feelings after all; he was a cupid and she was … well, her – a useless, damaged witch of unspecified heritage who didn't deserve love after what she'd done.

He glanced up at her, smiled. "I missed this."

His words, that look, made her want to cry, but instead, she nodded and gave her attention to her breakfast.

"I'm surprised you haven't jumped me yet."

"What?" Rinna's head snapped up. The spoonful of eggs on the way to her mouth dropped, landing with a splat on the edge of her plate, spraying across the table and spattering her Yummy Sushi pyjamas. She didn't seem to notice as she stared at him, her big topaz eyes widening, a stain of red painting her cheeks. "I wouldn't ... I didn't ..."

For a moment, Tamuel wanted to tease her for misunderstanding his words, but the need died as fast as it came. He had never been able to stand to see her pained in any way. So, rather than teasing, he gestured to the gem hanging against his chest. "For this. I thought you'd be more interested in looking at it than eating breakfast."

"Oh, I ... um ... Yes. Of course. I am. Very interested." She picked up her spoon, staring at the mess she'd made on the table and her pyjamas. "Oh, I'm sorry. Did any get on you?"

"None. But it did get on you." He waved a hand. Magic prickled in the air and the mess disappeared.

She swallowed hard. "Impressive."

"Hardly." It was the kind of simple spell she'd mastered long before they'd begun their training – where he'd struggled for a long time, his cupid and warlock powers not seeming to play well with one another. Until she'd befriended him and begun to help and they'd discovered their powers had a certain symbiosis together, hers helping to rope in his and allow him to get a handle on them; his feeding into hers, allowing her to do more complicated spells than she should have been able to at such a young age – an indication of the promise of the powerful magical practitioner she was bound to become. And it had grown. He sensed it before he even entered her room yesterday. Her power was a tang on the air, a constant vibration emanating from her skin, glowing in her eyes. But there was a strange wrongness about it. Was the wrongness why she hadn't used it to clean up such a simple mess?

And come to think of it, why had Dianna been so concerned with making certain Rinna had everything she needed? Surely someone with as much power as Rinna had in her little finger could summon anything she wanted? He half-expected her to click her fingers and call the HeartsBlood Gem to her. And yet, hands clenched in her lap, she asked, "Can you tell me how you came to get it? All the rumours I tracked down said it was used by the Vestal High Priestess Clodia and then lost with her when she disappeared."

He focused on her question – his could wait until she was more comfortable with him again. "It didn't disappear. It was tied into the garden of the Vestal Temple in Roma where Clodia laid her curse to take my mother's Goddess-given power for her own. She used it to amplify her magics to place the curse and channel the power into herself from my mother."

"What a misuse of its power."

He nodded. "Yes. We think that misuse was why her spell backfired. Rather than transferring the powers to Clodia, it transmuted them, pushing them down deep inside my mother, attached to her eternal soul. Her powers travelled with her through her incarnations but she wasn't able to use them because the transmutation had the unfortunate side-effect of energising Clodia's curse, like a battery."

"Why would it do that?"

"Protective magic going haywire? Clodia couldn't take my mother's powers as long as they were hidden inside her and the HeartsBlood Gem hid itself where it was last used until I found it. We planned to use it to reverse the curse, but Clodia had also been tied to the area." He told her of what had happened, of how they had almost lost everything until her mother sacrificed the power that should have been hers to open the rift into the Void and pushed Clodia there. The powers had disappeared into the Void with the evil priestess-witch.

"I vowed that night to do everything I could to get my mother's powers back. I've been following every lead for the last eight months. I managed to find out Hades and Zeus took Clodia from the Void and put her in Tartarus as punishment, but the power wasn't with her. I tried everything I knew to search for it in the Void, but nothing worked. My only chance is to speak to her."

"And you need the gem to do that."

His fingers closed around the blood-red stone. "She is tied to it in the same way my mother is. I think I can use it to get the answers I need, but also, to transfer the power from wherever it is back into my mother. But while there was a lot of research – primarily yours – that stated it could be used in this way, there was nothing to tell me exactly how. Nothing I've done has made it react in any way since Jules gave it to me."

"Of course it didn't. The gem, whether it is truly a piece of a Goddess' heart or not, was created by a Goddess aligned with mother nature. Its spells and power can only be untapped by a female with a like power."

"That makes sense. Although, if that's the case, then how am I to use it?"

"You'd need a female to help you use it. Although, given you inherited some of your powers from your mother, you most likely will only need the witch to act as a channel and not use her actual powers. It probably would have worked for you if your mother had just held it with you." She frowned. "But she should have known that if she'd held the gem even after she lost her powers – the gem would be happy to whisper its secrets to her. Why isn't she here with you?"

"Because I didn't tell her what I was doing when I asked for the gem."

"What?"

"She would never have agreed with my plan and would have tried to make me take back my vow. She says she's perfectly happy with her lot." He shook his head. "But I know she can't be. Not when it means she won't get to live forever with her soulmate, my father. Not when her human death will lead to his. I see the sadness in her, feel the pain of the loss that is to come in knowing her death will snuff both their lights from this world. And I can't ... I have to ..."

She placed her hand over his as he shook his head, words failing him. Her lips trembled a little, eyes full of an empathy he'd not felt from anyone but her in all his long years.

For a long, timeless moment, they stared at each other, hands gripping, her beautiful eyes on his, knowing, understanding; just as she'd done so many times when they'd been friends. It comforted him, wrapping him in warmth. He eased forward, his hand coming up to cup her face. "Rinna."

She turned her head, lips finding his palm; warm, her breath slightly damp as she pressed a kiss into his skin. Her eyes closed, long lashes a sweep of darkness against too-pale cheeks.

He held his breath, wanting her to stay where she was and yet move closer.

Her eyes opened, she looked up at him.

A punch in the heart, the stark want there. "Rinna," he whispered again.

An alarm peeled through the silence – the chronometer.

The sound broke the spell – of him, of her, of them. She jerked away, her chair skidding back, the nasty squawk vying with the alarm.

He blinked. Looked up at her. She seemed to be as shocked by what had almost happened as him. "Rinna ..." he began.

The chronometer beeped, a voice replacing the shrill alarm: *"The veil is thinning. Alignment adjusting ... adjusting ... The Underworld's position has changed. Time has shifted. One week in the Underworld is now equal to two hours in the Earthly Realm. The clocks will strike twelve on All Hallows' Eve in one and a half weeks Tartarus time. Allotted time lost: two and a half weeks. Alignment still changing. Further alarms will be forthcoming."*

He stared at the chronometer to verify the words he still couldn't believe. "Shit."

"You used my voice? How? Why?"

He looked up, met her confused gaze. "I pulled it out of my memory vault – I missed you. Besides, something about the specs reminded me of you. I should have known you designed it."

They stared at each other for a long moment until she blinked, took a step back. Cleared her throat. "Umm, well, we should get going before you run out of more time."

"You want to come?"

Her lips quirked. "You don't think I'm going to let you go wandering through the Underworld and into Tartarus alone, do you? You don't know anything about all the nasties down there that could stop you from getting to Clodia's cell."

"Isn't the Hells-Key supposed to help with that?"

She picked at her cuticles as she stared him down. "It doesn't shield from everything. And the Underworld will fight you all the way, especially if you don't know what you're doing."

"And you do? I got the impression you never leave these suites."

Another shrug. "I've been out. When I need to talk to an interview subject. You need me to go with you. Not to mention, you need my help to work the gem."

"You could tell me what I need to know now. And I could ask Dianna or one of the other Soteira to come with me. You don't have to come if you don't want to." What was he doing, giving her an out? He wanted her to come.

"Don't you want me to come with you?"

"I do ... I just ... I thought, after you believed I left and didn't write, that you wouldn't want to spend more time with me than absolutely necessary."

Her mouth worked for a moment and she looked down at her lap. "About that ... I ... I ... Maybe there is something to what you say about someone intercepting our letters." She cleared her throat, glanced up at him again. "Besides, I want to speak with Clodia myself."

He stared at her, expecting her to look away, but she didn't. Despite all the changes, the spark of the girl he'd once known was still within her. "Okay."

"Okay?"

He shrugged. "It makes more sense. We can save time by discussing the gem and the spells we might need to use as we travel. Now that I've lost a few weeks, it seems like the best option."

"Oh. Of course."

Was that a flash of hurt in her eyes? Damn, he didn't mean to make her feel rejected – he just didn't want his eagerness to show too much.

He leaned forward, stilled her fingers as they clenched in her lap. Her gaze met his, boring into him as she frowned a little. He wanted to kiss that frown away. He swallowed hard. "And it will give us time to discuss what happened after Eros took me. And maybe, we can make plans to find out why someone meddled after ..."

"After?"

"After we've finished here."

She looked down, the dark sweep of her lashes against the shadows under her eyes doing all sorts of things inside him – things he gathered close, not wanting her to see. No point in spooking her by the violence of his feelings. She could never love him back in the same way.

"Okay."

"So, you want to find out who kept those letters from us after we finish this?"

Her smile faded, replaced by shadows in her eyes. "One thing at a time," she whispered.

He nodded quickly. "One thing at a time."

She stood. "So ..." She cleared her throat. "I should go get changed and attach the Hells-Key. You need to do the same – that suit will get wrecked down in the tunnels."

"Dianna said there's clothes for me in the room."

"Good. Umm ... see you back here in a few hours."

"It will take you that long to get changed?"

She smirked, eyes glinting. "I see you are as yet to read the instructions for the Hells-Key. You'll need some recovery time."

He grimaced. "Does it hurt?"

Her lips curled into a small smile. "Not as much as you think it would given you have to attach it to your chest. But it does take something out of you." She backed up a few more steps. "I'll see you when you're ready."

"Okay. I'll ..." She'd already disappeared into her room, the heavy carved black doors slamming shut behind her. He let out a sigh. "Well, that went better than expected." She'd forgiven him – maybe – and she was helping him, so he would have more time to make certain that forgiveness stuck and maybe they could start up their friendship again. Life would be much more tolerable with Rinna in it.

He only hoped the Hells-Key spell wasn't as painful as she'd made it sound – although, considering Hades created them, it was probably going to be worse.

CHAPTER 7

amuel glanced at Korinna as she marched stoically at his side. She seemed nervous – shoulders held tightly, eyes darting around. Not that he blamed her. The journey was proving to be difficult. More difficult than he'd thought it would be with Hades' Hells-Key melted into his chest.

He touched the still-throbbing place where the Hells-Key had magically become a part of him half a day ago. By all the Realms, it had hurt.

He glanced at Rinna again, spying the red skin showing above the V of her dark grey, long-sleeved Soteira tunic. She seemed unphased by it. Yet his powers were still sparking and fighting it every step, not wanting to accept what was basically death magic anywhere near it. Rinna had been right – it had knocked him for six and he'd lost consciousness for over an hour. Then it had taken him another hour to stop his limbs from shaking so badly he couldn't even stand, let alone get changed. The upshot of which was he still hadn't gone into his mind vault to retrieve the memory of the sigil. A problem for when they returned.

He frowned down at the witch at his side. "Do you wear the Hells-

Key a lot?" That would explain why she wasn't affected by the magic of attaching it.

"No. I don't need it most of the time – only when I want to interview a soul who's down here that Hades can't bring to his palace for reasons of security. Why?" She glanced up at him, grimaced. "Still feeling it, aren't you? We could have waited a little longer – the chronometer hasn't gone off again and according to the map, the path to the Gates of Tartarus will only take us a few days at the moment."

"How long after that to Clodia's cell?"

She shrugged. "The map won't show us until we step into Tartarus. The Underworld and Hell Realms are too large to put on a hundred-thousand maps let alone one." She showed him the map. "This has been spelled to show the most direct route."

"Kind of like Google Maps."

"Google Maps?"

He shook his head. "Never mind. So it tells you how long the journey will be?"

"There is an indicator here." She pointed at an hourglass image where the sand shifted from the top bowl to the bottom. "However, because things constantly shift and change down here, it's never certain how long a journey will take." She glanced up at him again. "I wish we could stop so you could rest but now we're in the tunnels ..." She looked around them. "It's best not to stop."

"I don't need to rest." He waved his hand, not wanting to show weakness in front of her – he'd just got her trusting him again, after all. "I was wondering how come the Hells-Key didn't affect you like it did me?"

"Oh. Probably because it's not fighting against my magic."

"Why not?" It should have, given her magic was one of life and healing.

"I ... don't use my magic."

"What? Why?"

She shrugged nonchalantly, but something about the way she held her shoulders told him she was the opposite. "I just prefer to do things without it. I've not used it for a long time."

"But I can feel it."

Her gaze darted up to him. "That's not possible. I keep it locked down."

He waved his hand at her. "Well, you're not doing a very good job because it's all over you. You're glowing with it."

Fear sharpened her features as she looked down at herself. "I'm not."

"You are."

She looked up at him, eyes pained, pleading. "You're lying."

He couldn't stand that look in her eyes, so he smiled. "You're not glowing," he lied. She wasn't lighting up the tunnel, but her skin shone like it was moon-struck. Maybe he could see it because of the way their powers had always worked together. A thought to delve into another time.

"Then why did you say you could?"

"What I meant was that I can feel it in you, like a vibration deep down."

She took in a shuddering breath. "I'll have to tighten my shielding. Sorry if it's worrying you."

"I'm not worried. I always liked your magic. It's soothing."

She frowned up at him. "It's hardly that."

He wanted to press her but she flicked the map and stared down at it. "We need to take the next left."

He glanced at the map she insisted she be in charge of. He'd wanted to tease her about being a bossy-boots but the words caught in his mouth as she'd raked her glossy curls into a knot on the top of her head, told him to grab his backpack – she'd packed it for him while he was out of commission – and walked out the door.

"Wouldn't that right path get us there faster?"

"It would, except …" She tapped the tunnel that led off from it. "We'd have to go through the Banshee Hall – and trust me, you don't want to go there. Those girls could talk your head off."

She shook her head, a lock of hair falling down to kiss the skin of her neck. He wanted to brush it aside. Place his lips there instead.

His mouth dried. He coughed.

"Here." She folded the map up under her arm, then pulled a metal bottle out of the backpack he wore and handed it to him. "I packed a few bottles of water for each of us and some food – I didn't know how long we'd be gone and it isn't wise to eat anything you might be offered in the halls or tunnels of the Underworld or Tartarus."

"So I've heard," he rasped, his mouth as dry and hot as … Well, hell. He chuckled to himself then took a quick chug of the water. It went down too fast, making him cough and splutter.

She slapped his back. "Easy. We could be down here for days and you don't want to use up all your water before we're done."

"I am a cupid. I can do without food or water for some time."

"You've never tried to do so in the Underworld though, have you? Time isn't the only thing that's different down here. Speaking of which, what does your chronometer say?"

He glanced down at it. "The alignment hasn't changed."

"You have to take your time from Australian Eastern Standard time?"

He nodded. "I cast the spell that allowed me to come down here in corporeal form in the Coven library under my parent's Melbourne mansion."

"Weren't you worried they'd feel what you were doing and try to stop you?"

"Of course." His parents would never have let him take this risk. "I made certain they'd left for the Coven's Halloween party before I opened the portal from the library – nobody but my mum would come down there after hours, so among other considerations, it was the safest place to punch a hole through the weakening veil."

"I still don't understand how you managed to make the portal open. The spell from the Mysteries Grimoire must have taken huge amounts of magical energies to keep you corporeal and let you open the portal that brought you to Hades' Palace. How did it not burn you up?"

He cocked his brow. "That was the easy part. I used other magic to help power the spell."

Her brow furrowed more deeply, the look of consternation on her face bringing back memories of how she always looked when she was stumped. He wanted to run his finger down that groove and smooth it away, but put aside the urge as she asked, "How? That kind of magic doesn't just lie around waiting to be used. You were alone, so you couldn't syphon off power from anyone else, even if you had a want to do such a thing."

"I never said I was alone. I just said my parents weren't there."

"But even if you syphoned someone's power with permission, it wouldn't be enough. Not for you."

"Why'd you say that?"

"Well, that's not exactly how your powers work – you were always more of a giver than a taker. With me at least." She blushed, frown deepening.

"You're right, I didn't do that."

She nodded briskly. "As I said. And I know you didn't use the HeartsBlood Gem given you've been unable to use it. So, how did you do it?"

He blinked, lost in her eyes again as she stared up at him. "What?"

"Get here? Without the help of the HeartsBlood Gem. How did you get enough power to make the spell work?"

"Umm ..." He shot her a quick smile to cover his lapse in concentration. "Well, my mother's Coven have managed to build up quite a collection of grimoires and books on magic – both light and dark. Over the years, as Coven members have died, many of their spirits have stayed around to help guard and look over the connection. An underground chamber, the size of many football fields, was built on top of a couple of main lay-lines, with Stephens House constructed on top to conceal the entrance from unwanted eyes. It houses the Melbourne Coven's library as well as the Stevens' private collection. My mother, Jules, and my great-grandmama, Violetta, are the archivist and librarian and they continue to build and add to it."

"Making it the perfect place for your spell. I get it. But that still doesn't explain where you got the excess power to drive the spell. The power reserves for a spell like this to not only break through the veil, but allow you entry into the Death Realms while alive and corporeal are enormous. I mean, Hades himself had to bring me and the other Soteira down here and used considerable magics to do so – and while you are powerful, you're no son of a Titan."

"Yes. Well, there was also the power the Stevens' spirits gave me."

She frowned. "That might gain you enough, but only if you fully drained them." She gripped his arm, eyes widening, worry flickering there. "You didn't, did you?"

"Of course not. I would never use a spirit that way. Besides, they are too important to my family and I would never do anything to cause Mum and Dad more pain."

"Of course." She let out a shuddering breath, letting go of his arm.

It was his turn to frown – why did the thought of using up spirits like that so affect her? True, it was an evil thing to do – as evil as draining another magic user's powers without permission – but this felt more ... personal than an issue of morals. Did this have something to do with what happened to bring her here? What the fuck had happened at Pompeii? Was it more than the natural disaster they'd all been told it was? He didn't get a chance to ask, because, as her gaze met his once more, the words were lost to him.

"So ..." she said, clearing her throat and looking away. "The magic you've told me about so far would be enough to open the portal but it wouldn't be enough to keep you corporeal so you could bring the HeartsBlood Gem with you and then close the portal behind you cleanly."

Her shoulder brushed against his arm. Sparks shivered through him, making his cock twitch. He really wished she'd stop touching him so casually like that – especially given his cock didn't seem to know the meaning of a casual friendly touch from her. Thankfully, she didn't notice his pause.

She spun to face him on a gasp, continuing to walk backwards. "Don't tell me you left the portal open? Do you know how dangerous that could be? Anyone could stumble on it and fall through – or find their way from here to there."

He smiled down at her, her concern a balm. "I wasn't that stupid. The portal closed behind me."

She pressed her lips together, that little frown of consternation making his lips twitch as she said, "Then how?"

"Well, what I didn't tell you before about my mother is that she was allergic to magic."

"What? How is that possible when she had all that magic repressed inside her?"

"Remember I said how the protective magic went awry?" She nodded. "Well, the HeartsBlood Gem, in an effort to keep her safe, made her hyper-sensitive to magic."

"Another way to stop Clodia – or anyone else – from trying to steal the powers."

He nodded. "But the upshot was that her reaction to magic could be explosive. However, her work as the Coven's archivist – one of the most talented they've had in centuries – meant they had to do something about that little issue so she could work in a library full of magical books, grimoires and manuscripts."

A light lit her eye. "They created an ark, didn't they?"

He smiled brightly at her. "How did you guess?"

"It's the only option. Where did they put it?"

"Violetta created it and placed it in a secret cavern under the library that only the family spirits know is there."

"That amount of power ... it's incredibly dangerous. Surely she syphoned it off regularly."

He shook his head. "There wasn't anywhere she could syphon it too that wouldn't affect my mum. So she just kept making the ark larger."

Her mouth dropped open. "You tapped into that?"

He nodded, smiling widely. "It was quite a ride." She slapped his arm. "Ow! What was that for?"

"Do you realise how stupidly reckless that was? You could have killed yourself! Or set the entire building down on your head!" Her voice echoed sharply in the dark tunnel. "You could have caused an earthquake. Innocents could have been killed!"

"But I didn't," he said, grabbing her hand before she could hit him again.

She was trembling.

"Hey, hey, it's okay." He grasped her shoulders, stopped walking. "Nothing happened. The spell worked as it should and now I'm here with you, no worse for wear. Well, except for the bruising – you really know how to pack a punch." She didn't smile at his funning as she would have in the past. He brushed a wisp of hair from her cheek with his knuckles, too aware of the lemon and spice scent of her as it rose around him. He let go of her shoulder to cup her face. She still trembled, the shadow of something horrible flickering in her eyes.

He hated seeing it. Wanted to make that terrible look of loss just go away.

He leaned a little closer; her breath brushed against his cheeks. His gaze dipped to her lips. She bit into the lower one. He wanted to put his lips there, stop her from doing that. But first, he needed to find out why she was like this. It couldn't wait until later.

Pulling back a little, he asked, "Rinna, what happened at Pompeii? You know it wasn't your fault, right?"

She stared at him for long, silent seconds. Her mouth opened a little. He thought she was going to tell him.

His chronometer's alarm went off, screeching in the air for a few seconds that made them clap their hands to their ears, both their gazes going to the dial. It spun and shifted, the arms and gears clacking and whirring as the alarm cut off and her voice said, *"The veil is thinning. Alignment adjusting ... computing, computing ... The Underworld's position has changed. Time has shifted. One day in the Underworld is now equal to fifteen minutes in the Earthly Realm. The clocks will strike twelve on All Hallows' Eve in six days Tartarus time. Allotted time lost since last computation: five days. Alignment still changing. Further alarms will be forthcoming."*

"Shit." It was changing faster than he thought it would, even with Persephone's warnings that this All Hallows' Eve would be different.

"Something's not right," Rinna said quietly, her gaze still on the chronometer. "The Underworld should be moving further away from the Earthly Realm this All Hallows' Eve, not closer. It's not due to take that position for another fifty years, Earth Realm time."

"Ah, I forgot to tell you." He told her about Persephone's warning.

"Why didn't you tell me before now?"

"Would it have made a different?"

"Yes … No … I don't know. But I don't like to be left in the dark."

"That wasn't my intention."

She stared at him for long moments, biting her lip. "It will be okay. We still have time. We just have to hurry."

"And we weren't hurrying already?"

Her mouth quirked. "Not really." She glanced down at the map. "Rinna?"

She looked up at him. "I just … now that you're here … I didn't want it to be over too quickly. I … I missed you."

"I missed you too." His hands were somehow on her face again, his fingers stroking her cheeks. He wanted to kiss her, but he also still wanted to know what had happened to her. "Rinna …" The earth rumbled around them, making him stumble a step and let go. "What now?"

She glanced around, worry making her frown deepen. "We shouldn't have stopped." She turned to him, her hand slipping easily into his, tugging him into a walk. "We have to go."

"What are you talking about?"

"I know better than to stop in the tunnels. I shouldn't have indulged my need to …" The ground rumbled and tipped again, making them stumble back half a dozen steps. He grabbed a hold of her to steady her, but she was rock solid. More so than him. "Don't. We can't stop."

"But we're not finished here yet."

"Yes, we are. We don't have time for this." She jerked out of his hold, grabbed his hand again and pulled him into a brisk walk as earth around them rumbled, showering them in dirt.

He raised a shield bubble over them to protect them, then swung in front of her, making her stop, look up at him. He cupped her face again. "I always have time for you, Rinna. Always. And I want to know what happened to you. I want to know how I can help."

"Why?"

"I care about you. Alongside my family, you are the most important person in the world to me."

She sucked in a breath, her topaz eyes flaring gold, as if she was using her power. He could almost feel it licking inside him, twining with his, wanting to play – but he had to be imagining that because she said she never used her magic; had locked it away.

She licked her lips. "Don't say things you can't possibly mean."

"Why not? I'm allowed to give of my love. I just can't receive it in return." He swallowed against the harsh reality of Eros' curse.

The low rumbling suddenly turned into a roar and the floor bucked under them, sending the shield bubble, and them inside it, up in the air to smash against the roof of the tunnel. "What in all the hells is going on?" he yelled above the noise as they bounced back to the dirt and rubble-strewn floor.

"As I said, we don't have time for this. We've stayed in one place too long. We've got to move on."

The earth buckled again, sending the bubble bouncing back up the tunnel. He sent out ribbons of power, anchoring it into the wall before they lost more ground. "Is this what you meant when you said things changed down here? Is it because they have earthquakes?"

"Yes but ... this is far more dangerous."

"Why?"

"Don't you get it? We're both alive and corporeal. The Underworld is a place of dead things, not living beings. We're not supposed to be here and it knows it. It's trying to push us back."

"But you live in the palace."

"That's different. It's Hades' private space and he sets the rules there."

"He's the King of the Underworld. Doesn't he set the rules for everything down here?"

She shook her head, hands going out against the edges of his shield to steady herself – her touch was a caress on his magic that almost made him groan. Instead, he leaned in closer to hear her above the noise.

"... not the one who created this place. The old Gods did that – and it is still subject to the basic rules they set. The Living Realms are for the living, the Death Realms are for the dead. Even if you had more time, we would still have to hurry through these tunnels."

"I thought the Hells-Keys were supposed to allow us to slip through easily."

"This *is* easily for a corporeal being."

He shook his head at her. "And you've been down here before?"

"There were souls I needed to interview."

He couldn't help but smiling. "I always liked it when you were a little crazy."

"No time for insults – this will only get worse if we don't keep moving. It can't latch onto our essences as easily if we keep moving."

He let her go, turning to pick up the water bottle he'd dropped on the ground. "I'm glad you're here, given you're knowledge-girl."

She harrumphed at him as she resettled her pack on her back, but her lips were twitching. "Come on, non-knowledge-boy."

"That's idiot-boy to you."

Her snort of laughter had delight bubbling in his veins as they jogged forward, his shield protecting them from the ground that continued to rumble and shake around them. Something had changed between them. It wasn't what it was before, but he was willing to work on it with her to get it back there. She may not be able to love him because of his curse, but life sure was better with her in it, especially if he could help her to forgive herself for whatever she imagined she'd done. He wasn't going to let her disappear from his life ever again.

Whoever or whatever had kept them apart last time wasn't going to succeed again. If they tried that shit this time, they'd find out the hard way that this time he'd fight to the death to keep her with him.

As they jogged, the screams of the inhabitants of the lower chambers became louder and louder. The map indicated the most direct route was through the Morningstar's lands, the entrance to Tartarus currently closest to his kingdom than any other Hell Realm.

The faster they moved, the fewer the quakes around them.

"You get the feeling the Underworld still isn't happy we're here?" he said to Rinna, trying to make her laugh.

She just shot him a look. "Did you really think it was going to be easy?"

"No. Quite frankly, it's same old same old. I've come to expect things to always be difficult." Including, apparently, his relationship with her. At one time, it was one of the easiest things in his life; a blessing he'd never thought to have. Of course he should have expected it to get ripped away. He glanced at her as she jogged, a frown on her face once more. "What is it?"

Her shadowed gaze met his. "Has life really not been easy for you?"

"Why would it have been?"

She shrugged. "I don't know. You always seemed so charmed. Everything came easy to you. And you know … you're a cupid."

"Are you kidding me? I had to fight every day not to be left behind. Everyone was better at everything than me. And there wasn't a group I could truly belong to, not at the training camp and not outside of it." He'd got used over the years to being called a mutt or a mongrel. "But at least at the camp I had you. When Eros took me, I had no one."

"You had Eros."

He snorted. "Eros might be my grandfather but that doesn't mean anything when it comes to the other cupids or the job I had to do. He gave me the training the others get then left me on my own."

"Isn't that what happens to the other cupids?"

"Maybe. But they are made to be cupids – I'm not. Also, they don't have to deal with having both cupid and warlock powers. And they certainly didn't have the Gods and Goddesses interfering constantly; everyone always so interested in the cupid with a demi-God father and a reincarnating-witch mother tied to a curse. It felt like I was constantly under the microscope; everyone expecting me to fail or setting me up to fail."

"Did you?"

He shook his head, jaw firmed. "Not once. I wouldn't give those miserable sods the satisfaction."

"I had no idea."

"Why would you?"

They ran around a curve only to come upon another rockfall. "Damn it!" she said, instantly backing up while glancing at the map again. "That was the last path into the Morningstar's lands." They'd tried a dozen others before being turned around by rockfalls blocking the way or tunnels being cut in two by what looked like bottomless chasms. "Hades is going to be really pissed there's this much damage."

"This can't be the first time this has happened."

She shook her head. "No, but I can't remember it ever being this bad."

"Maybe the portents Persephone mentioned are causing even more havoc than we thought they would."

"Or, maybe the Underworld – or something – doesn't want us to get to Clodia."

"Why did you have to say that out loud? Now you've jinxed us."

She narrowed her eyes at him. "I did not jinx us. There is no such thing."

The ground rumbled again, bucking under their feet even though they were moving back up the tunnel. "You think?" he said.

She tried to look at the map as they jogged. "This way," she said, indicating a tunnel she'd chosen not to go down earlier.

It was darker than the tunnel they'd been in, doors lining either side a few metres apart.

A hand shot out between the bars of the cell as Tam jogged past. He dodged it. Another hand tried a grab at him from the next cell, its bone-like fingers scraping his shoulder, trying to latch on.

"Watch out," Korinna said, yanking him away. "You don't want to let them touch you."

"Why? What can they do?" He eyed the cell doors and the rickety-looking bars that didn't seem secure at all. From further down, a pathetic wail started, picked up by another soul, and another, until the air was full of wailing.

"Nothing magical," Rinna shouted over the din. "But they can tear at your flesh. And eat it."

"Ew!"

She shrugged. "Well, cupid flesh wouldn't sound so bad if you've not had anything to eat for thousands of years."

He twisted to look at the bony arm still stretched out, reaching for him even though he was too far away. "They've been here for thousands of years?"

"Earth Realm time. Here it's far longer."

"How can Hades stand having to come down here?"

She bit her lip. "I don't know. He doesn't talk about it and I've never wanted to ask." She'd always suspected it was torture for him, but it was a guess she didn't want confirmed; she hated to think that the God who'd protected and cosseted her and let her hide away in his home for all these years was being tortured by the job he was forced to do.

"No. I suppose I don't really want the answer to that question either," Tam said, echoing her thoughts.

She glanced at him. He frowned into the dark of the tunnel – the narrowest they'd been through so far – eyeing the bars of the cells and the darkness that hid untold torture within.

"Come on, we need to keep moving. But keep to the middle of the tunnel."

"You don't have to tell me twice."

They trudged on, winding their way through the tunnels, keeping to a brisk pace, eating and drinking on the move.

They spoke of many things as they walked over the next few days – or what passed for days in the Underworld. It was often hard to tell given there was no day or night – but somehow, she managed to keep him from asking what he'd started to ask before the first earthquake hit. She knew she couldn't keep his questions at bay forever, but she really didn't want to see the look on his face when he found out – pity or disgust, equally bad – and she certainly didn't want to have the conversation about what she'd vowed.

He didn't need to know she planned to die to fulfil it. That was nobody's business but her own. But she'd never been very good at lying to him. She rounded a corner. Maybe she could tell him the basics to stop him questioning further and—

She almost fell over the edge of a yawning chasm.

Tam's arm slammed out in front of her. "Careful."

"I see it as well as you," she said, shaking her head at him, more annoyed with herself than him. She glanced down at the map. It shouldn't have been there.

"This is ridiculous. We've been walking for two days. You need to rest. You're exhausted."

She glared at him, hating that aside from the few smudges of dirt on his face and the shoulder of his black tunic, he looked as fresh as when they started out. "I don't need a rest."

"Rinna. That is obviously untr—"

She held her hand up. "I don't need you to protect me. I've been looking after myself for almost two thousand years."

"Have you?"

The way his gaze flickered over her made her hyper-aware of the bagginess of her clothes, the shadows under cheeks and eyes, the paleness of her skin.

She bit the inside of her cheek as she backed away from the crumbling edge. "I can't rest even if I wanted to. It's not going to let us. We have to keep going."

He stared at her for a long moment, but when the earth rumbled below them and more of the edge fell into the chasm, forcing them back, he simply said, "Where to?"

She glanced down at the map – it shifted and changed, changed again, and again before settling, indicating a passage they'd passed half a day ago. It led into a larger chamber, one that had a tunnel leading straight to the Gates of Tartarus. She bit her lip. "Is there another way," she asked the map. It didn't alter.

"What's wrong?"

"Nothing. It should be fine. It's just, I've heard it's one of the worst parts of the Underworld tunnels."

"Worse than what we've been through?"

"Much worse."

He glanced back at the chasm. "We don't really have a choice, do we?"

"No."

The earth beneath them suddenly surged up, tossing them to the ceiling. Tam threw a shield bubble around them again before they hit the roof. He managed to right them as they bounced off the roof and keep them moving back from the chasm that widened with every rumble. The screams of the damned filled the air as one cell after another fell into the bottomless pit.

"Poor bastards."

Korinna nodded – it didn't matter that the souls here had deserved their incarceration and torture – being swallowed by the Underworld wasn't a final death she would wish on anyone.

They bumped up the tunnel, Tam trying to steady their progress, but they overshot the narrow entrance the map indicated they had to go down, the earth pushing them back and back. "This is ridiculous," Tam grumbled. "It's like it's trying to kill us now, not get rid of us."

"Who's jinxing us now?"

"It's not a jinx if it's actually happening to—"

She held up her hand as the hairs on the back of her neck stood up and a chill ran over her body. "Shh."

"What?"

She shushed him, listening. Then the sound she'd never wanted to hear again. "Hells, no. What are they doing here?"

"What?"

"Wraiths. Up ahead," she whispered, pointing to the glow that shone from the tunnel she'd planned to go down. Not the reddish-orange glow that lit most of the passages, but a sickly green one that writhed and moved, tentacles of it reaching out as if probing the air, seeking, hunting. The sound that had caught her attention – harsh whispers filled with screams – drew closer.

"Quick, we have to hide."

CHAPTER 9

Korinna rushed to the side of the tunnel, relieved to find that the fissure she'd noticed on the way down was still there despite all the earth's movements. In fact, she thought it might have widened a little. They could both squeeze in and hide until the wraiths were past. "Come on," she whispered over her shoulder.

Tam stood where he was in the centre of the tunnel, staring at her. "What are you worried about? Wraiths can't kill us. Not while we're wearing the Hells-Keys."

"Shh," she said, grabbing his arm to pull him into the mouth of the fissure. "They'll hear you."

"Still don't see the problem," he whispered loudly.

Of course he didn't. "They can't kill us down here like they can in the Earth Realm," she whispered as she pulled him closer, intent on squeezing into the small space. "But they can hurt us. Physically and spiritually."

"Spiritually? I've never heard they could do that."

Damn him for focusing on that part of what she'd said. "Yeah, they pull out your deepest secrets, your darkest emotions, and use them against you. But that's not what I'm worried about." She was, but she wasn't about to admit that to him. "You think the earthquakes and tremblings have been bad? You don't want to know what will happen if we spill blood down here. Now shut up and hide with me." Her lips were almost against his ear now – she really didn't want the wraiths to hear her. They were busy moaning – the shrieks of the stolen souls inside them coming out of their open maws – but if they stopped, they'd hear her and Tam clearly even if they were hidden by the crevice.

"What are they doing here?" he asked, finally using his inside whisper-voice. "With the veil fading tonight, I would have thought they'd have more auspicious places to be than down here."

"They've still got days, remember? Plenty of time to power up – which they'll need to do if they want to break through the veil and haunt more than these halls. Now shush and get in here. They'll still be able to see you." He nodded and pushed forward, crowding her. "Oof. When did you get so big?"

"Ms Korinna! Such a personal question," he whispered, his lips touching her ear, making her shiver as frissons of electricity rode through her nerves. "But I'm glad you noticed."

She would have smacked him for his teasing in the past – such a cupid thing to do – but she couldn't seem to muster the ability, her entire body revelling in the sensation of his warm strength pushing up against her.

He pushed closer. Her back hit rock.

"Am I in?"

She ignored the sexually tinged words whispered against her ear and glanced over his shoulder to the nasty green glow lighting up the tunnel beyond. The lips of the crevice were just beyond his back. He really was very broad-shouldered. "No. The fissure isn't deep enough for its shadows to hide you from the wraiths' glow."

If only she could take a chance and use her magic to protect him, but she couldn't risk it getting out of her control once again. Couldn't risk another mistake of judgement. Couldn't risk another person she cared for being killed. But then magic tingled in the air around them; a cloud of darkness starting to cover the entrance behind him. He was trying to protect them, but she wasn't sure it was going to be enough.

She opened her mouth to tell him he'd need to change his spell, but her jaw snapped shut as the wraiths' ugly magic whispered along the walls, calling to her. Whispering voices urging her to unburden herself of every hidden thing inside her.

She firmed her mind's shields against them but it wasn't quite enough. Memories she never let in, except in nightmares, flooded into her mind: the volcanic rumblings; the ruling council of Pompeii coming to her, worried, seeking help; her calming response that made them ignore what was so obvious – that she didn't have control over the sleeping volcanic God, Vesuvius, in the way she should. Instead of evacuating, they went about their business, trusting her; trusting her judgement.

That moment looped in her mind now as it did in her nightmares. So stupid and prideful to think she could handle it alone, that she didn't need to call Seph or Demeter for instructions on what to do. She'd been so hurt by Tam's leaving, his betrayal, that she was determined to prove she could do this without him or anyone.

She couldn't stop the images from playing out; when she'd headed out from her temple, past the still-worried people, soothing their fear with waves of her magic, a stupid, beneficent smile on her face; she'd felt so pleased with herself as she'd left them behind, laughing and smiling and shouting after her their love and worship as they must have done for her mother when she was their guardian, and headed up the volcano to soothe Vesuvius, to bind him with a spell of restful sleeping. But her magic faltered and instead of soothing Vesuvius into a peaceful, dreamless sleep, she woke him up. Her magic had worked fine as she'd transported herself back to Pompeii, her plan to get the people to evacuate. But even as the volcano belched more and more sulphuric clouds into the sky and the ground rumbled and cracked, the people went about their business, still somehow affected by her spell of calm even after she withdrew it.

Then before she could think what to do, the volcano erupted in a gush of fire and clouds of steam and poisonous gas. Her spell of calm finally broke, panic and confusion and terror tearing free. But as it did, she remembered a spell, one she'd read in a book that Tam had smuggled from the camp's library – one they shouldn't have had access to.

As the people started to run – too late. Far too late – and the deadly pyroclastic cloud swept towards them, she didn't give a thought to if she could do such a powerful spell designed for two or more spellweavers; only the words Tam had whispered to her as she'd read the spell that first time – "You could do this. You're powerful enough to do this alone." He'd been so sure, had made her so sure in that moment of panic that she could save the people of Pompeii despite all the signs telling her it was a Fated event.

She attempted to fold space, to transport the entire city and its people elsewhere. But the greatest magic couldn't fight Fate and the spell snapped back at her, the people of Pompeii paying for her hubris. Instead of transporting them and their city, it cut their souls from their bodies in one, horrifying instant and thrust them through the tear in space she'd created, sucking them into the Void.

They hadn't been killed by the pyroclastic cloud of super-heated dust that enveloped the city a moment later. They'd been killed by her.

They should have all gone to Elysium. Instead, she'd thought to vanquish destiny and had instead forced on them a worse Fate than the one designed for them.

She'd thrown herself forward, screaming her pain, her guilt, her loss, willing to join those souls lost in the Void … and collided with the shield that sprang up around the temple, protecting it and her from the force of the volcanic explosion.

Even after the tear had snapped closed, she continued to throw herself against the shield until her arms and legs and body were bloody and bruised, her voice nothing but ragged gasps, the image of Pompeii as it was swallowed in the volcanic cloud imprinted on her mind for all eternity. She barely noticed Persephone and Demeter arrive until they picked her up and carried her away. She tried to stop them, to stay, to undo what had been done, but they were implacable and she too weak in every way to fight them, the spell having drained everything from her except her life. She wished it had finished its job.

That feeling of helplessness, of being wrong, of choosing wrongly, had never left her. It pulled at her even now as the wraiths writhed their way forward, urging her to give up on a quest she was unlikely ever to finish. She wasn't strong enough. The Fates weaving of their threads might have made her spellwork falter but they hadn't affected her reason. She'd been prideful and selfish in thinking she could change what was meant to happen. She was a screw up. Why did she think she could make it right? Hadn't she learned she couldn't trust her decisions? Couldn't trust her instincts? She really should give up. Should just go out there and let the wraiths have her pain, her guilt, her secret. Not that it was truly a secret. Persephone, Hades, Demeter – they all knew what had happened; what she'd done. It didn't matter that they'd spent centuries trying to make her believe that she could have done nothing to stop the deaths and that what happened wasn't her fault. She knew those platitudes for what they were – the desperate words of people who didn't want to face that what had happened to the people of Pompeii ultimately *was* her fault. They might have been Fated to die but *she* was the reason their souls were lost in the Void, in eternal pain, rather than enjoying the bliss of Elysium, as had been their Fate.

She was responsible for that horror. An eternal horror. Unless she fixed it. But could she fix it? Maybe giving in to the wraiths' fatal call was her penance. That her soul deserved to be as lost as the Pompeiians were.

"Rinna, by the hells. I can't believe … What are you doing?"

She looked at her hands pressed against his chest. He was in her way. "I need to get out there."

"Why?"

She looked up at him. "They're calling to me. Can't you hear them? I need to go to them. They'll take it all. Everything I've done. They'll make me pay. Truly pay. I have to go. Let me go."

She pushed him, but he was a rock, immovable, his arms tight around her.

"No, Rinna. Don't listen to them. It wasn't your fault. What happened wasn't your fault."

"You know?" She gasped as her gaze met his; at the shadows of her grief and pain reflected there.

But then they were gone as quickly as they'd come and he said, "About Pompeii? Everyone knows the volcanic explosion was Fated. You couldn't have saved those people."

"I know that!" She wanted her voice to be a yell, but it came out as a harsh, pain-filled whisper. "But their souls. I lost their souls. And I have to get them back. It's my penance. At least, I thought it was. But maybe my true penance is giving up my soul." Her gaze slid to the green glow over his shoulder seen even through his shadow-cloak hanging in the crevice opening. She pushed against him again. Maybe she should use her magic against him.

"Rinna." His voice, a harsh explosion of air against her face as he shook her. "Look at me, Rinna."

She didn't want to, but something in his voice reached inside her, forcing her gaze to his.

"Don't give into them. Whatever pain they're calling to, don't give in to it. If you do, you will never be able to set right whatever it is you think you did. And you want that, don't you? To set it right?"

Yes. Yes, she did. With everything in her. She nodded.

"Then fight it. Fight the compulsion."

"I can't," she said, the wraith's call barbed tendrils in her mind. "I'm too weak. Always too weak. I missed the signs telling me I was supposed to let them go, to shepherd their souls to Elysium as they deserved. I thought I could fix it, but I just made it so much worse. I deserve everything bad coming to me."

"No." His arms tightened around her, his gaze a black blaze – he was using his warlock powers, building a shield bubble around them – why hadn't he done that before? – pulling the shadow-cloak around it, the sensation shivering over her like a caress. She should wonder why that was, but the ebony of his eyes captured her and all she could think of was him. There was nothing but black in his eyes now. It should have terrified but instead it fascinated her as it always had. This sign, of him using his warlock powers, had confused all their trainers and teachers; was something they'd never been able to train out of him. Why they'd ever want to, she didn't know – his black eyes were as beautiful and magnetic as the indigo gifted to him from his cupid heritage.

The shadow-shield he created pulled in around them. It should have been cold and frightening, but as it always had been, Tam's magic was a warm fur blanket brushing against her skin. His power – so achingly familiar – shivered over her, through her, its touch a caress, bringing light where there was darkness; hope where there was doubt; prying loose the wraiths' barbed tendrils, turning them to dust.

And as the tendrils disintegrated, Tam's words, a faint echo to begin with, grew louder, filling up her mind, pushing out the images that haunted her in her sleep, that had come to her with the wraiths' call, replacing them with a single image: her nestled in the safety and warmth of his arms, protected, loved.

Even though she knew it couldn't be true, that she didn't deserve it, she clung to it; it protected her as much as his shield did from the wraiths' compulsive call.

The shrieking came closer, the sickening glow lighting up the tunnel over Tam's shoulder – his power allowing her to see through the cloud even though she could no longer feel the pull of the wraiths. So clever, her cupid. One of them needed to see when the danger had passed; he had gifted that control to her.

Wraith tendrils writhed along the opposite wall, more tendrils appearing around the edges of the fissure, probing the shadow-shield.

She gripped Tam tightly – when had she stopped pushing at him and put her arms around him? – and pulled him even closer, his body a rigid wall in front of her, protecting her.

But what was protecting him? Was his shadow-shield strong enough to protect him from the wraiths' seeking tendrils?

The shadow darkened, but she could still see through it. The wraiths appeared, their forms constantly shifting, flickering between shapes and faces – all the souls they'd devoured. Their mouths were open, their horrifying, wailing song a warning. But like a siren's song, it called spirits to them even as it terrified.

Souls that had been freed from their cells by the earthquakes, but somehow hadn't fallen into the chasm, rushed up the tunnel, throwing themselves into the wraiths' embrace. Of course, one touch and they were gone – their screams adding to the wraiths' terrible song.

She shuddered. If not for Tam, that would have been her. If she'd gone to them, she would have failed. She couldn't fail. She couldn't.

Tam's arms tightened around her. Comfort? No. He trembled. Did he feel the wraiths' call sliding along his shield, and sought comfort from her? Or maybe protection? A foolish notion – someone as powerful as he didn't need protection from one such as she. And yet, he held her so tightly, trembling, his gaze never leaving hers as if seeking her strength, her support. What did he feel? What demons did he fight as the wraiths' tendrils slid over his shields? She wished she knew. Wished she could help him fight them. But she couldn't trust the choices she made with her magic.

So, she held on tightly, her fingers finding their way under his black top to his skin, pressing tightly, holding onto him as he held onto her.

They stayed like that until the wraiths' moans had disappeared in the distance – the widening chasm wouldn't have stopped their journey at all, especially fuelled by new souls as they were.

She relaxed a little, but for some reason, didn't let go of Tam as he let go of his spell. The darkness that had hidden them from the wraiths' glow slipped away.

"That was fun," he said softly, his breath moving over her face, their eyes still locked together.

"Fun?" she whispered.

His mouth quirked in the corner and she lost her breath. He was so handsome, his eyes indigo once again, his skin glowing a little from the power he'd unleashed. His smile widened as he looked at her, that little flicker at the corners of his lips and eyes that made things flutter in her stomach. "Maybe not fun. But at least the Underworld's stopped trying to kill us."

"Yes," she managed, her attention caught by the smudge of dirt on his brow. She reached up without thinking to rub it away, but her fingers caught in the softness of the hair that had fallen over his brow as he looked down at her.

"Rinna," he said, brushing her hair back from her face, his large palms cupping her cheeks. "You okay?"

She'd been dreading those words. She didn't want to talk about it – she'd already said far too much. So she just said, "I'm fine. Thanks for … that." She waved her hand to encompass the space behind him.

"You never have to thank me for helping you. I only wish I could have been there for you all those years ago. Maybe if I had, things wouldn't have gotten this bad for you."

She swallowed hard. She wanted to tell him not to waste his time or energy on saving her – she couldn't be saved – but instead, all that came out was, "We should get going."

"We should."

He didn't move. Not surprising given she still gripped him tightly, her fingers kneading warm skin. Their bodies pressed closer. He cupped her face. Her hands slid up his back and around to his chest, flexing against muscle and hot-hot skin.

He was broader across the chest and shoulders than she remembered, his muscles well defined. And standing like this, she realised he was taller now; over six feet by a couple of inches at least, enough that he had half a head on her, making her look up at him. She'd always hated having to look up to anyone, but with him … she didn't mind at all.

"Rinna," he said harshly. "If you don't stop, we're soon going to discover just how big I can get."

She licked her suddenly dry lips. "I don't see the problem." After what she'd just been through, she was desperate to feel something of life, of living; and the pull of him, the pleasant burn of his skin against hers was certainly that. It had always been like this with him. Right from the first moment she'd seen him; the teenager demi-God-cupid who should have hung with the warrior boys he was supposed to train with, but instead, when asked who he wanted as his training partner, had pointed at her. He'd won her friendship in that moment and her heart not long after.

She'd been so stupid to think he would have left her of his own free will with no word for all these centuries. He was her friend. Her best friend. As she'd been his. She hadn't doubted it back then when they'd been together. Why had she so easily doubted it after he left?

She wished she could take the time to find out who had got in between them and why. But once his quest was finished, he would go and she would have what she needed to finish hers. Whoever had got between them, whoever had wanted them to stay apart, would get their way.

Because no matter how much she loved Tamuel, it didn't matter. They had no future. Not simply because she no longer deserved to be loved.

She had made a vow and there was no backing out of it. No choice.

There was only choice in this. Only choice in the now.

And she chose to show Tam just how much she loved him. If not in words, then with her body and soul, giving all she was to him in *this* moment.

A moment she would carry with her, giving her strength until the very end.

She might not be able to trust her magical choices; might not be able to trust herself. But she could trust him. She always had. "I trust you, Tam. I want this."

Light flashed in his eyes, his fingers shifting in her hair. His gaze probed hers for long, breathless seconds.

She reached up, grabbed his head and brought it down to hers, taking his lips in an open-mouthed kiss, all tongue and teeth. He opened beneath her onslaught, the flavour of him – the tartness of red wine mixed with the sweetness of berries – filling her mouth.

She moaned. Kissing him felt better than she'd ever imagined – and she'd imagined a lot.

She was kissing her Tam.

No, not her Tam. This was a new Tam. A Tam who had grown into a sexy, handsome, powerful male, one who'd lived a life; who might not have guilt or regret, but had known pain. His pain resonated alongside hers, different but somehow the same. Why could she feel it like she did? There was no answer to be had right now, nor did she want one.

All she could think about was getting closer. She was sick of fighting it. Tired of going without what she wanted; what she needed.

Skin. She needed to feel skin.

She pushed his long coat away from his shoulders, pulled at his tunic, at the ties securing it closed. His hands were busy too. Air brushed her skin a split second before her fingers splayed over his naked chest.

"Rinna," he said, the sound desperate. A plea. "Not here. Not like this."

She wanted to answer his plea. He was right.

But sense didn't enter into the passion driving through her that she could no longer ignore; the edginess of her desire was akin to skating on the edge of sanity. She had to give in to it. To set herself free for just this moment. It might be her last chance to ever feel like this.

So instead of roping herself in as she knew she should, she let go.

amuel resisted, his fingers tightening on her face, trying his best to pull her away. "Please, Rinna," he said against her mouth. "Not like this."

She reared back. "Exactly like this."

"We need to talk about what happened with the wraiths."

"Later." She slipped a hand to the back of his head, fingers twining in the silk of his hair, holding him to her as she ran her other hand over the delicious planes of his chest, his shoulders, his back.

He sucked in a breath. "Fine. But it's not safe and …" He moaned as she licked his lips. "You deserve more," he choked out.

"No. I don't." She gripped his face. The place and time didn't matter. All that mattered was that she wanted him. Loved him. Always. She hadn't wanted to admit that love had stayed with her because it hurt too much; because she'd held onto her mad over the fact he'd left, even though she'd known – had *known* – he'd had no choice. She could admit that now. Just as she could admit to herself that she wanted him. And that this would be her last chance to do something about it. "The roof could come down around us and I wouldn't care."

"I would. I don't want you hurt."

"Protect us with your bubble then, because unless you tell me you don't want me, don't want this, it's happening."

His hands were suddenly in her hair, his thumbs brushing over her cheeks. "I want you more than I've ever wanted anything. But after. When I have time to worship you properly."

She shook her head, tears pricking her eyes, her throat thick. "No. Now. I need this now." Her fingers tightened in his hair. "Don't make me beg," she whispered.

"But the Underworld – won't it object that we've stopped in one place? The roof might quite literally come down on our heads."

"I trust you to shield us." She bit her lip.

His gaze dipped to it. "I hate it when you do that."

"Then stop me."

His eyes glowed, then his lips came down on hers and she was lost.

The earth bucked around them, widening the fissure, the rock behind her crumbling to the floor. She fell backwards, her arms tight around Tamuel, taking him with her.

She landed on a soft cushion of air, his shield a bubble around them, deflecting the spray of dirt and rubble coming down from the rocks above as the earth buckled and warped around them, trying to push them back. But the bubble was caught in the fissure and so were they.

"Clever cupid," she said as she broke from his kiss, her fingers gripped tight in his silky auburn hair.

"I try." His lips curled into the grin that seemed to tap something deep inside her, pulling on strings of desire that ricocheted through her, bringing fire in their wake.

She pulled his head back down so she could suck on his lower lip before tangling her tongue with his. His hands ran over her, cupping her naked breast – where had her undergarments gone? – the gem he wore around his neck warm where it touched her skin. He tore his mouth from hers – she whimpered her protest – but then blazed fire down her throat, across her chest to her nipple.

Ye Gods!

He ran his tongue around the taught peak before sucking her into his mouth, his other hand moving down her stomach, tickling through her curls and sliding into the wet heat hidden there.

"Hmm," he mumbled against her breast, the vibration of sound adding to the incredible sensation of his tongue on her skin. "Ready already?"

"I've been ready for a long time."

He raised his head, gaze grabbing at hers. No humour flashed in his eyes, just need and a longing so old she felt it in her soul. He held her gaze and moved his fingers across the sensitive nub between her legs, sliding his thumb inside her aching core.

She trembled. He repeated the movement, over and over while he watched her, his gaze glued to her face.

The trembling started small, deep inside her, but then expanded, radiating out, until she was nothing but the tremble and a hot rushing sensation she didn't want to come to completion. Not yet.

"Cum for me, Rinna. Let go."

"Not without you."

She grabbed for him – he still had his pants on. Damn. But almost like magic, the buttons and ties of the leather pants he wore that matched hers – like the ones they'd worn in training all those years ago; all the better to kick-arse in – came undone with barely a touch and they fell down his legs.

"Slow down," he said, as if shocked to lose his pants so quickly when she knew it was his magic that had helped her.

"Naughty cupid," she whispered against his lips as she took the full length of him in her hands. He hissed against her lips, the sound feeding her desire, bringing her pleasure like she'd never known. She'd held a man's cock in her hands before, but it had never been like holding his. Thick and long, hot and silken, it twitched as she stroked it.

"Keep that up and I'll never make it inside you."

She smiled against his lips. She was tempted to bring him to completion with just her hand on his cock and her tongue in his mouth, but ...

She wanted more. So much more. She wanted everything she could have in this bubble of time.

The earth below them groaned, the walls shook; the fissure opened wider, trying to push them out, to force them back where they belonged.

The bubble expanded, wedging them in tight. She expected the cushioning sensation that held her to loosen with its expansion, but it didn't – it still felt like she was lying on the softest down-filled bed.

Her cupid. Looking after her. As she always knew he would.

Keeping her gaze on his, she guided him to her centre. His hand had found her breast again, squeezed as she changed their positions so she was on top. Slowly, so slowly, she lowered herself onto the long, thick length of him.

She wanted to close her eyes to savour the feeling of him deep inside her, sliding deeper, but she didn't want to stop watching him. His face, it was an artist's rendering, an angel succumbing to earthly pleasure and she wanted to take in her fill.

"Rinna," he breathed – she loved the sound of her name on his lips. "By the Gods." His other hand gripped her hip as he filled her entirely in all the right ways.

He flexed his hips, edging up into her further – she didn't think it was possible. Pleasure shivered through her, a quake to match the shaking of the earth all around them. She arched backwards, one hand sweeping down his chest to his abdomen, the other reaching up to cover the hand on her breast. His fingers, so long and fine, strong but gentle, teasing her flesh.

"Gods, you are beautiful, my Rinna."

Her gaze slammed back to his. Nobody had ever called her beautiful before. She knew she wasn't. She was pleasant to look at, but her features were a little too off-kilter to ever be called beautiful – her eyes a little too large; her lips a little too wide; her chin a little too pointed – but in his eyes, she saw that she was. Beautiful. Goddess-like.

He said he wanted to wait so he could worship her properly, but she had no idea how he could worship her more than he did right now. It couldn't ever get better than this. Except ...

She began to move. He joined her, his hips flexing, his cock sliding in and out of her in just the right way, making all her nerve endings sing. She wanted to hold his gaze, to watch the pleasure mount on his face, but she also wanted his lips back on hers.

She leaned down, her breasts brushing over the planes of his chest, hands in his hair, tasting, sucking, tongues and teeth and breath mingled.

One.

They were one.

He rose up, arms going around her as he slammed in even deeper, just how she needed him to without even knowing she did. He held her face close to his, breath a harsh pant, brushing over her skin, moving her hair, his gaze meshed with hers as he moved deep inside her, the passion-laden hunger notching up and up.

"I want you, Rinna. I love you. I always have."

She gasped, pleasure dipping for a moment as his words hit. Undeserved. Besides, he was probably just lost in the moment. Men could say all sorts of things when they were balls deep inside a woman – or so the other Soteira had said to her.

Yet, she longed to return his words; but she couldn't do that to him. So she said, "I need you, Tam. I always have," and hoped it would be enough to carry him through any dark times ahead. She wanted him to remember this moment and smile, not grieve over a lost love that could never be theirs.

His eyes glowed at her words, the shield around them taking on the amethyst hue of his cupid powers sparking deep inside their hidden depths. A golden glow flickered alongside the blue, strengthening them – something new in his warlock powers? – then he moved faster. And faster.

His lips slammed back down on hers, his taste inside her, his scent covering her, claiming her. One hand held her hips while he stroked her breasts with the other. The sensation inside her squeezed tighter and tighter. He moved his hand down her stomach, his thumb slipping into the wet heat of her, finding the nub that was the heart of her pleasure. He pressed, once, twice, three times, pounding and pounding inside her as his tongue played with hers and ...

"Tamuel!" she gasped, breath sawing in her lungs, her throat, as fire sparked in her nerves, becoming a blaze, exploding out, lifting her up and tossing her higher and higher, lit everywhere by the glow – golden and amethyst and blue melded together.

His cry lit the air a moment later as he pulsed around her, inside her.

For a timeless moment, all she was aware of was him and her, their hands holding tight, the warm dampness of their skin sliding against each other as the pleasure trembled through them, his lips on hers as he whispered words of love, as if to breathe the life of them inside her. As if they were true. As if she deserved them.

She opened her eyes. Chaos reigned outside the shield, but she didn't care. Not when his head was buried between her breasts, his breath and silky hair brushing her skin in a delightful way she wished she had time to explore. She ran her hand up his back, into his hair – slightly damp. So was hers. She could feel it sticking to her forehead, her neck. "That was quite the workout," she said softly.

He chuckled, the sound vibrating through her. Ye Gods, she loved that feeling, wanted more.

But the Underworld had other plans.

The earth around them shook even more violently. The fissure widened. The shield trembled under the barrage of rocks raining down on it, but stayed strong – he was so powerful. To have kept the shield's strength up like he had while losing himself to pleasure with her ... remarkable.

As the earth bucked and trembled around them, Tam finally lifted his head, his mouth twisted in a wicked grin. "Did I just make the earth move for you or what?"

She laughed. She couldn't help it.

Then the earth spit the bubble out of the fissure and they were falling, falling, down through the crevice that had widened up the tunnel to swallow them whole.

CHAPTER 11

Samuel shifted, wrapping Rinna in his arms, throwing everything he had into the shield as they fell.

The world shrieked around them, spirits flying in a tornado-type whorl with them in the centre. He looked down, below the bubble, but could see nothing but darkness.

Fucking hells! What had he done?

He'd been stupid and reckless to give in to her demands. She was just reacting to the fact they were in danger. To the memories she'd somehow shared with him when the wraiths passed them. By all that was holy, what she had been through! Why had the Gods sent her there knowing she must fail? Why had they not told her? There was so much to delve into, so much to find answers for so that she might finally find some peace, and he'd meant to but then she'd kissed him and touched him and told him she needed him, and he'd been too weak to fight the need that always simmered below the surface for her. Only her.

But he should have done better. Been better.

Eternal bloody hells. He'd told her he loved her. What a gauche idiot. It wasn't like she could say it back. Nobody could love him. It was part of his curse.

He was the one who should be in danger, not her.

Well, he might have been a weak idiot, but he wasn't a powerless one.

The Underworld might not be happy they were trying to travel through it, but it wasn't going to force them back and he'd be damned if he would let it kill them. Hades had given him permission to be here and he was going to force it to see reason.

"Stop!" he yelled, his voice booming out of the shield as he roped in the magic inside him, utilising both his cupid and warlock magics, stronger than he'd ever felt them even when boosted by the power he'd borrowed from his family's hidden vault.

The spirits scattered.

The rocks stopped falling.

The shield bounced to a stop.

Everything fell silent.

Except for Rinna's gasp of breath against his ear.

She clung to him, her nails digging into his skin. She must be scared shitless.

Holding onto her, he guided the glowing blue, amethyst and golden bubble safely to the ground, noticing it now had little flecks of deep red flickering along its surface as well. He had no idea where the red, gold and blue had come from – maybe the Underworld had changed his powers. He'd ask Rinna, after they were safe. And after all the other things he needed to ask her.

He used his powers to clothe them and, with the earth finally silent and still, let go of the shield.

She didn't let him go, her body pressed tight against his. "You can let go now," he said softly. "It's safe."

She held onto him as she looked up – was she still frightened? "How did you do that?"

He shrugged. "I was going to ask you if you knew. My powers feel and look different here. I thought maybe the Underworld had affected them in some way."

She frowned. "I've never heard of that before but I guess it's possible. There's not been many living people with powers down here to test the theory. I wonder if Hades would let me have a control group …" Her words faded, frown deepening, then she shook her head. "None of that matters right now." She met his gaze. "Can you use your powers to get us closer to Tartarus?"

He shook his head. "I don't think so. Although, I don't think there's a need." He pointed behind her.

She turned slowly, not letting go of him – he was sorry she'd been frightened so badly. Although, now he thought about it, she didn't seem to be clinging to him in fright. He looked down at her. She smiled as his gaze met hers, touched his lips with her fingertips, rubbed her body against his. "If we have time, I look forward to you moving my world like that again."

Bloody hells. Joy sparked through him, filling his chest. Could he smile any wider? "Gladly." She might not be able to return his love, but there was no doubt she wanted him. It was something at least. "It's not like me to look a gift horse in the mouth."

"I'm a gift horse?"

He brushed his thumb over the crease of her frown. "The best gift with nary a horse in sight."

She laughed softly. "You're so silly." She leaned up and kissed him. "I'm glad you're my silly cupid. For now." Sadness filled her eyes for a second, but then she looked away, gesturing to the gate at the end of the tunnel. "Speaking of gift horses …"

"I know. Lucky, right?"

She shrugged. "Maybe. Or maybe the Underworld listened to you back there after all and decided the best way to get rid of us was to let us get here faster."

"Maybe. At least it's not trying to kill us anymore."

"It doesn't have to. Not when we are going in there."

He turned her to face him. "You don't have to come. In fact, don't come. I shouldn't have asked you to help me with this. I don't want you to get hurt."

She shook her head, the glow of something wild and reckless in her eyes that he'd never seen in her before. "I'm not backing out now. Not when we're so close. Besides, you have no choice. Clodia won't just tell you where she put your mother's powers. The only way is to use the HeartsBlood Gem and it won't work without my help. So, no more trying to coddle and protect me – let's go."

"When did you become so stubborn?"

"A long time ago," she said, eyes shadowed.

He knew he should ask her about the memories he'd seen, but now wasn't the time.

He held out his hand. She took it, then strode towards the towering gates made of bones so old they were black and shiny, glowing in the semi-dark in a way that made his skin crawl.

Korinna couldn't believe what she'd done. Or how keen she was to have it repeated. With him. Only him.

By all the hells. She'd never realised what making love could truly be like – although she suspected it would only ever be like that with him. Her Tamuel. Her best friend. Her forever love.

She wished things could be different, that they hadn't lost all those years, that—

Her thoughts came to a screeching halt as they drew closer to the gate, her mind filled with the screaming that emanated from the black bones it was constructed from; bones that were a warning as much as a method of trapping prisoners.

The Gates of Tartarus. Worse than the Gates of Hell. The entry into a world of nightmares worse than the one they'd just passed through. For in this place, Titans and the souls of creatures of terrible power were kept to be tortured for eternity. Most of them deserved it. Some were prisoners simply for getting on a God or Goddess' bad side. None could leave. Ever. There was no penance good enough to allow their souls a moment of peace.

The gates sang to her, the song an ache in her bones, her nerves, making her tremble. Similar to the wraiths' song, but instead of making her want to throw herself at them, they pushed at her to stop, to turn back, to run as far and fast as she could. Even with the Hells-Key sunk into the flesh of her chest, she wanted to run screaming in the opposite direction. Hades must have shielded her from the worst of it the few times she'd come here with him, because she'd never felt anything like this before.

Or maybe she'd been changed by the wraiths. She'd pushed those memories down for so long, but now they were at the surface and she was terrified of truly facing them again.

Tamuel clasped her hand tighter in his. She eyed him – he was pale but otherwise didn't show that he was feeling anything close to the terror firing through her veins. He glanced at her. Smiled. Gripped her hand tighter. "Here we go," he said.

She couldn't find her voice so she simply nodded.

They kept going. The gates didn't open. Would the Hells-Key work without Hades as escort? He'd let them come down here by themselves, so it should, but doubt dragged at her like a wet cloak pulling her into the dark of the ocean's depths.

They reached the gates. Tamuel kept walking, never letting go of her. He became transparent for a moment, passing through the gates successfully, his grip pulling her forward. She glanced down. She'd become transparent too. Then her hand passed through the gate.

Cold. So cold. The gates tried to grab at her, gripping her arm, her hair, her legs as she tried to follow Tamuel. It was harder, so much harder, to get through these gates than it ever had been. Her griefs, her torment, rising to sweep her away.

She gasped. She couldn't fight it. She'd be trapped in here forever as she deserved.

"Rinna. Let go. It wasn't your fault."

Tam's words echoed around her. She looked up. She could see him. He still held her hand, his gaze firm on her, full of belief in what he said; belief in her.

She had to do this. For him. For those lost souls. She couldn't fail now. Not when she was so close.

The pressure increased, slowing her passage, squeezing. Painful. She gasped, closing her eyes, pushing forward harder, trying not to panic. She had to get through. Had to. She couldn't get stuck here. Couldn't die here.

"You can do it, my love."

She opened her eyes, caught in Tam's gaze and knew what to do: there was strength in love even when it was undeserved.

She bore down, shoving the ever-present guilt and grief behind the wall of pleasure she'd experienced in Tam's arms only minutes ago. Filled herself with it; with the brilliant joy of him. She remembered every kiss, every touch, every desire-laden pleasure he'd wrought on her body to answer her craving, her hunger.

Let me through. Let me through.

It had to work.

A gasp was squeezed from her as the pressure increased. She grasped at the memory of him looking into her eyes and telling her he loved her.

With a pop, she staggered free, smacking into him, knocking him off his feet.

He instantly sprang up, hands out to catch her, but she was steady as a rock as she looked at him. "Glad to see I can knock you off your feet."

He smiled – ye Gods, that smile – and, "You can knock me off my feet any time, Rinna."

She looked up at him and ...

Laughed.

He laughed with her. The sound rang around them before being swallowed by the red-tinged dark and the screams that lived in the cavern walls.

They fell silent.

The shriek of the chronometer on his wrist broke the silence. The sound echoed dimly in the cavernous, dampening dark. She shivered as the tinny voice of the chronometer sounded, barely audible above the screams coming from the tunnels ahead.

"The veil is almost completed its thinning. Alignment adjusting ... computing, computing ... The Underworld's position has changed. Time has shifted. One day in the Underworld is now equal to half an hour in the Earthly Realm. The clocks will strike twelve on All Hallows' Eve in two days Tartarus time. Allotted time lost since last computation: four days. Alignment still changing. Further alarms will be forthcoming."

Korinna gripped his arm, staring at the chronometer. "It can't be right."

He looked grim as he shook his head. "It is right. Your design is perfect."

"But you only have two days to complete your task and return to point of origin before the spell expires. It's taken us more than two days to get this far; add to that whatever time it takes to get to Clodia—"

"Then we better hurry." He flashed her a cheeky smile. "Especially given I haven't yet gone into my memory vault to remember the spell to return."

"You didn't memorise the spell?"

He grimaced as he held up his scarred arm. "I didn't think I'd need to; and not all of us have an eidetic memory."

"How will we have time to get you back to Hades' Palace let alone find a quiet space for you to enter your memory vault? If I remember correctly, it always took you hours to navigate your mind's pathways."

"I've improved since then. It shouldn't take more than an hour."

"I see your mathematics hasn't improved. An hour on top of time we already don't have is still an hour too much!"

He shrugged, a mischievous look on his face. "I expect the Underworld will help there. I don't think it will take anywhere near as long to get back as it took to get down here."

She nodded. He was probably right. Even so, it wasn't good news. They had no idea how quickly they could get to Clodia. And while she was certain of the spell to allow him to use the HeartsBlood Gem to force Clodia to tell him what he needed, she had no idea how quickly it would work. Or if it would work for him if she didn't use her magic. So much could go wrong.

"It will be fine," he said, giving her hand a squeeze. "I'm pretty sure I'll be able to change a small part of the Eleusinian Mysteries spell to allow me to portal back from Clodia's cell." He glanced down at the damaged design on his wrist, frowned, muttered, "I think if I change the stroke here and put it there—"

"You think? You don't know?"

He shrugged. "I wasn't expecting Hades to break my arm and Persephone to damage the mark when she healed me."

"Well, he wouldn't want you parading down here with that."

"Yeah, I know. But I didn't intend to bump into him."

She shook her head at him. "You'll get trapped down here if you don't remember it right."

"I know."

She gripped his arm. "Not just trapped. You'll be a prisoner."

"I know. But the risk is worth it." He rubbed his thumb over her frown. "Hey, it will be fine. You know my mind is a steel trap. I've just got to get inside it. Besides, I have you here to help. Nobody was better at ancient spell work than you. I know you'll be able to tell if I do the mark wrong."

"I may not be able to without my magic."

He cupped her face, kissed her softly. "I believe in you."

And he did. It was so clear in his eyes, his trust. And something more. Could it really be love? No. She couldn't let that false hope in. But even so, his belief, his trust, it was bliss. She touched his cheek, wanting to give back some of what he'd given to her. "And I believe in you."

He kissed her again, a smile playing on his lips, but before she could lose herself to the madness of him again, he pulled back. "After."

She only nodded even though she knew there would be no 'after'. He would go back to his home and she would—

"Which way?" he asked.

She suddenly realised she had no idea where the map had gone. She'd dropped it when she'd grabbed him and kissed him earlier. He chuckled, then clicked his fingers, the map landing in her hand. She met his gaze. Even the dark angry terror of this place couldn't dampen the light in his eyes; it gave her the courage to smile and open the map. After finding where they were and where Clodia's cell was situated – closer than she'd ever dared hope – she pointed at a darker space in the wall closest to them. "This way."

Their footsteps were silent, swallowed by the walls and their screams.

<h1 style="text-align:center">CHAPTER 12</h1>

Tartarus didn't seem to object to their presence like the rest of the Underworld did. In fact, beyond the dim light that surged from side passages, flickering from red to green to blue to yellow then back to red, beyond the screams that rose as if from the rocks and soil, there was a pull here. A gripping; as if, rather than wanting them to go, Tartarus longed for them to stay. It had never been like this when she'd come to speak to prisoners with Hades as her guide. But then, his presence was enough to drown out anything else. At least, after what happened to her with the wraiths, she hoped that's what it was.

Close to the entrance cavern, they passed a passage; a sickly yellow light crept out of it across the floor. Voices whispered in the dark, enticing her into the light. Tam's hand tightened on hers as they edged past, his expression grim, his attention focused on the tunnels ahead. Somehow it made her feel better that she wasn't the only one affected.

Half a day's walk brought them to the point the map indicated was the entrance to Clodia's cell. Shrieking echoed out of the red-lit cave, agonised and rage-filled.

Korinna swallowed hard. Zeus and Hades must have been truly

pissed with the ancient witch-priestess. But then, as far as they were concerned, the sin of hubris really was the worst.

"Shall we go in?" Tam glanced down at the chronometer.

"Have we lost time?"

"It's still the same as before. We've got time if you want to take a moment before we go in."

She shook her head – even if they had all the time in the Realms, she didn't want to linger any longer than absolutely necessary. "I'm fine." But still, she hesitated; those shrieks coming from the cell rode her nerves, scraping at her skin. If not for Demeter and Seph, this was where she should have ended up; perhaps one day soon, it would be.

Tam touched her cheek. She tore her gaze from the nasty red glow at the mouth of the cell to look up at him. His smile didn't really reach his lips, but even so, it made her feel better.

"Korinna? You don't have to come in if you don't want to."

"Of course I do." She pulled away from him. His hand fell from where he'd cupped her cheek – she missed the warmth and certainty of that touch like an ache inside. But she swallowed against the need to throw herself into his arms and lifted her chin. "Let's go in."

The cell didn't have a door – although cell was a generous word for it. More of a long, narrow hall with high ceilings, damp and dank yet blazingly hot.

At the end of the hall was a pile of rocks where part of the ceiling had fallen to make way for the prism of red light that hung suspended from the ceiling. Inside that prism, the ancient witch's soul was trapped, forced to face the dark grey storm cloud that hung before the prism, lights flickering on its surface.

As they edged further along, keeping as far from Clodia as they could, it became clear that images played in the cloud. Images that explained why Clodia screamed and railed, her nails stretched like talons as if to tear the cloud and its images asunder if she could but reach them.

A man and a woman featured in those images. A woman with a face that reminded her of Tam's in the line of his nose and the shape of his mouth. The man had hair and eyes the colour of Tam's.

His parents. Well, his father and the reincarnated soul of his mother.

Behind them, jack-o-lanterns glowed on a table laden with Halloween-inspired food, orange and black streamers; paper skeletons and fake cobwebs hung from the ceiling and every available surface. His father – Sebastio, or Bastien as he was now called – was dressed in a Highland warrior costume, while his mother, Jules, was dressed in 1950s garb, her hair styled in glossy curls. The way they looked at each other ... She swallowed hard, blinking back tears.

Suddenly, Bastien let out a whoop, hugging Jules, lifting her up to spin her around and kiss her passionately on the mouth before setting her back to place his hand over her stomach.

"She's pregnant," Tam said, voice filled with joy. "I'm going to be a brother!"

He grabbed her up and hugged her, echoing his father's movements, his joy so strong it thrummed through her despite the fact this place sucked at joy, pulling anything of light and life and happiness away from those within its walls.

Clodia screamed, a sound of fury and frustration. "No. No. You don't deserve happiness. You don't deserve to have everything when I have nothing. No. No. No!"

Clodia's torture was Jules and Bastien's happiness.

Clever Hades. She was certain he was behind this torture; it really was the kind of ingenious thing he would come up with. Many of those in the halls of the Underworld were tortured by the guilt they felt over things they did wrong in their lives – it was one of the reasons she'd run to Hades and his palace because she felt she deserved to suffer the guilt in full and where better to do that? But Tartarus was different. It couldn't punish through guilt because many of its prisoners didn't feel such a thing. Clodia certainly didn't.

So, she was tortured with what she could never have.

It seemed to be working. She was a spitting, screaming, raging mess, her soul ragged and worn; nothing close to the powerful priestess-witch she'd once been.

"Clodia." Tam moved forward, his attention now fully on the ancient priestess-witch. "Clodia," he said, voice louder this time, his power sparking, adding an irresistible tone of command.

But Clodia's attention didn't flicker for a moment from the images playing out in front of her.

Tam took another step. "Clodia, I command you to heed me." The Hells-Key glowed on his chest, power emanating from it. The guards used their Hells-Key to make the prisoners obey basic commands. Hades had obviously given Tam the ability to do the same.

Clodia's gaze flickered to him, eyes widening for a split second as if she recognised him, but then the images on the cloud changed, pulling her attention back to them, her screams of rage starting up all over again. How her voice wasn't a torn, ragged thing in her throat was beyond Korinna to understand. Maybe that was part of the torture – that her screams would be forever.

Tam frowned and looked down at the Hells-Key. "Is this thing on?" He tapped it.

She touched his hand. "It's not a microphone – and yes, it's working. But I think Clodia is so far gone, it's not touching her in the way it should."

"Then how do we get her attention?"

"Take the HeartsBlood Gem out." He raised a questioning brow. "She once believed it was hers. I don't think you'll have a problem getting her attention with it." And when he did, once he used the spell, he would have what he needed and then he would go home and be safe.

Her heart ached. Oh Gods. She thought she had more time with him. Hadn't realised how much she'd been relying on being with him for as long as she could, holding onto every moment as if it were an eternity. For her, with her days numbered, it probably was.

That time in the bubble – it wasn't enough. She'd told herself it would be, but it wasn't. Not nearly enough. But there was nothing she could do. She'd come with him to help him with this so he would give her the grimoire and the gem. She had to do as promised and let him go, even though he was the only person who ever made her feel it was okay to be herself.

"Rinna? What's wrong?"

He touched her shoulder, turning her slightly to face him. She blinked against the hot tears pressing against her eyes, mouth twisting a little. "It's almost done. Then you'll be gone."

"What are you talking about?"

She shook her head, a tear tumbling down her cheek despite her best efforts to rope them back. She looked down at her hand captured in his and couldn't stop from twining her fingers with his, loving the strength and warmth of his grip. "Let's get what you came here for."

A cackle sounded from above them and they turned to find Clodia looking down at them, her eyes alight with evil. "So yummy. Your pain. Even with that Hells-Key doing its best to protect you from this place. From ones like me. I wonder, if I ate your soul, would it taste sweeter than that little palate cleanser you just gifted me."

"Clodia!" Tam said, fists tight by his side as he stepped closer to the prism, glaring up at her. "Leave her alone."

"How can I when she's pushing her guilt and pain out into this place? And it's enjoying it as much as I am." Her gaze moved to Korinna. "I know who you are. You are the Soteira who failed in her duty. The one who thought she knew better than the Fates and lost all those innocent souls to the Void."

Korinna gasped, her body tingling in a way it hadn't done since she'd last used her power. "You can't know that." Nobody but Hades, Demeter and Persephone knew that.

"Of course I can. Everyone down here knows what you did, Korinna Soteira."

"It wasn't her fault," Tam said, stepping in front of her. "They didn't tell her not to try to save them."

"They shouldn't have had to."

"Yes, they should! She was young and new to the role. They would have helped anybody else. And they certainly should have told her that greater magic had been wound into that line of Fate, which was what altered all her spells."

She staggered as if she'd been punched – how did Tam know all that? She'd never wanted him to know all that. But then his words caught in her mind as she turned to gape at him. "What do you mean greater magic altered my spells?"

Clodia's cackle tore through the air again. "She didn't tell you?" Her gaze pinned Korinna to the spot, stoppering the words of denial in her dry throat. "That's just delightful. Betrayed not just by him but by your Goddess as well. Honestly, you're almost too stupid to live. Perhaps that's why you're trying to die."

Korinna just gaped at her as Tam yelled, "That's a lie. Korinna wouldn't do that."

"Wouldn't she?" Clodia gestured at her, wincing a little as the red light flared around her. "Can you not feel the guilt emanating from her? The pain? The grief? So strong. So glorious. It was enough to crack through this prison and grab my attention. I wanted to gobble it all down. Feed on it. As every being down here wants to as well. Can you hear them?" She cocked her head, lips widening in a smile of madness as the screams rising from outside her cell turned to shouts of need and wanting. "They feel you. They want to gobble you up too. Your guilt and pain and grief will draw the torturers' focus away, giving the one who gets you a glorious reprieve. But they can't have you. I want you for myself. I am the one who deserves the reprieve."

"You deserve nothing," Tam spat. "Nothing but to return to your torture. After we get what we came for."

She laughed again, the sound deep, rich, enticing. "What? The truth?" Her gaze flickered to Korinna. "That they meant you to fail and didn't tell you? Not once in all these years?"

Korinna tried to deny her words, but her throat and mouth were so dry, fear and betrayal a stone in her chest she couldn't speak past. She was a fly trapped in amber – or like Clodia, trapped in the red light.

Clodia's laugh tore through the air.

"Shut up!" Tam yelled, fists shaking at his sides. "I will not let you torment her with your half-truths."

Clodia's mouth widened in an horrific smile, eyes dancing with unholy light. "Oh, this is too wonderful. That the son of my greatest enemies can be so clueless about the one he loves. It's delicious."

"I said shut up," he snarled at the same time Korinna choked out, "You really do love me?"

His focus snapped to Korinna, blue eyes glowing in the red-dark of the cavern. "Of course I do. I've always loved you. Since the first day I saw you at the camp."

"But … you're a cupid."

"You believed that old wives' tale? All cupids are capable of loving – even me. I just can never receive it because of my curse."

"What curse?" She'd never heard of a curse.

He waved his hand. "I will tell you all about it when we get out of here. Just believe I do love you even though I know you can never love me."

She shook her head slowly, all other worries swept away under the tsunami of his admission. "But … that's not right. I do. Love you. I've always loved you too."

He grabbed her shoulders, his blue-blue gaze searching deep within hers. "You love me? How is that possible? It can't be true."

"It is. But you shouldn't love me. I don't … I don't deserve it."

"What are you talking about? If anyone doesn't deserve your love, it's me."

Clodia's cackle cracked between them, tearing their gazes from each other and back to her. "How sweet. Two deluded souls so caught up in your own misgivings that you missed the fact you are both wrong. You were used as a patsy," she said, pointing at Korinna. "And your curse isn't what you think it is," she said, gaze flickering over him. "I would think you'd learned that after what happened to your parents, cupid. But please, keep up this little drama. Your pain is filling me up all the way over here. Yummy."

Korinna glared at her. "We're not here for your edification."

"Really? Because it's the only way you get to have what you want – all this drama of emotion is bringing me a clarity I've not felt for centuries. And isn't that what you need? Me in my right mind so I can help you?"

Tam growled. "What do you mean I'm wrong about the curse? What does it have to do with my parents?"

Clodia wagged her finger. "That's not what you're here for, is it?"

"You don't know what we're here for."

"Don't I?"

"Then tell us. Share with us what you know of the curse and where you hid my mother's powers."

"What about the lost souls *she's* aiming to find?" she asked, bony finger jabbing towards Korinna.

"What are you talking about?" He glanced at Korinna.

She shrugged, hoping he believed she was as clueless about Clodia's meaning as he was.

"So many misunderstandings between you. So many secrets and lies needing to be exposed."

"No!" Korinna lurched forward. "It is you who are full of secrets and lies."

"It takes a liar to know a liar." Her eyes gleamed darkly red as she swept her gaze over Korinna.

She trembled, hands clenching at her sides, unable to do anything to stop the ancient priestess-witch.

Clodia laughed. "Use your power, little witch. Unleash it as you did all those years ago. There's no magical energy of the greater Gods waiting to subvert it here. It's the only way to stop me."

"No," Korinna gasped. The witch couldn't be right. It had been her. Persephone would have told her if some greater magic had been at play.

"Ahh, but what of your lost souls? How will you get them to Elysium if not with a final burst of magic?"

Korinna shook her head, aware that Tam was looking at her with confusion. "I will use it then. Only then."

"Why then and not now?"

She tried to shut her mouth, but it was like the truth was being pulled out of her. This place. It had to be this place. So it could excel in its torture. "Because after that, nothing will matter. The souls will be safe."

"And you?"

She tried to fight it, but the words forced their way up, squeezed out her mouth on a hated breath. "I will be gone."

CHAPTER 13

*T*amuel stared at Rinna, her words a violent storm in his mind, his heart. "I saw your memories when we hid from the wraiths. Felt your guilt and pain. I understand how terrible it's been for you, Rinna, but how can you think to …?" He shook his head, unable to say the words.

Tears spilled from her eyes, her face a study in agony. "I wouldn't have. Not if I'd known you'd come back to me. That you did love me."

"Then take it back."

"I can't, any more than I can take back the spell that doomed those souls."

"Don't you mean the spell an Old One screwed with so that it wouldn't work?"

"No. That's not right." She jabbed a finger at Clodia. "She's lying."

"No, I'm not," Clodia snapped. "He's not the only one who's cursed."

"What do you mean?"

Her smile slowly widened. "They were always jealous of those of us with more potential than they have. It's why I landed here. Why they did what they did to you. It's quite clever if you think about it. You take yourself out of the picture and they keep their hands clean.

You were just too stupid and self-involved to see it." She pouted. "And just when you've discovered your true love. Too bad, so sad."

"No," Tamuel said, grabbing Rinna close against him. She was stiff, unyielding. Panic tightened his chest, breath catching in his throat. "No. There has to be another way."

"You can't stop it," Rinna said, her words a rumble against his chest. "I made a vow to make right what I did wrong."

"But it wasn't your fault. An Old One screwed with your spells."

She closed her eyes. "Even if that's true, it doesn't change the fact those souls have to be saved and I vowed to save them. The spell requires a lifeforce in exchange." Her lip trembled, tears streaking down her face as she opened her eyes to look up at him. "I love you more than life itself; would do anything to be with you, but—" She choked on the words, struggling for a moment before she said softly, "I made a vow. I wish I hadn't now, but I did. There's no escaping it." Her topaz eyes should have reflected the red light of Clodia's prison, but they didn't. They glowed with the eternal golden light of her power and something else.

Her love. For him.

It *was* true. How it was possible with his curse, he wasn't certain, but he couldn't deny the reality of it. The glow of it washed over him, connecting with him, pulling him into the depths of her, until he wasn't sure where he ended and she began. Her love was everything. It was truth and power and everything good.

She couldn't die. "No," he said again. "I won't let you. You need to come with me. We'll find another way. We'll visit all the Realms."

"I can't. I'm tethered here. I couldn't trust in my power when I made my vow, so I used the power of the Death Realms as a proxy. When the Eternal Well accepted my vow, it bound me to this place until I meet my destiny. I belong down here. You don'—"

He put his finger over her mouth. "I will not let you be stuck down here any longer. I will not let you die to fulfill your agreement with the Eternal Well when it was never your fault in the first place. You don't owe those souls your life. We'll find an answer. There's bound to be something in the Eleusinian Mysteries aside from the destructive spell you want to use. And this. We have this." He pulled the Hearts-Blood Gem from his shirt.

"Oh, my pretty, powerful friend," Clodia screeched. "You brought her to me."

"I didn't bring the HeartsBlood Gem for you. I brought it to use against you."

Clodia's eyes glowed. "It won't respond to you, stupid cupid. It's filled with Goddess-given power. It will only connect with feminine energy. So, *she* will have to use it."

"Rinna says I'll be able to use it as long as she's touching it."

"Does she now. Well, she'd be W-R-O-N-G, wrong. She would need to use her own power, and a significant amount of it to boot to override my will."

"But I can't," Rinna said, a sob in her voice. "I need to hoard as much of my power as I can for my final spell."

Clodia wagged her finger. "True. Pity you kept your powers subdued all these years, rusty and nowhere what they should be. Especially given you used such a large portion of them keeping *him* safe; fulfilling *his* quest."

Rinna's eyes widened. "That's not true."

"Isn't it? You've been leaking power ever since you saw him. You leaked it in the tunnels to help shield him from the wraiths; to speed you on your journey. It poured from you when you fucked him, and again when you helped him to stop you both from falling into the abyss. And it was your power that found the tunnel that led straight to the Gates of Tartarus."

"That's a lie! Tam did that all himself and … I … I'd know if I used my power."

"If you don't believe me, just feel inside. Your reserves of power are not enough to power the spell you wish to use. Not any time soon. You've wasted it on him." She pouted. "Who knows what will happen to those poor souls if they're in the Void much longer. When I saw them after his mother trapped me in there, they were getting rather ragged." A manic smile replaced the pout. "But, good news. You do have enough to do what I need you to do. And if you do, then I'll help you save those souls."

"You only help yourself." Tamuel grabbed Rinna's hands, trying to turn her away from staring at the witch-bitch, the expression of devastation on her face a different kind of torture. "We will find a way," he said. "There is always a loophole. You won't need to use all your powers and you won't have to die. I won't allow it."

"Allow it? Listen to you. Being all man-like and trying to play the hero," Clodia said. "But you can fix nothing. Only I know the way for her to succeed in her vow without giving everything. And maybe, just maybe, you might even be able to be with him. Although, why you'd want to is beyo—"

"What is your price?"

"Rinna, you can't listen to her."

Clodia smiled slowly, her gaze never leaving Rinna. "Surely my freedom is a small payment for the chance to live and be with cupid-boy forever?"

"Rinna, we can't set her free."

"*You* can't. But *she* can."

Rinna shook her head, gaze pinned on Clodia. "Even if what you say is true and my power is now not enough, I've looked and looked. There is no other way. My soul has to power the spell to open the rift and find the souls because I canted the spell that sent them there."

"True. But, you haven't been where I've been. You haven't seen what I've seen. You have no idea what can be done, especially with a little bit of Goddess-given power. Only I do. And I vow, if you free me, I will go to the Void and release those souls and send them to Elysium for you."

He gripped Rinna's shoulders, turned her towards him. "Don't listen to her. She's a liar. We can use the HeartsBlood Gem, get her to tell us what we need—"

The alarm shriek of the chronometer cut him off.

"The veil has thinned. Alignment finalised. The Underworld's position has changed. Time has shifted. The clocks will strike twelve on All Hallows'

Eve in two minutes Earthly Realm time. Fifteen minutes Tartarus time. You have fifteen minutes to return. Countdown has begun."

Korinna's gaze snapped to him, grabbing at his arm, fingers fumbling to undo the band of the chronometer. "You've run out of time. Give me the HeartsBlood Gem. I'll find some way of getting her to tell me what you came here for and get the information to you. But you have to go. Carve the spell. Do it now."

He grabbed her hands, stopped her from trying to remove the chronometer so he could carve the spell on his wrist. "I'm not leaving without you, my love."

She gripped his hands, leaned up and pressed her lips against his. "I can't let you do that. I can't let you make that sacrifice for me."

"That's not your choice to make."

"Yes, it is. I thought for so long I couldn't trust my choices. But I can. You helped show me that. You've saved me in ways you can't know. Now let me save you."

She kissed him again before he could protest, then before he could pull her close, she was gone.

He stumbled as the force of the magic she'd used to transport herself across the cavern pushed him back a step. "Rinna, no!" He raced after her, but she leaped to the top of the pile of rocks before he'd made it a couple of steps.

He flung his magic towards her, intending to stop her, but it bounced off the golden glow of power now emanating from her like a shield – how had he not realised that was her golden glow working alongside his magic earlier?

She flung herself from the top rock towards the prism, slamming one hand towards it, while the other pointed at him.

"Rinna, no!"

Light exploded around them, blinding him as power smacked him in the chest. He slammed into the jagged rock wall behind him; sharp rocks tore through tunic and skin. He ignored the pain – he'd known worse – and tried to push off the wall. But the wave of power wouldn't let him. Against his chest, the HeartsBlood Gem glowed brightly, pulsing with the power that flowed through it, keeping him pinned. He used his cupid and warlock power to fight its hold, but for every inch he fought to move forward, another pulse struck, forcing him back.

She was strong, so strong. Clodia was right about one thing – Rinna was strong enough to break the priestess-witch free, something only a very powerful God should be able to do. Her magic had changed, become something other than what it had been – maybe because she'd been living down here for too long; maybe because of what she'd done; maybe because it was always going to get stronger and change – and maybe that's why some Old One had screwed with her power and brought her to this point of thinking she deserved death.

Even so, she would have to drain herself dry to free Clodia from her prison. And that alone could kill her.

"Rinna! Stop!" The light had become so bright he couldn't see her, but he could hear her scream of pain and anguish, torn from her as she forced her magic to break the prism. "Rinna, stop. Please, stop."

There was an ear-piercing wail, an almighty crack. Then the noise and light disappeared.

He fell away from the wall, slamming onto his knees, light-blinded, ears ringing. Trying to blink away the light-shadow, he shook his head to clear the ringing from his ears. "Rinna?" She didn't answer. The only sound was cackling.

Clodia!

He rubbed his eyes, vision returning enough to see that Clodia was out of the prism, looking at the body lying on the ground at her feet. The ancient witch looked up at him as she brushed at her tattered tunic, frowning. "Well, that's a problem."

He didn't take any notice of Clodia, his attention solely on his love. Every part of him screamed in pain as he pushed to his feet then stumbled one step after another towards Rinna, his gaze never leaving her.

Smoke rose in wisps off the material of her tunic. Blood ran from a gash on her forehead. One leg and arm lay at a strange angle.

Still. So still. He couldn't even tell if she was breathing.

"Rinna," he said, her name a sob in his throat as he tripped over his feet, agony tearing through his damaged back from shoulder to hip with each step. But he didn't care, his entire attention on Rinna as he came down on his knees in the rough dirt beside her. "Why did you do that, my love?"

She didn't stir, but her chest rose up then down, the motion ragged. She was still alive. He reached for her, but hesitated, not wanting to cause her more injury. Instead, he leaned down, kissed her gently, hoping she would waken at his touch.

"You know you two are as sickening as your parents."

He glared up at the witch who'd caused this. "What did you do?"

She placed a hand on her chest. "Moi? I did nothing. She was the one who did it all. She freed me."

"Then why are you still here?"

Her eyes glittered. "There is something more I need."

"Ten minutes until the veil closes and you are trapped," the chronometer chimed in warning.

He ignored it. "I don't care about what you need. Now go and do as you vowed and let me save her."

Clodia's smile widened. "Ah, just a little problem with that." She pointed at Rinna. "Her power opened my prison, but she poured too much of it into shielding you. That backlash should have killed you. Now, to get out of here and make myself a body, I need power. Your cupid power will suffice. You opened the portal to get here with it, and along with the spell you got from that nifty grimoire those Eleusinian nuts wrote, it's all I need to get back."

"I will never give it to you. I will never set you free."

She crouched down in front of him. "Not even if it means letting her free of her vow?" She reached out as if to touch Rinna, but he slapped her hand away. She smiled, slow, nasty. "Not even if it means being able to take her with you so you can save her?"

"I can't take her with me. She's tethered here."

"The only thing tethering her here is that vow. But who's to say the Eternal Well would be just as happy for someone else to do it? She saw the truth in that," she said, pointing at Rinna. "Would you let her sacrifice be for nothing? I'm far more capable of completing her vow than anyone else. Give me what I want and that vow disappears. You can take her; save her. Give me what I need to gain my freedom and I will take up the burden of her vow. Agreed?" She stuck out her hand.

He stared at her. She was a liar, but something in her face told him she wasn't lying about this. He knew he shouldn't do this; knew she should never be allowed to go free after what she'd done; knew if she got free, she wouldn't cease her grasp for power. But ...

He looked down at Rinna. Her breathing laboured more with every minute he allowed to pass. He might be able to use the Hells-Key to call on Hades to help, but ... he was in the Earthly Realm at Persephone's party and he had no idea how to jerry-rig the spells on the Hells-Key to reach him there.

He took Clodia's hand. "Agreed."

Power burned along his arm, twining up hers, binding them to the promise.

When the binding was done, she pulled her hand from his. "Excellent. Now, to the good stuff." She clapped her hands. Her eyes glowed black.

Something tore deep inside him. He gasped, bending double at the pain that overrode the cuts and gashes on his back.

"Hurts, doesn't it? It's the very least you deserve for being part of taking what was mine. Now the spell." He cried out as something blunt jabbed into his mind, pushing, digging. "Ah, there it is." She began to carve the sigil on her wrist with a jagged stone she picked up from the floor. "Those Eleusinian priestesses were clever to bond blood magic with life magic. It should be unstable but it's not. Ah, one little change – I don't want to end up where you departed from, do I? There, that should do. Now, give me the rest." She reached out her hands, making a gathering motion. Something tore inside him, the pain so great, he could barely breathe.

"Ugh. So much love and hope and sacrifice in your soul, it sickens me."

"I hope you choke on it," he managed to gasp.

She only smiled at him, moving her hands faster, the threads of his amethyst cupid power glowing almost blackly-purple in the red light of the broken prism, shards of which still hung above them and lay on the floor, shattered, around them.

The pain intensified, blackness edging his vision. "I will find you. And I will get back what is mine."

"Now, now, don't be like that. I'm doing you a favour. When you are no longer a cupid, you will no longer be tied to your curse."

"You're lying. The curse is gone. She loves me. I don't know how but …" He blinked. Clodia had said he didn't understand his curse. That he'd not learned from his parents. That could only mean one thing … "She's my soulmate." The loophole Eros had woven into his curse. She was the cracked piece of mirror – the imperfect cursed soul equal and opposite to his. Together, they were whole. No longer soul cursed. They were free. That was why she'd always loved him. And he'd been too stupid to realise. Well, he'd make up to her for that when he got her out of here and saved her.

"How can you still hope when all hope is gone?" Clodia smiled, her motions jerky, vicious, as she manipulated his power, pulling it into her in larger chunks.

He gasped, the pain almost making him black out. But he held on; for Rinna if not for himself.

The chronometer screeched its five-minute warning.

"Time to go," Clodia said, yanking the final dregs of cupid power from him. He fell over Rinna as the evil witch waved her hand. Light flared brightly overhead and the remaining shards of the prism exploded. Somehow, despite the pain slicing through him, he used his warlock power and flung a shield around them to protect Rinna from the dangerously sharp slithers of light. Clodia might have taken his cupid power, a power fuelled by one of the strongest magics known to Gods or man – love – but she hadn't taken the warlock power he had from his mother.

The bitch-witch probably thought it was weak. But it wasn't. Especially when he was with Rinna.

He held the shield tight over them as the prism rained around them.

The chronometer buzzed again – four minutes.

Then the light vanished, replaced by the dark-red glow of the caverns.

He looked up. Clodia was gone.

A roar sounded deep in the earth, making the cavern tremble and shake. Was it an alarm sounding to indicate an escaped prisoner? Or was it Tartarus' anger over her escape? Did it even matter? He'd almost run out of time. He had to get them out of here. Clodia might have thought by taking his cupid powers she'd got what she needed to escape, thereby trapping them both here, but she hadn't.

It had been his warlock powers that allowed him to tap into the ark under the Stevens' library and get him here – like called to like after all. And it was his warlock power – still connected to that well of magic – that would get him and Rinna back home where he could call for help to save her.

Rubble fell from the roof of the cavern. The shield sparked with every hit; amethyst and gold. He tightened his control, amazed doing so barely took anything from him at all. Just as well – he needed everything to get them home.

The roar became louder, rumbling around them, making everything shake and shake until it looked like the walls and roof and floor were moving liquid. The sound of that roar – pure rage.

He empathised with that rage. Felt something like it inside him. He would use it to track down Clodia, to capture her with the Hearts-Blood Gem and make her tell him everything he needed to know to help him finish his quest. She might have thought to have outwitted him, but she hadn't. He had only agreed to give her what she needed to get out of this cell; he hadn't agreed to anything else.

But first, he had to get them back; he had to save Rinna. Thank the Gods he no longer had to go into his memory to remember the spell or change it as needed to travel from this place: in taking it from his mind, Clodia had unwittingly shown him exactly what he needed to do.

The chronometer buzzed the two-minute countdown.

Hurriedly, he removed the chronometer, shoving it into his pocket, then cut open his wrist with the knife Rinna had put in his backpack and drew the sigil on his wrist along with the change in destination, aware with every line he was running out of time.

One minute.

He began carving the sigil into Rinna's wrist.

Thirty seconds.

He picked her limp body up, holding her close, then as the chronometer counted down from ten, he canted the spell from the Eleusinian Mysteries.

Power gathered in him, punching through his skin, out of the sigils, the pain almost blinding. The world shifted, portals opening up around him, showing him all the Realms that could be reached through the veil if one only had the will and the right spell to traverse them.

Sensing more than seeing the one he needed, he stepped forward, grunting as Tartarus tried to pull him back, tried to keep him in its embrace. Or was it trying to keep Rinna? It couldn't have her.

He tightened his grip around his love as the chronometer intoned, "2, 1 ..." and threw himself forward, using up the last reserves of power he had in him, hoping he wasn't too late.

CHAPTER 15

Darkness surrounded Korinna. She was falling, falling. And as she fell, the darkness squeezed in around her. Smashing into Clodia's prison had been painful, a sensation like being torn asunder, but this ... this was something else. Like she was still in her body, being pulled out of it a bit at a time.

Oh Gods. It hurt. It hurt. She wanted to scream, but had no voice.

The squeezing intensified, then suddenly, it was gone.

Cool dark surrounded her.

Was it supposed to feel like this – her soul torn from her body and sent down into the Underworld? She'd not expected it to feel like sunshine and roses, but she'd not expected this.

A voice shouted in the dark, alongside a sensation of being picked up and carried then placed somewhere softer. Kinder.

It sounded like Tam.

Tam.

Her heart ached at the thought that she would never see him again. Never be with him again. His soul was bound for Elysium far in the future when it was finally his time to pass through the veil of death, whereas hers—

Her soul cried out at the unfairness. She'd thought she deserved this, but the loss of those souls – she knew now it wasn't her fault. She shouldn't be made to pay. She deserved love. As did he.

He loved her. She loved him. She wanted a life with him more than she'd ever wanted anything. But it didn't matter. She'd sacrificed to save him and now she was dead.

The darkness disappeared as light flickered and shifted behind her lids.

"Help. Help. She's barely breathing." Tam's voice rose out of the watery depths of noise, becoming clearer.

No. He couldn't be here. She'd saved him – hadn't she?

Yes. Yes, she had. So … this was her punishment. To show her what she could have had – if only she'd not been so stupid as to see what he had seen so clearly when he'd somehow seen her memories – then yank it from her.

"Here, let me in." Another voice. Deeper than Tam's and yet achingly similar.

Something warm touched her chest, radiating outward. She would have cried out at the shock of it, but didn't seem to be able to move or speak.

"Foolish boy." An older voice. A woman. "What were you thinking? To use such a spell on such a night."

"Don't lecture him, Grandmama." A younger woman's voice, patient, gentle. "I think he's been through enough. How is she, Bas? Is she breathing?"

The warmth wrapped around Korinna, pushing into her skin, into her muscles and veins and nerves, probing. "She's alive," the deeper male voice said – Bas? "But her injuries are severe. What the hell happened, son?"

"She gave her powers to allow Clodia to escape," Tam answered.

"Why would she do that!?"

"Violetta! Calm down. Let him tell us why he brought her here."

"She did it to complete a vow," Tam continued. "And I think, to save me. To give me the reason to remember the spell and get back here."

"Clodia is free?" the younger woman asked, her voice an aching whisper.

"Yes. I couldn't stop her."

"It will be all right, Julianna," the older woman – Violetta – said.

Julianna? Bas? Violetta? This was Tam's family. But why would her hell show her this? Was she not in hell being tortured? If not, then where in the Realms was she?

"Violetta is right, Jules. We won't let her get anywhere near you. Besides, Clodia is a spirit and she still has to find a way out of the Underworld."

"She's not a spirit anymore. She took my powers and used them to enact the spell from the Eleusinian Mysteries Grimoire and become corporeal."

"The Eleusinian Mysteries Grimoire! How did you get your hands on that, boy?"

"That doesn't matter, Violetta. What matters is that she's corporeal. Hades will be furious."

"Who cares about that overbearing bore? You and your father can deal with him, Bas. But a grimoire of that much power in the wrong hands—"

"My son is hardly the wrong hands, Violetta!"

"She took your powers?" Jules said softly, and even though it was barely a whisper, it cut across Bas and Violetta's arguing. "Oh, Tamuel."

"Only my cupid ones."

"Oh, son."

"Don't feel sorry for me. I gave of them freely in a bargain to save Rinna," Tam said grimly. "Dad? How is she? Can you heal her?"

"I can try, but it's going to take some time. Why don't you lie down and get some rest yourself? You look like you're about to fall down."

"He looks like skin and bone," Jules said, her voice a throb of caring. "You're lucky she didn't kill you when she took your powers."

"I had no choice. I had to save Rinna."

"You're just like your mother," Violetta said gruffly.

"No, I'm not. I still have my warlock powers. That's what got me back. What helped get Rinna here. You have to save her, Dad."

"She's very important to you then?" Jules asked softly, her voice accompanying a sweep of movement over Korinna's brow, through her hair; a soothing, caring touch.

Silence, then, "She's my best friend and the love of my life. My soulmate. She broke my curse. I would die for her."

She'd broken his curse?

"Oh, son." The soft sounds that indicated someone was being hugged, tears were being shed. "I'm so happy that the horrible curse Eros put on you has been broken. So happy you have found your soulmate."

Soulmate? They were soulmates? She wanted to look in his eyes, see the truth there, but the warmth had moved, shifting to concentrate on her leg, her arm, her chest; pain she hadn't noticed until now began to fire through her. She wanted to scream as bones snapped and reshaped inside her, but still couldn't open her eyes let alone make a sound or move.

A hand grasped hers – Tam's – and a calming tingle shot through her veins, alleviating the agony until it was a low throb of pain. She would have sobbed with relief but still nothing came. Something warm and hard was placed on her chest. "Rinna. Please come back to me. I love you. We have our future to plan together."

Then darkness took over her.

CHAPTER 16

Korinna woke to a bright light glowing red behind her closed lids. Warmth aligned along her back and legs and across her chest. A lovely warmth she wanted to curl into and never let go.

That warmth moved, shifting against her. A puff of breath against her neck.

She opened heavy lids and looked down. A male arm, its strong lines and fine dusting of dark hair, curled around her waist. Her fingers wrapped around that arm, hugging it to her. A fine scar ran over the back of his wrist and down onto a large, masculine hand with long, fine fingers currently cupping her breast.

She'd know that hand and arm anywhere.

Tam.

He was here? No. No. He couldn't be here. She'd saved him. She'd saved him.

"Shh, shh." His arm tightened around her as she jerked, panic taking her breath. "It's just a nightmare." A kiss to her neck then to her head, her ear, her forehead as he shifted behind her, moving to roll her onto her back.

He hung over her, his auburn hair bed-tousled, a hesitant smile on his lips as their gazes met.

"You were supposed to live." Her lip trembled.

"Hey, hey," he said, kissing the tremble away, his hand running up and down her side, chasing zaps of lightning along her skin. "I did. We both did. Although it was a close thing for you." He kissed her again and when he pulled away, his indigo eyes were dark with remembered grief. "Don't ever do that to me again." His other hand caressed her cheek, her brow, stroking her hair away from her face. She wanted to melt under his touch.

But ... "How is it possible?" She reached up, touched his face, her thumbs sweeping over his cheek, touching the grey hollow under his eyes before moving down to shape over his lips. He pressed a kiss against the tips, making them tingle. "You're alive. You're safe."

"And so are you. And free. We found the loophole. Your vow is now Clodia's to complete. And the moment she took it, your tether to the Underworld broke. I brought you to my family home to heal."

"But you didn't get your answer ... and that's all my fault."

"Not your fault. And now you are here to help me on my quest. Together we can track Clodia down and get my mother's powers back. Just like together we broke my curse."

"Oh." She remembered the conversation she'd heard after she thought she'd died when the pain was so bad. But she hadn't died. She'd been clinging onto life – clinging onto Tam, as he'd clung onto her, holding her with him. "We're soulmates." Her mouth twisted.

"That's supposed to make you happy."

"It does. So happy."

"So these are happy tears?" He swept his thumb across her face.

"Yes. What about these?" she asked, brushing her fingers across his cheek, capturing a tear that had fallen from his glorious eyes.

"The happiest of tears."

She reached up and pulled him down to her, losing herself in his kiss, in the feel of his hands as they roved over her, the feel of him under her fingers, delighted to find he had slept without a top on. She wished he didn't have his pants on.

"Hey!" he sat bolt upright, now completely naked. "You've got magic? How?"

He stared down at her, confusion all over his handsome face.

She didn't blame him. She was just as confused. She sat up slowly, leaning against the pillows stacked against the head of the huge comfortable bed they were in – his bed. "I've got magic." She'd thrown it all at Clodia's prison, to break it, except what she'd channelled to protect Tam. Her eyes flared wide as they went to his chest – bare of the Hells-Key and the HeartsBlood Gem. "The gem. Where's the gem?"

"Here." He touched between her breasts. "You're wearing it."

She looked down. It glowed softly red against the sheets she'd pulled up around her when she sat up. She hadn't even realised it was there.

"What has the gem to do with it?"

She took it in her hand. It pulsed at her touch, a voice sounding in her head, *"Hello friend. I saved it for you."*

"Oh."

"What?"

She held it out to him. "Touch it." He raised a brow but did as she bid. The gem glowed for him too, but when she dropped her hand, leaving it only clasped in his, the glow faded. She put her hand on it again. It pulsed brightly, almost happily. "Oh. I understand."

"What? I don't understand."

She met Tam's gaze. "It caught the magic I sent to you. I thought it would act as a conduit, sending the magic into you, so it was yours. So you could use it without me." An image flashed before her: of him calling for her, trying to get to her, his entire attention on her, desperate to stop her from sacrificing herself. "I didn't even know it would work – I had no time to prepare the stone properly. But it did it. It took my power and gave it to you." She frowned slightly. "But then, somehow, it gave it back to me. I don't understand how?"

He stared down at the gem, a small smile curling the corner of his mouth. "Clever, sneaky thing."

"What? Why?"

He met her gaze. "When my dad was healing you, I heard a voice telling me I had to put the gem on you and hold on. I didn't even question it. I just did it. It must have transferred the power then, when my attention was solely on you."

"But you didn't incant the spell."

"I didn't need to." His smile widened. "It responded to the strongest spell of all."

"Love," she whispered.

"Love," he repeated.

They held the HeartsBlood Gem in their hands, the red glow brightening as a whisper, so faint to be almost unheard, sounded around them. *"Soul cursed you both may have been, but love blessed is what you are now. With that love, you will do great things."*

"Is that the gem?" Tam asked.

"I think it is." They stared at it, wonderingly, their fingers tightening simultaneously. "Speak to us again."

The gem glowed brighter, faded, then glowed again, the voice louder this time, musically lyrical and yet husky and deep. *"You must find Clodia. You must bring her to justice. You must save us all from what she will do with a cupid's magic and the Goddess-given powers stolen from Julianna Stevens that she will go after now she's free."*

"But how?" Korinna asked, her voice croaking in surprise.

"I will guide you." The voice became faint again. *"But first, you must set me free."*

They stared at the gem, then each other, then back to the gem. "How do we do that?"

The gem's glow fluttered. The voice came, but was so soft, so distant, Korinna couldn't hear what it said. "I can't hear you." She looked up at Tam; he shrugged. "Say it again. Tell us how we can free you? How can you help us to find Clodia and do what we have to do?"

"Build your power," the voice whispered, only just loud enough that she caught the words.

She shook her head slowly, whispering, "I can't." Her powers had always been so big, and now, they were a quarter of that; enough to do simple spells but no more. Despite what Tam and Clodia had told her, she didn't know if she could trust herself to make the right decisions if her powers were returned to her in full. Look at the mess she'd made about the vow for one!

The gem fluttered brighter, the voice sounding louder. *"You can. Your power is not the source of your grief, it is its salvation. Trust in yourself. Trust in your love. Both of you. It will help more than you know. Strengthen yourself and all will be revealed. Even perhaps the source of what has tormented your souls and caused you to be separated this long."*

"How? When?"

The gem glowed sluggishly in their hands. Korinna gripped Tam's other hand, their gazes meeting, worried. Then a whisper sounded around them, distant and echoing. *"Share your love. Build the powers you were both left using family, hearth and home as your centre, as your strength. When the world renews and the hare and the Goddess of rebirth are in the zenith, my power will be at its height. In the days of Oestra, I will come back and tell you what must be done."*

"That long? But Clodia?"

"She can do nothing until then. Your mate was clever. He did not let on that the power she stole from him was not what powered the portal spell. She escaped, but only to the last place she had been. She is trapped once more in the Void. Even if she finds Julianna's Goddess-given powers, she will be unable to do anything until the days of Oestra when all power renews. Until then, protect each other and those you love. And keep me safe."

Tam looked deeply into Korinna's eyes and then back down at the gem. "I have the perfect place."

Lifting the gem, her fingers still entwined with his, he put the gem against his chest and canted:

"With powerful magic, the greatest of all

Keep this gem safe from evil and thrall

Wrapped in the embrace of my healed heart

Protected by the love of souls no longer apart

A part of her, a part of me

Three become one, until one becomes three.

Bound by the waning power of All Hallows' Eve

Willed with our love, so mote it be."

The gem glowed red and gold as the spell wound around their hands.

She gaped at him. "How?" He'd just used a spell she'd only ever heard rumour of.

"Demeter gave it to me long ago, the day Eros came to take me back. She said she thought I might one day need it."

"But it will only work between those whose love is true and deserved."

"Exactly."

The gem pulsed hot in their hands, and slowly melded with his flesh, close to where the Hells-Key had been not so long ago.

She hadn't admitted it, but there had been a kernel of doubt. Now …

She sucked in a breath and met his gaze. They had a lot to discuss; a lot to unwind of their pasts and who had tried to keep them apart; of who had used her to take the blame and why; and why nobody had told her that until Tam and Clodia. There was also a lot to figure out about what the HeartsBlood Gem had told them. But none of that mattered right now. All that mattered was what he was doing. What it meant.

She leaned forward and pressed her lips against his. "I love you," she breathed as she pulled back.

"As I love you."

He kissed her again, and she lost herself in the flavour of him, of the sensation pulsing through her as his tongue brushed over hers. Slowly, she became aware the heat had gone, her fingers flush against the smooth skin of his chest.

She pulled back a little and looked down.

The gem had vanished inside his chest, a faint pulsing glow the only sign it was there.

She looked up at him and smiled. "It's where it's meant to be." The HeartsBlood Gem, held safe with their love.

"For now."

"For now."

"Do you really believe we can do it?"

He nodded. "I believe we can do anything, together. And with the HeartsBlood Gem's help, we'll get all of the stolen power back, we'll make certain Clodia sent your lost souls to Elysium, we'll free the spirit from the gem and then we will have our HEA."

"HEA?"

He rolled his eyes. "How can someone so well-read not know HEA is Happy Ever After."

"I never read fairy tales. I never believed my prince would come to save me."

"He didn't. Well, not until after the princess first saved him."

"Yes, I did, didn't I?" She put her other hand against the warm strength of his chest, looking deeply into his eyes. "Our Happy Ever After. I like the sound of that."

"So do I."

They kissed again for long moments, until she pulled back. "What are we going to tell Hades? And Persephone?"

He groaned dramatically and fell back into the pillows behind her. "Did you have to bring that up now?"

She patted him on his chest. "Don't worry. I'll save you from their wrath."

"You better. No point me ending up dead now."

"I won't let him touch a hair on your precious head."

"So fierce." He tackled her to the bed, kissed her laughter from her lips. "I love you."

"I love you."

He looked down at his chest then back at her, his smile widening. "No longer soul cursed, but love blessed."

"Forever."

"Amen to that."

THANK you for reading the first part of Tamuel and Korinna's story. I hope you enjoyed it. There's still lots more excitement and discovery, passion and sexy-times, action and evil to fight for this cupid and his soulmate. To find out what happens next, look out for **Blood Cursed**, the next instalment of the *Gods Cursed Series*. Due out in **A Perfectly Paranormal Easter** – Easter 2022.

IF YOU'VE GOT A MOMENT, I would love it if you could leave a review for **Soul Cursed**. Reviews can help readers find books, and also help tell me where I'm going right and where I'm going wrong. I am grateful for all honest reviews. Thank you in advance for taking the time to let others know what you've read, and what you thought – you can leave your review at Goodreads, BookBub or the ebook retailer where you bought your copy. You can find links to the ebook retailers at my website here:

https://www.leislleighton.com/paranormal-romance-novels/#APPH

LOVE A FREE BOOK?

YOUR FREE BOOK IS WAITING

One Fate, one mate, a bond too strong to deny ...

Paul Collins, duty-bound Pack Warlock and seer, must marry a strong witch for the good of Pack McVale. But his hidden feelings for his best-friend's sister, maternal wolf Ivy McVale, make this a more difficult pill to swallow every day. Especially when they begin to mate.

Then Paul has a vision: If they mate, Ivy will die. Desperate, Paul uses his powers to change destiny and make Ivy think she's always hated him. He can deal with any punishment the Fates make him pay for tampering with destiny, as long as Ivy lives.

After recovering from a bewildering month-long illness, Ivy notices her nemesis, Paul, is tormented by something. And strangely, she is the only one who can feel it. Unable to endure such unhappiness—even if he does call her Poison Ivy—she is determined to help him, no matter the cost. Because Pack McVale cannot survive without him, and curiously, neither can she ...

Simply sign up to my newsletter and I will email your free copy of Witch Bound to you. You will also receive the latest on upcoming books, sales, giveaways and relevant bookish news.

Get My Free Copy of Witch Bound here:
https://www.subscribepage.com/w2g6b9

ALSO BY LEISL LEIGHTON

GODS CURSED SERIES

Love Cursed

Soul Cursed

Blood Cursed

Hearts Cursed

(Coming out Christmas 2022 in A Perfectly Paranormal Christmas
Anthology)

Fates Cursed

(Coming out mid 2023 in A Perfectly Paranormal Prophecy Anthology)

PACK BOUND SERIES

Pack Bound

Moon Bound

Shifter Bound

Wolf Bound

Witch Bound

(A Pack Bound Series Prequel Novella)

Soul Bound

(Dawn of the Curse: Book 1

A Pack Bound Prequel Series)

As well as writing sexy, dark paranormal novels, I write mysterious and
emotional romantic suspense novels.

COALCLIFF STUD SERIES

Climbing Fear: Book 1

Blazing Fear: Book 2

ECHO SPRINGS SERIES

Dangerous Echoes: Book 1

Books 2-4 in this series, (written by Daniel deLorne, TJ Hamilton and Shannon Curtis) are also available now at all ebook retailers.

ABOUT LEISL

Leisl Leighton is a tall red head with an overly large imagination. As a child, she identified strongly with Anne of Green Gables, and like Anne, is a voracious reader and born performer. It came as no surprise when she went on to a career as a performer, script writer, script doctor, stage manager and musical director for cabaret and theatre restaurants.

After starting a family, Leisl stopped performing and began writing the stories plaguing her dreams. She now writes emotional stories mixed with mystery and a little bit of what goes bump in the night. Her novels have won and placed in writing contests here and overseas. She is a passionate advocate for the romance genre, was President of Romance Writers of Australia from 2014-2017 and when she's not writing romantic stories of redemption, she is helping other authors reach their dreams with her Author Services.

You can contact Leisl through her website:

www.leislleighton.com

And if you want to stay in touch and be the first to find out about new releases, appearances, special deals and exclusive content and giveaways, sign up to her newsletter and pick up your free copy of Witch Bound here:

https://www.subscribepage.com/w2g6b9

And if you want to get to know the Perfectly Paranormal Anthology authors a bit more, get sneak peeks of what's coming up for the APP Anthologies, as well as giveaways, special offers and just some PNR fun, then join our Perfectly Paranormal Paramours Facebook Group.

Find us here:

https://www.facebook.com/groups/251663560162131

facebook.com/LeislLeightonAuthor
twitter.com/LeislLeighton
instagram.com/leislleightonauthor
bookbub.com/authors/leisl-leighton

ACKNOWLEDGMENTS

Thanks go to all the usual people: my hubby (the love of my life) and my boys (the other loves of my life); my mum and dad; my sister, brother and their families; my writing group friends—Anita, Marnie, Chris, Laura, Frana—I could do none of this without your love and support through the good and bad (especially in this last few terrible years). You give me the strength to keep going and the room to keep filling my creative well.

Thanks to Helen and Liz—your counsel and amazing friendships will always be missed but what you brought to my life will never be forgotten

Thanks to my agent, Alex Adsett, for encouraging me to go off and pursue getting these stories out there myself.

Thanks once again to my editor, Marnie St Clair—working with you is always a joy.

Thanks to Samantha Marshall for your amazing cover.

And a big thanks to my fellow A Perfectly Paranormal writers – this would not have been written without you. I'll be eternally grateful that you thought of me when coming up with the idea for this anthology. It is exciting that this story will live on both in the anthology but also as its own little can-do novella.

Finally, thanks to all the readers. I love writing my stories but it makes it all the more special to know you're right there with me enjoying my characters' trials, joys and general shenanigans right along with me. I hope my stories lift you up and give you all the feels because then my job is done.

GOOD RIDDANCE

MARNIE ST CLAIR

GOOD RIDDANCE

An Owlscroft Coven Novella
Book 2

Marnie St Clair

ABOUT GOOD RIDDANCE

Hunting demons is the easy part ...

Lone wolf Harlow Jackson is Owlscroft Coven's demon hunter – a role no one else wants but Harlow relishes. A role her coven is trying to take away from her, 'for her own good'. To make matters worse, she's also ended up responsible for Melbourne's newest magical visitors – on-the-run wizards Aiden and Elijah. Harlow doesn't want or need secretive Aiden's assistance, but it's not long before she has to admit Aiden is not only gifted at evicting demons, he looks pretty incredible doing it.

But when their past catches up with the wizards, Harlow has to choose between her coven and her new-found friends, between witch duty and wizard power, and between charting her own course and making room for love.

And that's before the most destructive demon known to witchkind arrives on the scene ... just in time for Halloween.

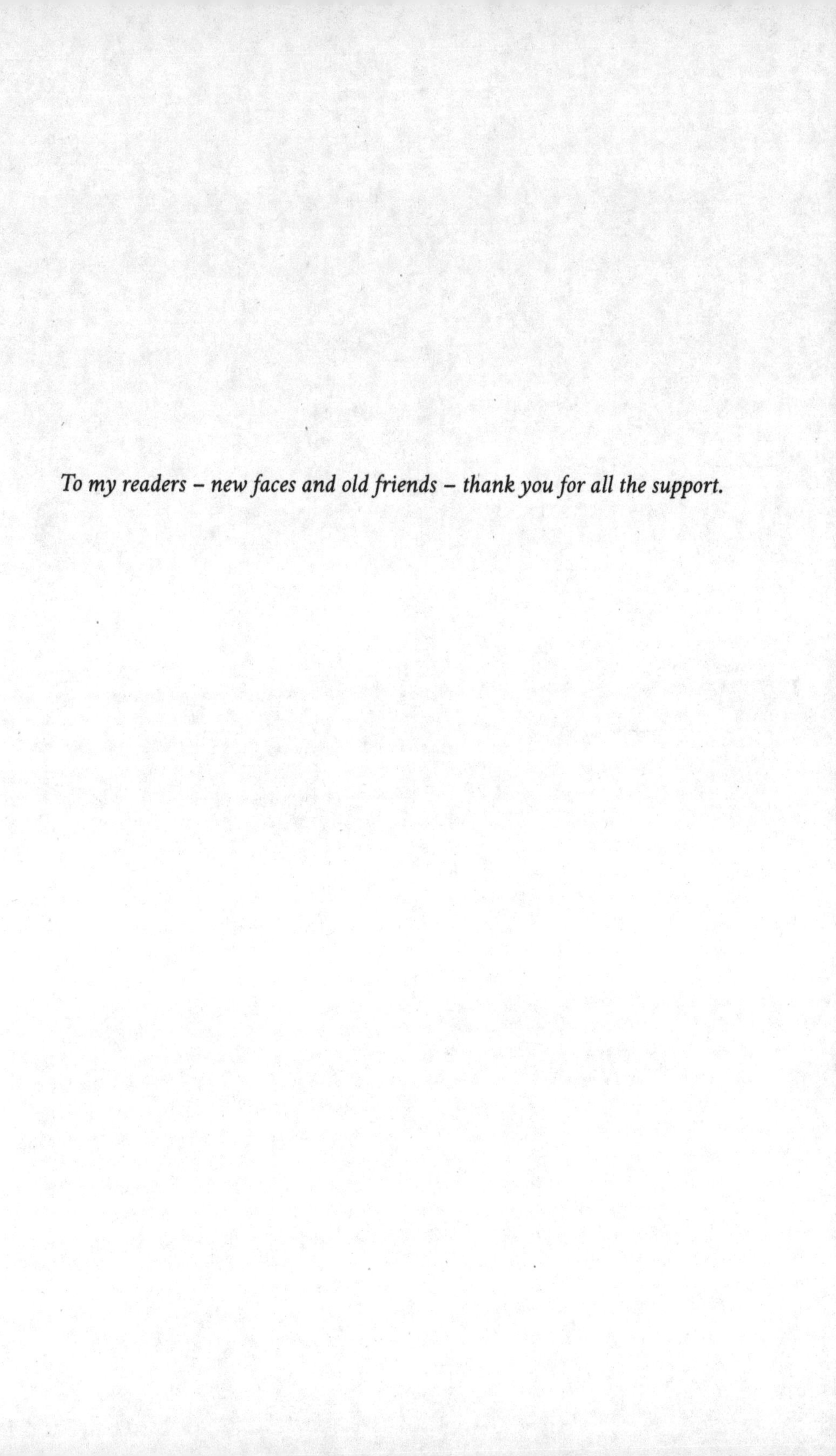

To my readers – new faces and old friends – thank you for all the support.

CHAPTER 1

People like to think they have to do something – something bad – to invite demonic inhabitation. Take a bite from the apple, so to speak.

There is some element of that – the more powerful demons are not going to waste their time inhabiting someone without the will and wherewithal to fulfill their ambitions. But mostly, demon inhabitation is a matter of luck.

And proximity to a portal.

I hate to break it to you, but all you have to do is walk past the portal at the wrong time and bam, inhabited.

That's where I come in. I'm Harlow Jackson, Owlscroft Coven's demon hunter, and I spend my life evicting demons from unwitting hosts.

This evening is my monthly catch-up with the Coven Council, where I fill the Council in on all things demon. We're in the ballroom at our covenstead, a Queen Anne mansion in the leafy environs of Hawthorn. Aunt Bernie, our Head Witch, and the other members of the Council are sitting behind a row of wooden desks set up at the front of the room. I'm standing, facing them, running through the latest stats.

"Big increase in numbers – as expected with Halloween in a couple of days." Demons get frisky this time of year. "Usual flood of Yellow; trickle of Orange, Violet, Green. One Indigo since last update. No sightings of Blue or Red." If those demon fuckers – an expression I use so often I shorten it to DFs – have other names, I don't know them. We call them by the colour their aura lights up when we cast a reveal spell. "All evictions successful; no known remaining active cases."

My reports are pretty much all the same, but the Council listens carefully. As usual, I've edited out any parts that are less than palatable – the close calls, the mad scrambles to hunt two demons at once, the times I barely manage to evict in time.

"Thank you, Harlow. Succinct as always." I suspect Aunt Bernie picks up on some of what I leave out. "And the wizards? How are things going?"

The wizards are Aiden and Elijah.

A vision of Aiden flashes in my mind – dark eyes, golden skin, sombre face – and a flush of heat follows. I shift from one foot to the other. "Fine."

Elijah, aka Jun Jie or just JJ, turned up in Melbourne from Singapore six months ago, on the run from another wizard who was trying to kill him for his magic amulet.

This is a common story in the wizarding world. It's all very Highlander.

Instead of introducing himself nicely, in true JJ form, he attempted to ingratiate himself by messing around with a batch of magic. It caused a lot of drama at the time.

Aiden followed shortly after. Aiden is JJ's uncle, and his main job in life is keeping his nephew alive. He has his work cut out for him. JJ's a doofus, a Cavoodle puppy – all big brown eyes, insane energy levels and poor decision-making. According to Aiden, JJ has a lot of raw talent, but this only makes Aiden's job harder because it's not balanced by any common sense.

I can relate because my sister, Everly, also has little regard for her safety or sanity. Not surprisingly, she and JJ have become fast friends.

"And Aiden ... You've told us previously that he's learned fast and is proving useful ... How would you rate his competence?"

After a prolonged and at times heated debate, the wizards were allowed to stay. Aiden promised their presence would not bring any trouble. He also offered to take on the dirty work – the jobs no one else in the coven wants to do. Which is how he came to assist me with my demon-hunting duties.

It wasn't something I wanted. I'm your classic lone wolf; I like to work alone. But it's turned out okay. Aiden listens and does what I tell him. He doesn't pry into my business, or share his own.

I can be reserved, but I've got nothing on Aiden.

"He's solid," I offer cautiously, wondering where they're going with this.

Truth is, Aiden's more than solid.

Wizard magic doesn't play nice with demons – some kind of strange feedback loop where attempts to evict actually make demons stronger. So to help me, he's had to learn how to use witch magic. He's only been doing it for six months, but he's already disgustingly good.

"Would you say that you trust him?" That's my cousin, Avery, lobbing another curve ball.

The short answer is, no. I don't trust anyone.

And Aiden? Less than most.

Melbourne is a magic city. Powerful. It would make a great seat for a new wizard emperor. Paranoid? Maybe. But I sense how much Aiden is concealing.

At the same time, I have no solid reason not to trust him.

I need to know where they're going with this before I can answer. "Why do you ask?"

"Can he man the portal while you take some leave?" Seraphina asks with her usual bluntness.

Sorry?

My displeasure must be all over my face because Avery and her mum, Aunt Lettie, exchange a here-we-go look.

"You haven't taken any leave in over a year." That's my mother; her tone is aggrieved, almost aggressive. She hates that I'm a demon hunter. Probably because it's the most dangerous vocation a witch can have. Most demons just try to evade me, but others turn nasty under the threat of eviction. There've been times when things have been dicey. I'd be lying if I said I don't count myself lucky to still be breathing.

"It's something Avery brought to our attention," Aunt Lettie interjects, attempting to smooth the not-unusual tension between Mum and I.

I shoot Avery an unimpressed look – it's exactly the kind of thing she would notice – and she mouths an apology. We're about the same age and we've always gotten on well. She probably didn't mean to do me like that.

"I don't want to take leave," I say.

Another set of exchanged glances passes along the row of desks.

"Think of it this way, Harlow," begins Avery. "Tired staff cause accidents. If we were a regular company, you'd represent a major OH&S breach. We'd be liable to be sued."

"We're not a regular company." Despite Avery's efforts to the contrary. "And I'm fine. No accidents."

"We can't have you working shift after shift with no reprieve," Aunt Bernie says in her brook-no-argument tone. "And while I agree that this would have been difficult previously, now Aiden is available to cover."

Not happening.

I know what everyone thinks – that being a demon hunter is the worst. Up all night every night, in mortal danger a fair amount of the time. But the truth is, I love it.

Truth is, I know with total certitude that I wouldn't survive in this coven without a role like this. I need my space, my autonomy – something sadly lacking in witch life. Until Aiden arrived, I'd worked alone for years. I wasn't supposed to – demon hunting's supposed to be done in pairs – but Judy, who trained me, moved overseas shortly after I started, to help her son and his family. It hadn't phased me one whit.

Truth is, I have no clue what I'd do on leave. I am not built to sit poolside sipping mojitos. I have no capacity for downtime.

"No. I would not trust Aiden alone with the portal. He could disappear at any second." My tone is cool; I am not taking leave.

They don't have a response to that. No one knows how long the wizards will stay.

"Well," Aunt Lettie says. "If you're sure you're fine without a break for a little longer."

"I am."

"But, of course, things will change when Claire and Lucinda complete their training," Aunt Bernie continues seamlessly.

The bottom drops out of my stomach. "Claire and Lucinda?"

Avery nods. "They've put their hands up for demon hunting."

Claire and Lucinda are coming towards the end of their neophyte year. They need to choose their speciality. I had no idea they were interested in my role.

"Then you'll be able to step back entirely."

I swing to Mum, who's trying not to sound gleeful, like that's not the best news she's had all year. She knows this will kill me. Her eyes soften as she looks at me, but her face has a determined set to it.

The twisting sensation inside me develops into a solid ball of 'no way'. No way am I stepping down. But as I glance along the row of faces, I can tell they've discussed it already and they're resolved.

I should have seen this coming. There's been cases in the past of demon hunters going nutty dealing with those DFs night after night, and the job's supposed to have a five-year limit.

That's not me. I'm fine.

But I'll be shunted on anyway. For my own good.

"You've done a superb job, Harlow. We can't thank you enough for your service. But you deserve the chance to live a normal life." Aunt Lettie's tone is soothing.

I'm not soothed. I don't want a normal life.

Especially not the witch version. The thought of coming to Owlscroft multiple times a week to work in a team on some minor but helpful task makes me want to leap from a tall building. I'd prefer to face a thousand Indigos.

And I'd have to find a day job. As the coven's demon hunter, I've been off the hook, but that's going to come to an end. "What am I supposed to do? Become a kindergarten teacher?"

There's a collective flinch at the bitterness in my voice.

"With your interest in martial arts, we thought maybe physiotherapy," Mum says tentatively.

Chalice. They've even discussed future career paths.

I'm pretty sure me and anything client-facing is not going to work.

Sound builds outside the ballroom. The hefty front door to Owlscroft opens and closes. Snippets of chit-chat drift in as witches mill in the foyer, waiting for the ballroom to open and all-coven to start.

All-coven.

I'll be expected to turn up. Every. Single. Week.

I glance out the window. It's getting dark. "I'll think about it. If there's nothing more, I need to get to work."

Aunt Bernie looks like she's not sure the conversation is over, but eventually she nods. I head for my backpack, which I dumped at the side of the room when I arrived, sling it over my shoulder and make for the door.

"Harlow."

I turn. My arms cross automatically.

Mum is tiny and blonde with delicate, even features she passed on to Everly. My dad is cut from a similar mould. I, on the other hand, am well on my way to six foot. I have dark, curly-tending hair, and though my skin isn't dark, it's more olive than pale. I used to harass Mum all the time about whether I was adopted, but she insists I wasn't. Just one of those genetic lottery freakeries.

"This is for the best," she insists.

I want to lash out because she's been waiting for this day for years, but the rules are not her fault. "Like I said, I'll think about it. I've got to get going." I give her a quick hug so she knows I don't blame her –

or at least, not entirely – and exit before I get drawn into other conversation as witches stream in for all-coven.

I wasn't even lying – I am going to think.

I'm going to think about how to prove to the Council that I should be allowed to continue.

And how to manage Claire and Lucinda.

They've never talked to me about demon hunting. They probably only want to take it up because of Aiden.

He's not exactly hard on the eyes.

But he may not even still be in Melbourne when Claire and Lucinda make their final decision. And just because they start training, doesn't mean they'll finish it.

The portal is not far from a McDonalds, which provides plenty of scope for loo breaks.

Maybe I'll forget to mention that.

CHAPTER 2

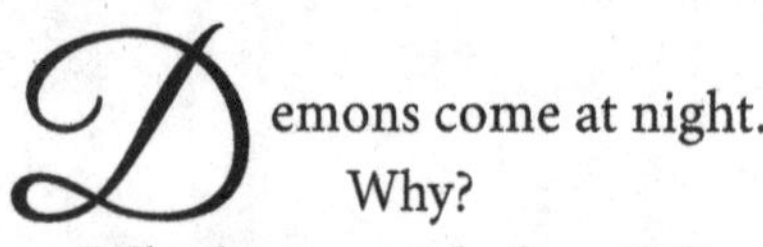emons come at night.

Why?

Who knows with those DFs.

Maybe it's easier to inhabit then. People are tired, loose, unfocused. Maybe it's when the portal is amenable to them pinging on through. In any case, my work day starts at sundown.

The portal is an old stone fountain in a small square in the CBD. You might have a question at this point. You might wonder, if we know what the portal is, why don't we just destroy it?

We've tried, multiple times, but a new one inevitably appears. Usually not too far from the last one, but it takes ages to track down exactly where – and Chalice knows what's crept through in the meantime.

So. No point.

I jiggle on the balls of my feet. I skipped the gym tonight to go to coven and I'm full of unexpended energy. The heat is finally here and, despite my earlier session with the Council, I'm basking like a savannah cat in the sweet spring air. As someone who spends all night every night standing around watching for demons, winter is not my favourite.

The only issue is, hot weather brings something else; something that is making my life problematic.

Horniness.

It's been a while. I'm not one for relationships, but with my gym-dominant lifestyle, it's not hard to find a guy. I haven't done that in months. Not since Aiden came to town.

Speaking of … Aiden's not helping me rein in my libido. He's doffed his winter layers, and he's in a black tank and black cargo pants. The tank sits close to his sleek muscles, leaving a lot of skin on display.

And his amulet.

It gleams in the low dusk light, the jade in the centre an alluring green, the weathered gold picking up hits of light. Between Aiden's golden-skinned muscles and the glow of his amulet, this is going to be a long summer.

I wish I'd made it to the gym. I stretch, fingers to the sky, then drop them to my toes. I stand and look around, making sure I know who's coming and going. I turn … and catch Aiden staring at me. I get a rare glimpse of the wildness inside. It stares at me – hot, hungry, with an edge savage enough to stop my breath.

It turns my belly to butterflies, sends heat through my veins.

He breaks eye contact and scans the square. Back to his usual control and composure.

My eyes flick to the small jade disk on his chest. "When are you going to let me touch it?"

His dark brown eyes are bemused. "I'm not."

He's told me that before; no one touches a wizard's amulet. But I'm nothing if not persistent. "No?"

"No."

"Never?"

"Never."

We'll see about that. The way that thing is calling to me, I'm not going to be able to resist for long.

"Eyes up, soldier." There's amusement in Aiden's tone, but also a certain degree of defensiveness. Wizards spend their lives protecting their amulets, and this is not the first time I've been caught checking it out.

I meet his gaze. "Maybe I'll just get one of my own."

Something flashes over his face, but he tamps it down and replies casually, "Good luck with that."

I cast a quick reveal spell on two older women in matching floral scarves and pearls. Neither of them lights up, so I continue. "How does one go about procuring an amulet? Apart from wrenching it from the neck of its still-warm previous owner?"

Aiden winces, but it does seem to be how most wizards do it. My gaze drops again to his amulet. "Is that how you got yours?"

"Harlow." It's a deep bass rumble that makes a shiver roll down my spine.

A group of young men pass the fountain. They're excited, talking at volume, on their way to a club most likely. One of them looks me over. "Hey, it's Trinity," he chortles.

I give the guy a hard stare; his laugh fades and he moves closer to his pack. But he's right. It's not shiny leather but I am in head-to-toe black. The dark helps me blend into the night, and the tough-girl chic deters some would-be approachers. I could deal with them but I prefer focusing on irritations of the supernatural variety.

"Your turn," I say to Aiden.

He mutters the words of the spell.

Demon inhabit
Show me it
True colour
Reveal me it

One of the boys lights up canary.

This is no surprise. A good 80 percent of what comes through the portal is Yellow.

If I had to guess, I'd say Yellows are at the bottom of the demon food chain. All they want is the experience of being human – to do the things we do, feel the things we feel. When they inhabit, they mimic being a regular person. They mess it up, of course, and harm to the host is always possible. Accidentally stepping out in front of a car comes to mind.

Aiden did the reveal, so I grab for the current batch of magic and cast an evict spell.

> *Yellow begone*
> *Back home now*
> *Leave the host*
> *Back home now*

The canary glow brightens then disappears. I turn back to Aiden. "You were saying ..."

The muscles in his jaw work. He gives me a dour look. He doesn't appreciate or approve of the way I constantly pump him for information about all things wizard.

I am obsessed. "Come on, I want to know how I can get one."

He hits me with an unimpressed Aiden look. "I'm not corrupting you like that."

His word choice plays havoc with my lustful tendencies. I resist the urge to throw him to the ground and straddle him, and content myself by allowing my gaze to trail over his biceps, his shoulders, his chest. "Maybe I'll corrupt you."

His eyes narrow; his nostrils flare.

He's not slow; he must know I find him attractive. And like before, I catch him looking too. But we don't acknowledge it; not out loud. I'm breaking our unspoken deal.

Which I know is a mistake. Aiden's the last guy I should be looking to start something with. Sure, he's hot as fuck but we work together. Add in my usual great form with men and it's a recipe for disaster. I'd get two weeks of delicious smutty steam, followed by a whole heap of awkward.

And I can't even think about having to report any entanglement and ensuing mess to the Coven Council.

Still. The desire is real.

As is the desire for an amulet.

Maybe I can ask JJ. Where to get one, that is. He wouldn't let me touch his; *he's* not even allowed to touch it. It's in a safe somewhere, waiting until he's old enough to start learning to use it properly. He hates that it's not on him but it's too much of a risk. If he accidentally interacts with it, a flare of magic may explode out, letting every wizard in the world know he's in Melbourne. So it's just sitting there. Unused.

Is it too late to switch teams? Can a witch become a wizard?

Not going to lie, I am envious of Aiden, envious of the wizard lifestyle. Wizards don't answer to anyone; they're free to make their own choices. "I'm serious. I'm ready to cross over to the dark side."

"You're not," he says curtly.

But I am. "I reckon I can handle it."

"You don't want to have to handle it."

But I do.

It's not that I don't respect my coven. It's not that I don't see the value in what we do. I know we make a difference, and I'm loyal. But as coven witches, we don't have the freedom to do much of anything – there's a limited number of spells we cast, a limited number of things we do. Helping others, mostly. The thought of having the freedom to explore, to chart my own course ... Besides, maybe I won't even have a coven for much longer. There's a huge chasm between me and the rest of Owlscroft, with demon hunting the only bridge. If they're going to burn it on me ... "Being a witch is boring."

"Believe me, it's far more interesting than being a wizard."

"How?" My utter disbelief comes blaring through.

He turns to face me more fully, expression serious. "All most wizards do is defend the power they've got and chase more. They'll do anything for it. Witches aren't ugly like that. That's rare in the magical world. You don't know how lucky you are."

His words stab at me. Lucky. Right. "Wanna swap? You can take my place in the coven."

He shakes his head, looks away and casts a reveal spell. Nothing.

I continue. "Aunt Bernie won't mind."

He folds his arms across his chest. "Bernadette would never accept me, or anyone, in your place."

It hits a nerve. Because, actually, she's pretty ready to shunt me on. "That's what you think."

He gives me a searching look.

But I turn, scan the square for new groups, trying to keep it together under a crash of emotion I'm not ready to deal with. "Anyway, I'm sick of Melbourne. I want to expand my horizons. Try new things."

There must be something in my tone, because he looks at me hard for a few seconds. "What's going on?"

My mouth skews. I don't intend to tell him. But then I do. "I'm being taken off demon duty."

There is a long moment while Aiden processes this. "When?"

I shrug. "Once I've trained new witches."

Two guys in short gym shorts lope past the fountain. I cast a reveal spell, and one of them turns Orange.

Orange. The crash it, burn it, blow it up crew. They live for explosions and general anarchy. They don't deliberately harm humans, as far as I can tell, but there is not infrequent collateral damage.

"I've got this," Aiden says, but before he can make after the Orange, a woman in a body-con black dress and sky-high heels pops up out of nowhere. Aiden does a quick reveal and she glows emerald.

Green. The second one tonight. We usually wouldn't even get two in one week, but it's almost Halloween, and thousands of DFs are pinging on over from Demonsville. It's like the portal stretches from pinhole to waterslide chute. Without Aiden, there'd be no way I could keep up. I'd have to leave Yellow, and sometimes Orange, to make sure I got Violet and Green. And I'd have to leave them all to hunt Indigo.

"I'll take the Green," he says.

I go to argue because we take it in turns and the Green should be mine, but he's already moving. I pivot and run after the Orange, tapping him as I pass. "Wanna see something cool?" I yell back over my shoulder.

I jog into a nearby alleyway, stopping halfway along. Yellows are the only demon I'll take out with an audience, because they literally just go poof. The other types fight eviction harder, and I've learned the hard way it's better to be alone.

He follows. Of course. Oranges live to see something cool. He peers around the alley, grinning. "What is it?"

"This."

He walks closer while I cast the evict spell under my breath. You can see the moment the Orange realises something's up. He flings out a hand, letting loose a stream of fire.

He's closer than I realised and I have to dodge, fast. I crash into the graffiti on the other side of the laneway. Pain spears through my shoulder.

He sends out another flame. This one's strong for an Orange – one round of the spell usually suffices. I hit the cobblestones hard then roll – crushing my shoulder – and leap to my feet.

Some witches fuss about the batch of magic they're using – is there enough of it, is this batch easy to work with? Some fuss about the spell, practicing the words over and over, getting them just right. Me, I just focus on myself, what I bring to the equation. I grab for some more magic, grind out the words, and put myself right behind my spell.

He shoots out a final flare in my direction, and I drop to a crouch, arms up, but the flame dissipates into the air before it reaches me.

Orange is begone.

The guy folds over his knees, breathing heavily, but he's fine. Or he's going to be.

His friend is hovering in the mouth of the alleyway. He's still hesitating there, unsure of what he saw, when I jog past. "Buy him a beer," I call back. "He needs it."

CHAPTER 3

I run back, shoulder jolting each time a foot hits the ground. Once I'm within range of the portal, I cast a reveal, praying we haven't missed anything. But the coast appears clear.

Aiden's not back yet. Not surprising – Greens take longer to dispatch than Orange. It's like they know what we're about before we even start evicting. They're hard to get alone and as soon as they're cornered, they're out to cause maximum drama – which I learned the hard way when I had to evict one in a restaurant a few months back. But they've got to go – they're sociopathic game-players who like messing with people's minds and hearts. Think white-collar sociopath and you're close. And they can last on earth for weeks if we don't evict, unlike Yellows, who'll disappear of their own accord in a few hours, or Oranges, who generally only last a day or two.

My phone buzzes. I grab it from my pocket. Mum. Chalice. She doesn't usually call me at work. I toss up answering in case it's an emergency, though it's more likely that she just wants to harrass me about tonight's meeting.

As much as she drives me crazy, I do feel for her. Neither of her daughters got hit with the fun end of the witch stick. I know she worries, but I can't do much about it. I keep myself as safe as I can.

I hit decline. I'm watching the portal by myself at the moment. I can't talk and reveal demons at the same time. Also, I don't want to talk to Mum right now.

A few minutes and five Yellows later, Aiden enters the square from the other end, a lean, graceful but deadly apex predator, walking through the dark of the night like he owns it. I wave so he knows where I am. He gives a single nod and heads towards me.

"All good?" I ask when he's close.

He nods. "You?"

"Why'd you take the Green?" I ask instead of answering. Come to think of it, he's been doing that a bit since I told him about what happened in the restaurant. Frowning, I add, "She was supposed to be mine."

He cuts a glance to me. Looks away. "Just the way it worked out."

It wasn't. Aiden knows how we allocate demons. We take it in turns; one does the reveal and one does the evict. And if he thinks I need protecting because of one little mishap—

My phone buzzes again. Unthinking, I grab it from my pocket.

Aiden's gaze slides down, then up to meet mine. "It's your mother," he says helpfully.

"Uh-huh." I shove the phone back in my pocket, where it continues to vibrate in reprimand. To fill in the time until it stops, I scan, identify a new group and cast a reveal spell. Nothing.

I don't know whether to make a big deal about the Green thing or not. I've been told in the past that I'm difficult to work with. Things are going pretty well with Aiden. I don't want to cause problems, and what's done is done. But ... "In future, we stick to the system. If you do the reveal, I do the evict."

He looks at me hard for a few moments. His mouth twists. He looks away and nods.

I should feel like we've cleared the air and we're all good, but there's still something unsatisfactory about the whole thing.

I move and he moves and we bump, his bicep against my shoulder. I wince.

He stills immediately, hand coming to my lower arm. It's a casual gesture, but all the nerve endings in the vicinity spark in delight. I have to concentrate to keep my breathing normal.

"What happened?" he asks.

"Just a bruise. Nothing major."

He exhales in disapproval. Still holding my wrist, his other hand gently pushes the sleeve of my tee up over my shoulder. His mouth skews. "If you're not going to fix that, I will."

I could; no one in the coven would take issue with me healing an injury caused in the line of duty, but I wouldn't usually bother. If he's offering … I'll take more of his hands on me. I nod.

Apart from demon hunting, Aiden doesn't use much magic. It's part of staying under the radar. But healing me won't take much. I feel a slight build in the underlying hum of magic he always has going on. He studies my arm and I study his face.

High cheekbones. Well-cut lips. Sharp jawline.

My gaze wanders lower. Long neck. Pronounced Adam's apple. Super interesting tendons.

One cord shifts as he moves. I could lean forward, take it in my teeth. Gently, of course.

Something warm and languid as honey flows through my shoulder, bringing comfort, ease and care. It's nice. I close my eyes and let the sweet balm flow through me.

When I open my eyes, Aiden's studying my face; like I was his moments ago.

He releases me and steps back. "How's that?"

Good Aiden. Always so responsible.

I rotate my shoulder, swing my arm around; it moves with ease. "Fixed. Thanks."

My phone buzzes again. Someone can't take a hint.

"You can take that," Aiden says, scanning the square. "I'll cover." When I don't do or say anything, he adds, "Take the call, Harlow."

I bristle, but he's right, I don't have the watching-the-portal-solo excuse anymore. Mum knows I dodge; she'll just keep ringing. Aiden will keep hassling. I grab my phone and answer. "Hi, Mum."

"Harlow. I was just about to leave a message."

Well. She got me to answer instead. "I can't talk long. Busy night."

"I was just … checking in with how you were. After the meeting with the Council tonight."

What does she expect me to say? Fine and dandy? Demon hunting is the only thing I can do, and they're taking it away from me. "I don't have time to get into it right now."

I turn to catch Aiden's reveal, but nothing shows up. Damn.

"I know it's not what you want, but it *is* for the best. And not just because of the danger, Harlow."

I grunt noncommittally. Mum doesn't seem to have taken my 'don't have time to get into it' on board.

"You can't keep living like you do. Up all night. Sleeping all day. We barely see you."

"I have a job to do, Mum."

"Yes. I know. And you have done it like no one else could. But it's enough now. It's time for you to focus on other things. A career that you can take forward and grow with. Friends. Relationships. You shouldn't be alone all the time."

"I'm not alone all the time." I realise with some surprise that that's true. I used to be, but I'm not anymore. I expel a breath. "Look, Mum, I happen to like my life. Just the way it is. I know you don't understand or approve, but … what's new."

She makes a wounded sound and I mutter a curse. Goddamn it. I had not wanted to get into this tonight. I make my tone gentler. "I want to keep demon hunting. I like it; I'm good at it; I'm not cray-cray." I sound defensive. I don't want to be. It's just, what happened with Aiden taking that Green before has put me on edge. I take a breath and say, "I don't need to step down."

And I don't plan to. I don't add that.

When I look around, Aiden is pointing after a teenager with green hair and Doc Martens. I nod to let him know I've got that he's going.

"Actually, you do. You know the rules."

Yeah. Well. I've never been good with rules. "What else would I do at Owlscroft?"

"You're so talented. There are many roles you would excel at."

"Like what?"

Mum doesn't answer. I sense she's trying to find something to say but coming up short. Other roles suitable for Harlow ... Searching ... Searching ... Searching ... Nothing. "Coven isn't everything."

My heart squeezes; a lump forms in my chest. "I know that," I reply brusquely. But the truth is, my job *is* my whole world. I may not be fully part of the coven – not like other witches – but it's my everything. And I know there's not much apart from demon hunting I can do but I wasn't expecting Mum to completely draw a blank like that. I thought she'd at least have options she thought were suitable, even if I know they won't work. What the hell else am I going to do with my life? My future stretches like a blank black canvas in front of me. "Look, don't worry about it, okay? I'm not going to hang around where I'm not wanted. I'll find something else. There's heaps of avenues to explore. Physio, like you said. Occupational therapy. Speech therapy. Osteopathy." I'm clutching at straws, reeling off a string of jobs I think go together. "It's not like I have to be part of a coven."

I am looking around as something to do while I talk but then I notice several fresh groups walking past. I've been drawn into the drama of my life instead of taking care of business.

"Harlow—"

"Wait on, Mum."

I press the phone against my chest and cast a couple of quick spells. It's wrong for me to think it, because they're never good, but I would really like a demon right now.

A Mafioso-looking silver fox in a black suit lights up Violet. Thank Chalice.

"Something's come up. I need to go."

"Harlow, I think you might have misunderstoo—"

"Demon, Mum. Gotta go."

I end the call and stalk after the fox.

Violets are sex fiends who can't get enough. They're not into force – thank Chalice – but their irresistible allure means it's not really consensual either. For either the inhabited or their bedmate-slash-mates. All parties involved are going to wake up thinking they've had the best sex of their lives. They won't be sure how they made it happen and they won't even necessarily regret it, but the fact that it wasn't a free choice gets to me.

Violets aren't dangerous, but I still get them alone when I'm evicting, mostly to preserve the dignity of the host in case anything untoward, like a stripping moment, occurs. Demons get desperate when they want to stay.

The guy knows I'm following; something about his gait has turned seductive. I take his hand and tug him through a dark doorway. There's stairs heading up to a nightclub, based on the steady thump of bass floating down, but no one right here. I drop his hand and turn.

"Evening, beautiful." His avid eyes are glittering. He likes what he thinks is about to happen.

His Violet allure reaches me more than usual; stirring something deep in my belly that travels like satin through my veins. Urging me to abandon sense and give in to hedonistic impulses. It'll feel so good, the glow of his eyes promises.

I don't doubt that it would. I'm tempted. I really am. It's been a shitty day, and using casual sex to work through stress is right in my wheelhouse. I like contact. I like it a lot. I haven't had it in a long time, and being around Aiden is stirring up all kinds of urges.

But this is a demon. Demon: bad.

I push through the stronger than usual resistance in my body. It's an effort; I have to work for it. Strive to recall that this is a Violet I'm dealing with, not the nice-looking guy underneath, and the demon has to go. I hold the line, muttering the words and holding my intent to evict firmly in place against my own urges, until the purple shimmers then fades.

A confused man stares back at me, trying to work out how he got here.

"Thanks for your help. You really saved my bacon." I'm not one to offer comfort, but I try to leave them thinking they've done something good.

CHAPTER 4

We barely draw breath for the rest of the night.

There is some cause for solace: no Blues, the charismatic actors, politicians and cult-leaders; no Indigos, the twisted pain and fear junkies; and no Reds, the total devastation warlords.

When the night is softening toward the grey of pre-dawn and the DF parade dwindles to nothing, we head back home.

Yes, the wizards and I live in the same apartment building, only a few blocks from the portal. A week after they were told they were allowed to stay, Aiden and JJ moved into a suddenly vacant three-bedroom apartment on the same floor as me. I've never asked but I'm pretty sure it wasn't coincidence.

Aiden hasn't returned to our previous conversation about my job coming to an end. We didn't have time while we were going after demons and now he's back to his usual unprying self. Which is a good thing. It's kind of disturbing that I said anything to him at all. I'm not sure when my subconscious decided he was my confidante. We work well together, but we don't open up to each other. He's a wizard, he's discreet to the point of secretive, and I'm very much aware he's not a permanent fixture.

We exit the elevator and head to my apartment. "Nighty-night," I say at my door. "HIIT at three?"

"See you th—"

Aiden turns. I swing too, body tense and ready, pulse spiking.

It's JJ. He's crept out from around the corner. His face is pale; his eyes are huge and glassy.

Aiden covers the ground in rapid strides. His hands land on JJ's shoulders and they engage in a rapid exchange in Hokkien. Aiden and JJ always use English around me; the use of Chinese confirms that something is very wrong.

Aiden's head drops; his shoulders bunch. There is an eerie stillness. The hairs on my arms stand up, all my witchy Spidey senses are on full alert. Then I am hit with an incredible wave of power. It crashes against me, through me. A roar that makes my teeth ache and my nipples hard. Pressure builds – in my head, against my skin. The danger is palpable.

If this was directed at me, I'd collapse in a heap on the floor. Incapacitated. Dead.

The wave falls away, drops to a gentle hum, leaving me once again capable of thought.

And my thought is – that came from Aiden.

I stare at him, eyes so wide I can feel the saucer shape of them.

He raises his head, twists it toward me, and I don't recognise him. The lines of his face cut differently. There's a cold ferocity there I've never seen before.

Who is this man?

He looks back at JJ. "Okay?"

JJ nods; he doesn't seem near as shocked and awed as I am.

"Harlow?"

"Yeah," I say, though I've got no idea what 'okay' means in this context.

Aiden releases JJ's shoulders and walks a little way back towards me. "Apologies for the Chinese."

Like that's what's worrying me.

He is once again the calm, reasonable, impeccably mannered

wizard I've come to know. But I've seen, and I can't unsee. I'll never underestimate him again. "Problem?"

He pushes a hand through his hair. "Jonathan's found us."

Chalice.

"I thought that was impossible." I, along with the rest of the coven, have been assured this will not happen.

"It should be." Aiden looks back at JJ. "JJ assures me he hasn't been anywhere near his amulet."

"I haven't! I swear I haven't!"

JJ's tone is full of earnest and I believe him. Unlike his uncle, JJ has no talent for deception.

I'm not sure that Aiden believes him though. Everything he's ever said has implied that amulets are temptation itself for wizards. JJ's not even allowed to look at his, much less use it. Even some wizard trying to kill him was barely enough to convince him that it should be kept out of the way in a bank vault.

"I take it we're safe for the moment?"

Aiden's gaze cuts to mine. "For the moment."

I turn and push open the door. "You better come in."

It's the first time Aiden's been inside my place, and I watch him take it in. It's a minimal, basic and functional one-beddie – lots of black and chrome and bare white walls. Nothing special but it suits me.

I wave them towards the one small couch and drop into a nearby dining chair. "So what happened exactly?"

JJ looks towards Aiden, who nods at him to proceed. "I was gaming with my friends and we reached Level 27. Finally." He stops and widens his eyes so I get how major that is. "It took us ages to clear the mages with the white—"

"JJ."

JJ refocuses. "We decided to stop for the night. I was walking home. It was just me; the others caught a tram on Swanston Street. And I was crossing Flinders Lane, and Jonathan just walked out onto the street!" JJ's voice gets higher and higher as he speaks. He is clearly still freaked. "He was looking around, up and down, up and down. I thought he knew I was there. I thought he was looking for me." His voice breaks; Aiden squeezes his shoulder. "I went into the 7-Eleven and hid at the back. Crouched down behind the shelves with the magazines with pink and blue quilts on the front. I was so scared. I waited and waited. I thought he was going to come after me, but he didn't. I crept towards the front and peeked out. He was still there, in the same place, just ..." His arms stretch wide, his face tilts to the ceiling. "Soaking up the ambience." He pulls his arms in. "I'm pretty sure he didn't see me."

"You're still alive," I say. But I'm not sure my joke is well-received. Too close to the bone.

"It makes no sense," Aiden says. "If he knows enough to come to Melbourne, how did he not feel you so close to him? Why has he not tried to attack us, or gone for the amulet?"

But there is no answer to those questions. "When was this?" I ask.

"Hours ago. I've been waiting for you guys to get back."

"You should have called," Aiden remonstrates.

JJ shakes his head. "You're busy. And I knew I'd be safe outside Harlow's room."

He knew he'd be safe outside my room? I shoot a narrow-eyed gaze at Aiden, but now's not the time. I look back at JJ. "Are you sure it was him? It sounds like he was acting like a tourist, not like a wizard on a mission to kill."

Aiden winces.

JJ looks at me as though I'm slow. "I'm sure. I mean, I know what he looks like. He's my uncle."

I think I am beyond shock. Turns out I'm not. "Sorry?" I scan between their faces, then land on JJ. "The big bad wizard you're on the run from, the one who's trying to kill you for your amulet ... He's your uncle?"

JJ nods. I switch to Aiden. "He's your brother?"

Aiden says nothing. Which I take to mean yes.

Wizards!

I am about to further express my amazement and disgust, but then

I catch the look in Aiden's eyes. A sadness so profound, I feel it in my throat. My chest.

His brother. Wow.

I change my mind. Being a wizard sucks.

I fold my hands in front of me. "Well," I say after a pause. "What now?"

Aiden stands. "We leave."

His words grab me by the throat, shake me around. I've known this was coming – they've always said they'd go – but it hits me hard enough that I struggle to breathe right.

This is it. They're going. No more Aiden.

Uncertain of what else to do, I stand too.

"We need to pack. As soon as the bank is open, we'll collect the amulet and head for the airport."

"Where will you go?" My voice comes out normal, but every cell in my body is screaming at me to stop them.

Aiden shrugs. "Anywhere there's a flight. Come, JJ. We need to move."

But JJ doesn't move. He stays on the couch, looking at his feet. "I don't want to go."

I have to stop myself from responding with a 'Good'.

I've never seen JJ go against something Aiden has said, and even now, he's not arguing exactly. It's more like a spontaneous emotional response that is pure JJ. I feel for him. JJ has made his feelings about his new life in Melbourne clear. He loves it here. He's enrolled at uni – same course as Everly. He's made friends there, and others he games with. He would stay here forever given the choice.

Aiden's jaw tightens. "You know what we have to do."

JJ stares at his feet.

"Now, JJ."

My hands come to my hips. "Or you could stay," I say.

Aiden's gaze cuts to mine. "We have an arrangement."

Sure. But that was at the beginning. Before we knew them. It doesn't feel right anymore. They belong in Melbourne. With us. I try to find some logical reasons to back up my feelings. "Jonathan wasn't supposed to be able to find you."

"No."

"But he has. And you don't know how. So what's to say he won't just find you again?"

Beyond the muscles in his jaw still working, Aiden doesn't respond, so I double-down. "Are you just going to keep running forever?"

"What's the alternative, Harlow?" he says brusquely.

"Stay. Deal with Jonathan once and for all."

He hisses through his teeth.

I realise what I've said. For wizards, "dealing with it once and for all" means someone's probably going to die. If not JJ or Aiden, then Jonathan.

But that's not what I meant. "He's your brother; can't you reason with him, or bargain with him or something?"

Is he considering what I'm saying? Impossible to tell.

I glance at JJ. There's hope in his eyes. I've got to try for the kid. "You don't have to go. Owlscroft will protect JJ."

Something flashes over Aiden's face. Surprise? Anger? Some hope of his own? It's impossible to say before it disappears behind the usual stony façade. "I won't put the coven in danger."

"We can take care of ourselves." We don't splash our power around like wizards, but we're strong. Pity the fool who takes us on. "And we can protect JJ. He'll be safe at Owlscroft."

It's a low blow – one Aiden's going to find hard to resist. But it's also true. Owlscroft is our beating heart; no one can find it who shouldn't. There's over 100 years of protective spells in place.

He exhales heavily, hands on his hips. "I'm not sure we would be welcome."

Neither am I, but I don't say it. I'll argue their case. I won't let anyone cast them out. "Let me call Aunt Bernie at least."

JJ turns to Aiden. "Please, Uncle."

Aiden's gaze is heavy on JJ. A muscle ticks in his jaw.

Is he wavering? I know the idea of relying on other people is probably killing him, as is the idea of bringing danger to town. But JJ is happy here, and Aiden cares about his nephew's happiness as well as his safety.

"We'll find a way to deal with Jonathan. We won't let anything happen to Owlscroft. Or JJ." I wait until he meets my gaze. "You've got me now."

He holds my eyes for so long, I'm sure he's going to say no. But then he gives one slow nod. "Make the call."

CHAPTER 5

I make the call.

It's not even five. I wish it were even one hour later so I didn't have to wake Aunt Bernie, who has enough to manage on a daily basis let alone having her nights commandeered, but in the end, I know she'd prefer to know.

We take the lift down to the basement, Aiden scanning the whole way. It's hypervigilant but low-key; nothing like his earlier display. What I witnessed then was a rare instance of him letting loose. Let's just say it's done nothing to tame my growing obsession.

We take Aiden's sleek black Lexus to Owlscroft. I'm pretty sure he doesn't have a driver's licence, but that hasn't stopped him from acquiring and driving a car. Same way not having a passport didn't stop him and JJ from flying to and taking up residence in Melbourne.

Wizards think the rules don't apply to them.

Because they don't.

It's a philosophy I wouldn't mind tapping into, but it's not the way we witches roll. We enrol in school, we take our driver's test, we fill out our taxes. We are very much in the system. Wizards are very much off the grid.

We climb in – JJ in the back seat and me in the front – and drive out of the hotel basement and onto the narrow, empty, one-way city street.

We're quiet on the drive over. I'm edgy, uncertain at what I'm going to find when we get there. Owlscroft's motto, though unspoken, is clear – we exist to protect and serve the people of Melbourne and surrounds. We don't exist to protect or serve stray wizards from Singapore.

But we won't abandon them. I won't allow it.

It hits me with renewed force; a punch to the guts. I don't want Aiden to go.

Not because he can't handle it. After what happened earlier, I know beyond doubt that Aiden is strong enough to deal with any threat. He doesn't need us – me – for that. But Jonathan being his brother … That tortured expression in his eyes. He shouldn't have to be alone in this.

When we arrive, the sky has lightened to pearlescent peach and aquamarine. We leave the car on the street, and head for the ornate wrought-iron front gate. It opens immediately – Aunt Bernie must have given it instructions.

Owlscroft is set back on a rise. We walk up through the irises and the poplars to where Aunt Bernie waits on the verandah, a large tartan shawl draped around her shoulders. "Come in. Quick, it's cold." She smiles at JJ as he passes – Aunt Bernie has a massive sweet spot for him – then closes the door resolutely and moves swiftly to the front, leading us to a little-used drawing room. "Aiden and Elijah, you can wait in here."

Aunt Bernie always calls JJ Elijah.

I peer in as the wizards walk through. There's an ancient couch, the television's already on and there's a pot of tea steeping. They should be comfy.

"Harlow, with me."

I exchange a last glance with Aiden, then follow Aunt Bernie.

"I've managed to rustle up Antoinette and Nicolette. You can bring us up to date in my office."

Mum and Aunt Lettie. Just what I need. "Yeah. Sorry about the time."

"No need to apologise, dear."

Inside, Aunt Lettie is her usual glamorous self – all shiny blonde bob and pearls. Mum looks more frazzled. It doesn't take long to bring them up to speed.

Aunt Lettie is the first to respond. "I understand the wizards have been very helpful, but the terms were always clear. I can't see why they'd expect we'd change them now."

I grit my teeth. Aunt Lettie is generally lovely, and I was hoping she'd be the most sympathetic to the cause. "They're not expecting anything."

"Well," she says with a Gallic shrug. "What's the problem? If they're happy to leave ..."

"I asked them to stay. I told them we'd offer refuge."

"Harlow." Aunt Bernie. Disapproving. I've gone beyond my remit.

"They deserve our help. Aiden's been working with me for six months; I'm not going to just abandon him."

"That's very admirable," Aunt Bernie says, "but we have to consider the danger."

"Jonathan's no danger to us."

There's a pause in response to that.

"I don't think I understand," Mum says. "You're saying this new wizard is dangerous enough that Aiden and JJ had to run from him, but we shouldn't be worried about him now?"

"Aiden can handle him." I don't want to get into it too much. I'm not sure my new insights into the extent of Aiden's power are going to help the cause. "He won't let anything happen to Owlscroft. And neither will I."

Aunt Lettie's head tilts. "I don't want to see Owlscroft involved in a wizard feud."

"It's not a feud. Honestly," I add when I see scepticism on their faces. "Aiden doesn't want to hurt his brother. He just wants to keep JJ safe."

"But if JJ's at Owlscroft, won't that bring danger right to us?" Mum asks.

I shake my head. "There's no way he'll find him here. JJ hasn't touched his amulet; he's not used any magic. And wizards aren't used to dealing with witches. He won't be expecting us to shield JJ, and he won't know how to counter or evade our spells." I have real doubts I'm convincing them but I persevere. "Jonathan doesn't give a shit about us. We're irrelevant to him. He has no reason to want to hurt any of us. He doesn't even necessarily want to hurt JJ. He just wants the amulet. All I'm asking for is a day or two for Aiden and I to deal with him."

"And how do you propose to do that?" Aunt Bernie, pragmatic as always.

I wish I had a plan I could lay out. "I don't know yet. This only happened an hour ago. But we'll work something out."

"I don't know, Harlow," says Aunt Lettie slowly. Which means she doesn't like the idea but she's leaving it to Aunt Bernie to be bad cop.

Mum's been unusually quiet this whole time. The expression on her face is ... questioning. I thought she'd be the hard no, but for some reason, she's not. "Look. I'm an Owlscroft witch. I wouldn't suggest this if I thought it would bring harm to the coven. But one thing I've always thought was true about Owlscroft, one thing I've always been proud of – we don't turn our back on our friends."

There's a long moment, then the strangest thing happens; Mum nods. "What about your demon hunting? Especially this close to Halloween."

"We'll work around it."

"Well, if you're sure there's no danger ..." Aunt Lettie shrugs again, hands near her ears. "I've said my piece. Your call, Bernadette."

Aunt Bernie takes a moment then meets my gaze. "You have three days. JJ must promise to stay within the Owlscroft grounds. If it's not resolved within that timeframe, we may have to revise our decision. You'll keep a close eye on the situation and report back frequently."

Relief floods me, loosening all my muscles. "Thank you. I'll go tell them."

In the sitting room, JJ is curled up on the couch, watching breakfast television and eating a bowl of porridge with milk and honey he's conned someone into making him.

Aiden is next to him, tense. When I nod at him, his head goes down.

I tell JJ he has to stay here, which he seems happy about. He can't hide out at Owlscroft forever, but it's a good temporary solution.

Aiden and I walk back to the car in silence. My arms are crossed against the cold. I'm still in a tee, the day hasn't warmed yet and the wind is slicing at my bare skin. It's also a good couple of hours past my regular bed time. We probably have a lot to discuss, but I'm not up for it right now. Aiden must feel the same.

We pass back through the gate. Aiden clicks the car open and I head to the passenger side. I go to open the door and slide in. It's been a big night and I'm tired and I'm not paying attention. I don't realise he's behind me until he's right there. I turn, confused, and find myself wrapped in him.

I'm instantly on fire, flames licking through me. His arms are tight around me. His heart is drumming fast and strong. Or maybe that's mine.

It takes me a moment to absorb what's happening. Then I soak it in. Soak him in. I rest my hands on his ribs, press my face against his neck. Smell fir with a whisp of smoke and man.

"Thank you," he says.

His mouth is near my ear; the warmth of his breath sends a jolt through me.

And then I'm released. Aiden walks around the car, opens his door and slides in. Meanwhile, I'm left facing the opposite end of the street. Unable to move.

I breathe in heavily, then release it.

What the hell was that?

Apart from the best hug of my life.

It's not like I don't have a certain degree of physicality with Aiden. We train together at the gym and spar at the dojo. I've always been aware of him. That was different.

My hand remembers how to work. I find the door handle, and slide into my seat.

Eyes forward, Aiden starts the engine and glides off.

Okay then. Maybe it wasn't a big deal. Just a rare show of emotion from a man whose nephew's been threatened. And I happen to be the one who delivered JJ to safety.

Maybe that's all that was.

On his side, at least. My whole body is still electric.

And if that's all it was, I get it.

There are many reasons why nothing's happened between us. I'm supposed to be keeping an eye on him for the coven – they're relying on me to know if there's something more at play, and I can't lose objectivity. I didn't trust him for a long time; I'm not sure I completely do even now. Not helped by the fact that I sense there's a lot he hides. And I get that he probably has his reasons, but it doesn't make trust easier.

And of course, if something did go wrong – which it always does, courtesy of yours truly – we'd still have to front up and work together every night. Which doesn't sound like fun, and worse, might compromise my ability to do my job.

He's a wizard, I'm a witch. His life is protecting his nephew; mine is protecting my coven, my city. Never the twain, right?

"So—" I stop to clear my throat, then try again. "Obvious question ..." One I've asked before but never got a good answer to. "Can't you just give Jonathan the amulet?"

It takes death to break the bond between wizard and amulet, but thankfully, JJ hasn't reached maturity yet – that won't happen until he turns 20 next year – and he wasn't able to bond with his amulet properly before Aiden whisked it away.

He gives me a fast but lethal sideways glance. "No."

"Why? I get that it's precious, but you could make this situation go away."

"It belongs to JJ."

I shrug, frustrated. Wouldn't they rather save themselves a whole heap of grief?

I'm not looking at him, but I sense Aiden taking in my dissatisfaction. He turns his head, looks out his window, then focuses on the road again. "JJ will be a powerful wizard. Others will be gunning for him; his life will be one of constant danger. The amulet makes him a target, but it also provides the means for him to protect himself. It's not something to be given up lightly."

I take a moment or two to process that. "Talk about a double-edged sword."

Aiden grunts in agreement. "I wouldn't have chosen this for him. I wish he hadn't found that amulet. But he did. It's his, and the burden of what to do with it is also his."

I cast a quick glance in his direction. This conversation has got pretty deep pretty quickly.

"I have sought to protect him – not just from others, but from himself. He's still young, he's not ready. I'm not either. I don't want to lose him."

Aiden is striving for control, but the edges of his voice are rough with emotion, and I can see it in his eyes when he glances in my direction.

"But he'll reach maturity soon, and I'll have to step back and allow him to make his own choices. Like I've made mine and other wizards have made theirs. I would like nothing more than to remove the amulet from JJ's life, but what he does with it is the most fundamental choice he'll ever have to make. It is not my place to take that from him."

It's the most Aiden's ever said in one go, and more than I was expecting in response to my seemingly simple question. I don't know what to say. But I feel the weight, the impact, of everything he just said; I want to give him something. "JJ's a doofus, but he's got a good heart. And he's got you."

He couldn't ask for a better role model than Aiden.

I don't prod further.

When we reach the apartment carpark, we agree to get some sleep then regroup to formulate a plan.

Back in my apartment, I shower, dress in a sleep tee and shorts and collapse into bed. I think I'll have trouble falling asleep, given the drama of the night, but I don't.

It's probably all in my mind, some kind of subconscious response to JJ saying that he knew he'd be safe outside my apartment, but I swear, when I close my eyes, I feel Aiden all around me.

CHAPTER 6

 wake refreshed and ready.

I shower, dress and head to Aiden's, tapping lightly on the door in case he's still asleep. I'm hoping for sleep-mussed and shirtless, but when he answers the door, he's not only clear-eyed but dressed. Damn.

He leads me in. Given his back is to me, I allow my gaze to roam all over him. From the dark hair, over the broad shoulders and back with its impressive well-cut musculature down to thong-covered feet. He's wearing another sleek-fitting black tank and all I can think is lucky tank.

I'm trying to shelve it. I really am.

I resolve to look around the apartment instead. I'm always a little in awe of what they've managed to do with the place. Admittedly, it's less of a dogbox than mine – three bedrooms compared to my one, and no, I don't know how they cover the rent – but it's more than that. It's, like, decorated. Sleek light-wood furniture, plentiful greenery, stoneware in neutral tones. Nice.

I take a seat on the couch.

Aiden sits on the one opposite. His hands come to a loose clasp in front, which has the effect of pumping his biceps.

Those muscles though.

"I've found a way forward," he says.

I manage to stop gawking at his arms and raise my brows.

"I've taken a vow. When Jonathan learns about it, he'll desist."

Every time I get to thinking I understand something about wizards, I realise I never will. "Do you want to explain how that works?"

"It's a special vow. One wizards use to bind themselves to a certain course of action. It involves handing over autonomy to your amulet, making any threat not only credible but inevitable."

I barely suppress a shudder. Hardcore. "What vow did you make?"

"To protect JJ."

"You already do that."

"By choice. Now I have no choice."

So, if it goes that far, if Jonathan doesn't choose to 'desist' … he could be choosing death? Another shudder passes through me. After what I experienced of his power last night, I'm assuming Aiden is the stronger of the two, but it occurs to me that I better check. "And you're confident that, if it comes to it … you'll be the one still standing?"

"Yes."

This is good news, but Aiden doesn't look happy. It doesn't take a genius to guess why. "It won't come to that," I add.

He nods.

"If it does … I mean, Jonathan attacked JJ in Singapore, and now's he followed you to Melbourne. If he doesn't make the right choice, he's leaving you with no choice. You shouldn't feel bad."

Aiden gives me a long look. "He's still my brother," he says quietly.

I try to imagine how I would feel if I had to take out Avery or Amelia to protect Everly. The horror of it forms a sick ball in my stomach. Unspeakable. I shift the conversation. "So, what's the plan?"

"If I remove the protection spell from the amulet, Jonathan will sense it and come to us. I'll tell him I've made the vow and ask him to make one of his own – to leave JJ and his amulet alone."

Something clinks softly in the breeze. I glance out to the small plant-covered balcony. They've even got windchimes. I look back at Aiden. "Great."

"There's one problem. I can't touch the amulet."

Right. And it can't be JJ – Aiden doesn't want him touching it. Realisation dawns slowly. I feel my eyes widen. "Me?"

"I hate to ask—"

"Are you kidding? How many times have I begged to try yours?"

He frowns. "You'll only wear it; not use it."

"Sure," I agree readily. But it does nothing to dampen my excitement.

"You're not bonded to the amulet, and you're a witch, not a wizard. Jonathan has no reason to attack you. And I'll be right there. I won't let anything happen to you."

"*I* won't let anything happen to me." I'm not worried. I just want it on me.

Aiden's frown deepens. He's not entirely comfortable with the plan or my level of enthusiasm. "Relax," I say. "I get it. I'll be wearing it; nothing more."

"We'll go get JJ's in a minute, but first … Have you ever heard of a witch wearing an amulet?"

I shake my head.

"Me neither. So before we try with JJ's …" He shifts to my side with his typical grace and draws his amulet over his head. "We should make sure there's no strange interactions."

"What, like growing a layer of iridescent scales? Or maybe my head will swell to the size of a hot air balloon and explode pink goo all over the place."

He gives me his patience-of-a-saint stare. I know he's right. And if something's going to go wrong, I'd prefer to know before we're mission critical.

He leans towards me, holding his amulet high. I lean in too. We're close. Blood rushes to my head, which may be due to Aiden's proximity, the prospect of his amulet around my neck, or both. My gaze drops to his mouth. Just a little further and my lips would touch his.

"Harlow." It comes out a little husky.

I meet his gaze, then duck my head. Aiden leans over, deposits the amulet around my neck, then sits back.

It nestles just below my collar bone, still warm from his body. Solid and hefty, I can feel its radiance spreading through my body.

It's a different sensation to witch magic.

We never have access to power like this. We never hold magic, never possess it in a source close to our hearts. We just use it. Pull it down from whatever batch is circulating at the time and weave it around the words of a spell. It's never ours.

But this magic is seated, trapped, in the amulet. Subjugated totally to the wizard's will, waiting to be unleashed on the world.

I want to unleash it.

If only I knew how. If only I hadn't promised not to go rogue.

But it's sort of mine for the moment. I place one hand under the amulet and another over it, cupping it, pressing its warm weight between my palms. Aiden shifts and I glance up at him. He's watching me, my hands, with a burning intensity.

It's clearly no easy thing for him to see his amulet on me. He's trusting me, big time. The knowledge sends a sudden rush of warmth through me. "Okay?"

"Just."

He's leaning against an arm of the couch. His eyes are heavy; there is colour along his cheekbones. "You look different," I say, squeezing, testing its hardness, the impression it makes on my skin.

"You're fondling my amulet."

Oh. I look down. It's an extension of him. I'm touching … him. An intimate part. No wonder I like it so much. I consider releasing it but he didn't ask me to so I don't. I rub a thumb over the jade. Aiden's breath hitches. I smile. "I think it likes me."

When I look up, the corners of his mouth are tipped up. Just a little.

I'm no artist, but the deep emerald colour with its light marbling is gorgeous. "Are all amulets this nice?"

"I'm fond of mine, but it's nothing spectacular."

I'm not sure I believe him. Not when I know how he conceals his power. "No one's ever come for it? Tried to take it from you?"

He shrugs. "Risk versus reward. It's not worth it, especially when there's not a high chance of success."

"And for JJ, the pendulum is weighted in the other direction."

"For the moment."

I slide my gaze to him, ask a question that's been on my mind since I was almost floored yesterday. "How strong are you exactly?"

He exhales sharply. "That's not a question I can answer."

"A wise wizard never shows the true extent of his power?"

"Something like that."

And that's as much as I'm getting.

"Aren't you going to ask how strong I am?" I can't resist adding, even though it's not a concept that really works for witches. Covens are strong; witches are 'useful' or 'talented'.

"I don't need to."

It takes me a moment to decide what that means and if I like it, but then a grin slowly spreads across my face. "I could do more with one of these." How much more effective could we be if we had access to magic like this? How much could we achieve? "Those DFs wouldn't stand a chance."

"It's not that simple," he says. "Especially with demons."

"I know you're all 'power corrupts', but what's the point of it if you don't use it?"

He doesn't answer. His gaze is fixed on his amulet, resting against my collar bones. "In any case, Bernadette wouldn't allow it."

"Probably not." Aunt Bernie runs a tight ship. I shrug. "Doesn't stop me being curious. I want to know how it works, what it feels like." Even locked down, Aiden's amulet hums against my chest. "Can I try yours out?"

His eyes flash. "No."

Gee. Touchy. "No, seriously. We need to run a few experiments. What if wearing an amulet interferes with my magic?"

"It shouldn't, and you won't need to use any while you're wearing it."

"I might. We don't know what's going to happen today and I have to be able to defend myself."

He doesn't respond. I think I'm wearing him down. "Come on, Aiden. This may be my only chance."

Again, no response.

"I taught you how to do it witch-style."

Something that might be a blush flushes high across his cheekbones.

He shakes his head, but it's more resignation than no. "One spell. A basic one. Witch magic only first, then you can try to add in the amulet."

Triumph pings in my gut. I resist the urge to fist-pump. It's limited, but it's something. "I'll do a colour change."

He nods.

I reach for a batch of squirming magic and bind it to the words as I cant.

Black to green
Black to green
Change Aiden's tank
From black to green

Aiden's tank morphs to deep forest. I look him up and down, lingering on all the many good bits. When I reach his gaze, it's a mix of heat and stop that.

"What? You look good in green. How do I activate this thing?"

He hesitates. He's making it into a big deal, assuming this is some huge responsibility; that he's opening some door that can never be closed, that I'm never going to be the same again. "It's a colour change spell, for Chalice sake," I snap.

He sighs. "I'm going to unlock it so you can use it now."

Whatever he does has that initial subtle hum singing. It's vibrating through me.

"You can feel it?"

Can I ever. I nod.

"Close your eyes. Focus on that feeling."

I close my eyes.

"Draw from the amulet, into you. Bring it into you. Your body, your whole being."

I've been waiting for this for a long time; I don't hesitate. I lean into it, connect with it, draw it into me. It's like bottled rays of sunshine, and I drink until I'm drunk. Power rushes through my veins, from my core to the tips of my being. Making me feel alive. Strong. Unstoppable.

"When you're ready, change my top back."

"How?"

"Just do it."

There is no need to wrangle this magic – no grabbing, wrestling, forcing. There's no outside carrier, like a spell. It's just me. My will. My absolute belief that when I open my eyes, that tank will be black.

I open my eyes; Aiden's top is black.

He locks the amulet down again immediately. The roar is back to a hum. It's a loss I'm not prepared for and I hate the sudden break. One hit is all it took. Already, I'm addicted.

"Happy?" he asks.

I am more than happy; I've experienced a total revelation. I don't think it'd be wise to admit that. "So my head didn't explode."

He holds out his hand.

Am I reluctant to give it back? You bet.

I get it. Or I'm starting to. Why wizards are willing to live and die for this.

I draw the amulet over my head and pass it over. And then I make a vow of my own. This won't be my last time using wizard magic.

CHAPTER 7

JJ's amulet is stored in a vault housed in an imposing gothic sandstone bank. The inside has been restored to its full Victorian glory – high-shine mahogany, light-pink plaster and ornately carved stone. It smells like dust, incense and old coins.

We are greeted by an officious concierge in black. Aiden produces ID and tells him we're here to access a safe deposit box; the guy points to a counter at the back. We head for it. Aiden flashes his ID again, there's some kind of security check process, and then we're led through a side door, down a set of sweeping stairs to the vaults below.

The main room holds a long wooden table and chairs. The space is dark and dank, with the subterranean chill and gloomy portraits adding to the spooky factor. The officer goes straight to one of the doors lining the walls. Inside, there's rows and rows and rows of slots. She unlocks a slot and then enters a key into the box. Aiden uses his own key and draws out his storage unit. She asks if fifteen minutes will suffice, then leaves us to it.

Aiden takes the unit to the table and then backs away. Back against the wall, tension is a live thing in his body. "You'll have to unwrap it."

"That bad, hey?" Because he is clearly a little on edge. I move closer and peer in at the unit's sole occupant – an ordinary-looking bundle of black cloth.

"An amulet like that? Yes."

Not just for wizards; even I'm feeling the tug. "I mean, Jonathan attacked JJ for it, so I figure it must be pretty powerful. Should I just take it out?"

"He shouldn't have shown it to him. And yes, but carefully."

I draw the black bundle out of the box, placing it on the table. "Jonathan's his uncle. JJ must have thought he could trust him."

Out of the corner of my eye, I see Aiden shake his head. "He should've known better," he says.

"Harsh."

"Wizards are not to be trusted. Not when there's that much power at stake."

"He can trust you." I flick a sideways glance at him. He's still tense. Too tense. "You could take this amulet anytime you wanted, but you haven't."

His dark gaze is piercing on mine. "Unwrap it," he says quietly.

I feel a little nervy as I peel away the cloth, but it's probably just Aiden's edginess reaching me. When I'm done, I almost laugh. It's small. It's old. The gold is tarnished and the orange-red stone embedded in the front – carnelian pops into my mind – is chipped. So this is the big deal amulet. The stuff of myth and legend; lost in the veils of time. "It doesn't look like much."

"Looks can be deceiving. Go slow." His arms are across his chest, one ankle crossed. Not taking any chances with himself. What does he think he'll do if he drops his guard? Lunge for it, knifing me on the way past? I know Aiden; I can't see it.

I study the amulet some more. "How'd JJ find it, anyway?"

"Magic."

Well, der. "I thought he wasn't old enough."

"He's not, but he managed to get his hands on a starter amulet – nothing powerful but enough for JJ – and he started to experiment. I ... wasn't aware. I noticed some magical surges and abnormal patterns of activity, but that's not unusual in a wizard approaching maturity."

"Where'd he find the starter amulet?" I keep my eyes down and my tone offhand, but I'm more than a little invested in his answer.

"He traded some of his father's artefacts."

I want to ask more about this magical market where you can barter your way to an amulet, but it's the first time JJ's father's been mentioned, and I don't want to move on like it's nothing. "Your other brother?"

"Yes."

I meet Aiden's eyes briefly, then return my gaze to the table. "Was he killed for his amulet?"

There's a heavy pause. "Yes."

"And that's when you stepped in to take care of JJ." I don't have to look at him to sense his nod. "And Jonathan? Did he help?"

"Jonathan was too busy with thoughts of revenge. All he wants is to avenge Wen Sen."

"Wen Sen?" JJ's father. And Aiden's Chinese name is Wen Yew and Jonathon's is Wen Long. I should have guessed Jonathon was Aiden's brother. I tilt my head as another thought occurs to me. "Is that why Jonathon wants JJ's amulet so bad? For revenge?"

"He's allowed his lust for revenge to consume him. He uses it to justify his thirst for power. A thirst so bad his own nephew is in danger from him."

If someone hurt Everly, I'd want revenge too. I hover a hand over the amulet.

"Go slow," Aiden cautions.

I close my palm over it. Aiden's got this amulet locked down pretty tight, but it leaps to meet my touch. It's trapped but it's still a huge presence. I know people think I'm foolhardy. It's true that I'm not a typical witch, but I have a strong survival instinct. I like facing danger, but I like surviving it too. And right now, that strong survival instinct is telling me to proceed slowly. For the moment, I just keep my hand where it is. I'm going to have the amulet around my neck soon; we might as well get used to each other. "What about JJ's mum?"

Another pause. "Collateral damage. I told Wen Sen he should swap out his amulet for something less desirable or find other lodgings."

Wizards have a bad reputation as man-whores. They impregnate then disappear, leaving behind their potentially magic male offspring. I hadn't considered that there might be a reason for this.

I replace one hand with the other and keep my eyes glued to the table. "Is that why you don't have a girlfriend?"

Yes, I'm shamelessly fishing. He's never mentioned anyone, and I'm assuming there's no yearning, abandoned woman back in Singapore, but I want to know for sure.

"Wizards shouldn't get involved. It's too risky."

I take that as confirmation, which I like. But it's dodgy logic, and a blanket restriction, and that I don't like. "Some people can take care of themselves."

He lets out a slow breath.

I look over my shoulder at him. His gaze shifts from my hands to meet my eyes. "No, I'm serious. Where would you ever find such a w —" I was about to say witch. "Woman?" I finish with instead.

I'm not sure why I'm pushing. It's not like I'm looking for a relationship, or anything even approximating. I'm totally up for some rough and tumble with Aiden, but I'm not built for something serious. I know that, but still, I don't like the fact that he's not even considering it.

"You think you could hold your own against a wizard?"

He's got a point. Not because witches aren't strong, but because so much of what we do is aimed at helping others. We don't go around attacking anyone; in turn, we're not often under attack. We don't have many spells for those kinds of situations, and we don't practice for them.

But I know I've got it in me. "If I had an amulet. If you taught me how to use it."

Enough with the caution. I pick JJ's amulet up and draw it over my neck.

I'm not prepared. It's Siberian steppes cold. A painful icy sensation seeps into my skin, burrowing down to the bones. And it's heavy. Unfathomably so. How can such a small item of metal and stone make me feel as weighed down as Atlas?

This is nothing like Aiden's. Aiden's was warm. Sure, it'd come straight from him and was full of his body heat – but it was warm *to me*. I suppose it's been around Aiden's neck the whole time I've known him; it must know me a bit by now.

This amulet though ... It's not happy I've put it on. It's still judging me. I'm not sure what it will do if I'm found unsuitable.

"Relax."

I look up. Aiden's gaze is locked on the amulet, his hands are in fists at his side. I can't help it; I laugh. "Are you talking to me or yourself?"

He doesn't want to see the funny side. "You. You can relax. It's locked down."

I know that. I'm not sure I'd still be breathing if it wasn't. "You really can't touch it?"

"No."

"What about when JJ starts to wear it? And use it. How's it going to be for you then?"

His arms cross his chest. "I'll manage while I train him. After that, he'll probably want to go out on his own."

I'm not convinced; JJ's pretty comfortably ensconced with Aiden and Owlscroft. But that's not even the point. The point is that Aiden needs to trust himself more. He can't live thinking he's like other wizards. He's not. Just like I'm not like other witches.

I take a few steps towards him.

"What are you doing?" His tone isn't panicked exactly, but it's close.

"Relax, it's locked down," I parrot back to him. He doesn't smile back. "In a few minutes, we're walking out of here together with the amulet around my neck. We're going to face Jonathan together. We need to know how close we can get."

I step closer. He shifts against the wall. "Don't push your luck."

I take another step. "I think you can handle it."

And another.

"Harlow."

It's a firmer warning but I don't stop advancing. Slowly; I'm bold, not stupid. "You've got all this power, Aiden, but what's the point if you run from it?" He has to know he can trust himself. I know he can. "You've made your decision and you've already proven you can stick to it. You don't want this amulet."

A final step takes me way inside his personal space bubble. His hand whips out, grips my waist.

I am close enough now to pick out the details, even in this gloomy space. His breath is coming fast, his colour is high. This started out being about the amulet; it's not anymore. He's aware of me in exactly the way I want and I'm buzzing with it, with our closeness.

"See?" I smile. "Nothing to worry about."

His hand squeezes, and I press forward a little more. Moving further into his space until I am standing between his legs and my chest is almost touching his. With him leaning against the wall, there's not much difference in our heights. Our eyes are practically level.

Despite the warnings, he hasn't attempted to distance himself. Good enough as an invitation as far as I'm concerned. Lungs tight, I inch closer and closer, until we're almost touching lips. Then I stop. His move.

Aiden looks down at my mouth, then back up. His grip changes, and he pulls me forward, hard and fast, so I collide against him. My pulse goes into overdrive; my breathing stutters. I smile.

Still holding my waist, his other hand rises slowly to cup my nape, sending a wave of sensation over my skin. I lean back into his grasp, a breath shuddering out. He's watching me in a way that makes me clench, ache and throb. The tips of his mouth kick up, just a little, and mine do the same.

Then his mouth descends on mine, meets it in the most firm, tantalising way I can imagine; bolts of delicious energy jolt through me.

I love everything about this kiss. The firmness of his lips, the way his hand cups my neck, the way he smells.

My arms snake up and around his neck. I run my hands through the dark silk of his hair, then run my nails against his scalp.

He makes a noise. A noise I like very, very much.

I press even closer, loving the feel of his solid body against mine. He seeks entry and I open. Our tongues touch, slide against each other and my stomach turns upside down.

There's a loud clatter and a heavy huffing down the stairs. That's our fifteen minutes. I pull back, Aiden releases me. But something of the energy lingers in the space between us. Aiden's breath is as heavy and uneven as mine; he's still against the wall, but there's a strain in his body like he has to check himself.

I bite my lower lip, trying to hold back my grin. It doesn't work. "Told you you could."

The bank officer hesitates awkwardly at the door like she knows what she interrupted. "That's time," she says apologetically. "Are you done?"

"Yes. Thank you," Mr Impeccable Manners says, recovering quickly.

We finish up and tumble out onto the street.

I sneak a sideways glance. When Aiden catches me, I grin. There's an answering warmth in his eyes. He almost smiles back.

And I almost take his hand. *Me*; taking someone's hand.

We need to shelve it. We've got somewhere to be and something to do.

I try to push my elation down, but it doesn't work. I've never felt this way before. So much so that it takes me a while to be able to pinpoint exactly what it is I'm feeling. When I do, I'm nothing short of amazed.

I'm giddy.

Giddy.

It's as strange to me as the amulet around my neck.

CHAPTER 8

We head to a set of sports ovals close to the river in Burnley. In an hour, the afterschool sports brigade will arrive, but for now, the fields are almost empty. Just a man in his fifties walking a tiny dog and a young mum reading something on her phone while her toddler joyously rides a trike a few paces ahead.

Seclusion was a key consideration in choosing a location for the showdown. This more than anything tells me that while Aiden is hoping his vow works, he's not one-hundred percent confident. He doesn't want witnesses to a wizard duel.

We set ourselves up in the stands, which gives us a good view over the fields and largely protects us from sight. It's weird being out like this in the daytime. Not that I'm entirely nocturnal. I get up sometime after midday and do regular-person things. Shopping, cooking, cleaning. Lots of time at the gym. But I'm not usually out in the sun. It's a somewhat uncomfortable reminder of the life that continues while I'm out to the world. As someone who moves through the night, I am missing out on the day.

Aiden removes the protection spell on JJ's amulet, and the persistent hum I've started to become used to spikes. It's restless, striving, struggling. Trying to get out. After being buried in a cave in Mongolia for a couple of millennia, I suppose that's reasonable.

We wait. The air smells of sunshine and the warm, dry spice of eucalypts. A gentle breeze sends leaves rustling. A family of magpies add their own warbles. In the distance, a tram is hustling along Swan Street. It's chill. Bizarrely so.

"Tell me about losing your demon-hunter role."

Now? We're doing this now? Jonathan might turn up at any second.

Or maybe I just don't want to talk about it.

But I was the one who brought it up last night. And it might have implications for Aiden too. Will he continue demon hunting while I'm teaching kindergarten?

Claire and Lucinda are surely hoping so.

"The job's supposed to last five years max for any one witch. I've been doing it for seven." And a large chunk of that has been as a sole operator.

He doesn't say anything. He knows I've left a lot out, and he's waiting. He's a good listener. Thoughtful and mostly silent.

"They're trying to sell it to me as a chance to study physio."

Aiden's brows go halfway up his forehead. "Do you want to study physio?"

I shoot him a get-serious look. Me; helping some old bird improve her balance? "They're trying to be … supportive. But, apparently, everything about the way I live is wrong and needs to change. They don't understand that I like my life the way it is. They don't understand who I am or what I want. They never have." I pause to draw breath. I am not usually a big talker, but Aiden brings it out in me.

"And when you say 'they', you mean …?"

"Mum, I suppose. She's never been happy with what I do or my decisions." She did support me earlier though. She was the one who listened when I said the wizards should stay. Confused, I change the subject. "Besides, I'm fine. I'm not going mental." I give him a loaded look. "I'll be relying on you to attest to that."

"When would I do that?"

"When I appeal the decision."

"Is it up for negotiation?"

"No, but I'm going to fight it anyway."

Besides, they have to find replacements, and I have faith Claire and Lucinda won't have the staying power required. They're young, they're fun-loving. Night after night of demon hunting? Who'd choose that?

Apart from me, of course.

Aiden takes a moment to walk to the edge of the row so he can look behind and around and make sure we're still clear. I check the other side. We regroup in the middle.

"Why five years?" he asks.

I cross my arms. "It's bullshit."

"Okay, but what's the rationale?"

"Dealing with demons on a nightly basis for years on end sends some witches cuckoo," I acknowledge reluctantly. "It's happened in the past. They become secretive. Start to show a certain reluctance to evict. A susceptibility to demon inhabitation."

Aiden exhales heavily. I'm not sure what it means, and I don't ask.

"It doesn't happen to everyone, and it's usually after ten years. Or longer. Five years is not that bad."

"You just said you've done over seven."

"I'm fine." But I can hear that my voice is strident. I take it down a notch. "It's not going to happen to me."

Aiden conducts another rapid surveillance of the fields, then looks back at me. "What about what happened with that Green?"

Betrayal. That's what this feels like. I did not tell Aiden that story to see it weaponised against me. But I think back to last night, how he stepped in to take the Green. He's obviously picked up on my sensitivity.

Some demons are cannier than others. Greens definitely fall into that category. It's like they know that I'm there to evict them before I even start. It's harder to get them alone and they're unpredictable when I do. They're master manipulators who get off on self-doubt, confusion and misery. Sometimes, I can feel myself succumbing to their manipulation. To their wide-eyed pleas – they just want to help the person they've inhabited! – and their subtle digs at me – who am I to evict them?

Earlier this year, I had no choice but to try to evict a Green in a full restaurant. Out of nowhere, she had a knife in her hand and up to her own throat.

"Disappear or she dies," she said.

I can't tell you how close that was. The Green would be evicting itself by killing the host, but I felt the intent to slice her throat so clearly. I'm not often scared, but I was then; scared that that woman would lose her life because of me. I almost broke, almost left the Green to play out its dramas over the coming weeks. I'd hung on by the skin of my teeth, sensing how close eviction was, praying it would take effect before any damage was done.

But yeah. Not an experience I'm keen to repeat.

I told Aiden that story so that he would know what to look out for with Greens, not so he'd throw it back in my face.

Besides, that's not an example of me losing the plot. Is it?

"Not the same thing," I say decisively.

Aiden doesn't look convinced but he drops it. "So, if you're not successful in fighting the decision, what will you do?"

That's the problem. I don't know. I don't want to leave my coven, but I can't see any future there. "The only thing I can do is hunt demons."

"That's not true," he says immediately. There's heat in his eyes; earnestness.

But I shake my head. I know myself. I know my limitations. I suck at following the rules. I don't play nice with others and I never fit in anywhere. I can't, or won't, compromise. Even when I was little, I was like this. I caused havoc at my first school. My desperate mother, knowing I'd have to one day cope with being part of the coven, sent me to a super-strict all-girls' school, hoping I'd get a clue on 'how to behave'. I didn't. I ended up expelled.

Being a demon hunter is the only way I've survived. I know the other roles within the coven, and none of them are going to work for me. It's not that I don't want to so much as I can't. I can't be like the other witches. And I don't really care about that, except it leaves me out of options.

I change the subject. "What would you do if you had to get a day job?"

"I had one. In Singapore."

I raise my brows. I only asked to change the subject but now I'm intrigued. "What?"

"I was a curator. At a museum specialising in ancient cultures of Southeast Asia. My team focused on war and martial strategy."

I grin. That might be the coolest day job ever. I wonder if he misses it. He probably can't wait to get back to his old life. "Are you going to stay when Jonathan's no longer a threat?"

He turns his head slowly, meeting my gaze, and there's something in his eyes that turns my stomach upside-down. "Do you want me to?"

My heart thumps. Twice.

I don't answer. I can't, even though I know what I want. I want him to stay. I almost have a coronary when I think about him going. But the word won't come out. My 'yes' is locked in a box buried under a pile of baggage.

I destroy relationships the second they start. Okay; not the second they start. I get a few good weeks in first. But then guys start making demands, setting expectations, assuming I'm going to go along with their plans, their prerogatives. I can't – I have a job to do. And even if I could, most of the time I wouldn't. Not if it wasn't something I didn't want to do. When they get that I'm not changing my life for them, the arguments start, like some kind of pissing contest I never signed up for. Maybe it's partly my fault – the kind of guys I go for – but I'm not interested in pushovers.

I don't want any of that to happen with Aiden.

He's still waiting for me to say something, but my words stick in my throat. I turn, scanning the fields to buy some time.

Then draw in a sharp breath and grab at his arm.

There's a man approaching. No dog, no toddler in tow. He's not moving like he's out for a casual stroll. There's a certain deliberate awareness to him.

I glance quickly at Aiden, who nods.

I release his arm and watch the guy pass through the gap in the low fence ringing the field. He stops, looks around. He hasn't spotted us yet, but he knows we're nearby. He starts towards us again.

Spiders skitter down my spine.

I clock his intimidating swagger. His focus. The menace I can feel from here.

I watch people all night long. I watch them before and I watch them after they've passed the fountain. And even though my conscious brain can't pick what the difference is, there is one, and my subconscious is well-acquainted with it.

The amulet has had most of its protection removed to get Jonathan here. I'm not supposed to use magic with it around my neck, but I need to work fast. I reach up for a batch and mutter the spell.

There's no way he can hear me, he's still too far away, but he must sense my witch magic because he stops, turns in a circle, trying to locate us.

Then he flares – a bright, saturated Red.

He narrows in on the stands. He's got a rough location.

Aiden pulls me down just as Jonathan's head swivels towards us. He slams protection back around the amulet, and around the two of us, constructing a tough invisible shell.

We are crouched close, all adrenaline-flooded limbs and raspy breaths.

For the moment we are safe, but we don't have long.

"What now?" Aiden murmurs.

Even this close, I can barely hear him over the deafening thump of my heart.

I have never encountered a Red before, but the advice is clear. Run.

CHAPTER 9

Jonathan's heading for us from the front. We slink down the back and jog to tree cover, praying the stands block us from view, before continuing to edge away. I look back constantly, but I can't see him. When we hit a path that takes us down to the river, we break into a full run, heading for the bridge to Hawthorn.

We haven't discussed it, but we're on our way to Owlscroft. It's the safest place to be right now.

If we make it.

I can't stop looking behind me. I'm so unnerved I almost expect Jonathan to drop from the skies above – sword raised as he descends, ninja-style. I ask Aiden over and over if he's following us. Aiden shakes his head but he doesn't slow his pace.

I can feel the cover of his protection, a weighty cloak of safety. Still, I am more scared than I've ever been. The kind of scared I didn't know I was capable of. The kind that makes my bones feel ancient and cold, that makes my tummy feel like it's full of ice, that freezes all thought.

I feel hideously exposed on the bridge. There is nothing above us and deep water below. Aiden's reinstated the protection spell, so

Jonathan shouldn't be able to track us, but he's had a fresh taste of the amulet, and he's inhabited by a Red. I have to wonder if the shields will hold.

We run and run, now through the plane tree–lined streets of Hawthorn. My heart is pounding, my lungs heave and my muscles ache, but I do not let up. Neither does Aiden.

When we finally reach the gate, it forces us to take a moment. Hands on hips, we walk in small circles, panting furiously.

Our breathing finally eases enough to talk.

"How bad is this?"

I grimace. "Bad."

"The usual evict spell doesn't work?"

"Nope." I don't remember everything I was taught about Reds, but I remember that much.

Reds are so rare that the known examples pretty much fit on one hand. They're close to impossible to evict but I'm going to have to come up with something, because this is not only a Red but a Red inhabiting a wizard.

Put it this way, it's not looking good for the fate of the world right now.

I look through the gate, up to Owlscroft. "I need to do some research." One thing is clear. This is not just an internal wizard matter anymore. It's demons, which makes it my problem. "And we have to tell Aunt Bernie."

The gate is sick of our procrastinating. The cranky old thing swings opens; taking the hint, we walk through. It's mid-afternoon. The day has turned quiet and still. Like it's holding its breath, waiting. Bracing for what comes next.

I sneak sideways glances at Aiden. His brother is inhabited by a Red. Who is after JJ and his amulet. It's horror story after horror story; I can't imagine how he feels. I try to focus on the practicalities. "This has to have something to do with how Jonathon found you, but I can't see the link."

Aiden's gaze travels between my eyes. "No," he says.

"But there is a weird link between wizard magic and demons."

Wizard magic and demons 'like' each other. If a wizard directs any magic at a demon, the demon 'feeds' on it and grows. Some wizards – bad ones, according to Aiden – ask to be inhabited, forming some kind of wizard–demon team.

"Yes."

"He still wants the amulet."

"I think that's a safe assumption."

I don't even want to think about what a Red could do with a powerful amulet in its death-and-destruction toolkit.

Aunt Bernie walks through the front door. I don't know what the gate has told her, but even from here, I can see her face is grave.

I bite my lip and trudge up the steps to the verandah, dreading having to tell Aunt Bernie what's happened. Before I can, her hands are on my cheeks and she is looking deep into my eyes. She releases my face, then draws me in for a quick hug. "Thank Chalice you're alright."

It's so uncharacteristic, I'm speechless for a moment before I recover and briefly explain the situation.

When I finish, Aiden steps forward. "Bernadette, I am profoundly sorry. If we hadn't come to Melbourne, Jonathan wouldn't have either."

Aunt Bernie's gaze rakes over his face. I can't judge by her expression what she's thinking. "You've done nothing wrong, Aiden. Nor has Elijah."

"I promised we wouldn't bring trouble."

Aunt Bernie tuts. "If that Red hadn't come here, he'd only be somewhere else."

Aiden doesn't look convinced. "I'll take the amulet and he'll follow. I'll deal with the problem somewhere far away. Where no one can get hurt. I only ask that you keep JJ safe."

Over my dead body is Aiden leaving by himself. I wait for her response, ready to go rogue if she agrees with him.

But her face softens. "I'm afraid that would be totally unacceptable, Aiden. I have no doubt that your offer is genuine, and every faith in your abilities and determination. However, Owlscroft would never willingly allow a demon to leave our jurisdiction. We do not shirk our duty. We will deal with the problem so nowhere else has to."

Sweet relief washes through me, almost sending my knees weak. Aunt Bernie. Legend.

"Inside with the both of you. We need to have a little think."

She is so calm that I can't help but feel reassured even though I can't see how this will be okay. We follow her into her office.

I start. "I need to spend some time in the library. I need to review everything we know."

"I'll check in with JJ, then join Harlow," Aiden adds.

"Good," Aunt Bernie says. "I'll phone the other major covens, let them know about our visitor. Maybe they'll have some useful advice. And all the other witches that held your position, Harlow."

I nod, but it's not a particularly promising avenue. Aunt Bernie has been Head Witch of Owlscroft for almost fifty years and hasn't lived through a Red. We leave her to make her calls. Aiden walks me to the library, so he knows where he can find me; along the wide hallway, out towards the back.

A series of loud thumps has me turning. JJ is descending the stairs, three at a time.

"Uncle!" He reaches the bottom on a run, only just pulling up in time to prevent a collision. "What are you doing here? Is Jonathan—"

His gaze locks on his amulet, hanging around my neck. His body draws up, stiffens. His hands form tight fists. His face morphs from his typical open smile to blank, slack-jawed nothing. He's still, very still.

Then he flies at me. And the look on his face … it's no longer blank. It's something very close to hatred.

Aiden moves fast, grabs him from behind, arms around his chest, holding him back from attacking me as I scramble backward.

"Take it off!" he screams. "It's mine."

"JJ. Calm," Aiden says firmly.

JJ is a little past a calm prompt. His face is beetroot and smooshed looking, his hair is wild, and he is struggling like a wild animal against Aiden's hold.

"I'm not using it." I have to raise my voice above the din he's making. "I'm just wearing it. Just for today."

He gives no indication that he's heard. He's still madly trying to break free.

"It's to attract Jonathan. So we can get him to leave." I don't say anything more. I don't know whether Aiden plans to tell JJ or not about the Red. JJ was pretty freaked this morning, and I wouldn't describe his current mental state as stable. "Honestly, JJ. I know it's yours."

There's still the occasional jerk but his movements start to lack force. He's running out of puff.

"You shouldn't be wearing it." His voice is still more shout than anything, but the initial rush of madness has subsided.

"Can I let go now?" Aiden asks.

"Yes," JJ spits. He has dialled it down from wild beast to sulky and mutinous, but when he looks at me, that hateful rage is still there. "Why are you letting her wear it?"

"I should have asked your permission. But there was no time, and as Harlow said, it's just to attract Jonathan. One day only." Aiden slings an arm around JJ's shoulder, trying to turn him, steer him away from me. "Let's take a walk. I'll tell you what's going on."

It seems to be working. They head back along the corridor. Then JJ turns and gives me a look I'll never forget. Don't get me wrong, I have a lot of time for JJ. He brings a certain amount of levity to a world gone mad. But you would not know it at this moment.

No one touches a wizard's amulet. Aiden's said those words to me over and over again. Now I know why.

I stand a moment, hands on hips, shaken.

Or maybe I'm just procrastinating. Usually, the coven library is one of my favourite places in the world. Right now, I don't want to go in.

I've been recalling more and more of my earlier studies since we ran from the ovals, and I'm pretty sure what I'm going to learn. Given the difficulty evicting and the horrific havoc Reds wreak, strong consideration has to be given to taking out the host. As powerful as a

Red is, its host is human. If the host dies before the demon has a chance to respond, it's automatically evicted.

Killing is not what we witches are about – but it may be the only viable course of action.

I take a deep breath and turn.

I can't risk eviction not working. And I can't risk losing Aiden in a failed attempt.

But Aiden's got just as much skin in this game as I do; Jonathan's his brother and Aiden's already moved his whole life rather than harm him.

His brother; my coven.

What if we can't agree?

I spent a lot of time in the library in my neophyte year – first when I needed alone time, and then just because I liked it. The walls are a deep, dark red, but you can't see much of them because they're lined from skirting board to ceiling with stacked shelves of books. The antique Persian carpets and constantly crackling fire add to the cosy vibes. The fire was a gift from the first Head Witch. It's not real, but the warmth is and so is the cheery glow, and that's what counts. The rest of Owlscroft is always arctic, so this is a welcome addition.

The library has a decent section on demons, despite its somewhat niche status, and that's where I start. Witches aren't anti-technology, but we're not in a mad rush to digitise everything either. Some of these texts are ancient. Most date from the nineteenth and early twentieth centuries, and they have coloured cloth or leather covers with copious gilt. I have memories of flicking through most of these in the early days, but to be honest, I skimmed most of the material on Reds. I had my hands full learning how to evict the demons that come through on a frequent basis, and I put Reds to the side. Until now, I've had no need to come back.

I grab the most basic of the demon-hunting texts, and collapse, legs crossed under me, in the nearest armchair. A cloud of dust lifts, dances in the air around me, caught in the light coming off the cheery flames. It's nice. I wish I were here for a different reason.

The chapter on Reds is short. We witches just haven't had the chance to gather much data. But to summarise, they're dangerous. Think large-scale humanitarian disaster – military coups, genocide, widespread rape and torture. They can last on earth for decades, and can and will destroy anyone who gets in their way. Among their other terrifying abilities, they can 'crush hearts' at will, of anyone or thing they can see.

My stomach clenches. Juicy.

The basic recommendation, if you're one of the unfortunate witches to whom it falls, is beheading from behind.

Yes, actual, literal, manual beheading. Death needs to be unforeseen and instantaneous. You can't leave even a single moment for the demon to respond or you'll find yourself without a functioning cardiac unit. Spells to protect the heart have not worked.

I have to close the book a moment. I'll do what's necessary, but chopping someone's head off? It's not just a bad taste in my mouth, it's a revulsion that has nausea rising from the pit of my stomach. I can't reconcile myself to having to do that.

But I know why it's come about. Witches have no magic to kill.

That's not strictly true, there's whispers of it, but it's not taught; it's not even accessible. I wouldn't even know how to start finding out about it. It's the biggest taboo we have. Instant excommunication. We would never use it, even on a Red.

I'm returning the book to the shelf when Aiden enters the room. He comes to stand in front of the fire; he looks depleted and I haven't even told him what I've found yet.

"How's JJ?" I ask.

Aiden looks at me a moment before responding. "It's not easy seeing your amulet on someone else."

No. I'd gathered that. I scan the other books on the shelf.

"He'll be fine." He takes a seat on the floor, cross-legged. "I need to spend some time thinking about this. Then I'll help with the research."

I nod. To be honest, it's a relief. I'm not relishing telling him about the beheading. Maybe I can find us another option.

I grab a book pertaining to the major demons – the Indigos, the Blues and the Reds – and return to my chair. Flicking through, I can see it includes some other ideas. Hiding while casting the eviction spell. Whole-coven casting from a distance. Drawing the demon closer to the covenstead to harness its protective power. And then I hit a footnote that reveals that none of these have resulted in success.

Chalice.

I move on to a specialist Red compendium. It dates to 1856 and contains, among other things, an account of the 13 known encounters with a Red in the history of Ireland.

Not going to lie, it's grim. Credit to the author. The full gory reality of encountering a Red is certainly brought to life. Depressingly, regardless of where they start, most cases end up with beheading. Which, I note, is not always successful on the first attempt. Reds being what they are, covens have no option but to keep sending witches after them. It can cause quite the gap in coven ranks by the end. My stomach drops as I think about that happening to Owlscroft. If I fail, who will they send next?

I pour over the details of the non-beheading attempts. Again, not light reading. In the rare cases where an eviction spell has actually worked, the host has died anyway. As has the witch or witches who cast the spell and anyone else in the vicinity.

So really, how would you like your death served? With cold homicidal intent and minimal collateral damage? Or with kind intentions to preserve life that nonetheless result in carnage?

Panic and dread build, tightening around my lungs. I get that dirty, clammy feel of fear sweat. My bones feel heavy and ancient. I could do with some of Aiden's chill. He's sitting, still and poised as a cobra, eyes closed. I drink in the clean lines of his face, his well-cut lips, and hope that, wherever he is right now, he's having more success than I am.

I return the book to the shelf and scour for others. I almost miss a slim booklet nestled among the others. A flick-through reveals it's a treatise from a Russian demon hunter from 223 years ago – not on demons per se, but portals. Portals. My pulse speeds at the promise of it and I take it back to my seat.

The author, Alina, made an extensive study of the metaphysics of portals, arguing that demon hunters could strengthen their chances of success by casting a spell on the portal itself, so that it sucked in the demon as the eviction spell worked to dislodge it from the human host.

I sit up straighter. Finally. This is the kind of thing I was hoping for.

She also posited that the portal changes in nature through the year, to explain why so many demons appear around Halloween, and particularly on the night itself. That same factor that widens the portal should also allow for a better chance of successful eviction. Which means, if we want to maximise our likelihood of success, tomorrow night is the night – with the zenith coming at what's been translated as 'the wee hours'. Shortly after midnight?

I keep reading, sure I'm on to something. But the text stops abruptly, and the next page is a postscript, written by a member of Alina's coven. Alina had put her theory into practice. She had succeeded in evicting the Red. The host had lived; Alina hadn't.

A stab of sorrow for this brave, determined and unconventional witch has my head bowing. Alina should have lived to finish her research. But I can use what she started.

I look across at Aiden. He's watching me with fathomless eyes, one leg up, an arm resting atop. My heart leaps inside my chest, my stomach twists tight, and the rest of the room fades. I take a sharp breath and hold it; for a second, I forget all about demons and beheadings. "Hi," I say.

"Hi," he replies, rising gracefully in one swift motion and heading towards me. "What did you learn?"

I look away. There's no good way to say this. I grit my teeth and plough on. "Our best chance is to behead Jonathan."

He comes to an abrupt halt. I've killed the mood entirely.

"There's a slight chance of successful eviction – a mostly untested experimental procedure – but even then, one of us is likely to die. Maybe both."

Aiden's not breaking the uncomfortable silence.

"I'm sorry," I add.

He exhales.

I try again, a little gentler. "A normal eviction spell hardly ever works. And even if it does, by some miracle, all of us, including Jonathan, are likely to die anyway. That's why the recommended course of action is to …" I can't say it again. "The host dies, but if all goes well, no one else does, and the Red's gone."

He pushes two hands through his hair, then lands them on his hips. "I have another idea."

I brighten. "Yes?"

"We ask Jonathan to help."

For a long moment, I have no words. From my reading, we're not going to have time to ask for anything before our hearts are crushed. "You plan to ask a Red demon to evict itself?"

"Not the demon. Jonathan. He's a wizard; he can use his power."

I don't know how to talk to an inhabited human. I don't know if it's possible. Will it be different with a wizard? And what makes Aiden think Jonathan will want to help? "He's already attacked JJ. You took a mortally binding vow because he's so full of power-lust. Now he's inhabited by a Red and you think he's going to make a different choice? You know how it works. He probably invited inhabitation, and the Red wouldn't have chosen him unless he had that in him."

His eyes have that heavy soulful look they get sometimes. "Everyone has it in them."

His words are beyond heavy; they're soul-crushing. And I'm not sure they're true. "Not everybody acts on it. You don't." I put my hand under JJ's amulet, lift it towards him. "You are coping just fine with this dangling in front of you. Jonathon? Not so much."

His jaw tightens. "We can't condemn him based on something he hasn't done yet. We can't just … choose to kill him. We have to evict. It's what we do."

I want to agree – eviction *is* what we do – but I just don't know. I don't want to kill but I also don't want to die. And I don't want Aiden or JJ to die either.

"I know he's still in there. I know he doesn't want this."

I start to shake my head. I mean, it's an idea, I just don't think it's an idea that will work.

"What about the experimental procedure you mentioned?"

"It may not help."

"Tell me anyway."

I tell him about Alina's portal hypothesis. Aiden listens intently, serious tilt to his head, fire lighting his dark eyes to a warm chocolate. When I finish, he nods. "Our approaches are complementary. My approach increases the push; your approach increases the pull. We can use both. No one needs to die."

Aiden is a lot more optimistic than I am. But I guess he's right. It's worth a go, and something in me is excited to discover if it will succeed. Halloween's tomorrow; we have tonight to experiment.

"We have to practice," I say. "Alina left a form of the spell. We need to test it, tweak it to be even stronger. See if we can get it to work on the demons that come through. And if it doesn't work ..." I look at him. I don't want to say it, but I need for us to be real here. "I'll do it."

"It will work," he says firmly.

I can only hope he's right.

It's almost time for our shift to start. Aiden goes to check in on JJ and I go to talk to Aunt Bernie.

I can tell the phone calls have not gone well. She's trying to keep it together, to be the calm and confident leader we need, but I can see her sadness and her worry. "If you need the sword ... let me know. It's locked in a cabinet upstairs."

Well. That's confronting.

"I'm so sorry, Harlow. It's terrible when a witch has to deal with this."

She's not wrong. "Witches help people. We preserve life; we don't take it." I'm not sure why I'm saying this; I just need to voice it.

Her head tilts. "Yes."

I bite my lip. "But what if trying to preserve life only leads to more death?"

Her eyes are full of emotion. "You're our demon hunter, Harlow. We will support whatever decision you make."

But it affects her. It affects everyone. If I fail, Owlscroft will continue trying. They'll send other witches. They'll have to. Whether Jonathan leaves Melbourne or not. And other covens will as well.

We have to make Alina's spell work.

"I have a favour to ask."

Her brows shoot up in surprise. I'm not one to ask for favours.

"Don't tell Mum. Please. I'll tell her after."

"As you wish." I can't tell if she approves of my request or not, but if Aunt Bernie says she won't tell, she won't.

I head out to wait for Aiden. I've always made my own decisions. Insisted on it.

None of them have been quite like this.

CHAPTER 11

Four seasons in one day. Something all Melburnians learn to live with.

In the hours we've been buried in the library, the weather has turned; it's not cold but a sleety drizzle is falling.

We catch a tram back to the city. It's standing room only, and we grip the rails overhead as we rattle along Swan Street. Forced close together, our gazes are locked; we collide when the tram lurches, and sometimes when it doesn't. I want to ask Aiden if he's okay, but it's not the best location for a conversation about demons and beheadings.

Still, my body lights up each time my skin makes contact with his and I'm hungry for more. It's the only thing making me feel okay. I assume it's the same for Aiden, because his hand winds up on my hip. Something I'd usually hate, but this time, I lean into it.

We jump off and collect Aiden's car. After what happened earlier this afternoon, we've agreed we need a quick getaway option in place. Aiden drives the short distance to the square. He parks in a loading zone and makes it so that the car is invisible to everyone passing, including City of Melbourne's overly vigilant parking inspectors.

We're a little early; it's still light. A man on the other side of the fountain is shuffling to a bass-heavy house tune. It's not clear if he's doing it for money or just coz, but he's attracting quite a crowd.

We cast Alina's portal spell.

> *Take it back*
> *Pull it back*
> *Return it*
> *To its proper place*

It's a translation of the original Russian; we won't be able to test whether it works until the demon parade starts, but we've cleared the first hurdle – the portal doesn't throw it back in our faces.

Thanks to Alina, I am thinking about the portal in a whole new way. I've always considered it this fixed thing we can't control. We tried to shut it down, but when that didn't work, we gave up. Now I'm wondering if we tried hard enough. What is a portal anyway? Is it something demons made? But it doesn't put up any resistance to taking them back when we evict; does that mean it's not on their side?

Excitement buzzes through me as each question hurls itself into my mind. Someone should continue Alina's research, but for now, I have to shut down my curiosity. We need to focus.

The night starts as usual, with a series of Yellows. Yellows aren't challenging, but the speed at which they now pass back through to their side of the universe is astounding.

I look at Aiden and grin. It works.

It works so well that when an Orange lights up, we decide to evict on the spot rather than chase it into a laneway. With the portal's extra pull power, there's no flames, no explosions. The demon is simply gone.

This is going to revolutionise demon hunting. "We have to document this," I say. "We can't just leave future witches with the mess we're in. We have to get them better tools, better processes."

The pace picks up. We're not sure how quickly the portal spell fades – we recast it when we have a spare moment to keep it topped up – but Yellow, Orange, Violet, Green, they all fly back through within moments of arriving. It's so satisfying.

A woman in a houndstooth silk blouse and red stilettos sweeps past at a rapid clip. She looks a little like Cruella de Vil. When she lights up Blue, my pulse spikes. Blues aren't as violent as Reds but they're incredibly difficult to evict. Definitely a demon to take on in a team.

I look for Aiden but we just had a multitude of lesser demons come through in quick succession and he's across the square, pursuing a Green who slipped away.

I look back at the Blue. We don't want *her* slipping away. Besides, this is a chance to practice on a powerful demon. If we're facing a Red tomorrow night, we need as much practice as we can get.

I step out in front of her, blocking her path. "I really need to talk to you."

She comes to a halt, elegant brow raised.

"It's got to do with your mission. It's important." I signal with my head towards the fountain.

Blues always have a mission, and everything's always important. She follows. Once she's close, I grab for some magic and cant the spell, quietly but firmly.

The Blue has only just come through; it's still getting its bearings. But her radiant blue eyes show growing awareness of what I'm trying to do.

Awareness, but no fear. She's in no way threatened by me. Even with the stronger portal, she's resisting easily.

When I'm done, she smiles, and suddenly, I'm the one who's apprehensive. A quick glance across the square reveals Aiden's still occupied. I should have called him; waited. Now I'm alone with this.

And I'm going to have to deal with it. I look back at her, braced and readying for a second run-through of the spell.

She laughs, light and bell-like. "What's your name?"

She's stunningly pretty. Her black hair is as shiny as I've ever seen; it's in a classy up-do, with a few wispy tendrils sweeping down to frame her exquisite, heart-shaped face.

I straighten from my combat-ready stance. "Harlow."

Her skin is flawless. And those eyes – they are deep, sparkling sapphires. They hold a wealth of power, wisdom, experience. They see me. They know me. *She* knows me. My apprehension fades. Everything fades. Except this dazzling woman.

She is glorious. Mesmerising. My heart swells with admiration.

Why should I try to evict? I don't want to. Who's to say the earth wouldn't be better with her here? It's not like humans do such a good job running the joint. I am dimly aware of my evict spell; it's still trying to work. I consider trying to cancel it, but there's no need – she's withstanding it with ease.

Her smile grows broader, her head tilts. She's taking me in, assessing me.

I hope she likes me. I want to please her, serve her. I want to know everything about her. "What's your name?" I ask.

Her smile twists; her eyes narrow.

I've said the wrong thing. I've disappointed her. I feel sick with it. Sour acidic bile coats my tongue. Nausea has me taking a step away; then another. I stop, silently begging her forgiveness. She tosses her head to the left, and I look, desperate to win back her favour. Cars speed by. I am transfixed; I can't look away.

I feel horrible. I'm not worthy, I've let her down, and it's awful. If I threw myself onto the road, under a car, that awful feeling would go.

Would that please her? I look back; she tosses her head in the direction of the street again.

My light, my essence is falling away. I can't find it in myself to care. There's no reason for me to stay. Step by backwards step, I stumble towards the road.

"Harlow!"

The shout of my name cuts through the fog, snaps me out of my listless fugue. I wrench my head around to see Aiden halfway across the square, wondering what the hell is going on. My feet keep trying to shift backward, but I plant them, scrambling to claw back to myself. I shake my head clear, desperate to regain control, awareness. I know what's happening. Cruella's decided I'm not so harmless after all; that I'd be better splattered on the street.

"Harlow. Look at me."

Her voice is a siren's call I cannot resist. As I meet that glow of blue, a fresh blast of compulsion sweeps over me. It's a special kind of torture, to be aware that you're being played, but unable to fight it. I shudder. And I step backward.

From the corner of my eye, I see Aiden running, but he's not going to make it in time. If I don't want to end up roadkill, I have to save myself.

I dig deep. I do what I always do and I get behind myself. I am Harlow Jackson. I am Owlscroft Coven's demon hunter. I am not throwing myself under any car.

I fight another backward step. The effort of it has my breaths coming in jerks. When I plough one foot forward, it's like walking into a hurricane of sickness, every step courting disease and death. But the harder it gets, the harder I push; the worse I feel, the more determined I become.

I get back behind my spell. It's still there, trying, but without my will behind it, it's useless.

I push it at her. Everything she throws at me, I absorb and I use it to grow stronger. My power swells, courses through my veins like lightening. I am inviolable.

I cannot fail. I will not fail. I will prevail. I know it. It beats through me, as surely as my heart does.

The Blue is not scared. It laughs, loving my spirit.

As I watch, the woman collapses to sit on the edge of the fountain, head in her hands.

But me, I still see the potential, the wonder of the glittering future that could still be.

I could gather millions to me, to my cause. I could hold all those souls in my hand, each of them willing to take a bullet. They would adore me. I would rule the world.

It rushes through me – a thrill that nothing could ever, will ever, match.

"Harlow!"

Aiden. Aiden would worship me too. He would fall to his knees and adore me.

He's in front of me, hands on my shoulders. His face is taut, drawn; his eyes are huge. "Fight! You must fight!"

Fight what?

Oh.

Goddamn demon! It's left Cruella and it's trying to inhabit me. And I'm on the verge of going along with it.

I scramble for defences, claw to hold on to what I know is true. Demons serve only themselves. They seek to control and harm, for nothing more than their own amusement. They must not be allowed to win.

Still the vision of a bold and bright future is fighting to take hold in me.

"No. No way. No." I don't know if I say it out loud, but I say it with every fibre of my being.

Not happening.

I gather and I push at the Blue. Push it to the edges of the portal, which Aiden has given the pull power of a black hole. I advance, shoving everything at it, willing to go through myself if it comes to it.

The Blue loses its footing; it is sucked back in and shredded like bad rubbish.

Good riddance.

I collapse, barely managing to land on my bottom near Cruella on the wall of the fountain. Panting heavily, forearms on my thighs, I lean over; an emptied-out shell. Aiden crouches in front of me, hands on my knees, eyes worried.

I shake my head. I'm fine. Or I will be.

"You okay?" I ask Cruella. She's pale and a little glassy-eyed but I'm pretty sure she's doing better than me at this moment.

"I think so. Just felt dizzy all of a sudden."

"It's the weather," I offer blandly.

She smiles weakly and struggles gamely to her feet. Aiden rises and extends a hand to assist, but she shakes her head. "I'm good."

She sets off, slower than previously but gathering pace as she steamrolls on. She'll never know how close she came.

Unlike me. I look up – I have never seen Aiden so pale; he knows.

"On the plus side, the portal strengthening spell worked on a major demon." My tone is nonchalant. It's not how I'm feeling but I'm grateful for it.

"What happened?" he asks.

I breathe out. It's not something I want to admit but I owe it to him to be honest. "I bit off more than I could chew." I shake my head at my own audacity. "Everything was going so well. The portal spell was working and I thought … I'd see if I could take on a Blue." By myself.

He doesn't say anything; he's waiting.

I attempt a smile. "The portal spell works, Aiden." What happened back there … it wasn't the portal spell not working. I just … I fell for a Blue. "And if Alina's right, the pull will be even stronger tomorrow." I stand. Still a little shaky but better on my feet. "You were right; we can do this. And we can practice and tweak more. Then we'll get Jonathan to come to us, and we'll evict."

He stares at me for a long moment. It's what he wanted, but he doesn't look happy.

His gaze drops to JJ's amulet. I'd forgotten about it. Weird, considering how heavy and uncomfortable it was at first. But it's been against my skin for hours, and it's warmed up.

"Aiden." I wait until he's looking at me. "We can do this."

Aiden makes a movement with this head that's not quite a nod but eases the tension. "We'll talk about it later," he says.

I want to ask why the tables have turned; why I'm now the one who wants to try to evict. But he's right; we need to get back to work.

Hours later, we're on our way home.

I'm so tired I'm contemplating just stretching out on the pavement. My gaze flashes to a young blonde woman, hurrying along the street towards us. Her arms are wrapped around herself, her head is down, and it's so unexpected it takes me a moment to realise it's Everly.

She slows as she draws near. She's not crying at the moment but it's obvious she has been. She's pale and her eyes are red and puffy. Chalice. She's seen something. With her doll-like features and peaches and cream complexion, Everly looks fragile. She's not. She's the strongest witch I know. If she's been crying … it's not good.

As a future witch, Everly can project some part of herself forward into the future and 'see'. When I said being a demon hunter was the most dangerous job a witch could do … Future witch comes pretty close. The further forward she goes and the longer she stays, the greater the chance she'll never come back. Or not in one piece, mentally, at any rate.

She stands at a distance in front of us, arms still crossed. "I need to talk to you."

She looks significantly at Aiden, who graciously slips away to rest against a building further along the block and wait.

"Did JJ tell you?"

Everly's face screws up. She nods.

"So what is it I need to know?" I don't ask for everything. Everly can be cagey about what she reveals. Understandably.

She swallows, looks away. "Two wizards, black hair. Face down on the ground."

Jonathan. Aiden. I'm standing still on flat pavement but I feel like I'm about to lose my footing. It's one thing to know our chances of survival aren't high, it's another to visualise it.

"Am I dead?" I might as well just get to the point.

"You wish you were."

That gets to me; a knife twisting inside my gut. I pull myself together. Tell myself it's been a long day. And that while what Everly sees is true, it's just one truth. "Do I want to know what that means?"

She scrubs at her eyes, looks away. "You have a choice to make. Make the right one."

"Everly—"

She interrupts. "Please, Harlow. I've never asked you for anything. I know this is a lot, but … don't take any risks. If there's a safe option, take it."

Everly and I have a strange relationship. My fault, probably. I can't imagine it was easy for her growing up with me as big sister. Always in trouble at school. Always in trouble at home. We're not 'close'; not like Avery and Amelia. We've never confided in each other, gone on shopping sprees, giggled about boys, or whatever the hell else sisters are supposed to do.

But that doesn't mean I don't love the shit out of her. I like her and respect her and I would lay down my life for her without a second's hesitation.

"Please, Harlow."

"Yeah. Got it." I trust my sister; I trust her visions.

Everly lives at home. Aiden and I get her into an uber back to Camberwell, then trudge back to ours. He must know Everly's visit has something to do with what's going on, but he doesn't ask and I don't tell.

CHAPTER 12

We need to make a decision. Plan A or Plan B.

It'd be nice to be able to hedge our bets; have the sword at the ready if eviction doesn't work. But we won't get a second chance. If we dither about, we lose our element of surprise and achieve nothing. Guaranteed.

Everly's vision … Despite what Mum thinks, I don't have a death wish. And I can't allow anything to happen to Aiden. It's sad that his brother has been inhabited by a Red DF; I don't want to make it sadder by failing to evict and dying in the process.

But the portal strengthening spell has changed everything. It's working; except we don't know if it will work on a Red. I just wish we had more time to experiment.

When we reach my apartment, I unlock the door and nudge it open, but I don't make any move to go in. The past two days have been intense, and there's worse to come. "We should talk. We need to decide."

"Tomorrow," he says.

I cross my arms. "Do you want to know what Everly said?"

"Not tonight. No more. Tonight we sleep."

Something in me unknots and I lean against the doorframe. I

needed to hear that; I need the space. And he's right – nothing will happen before tomorrow. We don't have to do this right now. "Okay." I wait for him to turn and walk away, but he doesn't.

"I'll sleep here with you tonight."

My heart stops, then races. A sudden sizzling heat flushes through me, reenergising a body I thought was done for the day. I shift off the door, alert and aware.

I must look like I'm about to pounce, because he adds, "I'm not risking Jonathan finding you."

Yeah. Makes sense. Okay. No biggie.

I try to tell my pounding heart that.

I could argue about not needing protection. I would usually, just on principle. I don't need him here. I can take care of myself. But I want him with me. I want to be with him.

I push the door wider and walk through, leaving it open. Aiden nudges his shoes off at the door. We stand in my living room, a few paces from one another, a sudden tension weighing on the room. Then Aiden drops to the couch. "I'll sleep here."

Not if I have my way, he won't.

Or at least, not alone. I reach down and pull off my boots.

I have hit an over-stimulated state of second-wind frenzy. I know I need to sleep, but I am too juiced. And hey, we'll probably die tomorrow. Or I'll wish I did, whatever that means.

I can't leave things like this.

I have feelings for Aiden, feelings of a very lustful kind, and I want him to know. I do it my way. I strip off my t-shirt and fling it to the floor.

I see heat. I see yes. Then the mask drops. "Not tonight," he says, shifting so he's not facing me.

Yes tonight. "Don't try to tell me you don't want to."

His jaw clenches. "I don't always do what I want."

Try never; he never does what he wants.

I undo my jeans, push them down and step out of them. He's studiously not looking, so I walk to stand right in front of him. I'm in a crop top and undies. His gaze fixes on my middle region – the skin of my stomach, my hips. It rises, skimming over my breasts then up to meet my eyes.

"Your turn," I prompt.

The tips of his mouth quirk up, but he shakes his head. "Not the right time."

I beg to differ. It might be our only shot.

He makes as if to get horizontal and sleep. I move closer and I don't stop. Not until I've pushed him back against the couch, and I'm leaning over him, one knee between him and the back of the couch, one knee between his legs.

His hand is on my waist again. Holding me back? Holding me close? Just because he wants it there? As always, he is a mystery.

But I like the way it feels.

I am in his space. If he didn't want me there, he could push me away with ease. But he's not doing that. He's as still as a snake. A cobra, biding its time.

My gaze drops to his lips. Then returns to his eyes. His breath is heavy. There is a stain of colour high on his cheekbones, a tension radiating from him that lets me know holding back is hard.

Good. It should be.

"Come on," I say. "Live a little. Before we don't have the option anymore."

His hand squeezes my waist, and my pulse goes staccato, but then he says, "We do this now, there's some part of us saying we think this is our last opportunity. I don't want to put that out into the world."

"I don't believe that." It's sex. It's good.

Especially with Aiden. I try to drop further forward, but meet resistance from his hand, which again squeezes my waist, sending a knot of coiling need spiralling through my belly, and lower. My breathing turns husky. Aiden's nostrils flare. His eyes scan mine. And then he lunges.

I'm flipped and pinned against the back of the couch, head deep into cushions. One hand is still at my waist, gripping with delicious force, the other captures mine and pushes it against the couch next to my head.

His face is close. His body is hot and heavy on mine. I smell mountain fir-tree and smoke and man. This is all I've wanted for the longest time.

I snake my free hand under his tank, up his back. I scrape my nails back down – not too hard, but not too light. His eyes close, he makes a sound and his mouth crushes to mine.

My body rises up into his. Chalice!

He breaks the kiss and draws back. I try to follow but he's got me pinned. I try to bring him back to me with the hand that's between his shoulder blades, but he's not having a bar of it.

Every nerve, every cell in my body howls in frustrated denial.

"I need to know this isn't just about what might happen tomorrow." His voice is roughened with desire, but I don't doubt he has enough control to stop right now, no matter how much he wants it.

I don't want to talk. I want him. But as I stare at his lips and throb with my need to have them back on me, I know I'm not going to get anything unless I give a little more.

I'm good at taking my clothes off. I'm good at making the first move.

I'm crap at confessing my feelings.

"It's not," I say. "I've wanted to jump your bones for ages."

Is that enough?

The hand at my waist comes to cup my neck, my face. A thumb strokes across my jaw, feather-soft. He looks into my eyes for what feels like eternity. I've got no idea what he sees, but when he lowers his head and covers my mouth with his, it's so tender I almost panic and push him off. Rough and tumble I can handle; this might kill me.

He kisses along my jaw. It feels good, but I turn my head, stopping him. "I don't do this."

"Don't do what?" he murmurs.

"Relationships."

He pauses, then nips at my lobe. I arch up. I almost tell him to do it again, but I need to be clear. I wouldn't have brought this whole thing up; I would have jumped straight to sex. But since he did, I've got to be honest with him. "I'm not girlfriend material. I'm too full on, and I don't like compromising."

I feel something like an exasperated chuckle near my ear. "I know who you are, Harlow."

He does but not in this way. "Guys are cool with me at first, then they're not. They start expecting me to go to their sister's birthday dinner. Shit like that. They get sick of hearing no all the time."

He pulls back, looks me in the eyes. I'm expecting something serious, but he says, "I don't have a sister."

I let out a quick amused huff. "You know what I'm saying. It's not about their sister; it's about me … doing what they want."

His eyes turn serious. "I know what you're saying. It's their problem. If they're not enough for you, if they're threatened by you, that's on them."

"It's me too. They start pushing, I push back." I'm no saint; it's a mutual destruction.

"That's not going to happen with us. I don't need to throw my weight around, assert myself over you to prop up my own ego."

I realise with something like wonder that he's right; he never has. He listens to everything I say about demon hunting, he's let me teach him. All without a flicker of fragile ego.

"We're a team. We respect each other. As equals."

I breathe out, my heart swelling and softening as his words wash over me. Equals. Respect. It's all I've ever wanted. It's a revelation and I'm light-headed with it. This is what I need, this is what's been missing.

My eyes smart, fill with liquid.

His expression turns tender, he brushes a thumb across my bottom lip. "Coming to Melbourne, meeting you is the best thing that's happened to me. I didn't have a life before you. I was alone, consumed by grief and fear. You changed everything." His hand cups my jaw, he drops the lightest kiss on my cheekbone. "I've tried to keep my distance because wizards are trouble, but all I want is to be with you. You're everything to me, Harlow. The only one. I need you in my life. All the time. For good."

He's making me ache; I am raw, bruised, open and vulnerable like I never am. I want to tell him how I feel but I don't know how to make those kinds of declarations. "Aiden," I say. "I'd walk through fire for you. Kiss me."

His mouth meets mine in a return of the earlier fury. His kiss is primal, demanding. Bone-melting heat and a clash of tongues and teeth. It's hard to break away but I want skin. I twist and sit, straddling his hips. I tug off my crop top. His hands are on my breasts immediately. My head drops back and I press forward. When his thumbs rub over my nipples, pleasure flares deep in my belly. I gasp and squeeze his ribs with my thighs, but I'm too impatient to linger. I reach down for the hem of his tank and draw it over his head, throwing it aside with relish.

Finally.

I sit back to admire; my mouth goes dry. How could one man be so golden, so gorgeous, so beautifully, perfectly muscled? I put my hands on him, loving the feeling of his heavy shoulders and chest under my palms. I brush my fingers over his nipples and down; he shudders and tugs me back to him.

There is fire in my blood when he kisses me, hands moving all over me. I have always liked sex but this is something else. An intoxicating drug I could easily become addicted to. Maybe already am.

He shifts me off so he can stand and remove his cargoes. I rid myself of underwear and lie back to enjoy the show. The light is still dim; the sun's not up yet. But it's enough to see by. And appreciate. Again, I'd like to linger. I'd like to sit and put my hands on his hips and tug him towards my mouth. Next time. I just watch as he sheathes himself.

He lowers himself so that his top is braced over me but his bottom half is deliciously heavy, his erection a rod against my belly. He returns to kissing me and when I wrap a leg around his hip, he pushes me wider and enters in one smooth motion.

Chalice. It's so good I think I'm going to sublimate on the spot; literally just go up in flames. His hand cups my butt. He draws back then pushes again so slowly I moan. Luxury. Pure luxury.

And that's where the slow part ends. Wildness takes over, and it's fast and powerful, lighting up my entire body until it explodes in a volcano of pleasure.

I'm ruined for all other men and I love it.

Afterwards, when our breathing has slowed and our skin has cooled and I can no longer resist the tug of sleep, I hold on long enough to make a couple more vows. I'm not letting him go. And we're not dying. We're living so we can do that again. And again.

AT SOME POINT we move to my bed and indulge in another round.

I wake feeling refreshed. Having Aiden here feels natural, and I take shameless advantage of him all over again. Things progress to a strangely normal morning. He makes coffee; I make toast with butter and vegemite. I can tell he doesn't approve of this as a breakfast food, or probably any kind of food, but I make him take a bite and he politely chews.

"So. Everly," I say, when I can't avoid it any longer.

"Yes," he says.

"She saw you and Jonathan, face down on the ground."

"You?" he asks.

"Still standing, apparently."

He nods.

"Everything Everly sees is the truth, but it's only one truth. Things change. It may not turn out that way."

"Of course." He seems oddly unconcerned.

"We don't know what's going to happen tonight, but I want to try for eviction. I think we can do it." I'm not going to let Aiden die.

"I agree."

It feels too easy, but there's nothing more to say.

He leaves to shower and change. I do the same.

A little while later, there's a knock at the door. I grin because he's too polite, but when I open it, it's Mum.

She doesn't look as bad as Everly did, but I know immediately that she knows. "Aunt Bernie said she wouldn't tell you."

"She didn't. Everly was a mess when she got in."

My bad. I should have told Everly not to say anything. "It's going to be fine," I say. "We've got a plan; we're going to stick to it. I know it's probably not what you want me to—"

Her hand comes up. "You'll make your own decision, Harlow. You always have and you always will. That's not why I'm here."

I blink at her.

"I think you misinterpreted me the other night. When I said coven wasn't everything, I meant you don't have to sacrifice your whole life for it. Like you have been. For years."

My hand comes up to the back of my neck. "It's what I wanted to do."

"I know. But there are other things in life, and you deserve those too."

"I think—" I break off. My mouth quirks. "I think I might be getting some of those."

"Good. But what I really want to say is—there will always be a place for you in this coven. No one has done more for Owlscroft than you. No one. Stepping down from demon hunting doesn't change that."

I want to believe her words, but when I exhale, it's shaky. "I know that's technically true. And you were right about my time being up." I think about the Blue and how close I'd come to losing everything. I try not to let it show as I say, "When this is done, it'll be time for me to think about doing something else. I just ..." I shake my head. "I'm not sure what else I can do."

"Do what you've always done, Harlow. Define your own role. Come up with some ideas on how you see yourself contributing. Bring them to the Council. We'll support them if we can. We know what you're capable of; we don't want to lose you."

Define my own role. The words break through the heavy cloud that's been dogging me for days. I feel lighter, like my future is once again full of possibilities. "Okay. I will." I offer her a smile – something softer than my usual grin.

Her eyes fill. "Harlow, I'm not saying this because I think it's my last chance, but I have to say it … I need you to know how proud I am of you."

It takes a moment to sink in, then warmth rushes through me and I'm blinking for a different reason.

"I'm sorry I've made you feel like you wouldn't have a place in the world just by being who you are. It was my own fear. You're so fearless, so sure of yourself, and I was always worried that you wouldn't fit in, that you wouldn't find happiness. But you have found your way, like you always told me you would. You fit in perfectly; in your own way. And how you're standing up and fighting for your friends—" She breaks off, hand in front of her mouth, choking back a sob.

I give her a hug. "We're going to get through this. Aiden and I."

She nods furiously. "Oh, I know you will."

"I'll call you tonight. After."

"I'd appreciate that. You know I'll be waiting by the phone."

Yes. That's why I offered to call.

"I'll leave you to it." She gives me a parting kiss on the cheek.

"Mum …" She turns back. "Aiden and I aren't just friends."

"I know that too, Harlow," she says with a smile. "Why don't you bring him to lunch on Sunday."

CHAPTER 13

The last of the sun's slanted rays turn the buildings surrounding the square gold and pink. The fountain bubbles merrily, and witches, vampires and ghouls stroll past.

The costumed variety, that is – Halloween is here.

Halloween's been slow to take off in Australia. It's spring, and everything is getting lighter, not darker. We don't have the frost-breath cold, the bare ghostly branches or the fallen leaves, but we don't let that stop us from dressing up and enjoying the occasion.

Not Aiden and I, of course. No trick or treat for us. It's our busiest night of the year.

We strengthen the portal and wait until the sun dips below the horizon, the wild colours leave the sky, and the demon parade starts.

A few hours in, a grey-haired man in a business suit lights up Indigo.

I hate all demons, but Indigos? Special place in hell, so to speak. They're incredibly dangerous – the most dangerous apart from Reds. They'll hurt you if you give them any kind of chance. Which I don't. There's a set procedure to follow – they need to be led somewhere totally secluded and restrained – rope, handcuffs, whatever – before eviction is attempted.

I hate Indigos but I love hunting them. Nothing gives me more satisfaction than knowing there's one less Indigo walking the streets.

We'd usually follow it out of the square. But we've got the portal spell to help now. It's a risk, but it's getting late and we have to practice for the Red. I won't attempt it alone this time. I raise my brows at Aiden. He nods and concentrates on strengthening the portal to maximum capacity.

It's not hard to get the Indigo to come close. It's late, the square's almost empty, and I'm a lone female. It's Indigo heaven. I turn, hunch my shoulders, gaze around anxiously, trying to look lost, upset. Vulnerable.

Of course, sick fuck can't resist.

With my back to him, I pull down a batch of magic. I cant the words; focused, determined. The batch is skittish. It doesn't want to go near the Indigo, and I get that. Indigos are skin-crawling. But we all have to do what we have to do, and that includes reluctant magic. I bind it tightly to the spell, then turn, pushing it towards the host.

His face turns nasty as he becomes aware of what I'm doing. They can't crush hearts at will, but Indigos are brutes. Given half a chance, he'll destroy me with his bare hands.

He descends on me, movements sloppy but fast, bringing his gut-turning wrongness closer and closer. Oranges burn, Violets seduce, Blues mesmerise – Indigos, they freeze. Paralyse. Weaponise fear, so that it turns their victim into a deer in headlights – incapable of fight or flight.

His gaze is fixed on me; he's already casting ahead to what he's going to do; how I'm going to suffer. I am usually impervious. The violent perverse fantasies only make me more determined to shove any Indigo back to Demonsville. But this time, the fear, an icy mess like a poisoned slushie, soaks into me, weighing me down, rendering me slow. Rendering me prey.

Aiden's getting twitchy on the sidelines, ready to drop the portal strengthening and physically intervene. I shake my head at him. I am no one's prey.

No way is this demon staying in this world.

I back my spell, push it forward into combat.

And that feeling from yesterday – the certainty that I am strong enough, that I will prevail – rises in me. Lightning in my veins, every cell vibrating with it. It comes quicker than yesterday and it's stronger. There's not a sliver of doubt in me. I can do this; I can do anything. Power pulses through me; I am alive with it. I am invincible.

I shove forward, relentless, in total control.

The pressure quickly becomes too much and the demon jumps from the businessman. The man falls forward, hands on his knees, breathing heavily, and I steel myself as it tries me instead. Visions of blood and pain and defilement fill my head; the abhorrent slaking of blood-lust. It might appeal to some but I am never going to be susceptible to an Indigo. I push it towards the portal, feeling some of Aiden's energy in its determination to suck the demon back.

The Indigo loses its grip and vanishes.

I am flooded with elation. Euphoria beats through me. I just dispatched an Indigo in a hundredth of the usual time and effort. The Red won't stand a chance.

Aiden is not smiling. He watches me carefully, hands on his hips.

"What?" How can he possibly have an issue? That was awesome.

"How did you get around the protection spell?"

My face screws up. What protection spell? But there is only one that could be relevant. I look down at the amulet, then back up. "I didn't."

"You did." His head cocks to the side. "You didn't realise?"

I shake my head slowly. "It wasn't deliberate." That lightning in the veins … That was the amulet? I frown. "I thought wizard magic didn't work on demons."

"It doesn't."

I shrug. "It did just then." I give him a half-smile. This is good news, surely.

He doesn't return it. "You shouldn't have used it."

I'm confused by his attitude. "It wasn't deliberate. It just happened." The amulet must have realised what I was doing and decided to pitch in. "Aiden …" I start, then stop to gather my thoughts.

JJ's amulet was lost in a cave for a thousand years. Maybe it wanted to be lost. Maybe it kept itself hidden. And when it was found, it was by JJ – a wizard who hasn't started using his power. Maybe it doesn't like wizards; at least the typical kind. And it doesn't like demons either. "The amulet … It wants to help."

"We can't assume that."

A new insight strikes. "Yes. We can. That's twice it's happened. It helped last night too." His gaze narrows. "I didn't realise; I just worked it out now. We should use it on the Red."

He shakes his head. "You haven't tried to use it deliberately. We don't know what would happen if you did."

Okay. He has a point. But still. "We need to investigate further."

"There's no time. We stick to the plan."

The immediate dismissal stings. "If we have something that can help, we have to use it. This is Jonathon's best chance. And ours."

"No. As soon as we get Jonathan here, you take it off."

"But—"

"This is not up for discussion."

Not up for discussion? "My job is to protect my coven. I decide how to do that."

"Not when it comes to JJ's amulet."

"I'm the one wearing it!"

Aiden's mouth twists. "You will not use it. I will not allow it."

He's said the wrong thing. I'll do anything and everything to keep my city and my coven safe. "You think you can stop me?"

His face is set in firm, stern lines that telecast 'yes; he does'. "Don't make me."

The threat of his power is like a living thing. My own rises to meet it. We eye each other; defensive, suspicious.

Are we at this point already?

One night! I got one night with this man. And this was the one I really wanted to break my losing streak with. "I thought you were on my side." There is bitterness in my tone, to match the bitterness in my gut. I must have believed this time would be different.

His eyes widen, just a fraction. "I am. Always." He takes a moment, scans the square and casts a quick reveal spell. "Being on your side doesn't mean I go along with everything you say."

Of course it doesn't.

Is that what I think?

I don't want what I saw in my fantasy as a Blue – Aiden falling to his knees and worshipping me. We work as a team; as equals. That means listening when he disagrees. Because if he's saying no, he has his reasons.

I take it down a notch. "Explain to me why we wouldn't use it when we know it works."

Aiden breathes out. He looks at me and his face softens, his eyes fill with an aching tenderness. "You know how close you were last night."

He's trying to protect me. From myself.

It's a stab to the heart; right where I'm softest. "That Blue … I just wasn't prepared." My mouth skews. It wasn't only a lack of preparation. First the Green, then the Violet …

"It's the amulet," he says gently. "It's making you vulnerable."

My head drops. I wish he was right. "It's not the amulet." My voice is so quiet, it's almost a whisper. This is so hard to admit – to him and to myself. "It's me." Everything my coven has been saying is right. I've been doing this too long, with too few breaks, and my immunity to demons is fading. "I'm losing my ability, my will to fight them."

He has gone very, very still. He's suspected some of this, I'm sure, but not the extent.

"I know," I say on a half-chuckle. "As usual, my timing sucks."

He tuts at my inappropriate attempt to lighten the mood and wraps his arms around me. His warmth, his strength – they make me feel a thousand times better. "We'll get the sword," he says quietly.

His words have me drawing in a shaky breath; a lump forms in my throat.

He would do that. For me.

Has it come to this? I draw back and look into his eyes. Losing his brother like this would kill him. Everly's words come back to me. A choice – the need to make the right one, the safe one. I don't want to die. I don't want Aiden to die. But he's had too much loss, too much grief in his life, and I'm not willing to accept more for him.

I just need to hold on a little longer. And I will. My days as a demon hunter are numbered, but I can take out this Red. "I've got one more big one in me. I know I do."

His hold tightens. "I can't risk it. Not with you."

It's a risk either way. I shake my head. "We don't need the sword. We just need to work together."

A faint buzzing reaches my ears. Aiden swears. Retrieving the phone from his pocket, he fires off in rapid Chinese, then ends the call and rests the phone against his chest, head down. "Jun Jie," he intones heavily.

"What's going on?"

"He's holed up in the restrooms at the KFC on Russell Street. He's sure he saw Jonathan; thinks he's following him. He's too scared to leave the toilets and find out."

Chalice! We don't need this right now. "What's he doing outside of Owlscroft?"

Aiden shakes his head. "He was upset." He looks pointedly at the amulet around my neck. "He snuck out to the city to see friends, play some games, blow off some steam."

"But tonight of all nights."

"Yes."

"Far out. Only JJ."

"Yes." Exasperation drips from his tone.

"Is Jonathan stalking him or is he just being paranoid? How did he find him?"

Aiden shakes his head. "I don't know. We don't know how Jonathan found us in the first place."

"But why would he stalk JJ? He hasn't got the amulet. Surely Jonathan knows that."

"Wizards don't like being separated from their amulets. He's going to assume it's on JJ. By the time he works out he doesn't have it, it might be too late."

I groan. There's no other option. "Go. Rescue JJ. Uber him to

Owlscroft and get back here as soon as you can." I glance at my watch. It's just before midnight; there's still over an hour until we planned to start. It'll be tight, but if Aiden works quickly, it's doable.

Aiden looks torn. I can see he's still thinking furiously, trying to find a solution that involves both staying with me and rescuing JJ.

I step closer, put my hands on his arms. "Go. If Jonathan is stalking JJ, he's not going to turn up here. I can handle the portal alone for a while. And you're not going to be able to focus if you're worried about JJ."

His hands come to my face, framing my jaw. "You will keep yourself safe," he says.

"Yes," I agree.

He drops his head and kisses me lightly.

"Go," I say.

He nods and jogs off in the direction of the KFC.

Demon hunting is easier with two, but I did this job for a long time by myself. I get busy evicting.

When things start to quieten and the square is all but empty, I become aware it's been a while. This is it; the wee hours. I feel edgy, not quite right. I'm thinking about calling Aiden when the hairs on the back of my neck stand on end. I turn. I'm sure I've seen something but it's only a young woman in a black witch's hat and cape, disappearing into a dark side alley.

My gaze shifts further to the left.

It's JJ. He's walking towards me. He's alone.

My stomach drops. Something's gone wrong. I run towards him, waiting for Aiden to show up.

"Okay?" I ask once I'm close.

He smiles. "Hi, Harlow."

He seems okay. I look in the direction he appeared from, but Aiden's not there. "Where's your uncle?"

"I don't know."

"Did you see him at KFC?"

"No."

"He went straight there after you called. You were supposed to wait for him."

He shrugs. "I didn't want to."

My mouth skews. My hands come to my hips. "What about Jonathan? I thought you were hiding from him."

"Jonathan's on his way home."

What? "You talked to him?"

"Yes."

My gaze drops to JJ's throat. Maybe Jonathan realised JJ didn't have the amulet and decided to leave him alone. It doesn't sound very Red-like to me, but what do I know?

"Okay," I say, attempting to get my bearings. I can only assume Aiden's still at KFC, looking for JJ. Who's here. Safe and sound. "Look, why don't you just uber back to Owlscroft? I'll wait for Aiden to show up here."

Actually, I'll call him. Tell him the JJ situation's been dealt with, and Jonathan's … heading back to Singapore. I bite my lip. That can't be right.

JJ's gaze is fixed on my chest. "You shouldn't be wearing my amulet."

Um. Okay. We're doing this again. "Aiden told you what's going on. It's temporary."

"He shouldn't have given it to you."

I should be expecting it by now but I'm a little unnerved by the intensity in his tone. It's not like I'm hurting it; I'm not even using it. It's just hanging around my neck. "It's for safekeeping. With a little demon attraction mixed in. Don't worry about it."

"I'd like it back now."

I look at him.

"Please," he adds.

Polite but insistent.

"I can't, JJ. Aiden wouldn't want me to give it to you." And besides, we still need the amulet to tempt the Red here. Speaking of which … I check my watch. Quarter-to two. I need JJ gone and Aiden here. "JJ, can I get you to—"

"It's not yours."

Chalice! I don't have time for this. "Everyone is aware of the fact that it's yours. Believe me. You'll get it when you're ready."

"I am ready."

"No, you're not."

"It's not for you to say."

"It's not me saying it; it's Aiden."

"It's not for him to say either."

I become aware that the whole time we've been having this conversation, JJ's been moving closer and closer. For some reason, I've been backing away.

Backing away; me.

I pull up. I stare at JJ so hard I'm almost squinting; a wave of prickles washes over me. "JJ?" There's something different about him. "What's going on?"

"I want my amulet."

"Yeah, I get that. Let me think." I shake my head slowly and turn as if considering his request, but under my breath, I'm muttering a spell. It feels hideous having my back to him, like spiders are crawling across my nape and up and down my spine. I turn my head slightly, just enough to see the Red radiating off him.

Oh hell no.

CHAPTER 14

*H*ow did this happen?

Is Aiden okay?

Why is my heart still beating?

I want to ask all these questions and more, but I don't. JJ's not going to answer; JJ's been inhabited.

And the last one, I can answer for myself. It's the amulet around my neck. With it on, I'm protected. Wizard magic and demons don't mix. If he tries to crush my heart while the amulet's around my neck, who knows what will happen?

For the moment, he's not risking it. Especially because he probably doesn't know that I know he's inhabited. JJ's never been involved in our demon hunting; he likely doesn't realise I've cast a reveal spell. So he's playing nice, waiting to see if he can talk me into just giving him the amulet.

I'm not going to, and eventually, the Red is going to get frustrated and come out swinging. He'll risk the potential damage to get what he wants.

But it gives me time to figure out what to do.

I can try to run. Find Aiden; regroup.

I can stall, keep JJ talking, give Aiden a chance to get his arse back here and help me.

Or I can deal with this Red on my own.

It's Halloween. The portal's been gaining in pull power all evening, and the time to cast an evict spell is nigh. I told Aiden I'd keep myself safe, but that was before either of us knew JJ would turn up, inhabited.

And if Aiden's not here, he can't end up face down on the ground.

My hands go to the amulet; JJ is riveted. I inch slowly towards the fountain, talking the whole way. "I know what you mean about Aiden. He can be stupidly overprotective. Maybe you *are* ready for this."

His breathing accelerates in anticipation.

I cup the warm weight in my hands. "Aiden's not here right now. I'm the one wearing it so I suppose it's up to me. Maybe I *should* give it to you." I loop my thumbs under the chain, as if I'm about to draw it over my head.

He closes the gap between us, waiting for the moment it's off me and he can pounce.

I drop the amulet back around my neck. His gaze flicks up to mine, a mixture of JJ sulky and Red fury.

"JJ. You've got an inhabitant. Can you feel it?"

Aiden thought he could ask Jonathan to help; I'm asking JJ. Aiden says JJ's powerful; I just have to hope that he can tap into some of that. And that he's still in there somewhere; that the Red hasn't taken full possession yet.

He smirks. It's JJ's smile and it's not JJ's smile, and it's the most unnerving thing. "Yes."

"It's a Red. A demon. I need your help. We'll work together. You push, I pull. Can you do that for me?"

The smile falls from his face. "No."

"We have to evict it. Get it out."

"Why? I like it."

But the JJ I know wouldn't want to be inhabited by a Red. I don't know exactly what happened to get him to this point. He was upset about me wearing his amulet; angry and resentful, and it's clearly made him vulnerable to inhabitation. I think Jonathan must have tracked JJ down, but when the Red saw JJ's potential, it decided to inhabit him instead.

And now JJ thinks he likes it. He doesn't; he's being manipulated. After last night, I have some sense of what that feels like. "You don't. It's showing you a fantasy; one I know you don't want."

With or without JJ's help, I have to evict. I reach up and grab as much magic as I can. I say one round of the spell, calm and strong and allowing for no uncertainty.

This is going to work. It has to.

His eyes flicker. "What are you doing?"

He can feel it then, the eviction spell. It's not working yet, but I'm just getting started. "Getting rid of the demon. Feel free to chip in."

A cold fist wraps around my heart. I draw in a sharp gasp against the sudden pain and stumble forward before steadying myself, placing a hand over my chest, as if that could help.

"I want my amulet."

I need to focus on my spell but it's hard with the icy squeeze. I need all my attention just to breathe. I try again to get JJ to help. "You don't want to do this, JJ. This is not you. You know I'll give the amulet back when Aiden gives the word."

A sob breaks from his throat. It's JJ, but it doesn't last. The fist around my heart squeezes. It's not crushing my heart – not yet. It's testing what it can do with the amulet around my neck.

I need to work fast. The pressure builds as I cant the spell again. Slowly but steadily, he's exploring how far he can push. What's going to happen if he keeps crushing. Whether it matters that Aiden's protected the amulet. Whether it matters that I'm a witch.

I break on a sob, stumble again. Pain is spearing through me, and Chalice, it hurts. I'm being squeezed to death from the inside, my heart compressed by an ever-tightening vice. I haven't completed the second round. I need to finish it but I can't. My panic is growing. I can barely breathe, let alone speak.

The screws tighten. I almost black out, fall to my knees. My hands are at my chest, uselessly clawing. If I could crack my ribs open to ease some of the horrendous pressure, I would. If I don't do something, I will die.

Please. Help.

I yell the words in my head, begging the amulet to intervene. I can feel it – the ebb and flow of power swirling through me – but it's hesitant. Then I work out why. JJ is its true owner; it doesn't know what to make of this situation. It does just enough to allow my heart to keep beating.

I hear Aiden before I see him; footsteps covering the ground at speed. I manage to look up. The look on his face is pure horror, the whites of his eyes shining bright.

"Run." When he wasn't here, he wasn't in danger. I want it to come out as a scream, but it is barely audible. He doesn't run. On my knees, struggling to get breath into my lungs, I watch as he strengthens the portal. Nothing happens. He tries an evict spell, but it's nothing to the Red. The Red is ignoring Aiden, still fixated on the amulet, trying to work out why my heart's still beating against the force of his crush.

Aiden swings to JJ, desperation written all over his face. "JJ! Push it out!"

There is a pause, then a sob. "I can't. I don't know how." It's a whimper; a flash of the real JJ.

The Red takes possession again and it's not happy. I grunt, double over in agony as my chest burns with ice, hands on the concrete to prop myself up. My vision keeps blacking out. I can hear the desperate rasp of my breath.

The Red is trying to kill me now, there is no doubt. The amulet is protecting my heart for the moment, but it won't do more than that.

That's not JJ; it's a demon, I yell at it.

But the line between demon and human is thin, and the amulet wants to serve its master. Inhabited or not.

"Use the amulet, Harlow!"

I want to laugh. I would if I wasn't in such wretched pain. It's not like I haven't begged for help. "It's JJ," I manage. "It won't go against him."

Aiden looks to JJ, then back to me. "You said you have one more in you. Promise me you'll evict, even if it kills me."

I gape up at him. I must be in even worse shape than I thought because his words make no sense. His head goes down, his shoulders bunch, there's an eerie stillness, then Aiden's power sweeps through me. Wizard power. But he's not directing it at me; he's directing it at JJ.

Wizard magic and demons don't mix. What's he doing? He's going to make the demon stronger.

Aiden's efforts distract the Red enough to loosen the vice around my heart. I fall forward on my hands, looking up at Aiden and sucking in oxygen like I'll never get enough.

"I push, you pull."

I hear his words but in my haze, they make no sense. Nothing makes sense. I need to get back into the game.

Aiden locks gazes with me. "I love you." He turns to JJ, drops his head back, spreading his arms wide, opening his chest. "You'll get further with me. I'm stronger than JJ and closer to evil than he'll ever be. Inhabit me instead."

No.

No. No. No.

JJ slumps then falls unconscious to the ground.

Aiden's whole body jerks. He lowers his arms, his head. It's there in the stiff, unyielding lines of his body. When he turns to me, there is no hint of his earlier tenderness. There is only cruel domination.

He is a warlord, come to decimate.

I struggle to my feet, everything in me hurting.

I look at the Red; it looks back. Aiden-not-Aiden.

He's trying to bend me to his will. But I will not succumb. One more big one, and I have to make it stick. I grab more magic and start.

The Red grips my heart, fierce and unrelenting. I know I've got seconds to live. Through the overwhelming numbing pain, I force the words out. The amulet is no longer confused. I am not its true owner but it knows me. And it hates demons. It throws a shield up around my heart – a true impermeable barrier – and then another one around the whole of me. The Red can't get to me.

I focus. I put everything into it, drawing on every drop of power I can squeeze from myself, from the amulet. Energy runs through me, a tornado, wild unfettered power beyond anything I've experience before. I am lightening. I am the storm. And I am coming for the Red.

The Red gives up on the heart crush. I see the cold ferocity in his eyes. He's going to break the shield around me and rip the amulet from my neck. Rip my throat out for good measure.

I don't know how long the amulet can hold out against him.

I give myself, and the amulet, full rein. I push everything I am at the Red but it's not enough. I need help. I need Aiden.

"Aiden, you have to fight. I pull, you push, remember?"

Aiden's head cocks, but all I can see is the Red.

"Push, Aiden!" I hiss.

He is closing in. Beating back my efforts to evict.

If I can't get this to work, I'll lose Aiden forever. He'll be a warlord or he'll be dead. I promised him I would evict.

The Red takes another step closer. Beneath his fury, I can see Aiden. The man I love.

I can't lose him.

I can't.

I love him. I love him. I want to spend my life with him.

All the stupid things I've told myself, allowed myself to believe … And now all I want is a future with him.

"Aiden, I want you to stay."

He pauses.

"Of course I want you to stay. I should have said it when you asked. I want you to stay and I want us to be together. A team. For good."

It might only be for an instant, but I swear it is Aiden, not the Red, staring back. I let out a tortured gasp. He's still in there.

"Whatever comes next, I want to share it with you. But first, I need you to get rid of this demon."

I curse my own bullheadedness. Why have I not said this before? Why have I not told him how I feel? Because I was scared. But I'm not a coward. I pour all my feelings, everything I am, into making this work. "Aiden, I love you. Please, please come back to me. I need you."

Something flares in his dark-brown eyes, something that is wholly and only Aiden.

And then I feel him. His incredible force. It starts small but it grows. His head is down, his focus is absolute. He is expanding from the inside, giving the Red nowhere to lodge. It is freaking awesome.

I get back behind my spell, and I give everything in me.

The Red fights, ferocious in its desire to stay in this world, but we are a team and we are relentless.

And then it's gone.

Aiden lands on his knees then plunges forward.

Two wizards. Black hair. Face down. But one is JJ, not Jonathan. I give him a quick glance, check his chest is moving.

Then I'm at Aiden's side, running my hands over his face, his neck. Checking for breathing, a pulse. If he hasn't made it ... If I've made the wrong choice ... I won't want to live.

With a groan, he pushes himself to his side, supporting himself on his elbow, head still down. I can hear his ragged intakes and exhales. "JJ?" His voice is raspy.

I take another quick glance to confirm my earlier judgement. JJ's out for the count but his chest is rising and falling. "He's okay."

They're both alive. I can't believe it.

With a monumental effort, he looks up at me. "Say it again," he wheezes out.

Heat flushes over me.

"Say it again. Now that it's not to save me."

I know what he wants to hear.

Is it different, putting it all out there now, when there's no clear and present danger? Hell, yes. But he needs to hear it. And I want to say it.

"I said I loved you. I said I wanted you to stay with me in Melbourne. But on reflection, I don't think that's going to work."

He looks at me, still. I lean forward and kiss him.

"I've got an idea of what comes next," I whisper, drawing back a little. Mum was right. I do know myself. "We're going to need to travel."

For the first time ever, Aiden smiles back.

EPILOGUE

Across the back seat of JJ's ancient little green Toyota, I link my fingers through Aiden's. These past weeks, I've barely let him go. Craving him like a drug, an addiction I have no intention of fighting.

"Move, JJ! You have to be in the right lane." From the front passenger seat, Everly casts rapid glances back over her right shoulder, checking the coast is clear. "Go!"

JJ doesn't go. "You said we're turning left," he says mutinously.

"From the right lane!" She glances over her whole shoulder again. "Bloody hell! We've missed our chance. You'll have to take the next exit."

I swap a quick grimace with Aiden. Things between JJ and Everly are not good.

We're on our way to the airport. Aiden and I have a flight to snowy Russia.

I want to see the portal Alina was working with. I want to rummage through the Moscow Firebird Coven's library and see if she left anything else I can use. I want to talk to her coven – see what stories they may still have about Alina, and how they handle demons now.

It's not sitting by a pool sipping Mai Tais – but it's my kind of leave.

And Aiden's, thankfully.

Everly makes eye contact with me in the mirror. "When's the flight back again?"

"Gets in at eight in the evening on the thirteenth."

Our trip's only a fortnight. I wouldn't mind going for longer, touching base with some of the other European covens, but it's what I can get at the moment. Judy is covering the portal while we're away; Claire and Lucinda are helping her. They still want to go ahead with demon hunting – we'll start training properly in the new year. Soon they'll be fully up to speed and Aiden and I can leave it to them. I can't wait.

We'll be on hand, of course. We'll be on hand for all the covens of the world.

This is what we'll be doing from now on – researching everything demon, demon realm and portals; developing better ways to deal with those DFs; and acting as consultants and support for any demon hunter who needs us. Being the only ones to successfully evict a Red with no casualties gives us a certain cachet. When I put the idea forward, the Coven Council, and other covens around the world, were keen as mustard.

"I'm driving next time," Everly snips at JJ.

"It's my car," JJ shoots back.

"I'm a better driver."

"In your dreams."

"Jun Jie." That's Aiden, rumbling out a warning.

JJ changes into an inappropriate gear in response.

Aiden's jaw is tense; I catch his eye, give him a 'Don't sweat it; Everly deserved it' look. Aiden gives me a half-smile and falls back against the seat, looking out his window. JJ is still living at Owlscroft. Aunt Bernie offered and JJ readily agreed. I don't think Aiden would have left him otherwise. Even so, I know he's still worried. I want to tell him JJ will be fine while we're away – that Aunt Bernie will take care of him – but I know it won't make the worry go away.

Physically JJ is fine, but being inhabited by a Red has changed him. He's not the happy-go-lucky, video-game-playing, not-quite-adult he was a month ago. He's retreated into himself, only emerging to make the occasional sullen remark. He's stepped back big time from Aiden – which honestly was pretty overdue anyway. But he has no interest in his amulet; he even tried to get me to keep it. I still want an amulet, but I won't take JJ's. It's back in the bank vault for the time being.

He was able to tell us at least some of how he came to be inhabited. It wasn't Jonathan who found JJ; it was JJ who found Jonathan. Everly confided in him her vision of the future – of Aiden lying dead on the ground. JJ decided he'd deal with the problem himself. He stole the beheading sword and snuck out to confront the Red – invincible teenager style. The Red decided he liked the cut of JJ's jib and jumped ship.

Everly feels terrible; she blames herself for what happened. And somehow that's translated into her being constantly catty and snipy to JJ. She also watches him like a hawk, like Mum on her worst day.

They were friends before this happened. They're still together all the time, but are they friends? Not clear.

We finally pull up in the drop-off zone. Everly turns. "You remember my order, right?"

"Snow globe. Pretty not tacky."

She grins and bats her eyelids. "Make that extremely pretty."

I roll my eyes. "Anything I can try and get for you, JJ?" I ask as I unbuckle. "Last chance."

"New life? Do they sell one of those in Moscow?"

Aiden's hand stills on his buckle. The grin falls from Everly's face.

I decide to take it as JJ's new morbid humour. "I'll keep my eyes open."

I think maybe his mouth twitches.

We say our goodbyes and grab our bags. I make sure I've got my notebook with our list of priorities. Aiden's brief time as a Red provided many insights, including how Jonathan found them in the first place. Still seeking to avenge JJ's father, Jonathan sought inhabitation through the Singapore portal. When the Red learned of

Jonathan's search for JJ's amulet, it recognised Aiden because of Aiden's work as a demon hunter – all the demons he's evicted took some kind of visual of him back through the portal – and knew roughly where to find him and JJ.

We had no idea that demons took memories of their time on earth back. It's ground-breaking information, and requires much further research.

Which we're about to get started on.

Together.

~

I HOPE you enjoyed Harlow's story! For Everly's story, stayed tuned for the next volume of the *A Perfectly Paranormal* series, *A Perfectly Paranormal Easter*, coming in April 2022.

ALSO BY MARNIE ST CLAIR

If you enjoyed this story, you may enjoy my other works:

Bad Batch

An Owlscroft Coven Novella, Book 1

(In A Perfectly Paranormal Valentine)

No Place Like You

A sweet but sizzling rural romance

Blue Steal

A witty and suspenseful romantic mystery

ABOUT MARNIE

After years of forecasting the price of tea in China, Marnie St Clair finally shut down the spreadsheets and got serious about her passion for romance, especially the kind that blends charm, humour and a dollop of magic and mystery.

A country girl at heart, Marnie now lives in Melbourne, Australia, with two surprisingly civil teens and a weatherman husband. She likes prosecco, cottage gardens, driving at night, sandalwood-scented anything and a really strong cup of coffee. Or preferably two.

You can contact Marnie through her website www.marniestclair.com, where you can also sign up to her newsletter to be the first to find out about new releases, special deals and exclusive giveaways.

And if you want to get to know the Perfectly Paranormal Anthology authors a bit more, get sneak peeks of what's coming up for the APP Anthologies, as well as giveaways, special offers and just some PNR fun, then join our Perfectly Paranormal Paramours Facebook Group.

Find us here:

https://www.facebook.com/groups/251663560162131

facebook.com/Marnie-St-Clair-1424659434526822

instagram.com/marnie_st_clair

ACKNOWLEDGMENTS

A big heartfelt thanks to the *A Perfectly Paranormal Anthology* contributors – Hellucy Howe, Leisl Leighton and Samantha Marshall – and former contributor Georgia Tingley for inviting me to be part of the group. *A Perfectly Paranormal* has been a blast to be part of and I look forward to future instalments.

Thanks as always to lovely Mady (no sister like you) and my writing group pals Leisl and Frana for the continued support and friendship.

A million kisses to my biggest support and own personal weatherman.

HEADLESS

SAMANTHA MARSHALL

HEADLESS

A Merged Worlds
Novella

Samantha Marshall

🌸 Created with Vellum

ABOUT HEADLESS

What would you do for redemption?

Being a demon isn't easy. Ivory would know: she's spent most of her life as one. Survival is a day-to-day balancing act; she doesn't have time for the tall, dark, handsome – and headless – ex-knight who claims she's the only one who can help him on his ancient quest.

Yeah, right.

Devlin didn't think his un-life could get any worse. With his honour in tatters and long, lonely centuries behind him, all he wants is a chance to atone for his sins and break his curse. It seems simple enough, except the demon who can break said curse has better things to do with her time – like running from the Demon Hunters who followed *him* to town, destroying the meagre existence she'd eked out for herself.

Oops.

Still, Devlin's as determined as Ivory is ornery – and with a common enemy forcing them to work together, he's got a second chance to change her mind. All he has to do is turn up the charm, appeal to the sense of honour his sinfully delicious demonic companion doesn't have, and hope she doesn't mount his head on her wall as a trophy – or worse, his heart.

*To Disney's Halloween Feast, which first introduced me to the concept of the
Headless Horseman.*
*To the Monster Mash, and the Time Warp, upon which my love of both fun
and spooky are built.*

*To Big Boo's Haunt, where I learned to love cute little ghosts with their
tongues hanging out, and to Mad Monster Mansion, where I laughed every
time I got turned into a pumpkin and flushed down the toilet.*

*To Terry Pratchett, who had me falling head over heels for Death the first
time I ever read him, and is consequently responsible for my fascination with
skellingtons.*

*To Link, who taught me that monsters disappear when the sun comes up, and
that it's okay to put ghosts in a bottle until you're ready to face them.*

*To the Scarlet Monastery Graveyard, which I visited every year without fail
and still managed to never get hold of the elusive flying horse. To Shtinky,
who got the horse first try and rode it everywhere for the next fifteen years
with a smug look on his face.*

To Illidan, who taught me that demons could be sexy.
*To the friends who have never questioned my penchant for drawing ghosts,
reading vampire books, howling at the moon and just generally being kooky.*

To everyone, everywhere, who loves a bit of Halloween aesthetic all year round, just like I do.

Most of all, to those beyond the veil. I hear you.
♥

BEGIN AS YOU MEAN TO GO ON

Trees loomed ahead, and Devlin's fingers tightened on the wheel as the RV bumped off the road and onto the grass. Despite reading the operations manual from cover to cover several times, in the heat of the moment he couldn't remember which of the various pedals was for acceleration, braking or, in a twist of creative inspiration he'd never understand, the built-in drinking spout which jettisoned water in case of an unreasonable thirst.

He stomped down hard with his left foot and yelped as said water splashed across his chest. Not that one, clearly – and those evergreens really did look quite menacing, now that he was close enough to make out individual branches. Shifting his foot to the right, Devlin stomped again and the RV jerked to a halt, momentum throwing him against the dish-like centre of the steering wheel hard enough to set the horn blaring – a sound that cut off as the vehicle rocked back on its axle, returning his body to the seat amidst a symphony of clanging pots, clattering crockery and Bailey's indignant shriek.

"My pardon," he called, offering a sheepish grin. Bailey glared from where she now lay upside down on the floor after tumbling off the RV's bed, blankets tangled around her legs. Devlin sighed, pushing himself upright. "Stopping is more complicated than it at first appears."

Bailey curled a lip.

"Are you injured?" Devlin tried to peer down the length of the vehicle, but his head had lodged at an awkward angle on the dash. When Bailey didn't answer, he braced against the steering wheel and leaned over until he could tangle his fingers in his own hair. Ignoring the sharp tug against his scalp, he positioned his head under one arm and levered out of the driver's seat.

Perusing one's environment from one's own armpit had taken some getting used to – and a revised hygiene routine – but after more centuries than he dared record, Devlin had become accustomed to it. He'd become accustomed to a lot of things, the sort of things he'd never imagined having to become accustomed to until his head was permanently separated from his body. Such was the nature of being cursed.

"Hold still a moment, or you'll make it worse." Devlin sat his head on a stack of books so that he could see both his body and Bailey, then set about disentangling her legs from the blanket and getting her back onto the bed without either of them tripping over one another. That trick alone had taken him decades to perfect – though perfection, really, was in the eye of the beholder, and Bailey wasn't the kind to be impressed when one poked her in said eye because he'd placed his head at a strange angle and couldn't quite see her face.

He took a half step back from the bed. "Better now?"

Bailey narrowed her eyes at him.

"I'll take that as a yes. Will you accompany me on my errand, or am I going alone?"

Her eyes narrowed further, until her irises were little more than baleful slits.

"Alone it is." Devlin straightened the clothes he'd obtained at their previous rest stop.

He was still becoming used to modern clothing, but the tight denim he'd acquired felt somewhat, if not exactly, like his old leather breeches and the black t-shirt, though a little snug, was reminiscent of the linen shirts he'd once worn beneath his tunic. Since the shop owners had screamed and fled when he'd accidentally knocked his head off on a low-hanging display, Devlin hadn't been able to ask about armour or even pay for his items – but he'd found a stand of leather jackets that, whilst their protective value appeared doubtful, were lined with fleece and had a nice, high collar.

Devlin picked up the roll of flexible, adhesive cloth he'd discovered in the RV's bathing room and examined the box. "This ... kinesio-tape claims maximum adhesion with minimal skin irritation, and yet my head still fell off. Maybe I didn't use enough?"

Bailey rolled over to stare at the wall.

"I apologised for the sudden stop," Devlin grumbled, pulling the roll of tape from the box. It was a brilliant lime green with a removable backing protecting the sticky side. "I cannot do this alone, Bailey. Please."

She heaved a dramatic sigh, then shuffled to the edge of the bed and picked his head up by the hair. While Devlin faced the mirrored closet door, Bailey held his head on top of his neck so that he could secure it in place with the tape.

"Is it on straight?"

Bailey eyed him up and down, then jerked her chin in a nod and returned to the bed.

"Are you going to cease talking to me for the rest of the day?" Devlin snipped off several long lengths of tape and began wrapping the stuff around his neck as best he could. When he had a band as wide as his four fingers, he stopped and jumped up and down in place. "I'm far more hopeful about this excessive amount of tape. My head feels almost solid."

Bailey grunted, but some of the tension eased from her shoulders.

"Do you think I should take my sword?" Devlin twisted to look out of one of the RV's windows, eyeing the township beyond. Nobody in this new, modern world carried swords and the few times he'd tried, he'd had a less than ideal reception. He clicked his tongue against his teeth. "No sword."

Bailey sniggered.

"I fail to see the joke," Devlin snapped, snatching his leather jacket from the hook on the back of the door. "You're not the one facing a journey without her sword strapped in place atop her armour."

He drew his jacket on, then picked up a striped black and grey scarf and wound it around his neck to hide the tape. Tucking the ends of the scarf into themselves, Devlin fastened the jacket via the unusual but convenient contraption he'd learned was called a zipper, and held his arms out for inspection.

"Well?"

Bailey's eyes drifted unerringly to his hair, long enough that one of them could grab it in order to carry his head around. At the current moment, it stuck up at all angles, testament to the fact that they'd both been doing exactly that.

"Not much I can do," Devlin muttered, trying to fix the unruly mess as best he could. "If I comb it, I run the risk of dislodging my head entirely."

Bailey's lips pressed together but laughter shone in her eyes. Devlin grumbled as he stomped back to the front of the RV, snatching the silver key from the ignition and sliding it into his pocket.

"Defend our home then, if you're not coming along." Without bothering to wait for her answer, he opened the door and climbed down to the ground.

A chill wind swept the grassed area in which he'd parked the vehicle, swirling dust and leaves before it. Devlin was glad of his scarf and jacket as he closed the door of the RV and made his way towards the small cluster of shops on the other side of the road. Clouds hung overhead, dark with the threat of rain, and the early morning saw a thin fog curling against the ground much like a lazy cat.

He risked a glance down at his palms, still bearing the same callouses they had at the moment of his ... not quite death. Broad hands, flecked with scars he'd earned honourably – or at least, that's what he'd thought at the time. Devlin clenched his hands and shoved them in his jacket pockets. His neck itched the further he went and every curious face that turned his way made him flinch – but nobody screamed or backed away as he rounded the front of the nearest building, following the phantom tug in his chest that had led him on such a wild chase.

The shops were clumped together in groups of two or three, with neatly swept front steps and coloured awnings. Gut twisting, Devlin hesitated outside a shop with stylised letters on the door and magical paraphernalia in the windows. If he were to progress further, to reach for the one and only thing that could absolve his many sins, he would have to confront a creature he'd once sworn to hunt and destroy; a creature to whom he now owed a terrible debt.

Shame burnt his cheeks as he studied the shiny brass handle before him. Had he really come so far only to balk now? He thought of all the long, lonely years he and Bailey had been trapped in their secluded hollow and frowned. He owed it to her, to his sins, and to himself to set things right once and for all – to have courage, even in the darkest times.

Squaring his shoulders, Devlin opened the door and went in search of a demon.

2

MIND YOUR MANNERS

Tucked in a chair by the open fire, Ivory hummed softly to herself as she ground pestle into mortar. It was well past the time she usually lingered at Mystic Madhouse, and she certainly wasn't of a mind to turn the raw materials she sold into actual products, but ... with Halloween only a few days away, the little shop was overrun with requests for outlandish ingredients and pre-brewed potions. Jacinta had reached out for help and though Ivory didn't much like being beholden to anyone, she did owe the businesswoman a favour or two.

Ivory glanced over the meticulously detailed potion recipe on the arm of the chair and then down at her mortar and pestle, judging the state of the ingredients inside. Being what she was, she didn't need the recipe for more than the list of components – nor did she require the ridiculous verse the author insisted must be chanted while the mixture was formalised into a whole.

Dipping a clawed finger into the mortar, Ivory drew out the tiniest sample of her work and flicked it into the open fire. A great hiss went up, as though some horrid beast crouched among the logs, and the flames flared momentarily blue before returning to their normal orange and yellow.

Perfect.

"Um ... Ivory?"

Swallowing a sigh, Ivory glanced towards the doorway where Jacinta stood wringing her hands. "What is it?"

"There's a ... uh. Someone here, that I ... um. I need your help."

"*My* help?" Ivory tipped her head to the side, brow furrowing. Jacinta was a powerful mage, the left forearm bared by her sleeveless dress marked by two thick bands of sapphire blue that warned anyone who cared to look that she was well and truly capable of defending herself. "What for?"

"It's ..." Jacinta trailed off, pinching the bridge of her nose. "You'll see. Please?"

Please. Ack. Ivory made a face, the very air souring with the taste of such a pathetic word. Still, Jacinta had opened Mystic Madhouse to her when she was starving. When nobody else would so much as twitch aside their blinds, the mage had offered kindness and acceptance – a gift Ivory had snatched with greedy hands, even as she hated herself for needing it.

"Fine," Ivory groused, rolling out of her chair. After a final grind of mortar against pestle, she tipped the mixture into a jar, screwed on the lid and dusted her hands together. "I can finish the liniment later."

Jacinta's gaze tracked to the recipe balanced on the arm of Ivory's chair. "I thought it was a draught?"

"A liniment will work better."

"The recipe says—"

"The recipe is stupid," Ivory snapped. "As is whoever wrote it. Were they watching old cartoons about witches while they squiggled in their fake pigskin notebook?"

Jacinta rolled her eyes. "You really are a bitch, you know that?"

"Thank you." Ivory followed the other woman out the door and down the short flight of stairs to the main shop. "Are you sure want me going out there? Looking like *this*?"

"I need you to," Jacinta said, her expression sombre in a way Ivory had rarely seen. "Pl—"

"Don't say it," Ivory snapped. She dusted her hands on her jeans, then blew out a breath. "Fine. You were warned."

Mystic Madhouse was set out much like a conventional grocery store, with neat aisles running parallel down the length of the floor. The sales counter was at the back of the area, blocking access to the rest of the building, and the glass windows at the opposite end let in enough light to see by without blinding. For the most part, the shop was functional more than ornamental – but with Halloween only a matter of days away, jack o'lanterns dotted every available surface while cheerful bats and smiling skeletons peered down from the ever-green garlands framing the walls and windows.

A man stood at the counter, his eyes a peculiar shade of light green that was anything but natural. Long lashes lowered to half-mast as he turned those eyes on her, giving him an air of menace that immediately piqued Ivory's interest. He was almost obscenely tall, with shoulders broad enough to block out most of the light from the windows. Though shadows clung to his form, they were no impediment to Ivory's vision; she drank in the rugged lines of his face, from his shaggy, dark brown hair to the slight scruff on his jaw and the tiny scar that bisected the skin just below his left eye. A striped scarf poked from the high collar of a black leather jacket, below which Ivory glimpsed jeans that fit tight enough to show off unfairly muscular thighs.

Handsome wasn't a strong enough word to describe him – in fact, if she'd been the poetic type, Ivory fancied there wouldn't *be* a word to accurately portray the look of him correctly. If that wasn't bad enough, he opened his mouth and the words that poured out were guttural and deep, the intonation in his voice striking against Ivory's soul as though she were some ritual instrument he alone knew how to play. Her breath caught as the sounds rolled over her, *through* her, and when he stopped, she could only turn to Jacinta and gape.

The mage spread her hands and shrugged. "I have no idea what he's saying. Do you?"

Ivory swallowed, and when she turned back to the man, found him eyeing her as intensely as she'd been eyeing him. She lifted a hand to the black horns that curled from her skull just behind her temples, somewhat reminiscent of a ram's but much, much deadlier. Even after all these years, instinct screamed at her to cover them, but instead, she tugged one of her black dreadlocks and tried to recall how Jacinta addressed her customers.

"May I help you?" Ivory offered, speaking in the same language he'd used.

The man frowned, looking for all the world as though he'd bitten into a sour lemon. "I come seeking a demon."

Ivory snorted. "There's only one kind of man who goes looking for demons – and if you're going to try and murder me in this store, Hunter, it'll be the last mistake you ever make."

"You misunderstand. I am no Hunter," he replied, the gravel in his voice rasping over her skin until Ivory fought the urge to shiver. "You, however, appear to be a demon."

"What gave it away? The horns, or the claws? The black eyes, perhaps? Or maybe ..." Ivory drew her lips wide in the parody of a smile. "The fangs?"

The stranger touched a scarred hand to his breastbone. "I know because I can feel it."

Ivory took a second look at the way those pale green eyes seemed to flicker with their own internal light and felt her heart skip a beat. "You're a demon, too."

The man jerked backwards as though slapped, making a swift grab for his head. When he lowered his hands a moment later, his expression was so conflicted that Ivory let out a dreamy sounding sigh. He was so full of angst, so gorgeous and tortured, and it was *perfect*.

"I was not always a demon," he muttered. "I was cursed by one, and I deserved it. For eons, I've endured my punishment without complaint but now ... now that I'm free to travel the Earth, I wish to atone for my sins." Drawing himself up to his full height, he pinned Ivory with those bright eyes. "In order to repent, I need the curse broken – and my quest has brought me here."

An ancient demon, a curse, and a quest? Ivory snorted. If the guy in front of her wasn't so clearly brimming with demonic energy, she'd have laughed him out of the store and then kicked his ass all the way down the street.

"What does he want?" Jacinta hissed from behind the counter.

Ivory switched languages, darting a glance at her employer. "To have a curse broken."

"A curse?" Jacinta raised an eyebrow. "I could take a look, I suppose—"

"A demonic curse."

"Oh." She shrugged. "Nothing I can do about that."

"I know." Turning back to the towering stranger, Ivory spoke in his language again. "Jacinta can't help you. Her magic is strong, but not in the way you need."

He frowned. "Unless you're the one named Jacinta, then it is not her help I'm seeking."

"Me?" Ivory took a half step back, then laughed. "Wait, wait, wait. You think *I* can break your curse?"

"You must." Bracing both enormous hands on the counter, the man leaned forward. "Though we've never met, the tug of my curse does not lie. You are the one, the descendant of she who bound me." His fingers curled, as though he might sprout claws and dig them into the wood but, to Ivory's disappointment, nothing happened. "It is you and you alone who can break the spell and allow my debt to be repaid. Please."

Ivory curled her lip. Please, this. Please, that. It was what everyone said to get what they wanted – but the moment they had it? She was little more than a novelty whose shine had worn off, revealing the monster underneath. Gods, she hated that word.

"Not in the shop!" Jacinta yelped, tugging at Ivory's sleeve for attention. "It took me forever to fix the damage last time."

"What?" Ivory blinked at the mage, then belatedly realised she'd bared her teeth on a threatening hiss. Forcing her body to relax, she shook her head. "Don't worry; I won't break anything."

The man's gaze lit on Jacinta's smattering of freckles and neatly styled brown hair, and his expression softened. "Peace. As soon as your colleague and I reach an arrangement, I'll be gone and you'll be free to go about your business."

"She doesn't understand you," Ivory growled. "You have to speak English."

He blinked. "Am I not?"

"No." Ivory rounded the corner of the desk, ignoring Jacinta's pleas for them to take the situation outside. "You're speaking demonic."

Astonishment blanked his features before those lashes once again lowered to half mast. "Well, that explains a great many things. Perhaps when you break the—"

"No," Ivory repeated, moving forward until the toes of her shoes bumped his boots. "Find someone else to break your curse; someone who doesn't mind being ordered around."

"Ordered? I asked," he protested, holding both hands up in placation. "I spoke from the heart."

Ew. Ew, ew, ew. Ivory set a hand against his glorious chest and shoved until the stranger backed up several steps. "For the last time, no. Now get out of this shop, or I will throw you out."

Surprise and hurt shifted quickly to anger, those bright eyes snapping with demonic fire. "I should like to see you try."

Laughter bubbled in Ivory's chest and she darted closer, swiping out with clawed fingers. In a move so swift it was a blur, he wrapped a hand around her wrist and twisted. She went with the motion, leaping onto the counter and cartwheeling through the air to land on the opposite side. The stranger released her wrist with a grunt and she smacked his arm aside. With a sharp twist of her body, Ivory curled her free hand in his jacket and tucked one foot behind his ankle.

Jacinta screamed. Remembering that she wasn't supposed to damage the shop, Ivory resisted the urge to toss him over her shoulder and instead swept the man's foot out from beneath him, dumping him flat on his back at her feet. He hit the floorboards hard enough to shake the entire building, but it wasn't the unusually heavy impact that took Ivory's attention – it was the moment his head detached from his shoulders, rolling across the floor to lodge against a rack of tarot cards like some macabre sort of bowling ball.

"Damn," said the head. "I should have used more tape."

Jacinta screamed again, only this time it was a very different sort of scream; one that wasn't in warning but in anger. Glass tinkled, magic crackled in the air and before Ivory had a chance to so much as blink, the front of the shop exploded.

TAINTED AT BEST

*I*f Devlin was honest with himself – and after thousands upon thousands of years with only Bailey for company, there was no reason to lie – he hadn't been prepared to come face to face with the creature he'd sought for so long and find her ... beautiful.

Gorgeous.

Bearing the sort of face greater men than he would compose ballads about, and the sort of body that those greater men would have wept into their ale over. And since he was far, far removed from those greater men, Devlin had even found her demonic attributes attractive, wondering what it'd be like to run his hands over her horns or feel her sharp teeth grazing his skin.

Clearly, he was depraved.

Maybe even insane.

Probably both, since what he thought had been a respectable speech had sent her into a rage. And now, here he was, his head jammed most embarrassingly underneath a shelf, able to do little more than watch while his body was picked up by the force of the explosion and tossed against the shop counter, flattening the demon in the process.

"Jacinta?" The demon shoved his body aside and dragged herself upright. "Jacinta!"

Coughing preceded the mage, chest heaving as she staggered from the back room. "I'm fine. The shield spell won't hold long, so – holy shit!"

Devlin grimaced as the mage's eyes locked on his stump of a neck. The demon, too, seemed transfixed as he stood and dusted himself off before reaching to dislodge his head from beneath the shelf.

"Is he … is that …" The mage shook her head as though to clear it, her face turning green, then white, then green again.

"It's all right," Devlin muttered, tugging the remains of the kinesio-tape from his skin. "I won't hurt you."

The mage lifted her hands and swallowed. "Ivory?"

"He says he won't hurt you," the demon – Ivory – said, peering around Devlin to look towards the front of the shop. "And right now, he's the least of our worries. There are Demon Hunters out there."

"Hunters?" Jacinta frowned. "I haven't said anything, I swear."

"I know." Ivory hissed out a breath. "Either they've picked up my trail some other way … or they're here for him."

"Me?" Devlin frowned. "It's possible. I had a few, er, unusual occurrences on my way here that may have drawn undue attention."

Ivory raised a sculpted brow. "I can't imagine why."

"Yes. Well." Devlin tucked his head under one arm and tried not to pout. "Keeping my head on top of my shoulders is more difficult than it sounds."

Ivory ran a hand over her face, and Devlin took advantage of the moment to inspect her more fully. She had a wealth of ebony hair that fell in thick dreadlocks to her waist, the foremost of which were secured at the back of her head with a tie. Her almond-shaped eyes were obsidian jewels, set in a delicate face with clear skin just a hint too pale to be natural. A silver hoop pierced one nostril and the sharp horns that curled from her temples were also black, as were the tips of her fingers and her curved claws.

She was breathtaking, even in her simple, torn jeans and the snug navy tank that showed off flared hips, rippling muscles and breasts that, were he of a ravishing mind, Devlin had no doubt would fill his hands to bursting.

And, oh, the more he looked at her, the more he was of a ravishing mind.

"Regardless of who they're after, there are Hunters at my door," Jacinta said, her voice strained.

Reminded of the threat, Devlin turned towards the front of the shop as another explosion slammed into the windows. Though this one bore no shockwave thanks to the mage's shield spell, the entire building creaked and smoke obscured the street beyond.

Ivory sighed and dropped her hand. "You're right. We'll have to run."

"You don't want to fight?" Devlin frowned as he glanced between the two women. "You both seem skilled and I was once a Knight of the Round Table."

"A knight," Ivory repeated, disbelief thick in her voice.

"Yes."

"Without a head?"

"I ... Yes."

"Or armour."

"Indeed."

Ivory pursed her lips. "And your sword?"

"I didn't bring it."

"So, then, Sir Useless—"

"Devlin," he put in quickly, sketching a deeper bow than before. "Sir Devlin, my lady."

"*Sir* Devlin," Ivory drawled, leaning one hip against the counter. "I don't know how much experience you have with Hunters, but they're like a hydra; cut off one head and two more will spawn. When they return, they'll do so en masse, and Jacinta will lose everything." She drummed her fingers on the countertop. "If we run, Jacinta can claim we attacked her and then fled."

"I'd never say that!" Jacinta thumped a fist against her chest. "This is my shop, and I offered you a safe space within it. If those Hunters think—"

"Stop. We both know this is pointless," Ivory snapped. "I won't have your death, or worse, on my conscience."

Jacinta pursed her lips, fine lines of strain developing at the corners of her eyes. "All right. I can buy you enough time to slip out the back, but that's about it."

Ivory nodded, and though her expression was firm, the look she shared with the mage was almost ... sad. "Thank you," she murmured. "For everything."

Jacinta nodded once, then lifted her arms. The two blue bands inked into her skin began to glow, the same light trickling from her fingertips as she traced arcane symbols in the air.

"Come on." Ivory grabbed Devlin's wrist and hauled him through the doorway behind the counter. "This way."

The back portion of the building consisted of two downstairs storage rooms, a short hall and a staircase, beneath which nestled an unassuming wooden door. Ivory released her grip on Devlin's arm to flatten herself against the wall, opening the door just enough to peer outside.

"It's clear for now, but that won't last." She flicked a glance over her shoulder. "Be ready to move, Sir Useless."

Devlin opened his mouth to reply but the words died in his throat as Ivory licked one of her fingers then drew it across the locking mechanism. Where her skin touched, she left a black smear that began to smoke and sizzle, melting the metal like so much candle wax.

"Amazing." Devlin edged closer, lifting his head to examine her handiwork. "How did you do that?"

Ivory didn't answer, striding through the door and into the open air beyond. Devlin followed her into a small courtyard nestled between the buildings. There was a herb box on one side and a two person outdoor setting on the other. Neatly swept pavers were bordered by a half-height brick wall which separated the back of the property from the narrow roadway beyond. He turned in time to see Ivory close the door, licking her finger to run a second black smudge over the outer edge of the metal security screen so that it, too, melted into the frame.

"My vehicle isn't far from here." Devlin pointed across the road where the RV's bulk could barely be seen through the trees. "If we can reach it, we can leave."

"That's not going to work." Ivory shook her head, long dreadlocks quivering as though they had a mind of their own. "The Hunters will have people watching any new or suspicious vehicles – assuming they weren't already tracking you before you arrived. You're better off cutting your losses while you can."

Devlin froze. "I can't leave my vehicle; Bailey's in there."

"So call Bailey and tell him to run for it," Ivory growled.

"Bailey is a she," Devlin huffed. "And I have no way to contact her apart from appearing in person. If we work together, you and I can overcome any trap the Hunters may have lain."

"What? Oh, no." Ivory leaped back as though burnt. "Considering you brought the Hunters down on my head and ruined what little of a life I've been able to create in this town, you're lucky I saved your ass back there as it is." She reached behind her, drawing the tie from her dreadlocks so that they tumbled around her face in gorgeous disarray. Devlin was so distracted by the silver clips and coloured beads woven into the foremost locks that he almost missed it when she said, "This is where we part ways, Sir Devlin."

There was no mistaking the bite of mockery in the way Ivory spoke his name. Devlin drew himself up to his full, headless height, adopting his haughtiest expression. "I will accept my fault in this matter, though I swear it was unintentional – but I must argue with your determination to part from me."

"Oh?" Ebony eyes drilled into his. "Because you need my help?"

"Yes," he admitted, "there is that. However, by your own admission, Hunters are not easily dissuaded. We stand a better chance of escape if we work together ... and I am worried for Bailey."

"Dammit." Ivory spat on the ground; her saliva shrivelled the grass where it landed. "I'm going to regret this; I just know it."

Devlin brightened. "You're going to help me?"

"And *you're* going to help *me*." She bared pointed teeth. "The deal is simple: I'll help you liberate Bailey and the RV if you agree to take me out of town, to a safe place of my choosing."

"Deal," Devlin offered his hand to seal the bargain, but Ivory merely raised a brow and stepped away. When she continued to watch him in silence, he sighed and dropped his arm. "Let's go."

Keeping his head tucked close to his chest and his body low, Devlin hurried across the road and into the trees that surrounded the RV. Ivory kept pace by his side, eyes partly narrowed and jaw clenched tight. Her movements were fluid and her steps silent, a feat that made Devlin feel like some sort of intruding brute stomping through the woods when, in reality, his own footfalls were so soft, most creatures would never hear them.

From the way Ivory kept glaring, she wasn't most creatures.

By the time they reached the small clearing where the RV was parked, he'd seen and scented three intruders; one high, watching from the limbs of an ancient tree, and the other two crouched deep in the underbrush on either side of the RV's single door, mostly camouflaged by their brown leathers.

When he glanced at Ivory – whose nose was raised to the air in a move that highlighted the length of her pale throat – she flared her nostrils and held up three fingers, pointing to each of the Hunters he'd already identified.

"No weapons," he mouthed. "You?"

Ivory flexed her fingers in such a way that he had no choice but to blink down at her claws – which grew as he watched, along with her horns, until they seemed far too large for her delicate head. The black of her irises bled outward, overtaking the whites and when she smiled, her pointed teeth were twice as long, barely contained within her mouth.

"Incredible," he breathed, rubbing at the sudden ache in his chest. Ivory was as deadly as she was beautiful, and he longed to pull her close and explore her altered features – but then she jerked her chin towards the Hunter in the treetops, reminding Devlin they'd come here for a reason.

He grunted an affirmative and began circling quietly through the trees towards the nearest of the Hunters on the ground. The man had a high-powered crossbow tucked under his chin, finger resting lightly on the trigger as he aimed at the RV's door.

Devlin smiled.

Time to demonstrate exactly what it meant to be a Knight of the Round Table.

DAMSEL IN DISTRESS

*L*eaving Devlin to handle the Hunters by the RV, Ivory shimmied up to the base of the tree, pausing to toe off her boots and let the claws on her feet grow to match the ones on her fingers. She should have walked away from the damnably handsome Sir Devlin when she had the chance – or, more accurately, tossed his ass out of Jacinta's shop the moment she'd heard him speaking demonic. Except she hadn't, and now she was here facing down Demon Hunters alongside a man whose head wasn't anywhere in the vicinity of his shoulders, all because she couldn't leave an innocent woman trapped inside the RV.

Bloody bleeding heart – will you never learn?

Swallowing her growl, Ivory dug her claws into the tree and began to climb. Her quarry perched about halfway up, his butt wedged in a sturdy fork while he straddled the thicker of two branches and stared through the scope on his crossbow. Ivory licked her left thumb as she drew level with his knees, causing the liniment on her claw to hiss and smoke. The Hunter gasped and twisted towards the noise, bringing the crossbow to bear with superhuman speed. Clenching the trunk between her thighs, Ivory blocked the weapon's progress and yanked on his wrist, bending the Hunter almost double so that she could wrap clawed fingers around his throat and sink her thumb into the flesh beneath his ear.

"Oops." She smiled as his eyes turned glassy. "That'll teach you, won't it?"

The Hunter's lashes slid shut, his body sagging in her grip. The crossbow tumbled from his hands and Ivory caught it before it could clatter against the trunk. Bracing against the tree, she wrestled the Hunter back into the same position she'd found him, then used his belt to tether the weapon further along the branch so that when he opened his eyes, he'd be staring at the poisoned tip on the end of the bolt. Licking one of her other claws, she wiped a cloudy smudge over the crossbow's firing mechanism. It automatically began to melt, crumpling until the weapon was completely unusable – though the Hunter wouldn't realise that when he woke up.

"Sweet dreams," she whispered and then, spotting Devlin in the clearing, dropped to the ground. By the time she straightened, her claws, teeth and horns had shrunk to their normal size.

"Did you kill him?" Devlin asked, waving a hand at the tree behind her.

"Of course." When he blinked, she snorted. "So gullible. No, he's not dead, just unconscious."

Devlin's dark brows beetled and Ivory was delighted to discover that he was just as handsome when annoyed. Perhaps more so, considering his eyes darkened and his jaw clenched, emphasising the scar on his cheek and the press of his lips against one another.

"You honourable warrior types are all the same," she muttered, rolling her eyes. "I'd like to point out that I'm not asking if you killed *your* allotted assholes or not."

His frown deepened. "Of course I didn't."

"Right. So, are you going to disapprove of me all day, or are we going to get out of here before these cockwads wake and we *do* have to kill them?"

Devlin shifted his head back and forth in his hands. Ivory would have bet everything she owned that he debated whether or not to climb the tree and see if the Hunter really was still breathing or not. In the end, he grunted and turned to the RV.

"Bailey?" he called. "I'm opening the door."

There was an oddly heavy thumping from inside the vehicle. Nodding in satisfaction, Devlin drew a key from his pocket, set it in the lock, and twisted. The door popped like a pressurised hatch, sliding aside to reveal the few steps into the RV. Ivory got a glimpse of the driver's seat and a set of overhead cupboards before an enormous black shape barrelled down the stairs and onto the grass.

"What in the world is *that?*" she demanded, unable to contain the utter astonishment in her voice.

Devlin raised an eyebrow. "That? You mean Bailey?"

"*That's* Bailey? I thought Bailey was your lover!" Ivory stared at the creature and shook her head.

The easiest word to describe Bailey was 'horse', though even as it popped up in her head, Ivory knew the term to be woefully inadequate. Bailey was taller and broader through the chest and shoulders than any horse Ivory had ever seen. Her coat, mane and tail were a shimmering, glossy black and her eyes the same pale, demonic lime green as Devlin's – only her pupils were slitted like a cat's, rather than round like a horse's should be. Her hooves were big enough to crush dinner plates and surrounded by long, silky fur that flipped and danced as she pranced in place, head high and nostrils dilated.

"My lover?" Devlin's whole body shook with laughter. "No, Bailey is my companion. Once, she was a destrier, the noblest of knightly steeds. But since the curse ..."

"Deathcharger," Ivory breathed, clasping her hands to her chest as Bailey opened her mouth to reveal long, pointed fangs. "Oh, she's beautiful. Aren't you, girl?"

Bailey postured and snorted smoke for another moment or two, then, ears flattened against her head, extended her nose to sniff Ivory from hip to shoulder.

"She's very intelligent," Devlin began, looking somewhat ill as Bailey's fang-filled mouth came ever closer to Ivory's throat. "And can be somewhat ... ah ... temperamental."

"Hello, gorgeous," Ivory murmured, staring into Bailey's luminous gaze. "I know all about being called temperamental – it means people don't have the fortitude to handle us as we truly are. Don't listen to Sir Useless, hmm? You're perfect." She lowered her voice to a whisper. "We are kin, you and I."

Bailey made a sound that might have been a whinny, but for the echoing edge of a demonic squeal. She rubbed her cheek against the side of Ivory's head. With a laugh, Ivory threw her arms around the deathcharger's enormous neck.

"If you're finished making acquaintances," Devlin grumbled, "we shouldn't linger long."

Bailey snapped her teeth at him.

"Still displeased with me, I see."

The deathcharger rumbled, the sound so close to the spoken demonic language that Ivory strained to make sense of it.

"I did *not* bring the Hunters down upon us," Devlin protested, crossing his arms over his chest. "It was simple misfortune that they were in the area."

Ivory choked on a laugh, and Bailey snorted in blatant disbelief.

Devlin growled and stalked off towards the RV. "Fabulous. Now there are *two* of them."

Ivory buried her face in Bailey's mane to hide her laughter, and the deathcharger immediately used her giant head to tuck their bodies even closer together. Her soft, velvety nose moved over Ivory's dreadlocks, chest expanding as she drew deep lungfuls of her scent. After a while she made a noise that sounded an awful lot like, "Okay?"

"Yes, I'm okay." Ivory stepped back to offer her first real smile in years. "Though your master was nearly caught."

"No," Bailey huffed. "Friend."

Ivory's smile widened. "My mistake. Nobody lords over a deathcharger."

Bailey dipped her head in a nod but her eyes drifted towards the trees, one ear flickering. "Go."

"Are there more?" Ivory lifted her nose to the air but couldn't smell anything more than the sulphuric scent of demonic horse.

"Yes." Bailey nudged Ivory towards the RV. "Go."

Torn between the misery of fleeing – again – and the idiocy of making a stand, Ivory allowed herself to be herded into the RV, Bailey managing the steps by the simple expedient of jumping over them, her ridiculous bulk landing neatly inside with the temerity of a mountain goat.

Devlin was already in the driver's seat, head propped in his lap so that he could see where to insert the crystal key. Taking a seat on a nearby couch, Ivory watched in amusement as Bailey moved to the back of the vehicle, climbed onto the bed as though it were a dog mat and curled up with her legs tucked beneath her. The RV rumbled to life and Devlin hemmed and hawed over the instruments until he located the gearshift, put the thing in drive and lurched awkwardly forward.

"Stop!" Ivory shouted. The RV jerked up short, a small jet near Devlin's shoulder spitting a steady stream of water all over his chest.

"Again?" He patted ineffectually at his leather jacket. "Why is that pedal even down there?"

Ivory surged out of her chair. "Do you have any idea what you're doing? We almost ran into those trees!"

"I am relatively inexperienced with this vehicle," Devlin snapped. "I read the operating instructions but they made no sense and when I asked for advice, the woman ran away screaming."

Ivory covered her face with both hands and counted to ten. When she lowered them, she spoke as calmly as she knew how. "Get out of the damned chair. I'll drive."

She expected him to argue but instead, Devlin's face lit up. "You will? Wonderful! See, Bailey? Someone who can help us, at last!"

"I'm helping you get away from the Hunters so that I can also get away from the Hunters," Ivory reminded him, but it was impossible to stop the smile that flirted with her lips as Devlin scooped up his head and rocketed out of the driver's seat. "Once we're safe, we're going our separate ways."

Rather than moving to the comfortable couch as she'd anticipated, Devlin strapped himself into the passenger seat and angled his head so that he could watch Ivory put the RV in reverse and carefully back away from the pine trees looming in front of them. When she executed a three-point turn he applauded, eyes wide with boyish excitement.

The road was uneven but the RV's suspension was excellent, and Ivory accelerated with little more than a glance in the mirror to ensure everything was as it should be. They'd been driving a little over five minutes before she clicked her tongue against her teeth. "Damn. We're being followed."

Devlin unclipped his seatbelt and turned to kneel on his chair, lifting his head into the air so he could see out the back window. "A car and ... what are those smaller things?"

"Magebike," Ivory grumbled. Whoever decided to take the remnants of humanity's motorcycles and cram their engines full of power stones deserved to be hauled off and shot. Fast, silent and horrifically dangerous, magebikes were as likely to spark out their power cores and explode as they were to take their rider from point A to B, but for those more magically inclined beings – or ones with more ego than sense – they were a popular choice.

Ivory pushed the accelerator to the floor and the RV picked up speed as best it could. The sleek black car, flanked by the two mage-bikes as though they were starring in a movie, drew steadily closer and she gnashed her teeth. "They're going to catch us."

Devlin sighed. "So be it. Although this time, we may have little choice but to kill them."

"Well, duh. They're trying to kill us, after all."

"I'm glad we agree." He slid her a sideways glance. "Can you manage the vehicle in this situation? Because if so, Bailey and I will confront the Hunters."

"Manage the – what are you talking about?"

Devlin didn't answer, disappearing towards the back. When he returned a few moments later, he had a sword strapped to his shoulders and Bailey hard on on his heels. "Slow down a little, so they think they've caught us."

Mad. The man was utterly, utterly mad – but as he wedged his head on the dashboard, his nose pressed to the windscreen, Ivory lessened the pressure she was applying to the accelerator and the RV slowed.

Devlin stretched out a hand and Bailey immediately put her nose in it, giving him a reference point. She whuffed against his fingers and on the dash, Devlin's lips twisted into a smile. "Forgiven?"

Bailey nipped.

"Ah. Fair enough, I suppose."

Ivory wanted to ask what that meant but before she had a chance, the two magebikes shot past the RV and pulled in front of it, boxing the vehicle between themselves and the larger car behind. The RV's door slid open on a hiss and Ivory watched in astonishment as Bailey hopped down the steps and out onto the road as though the motor home were standing still.

"Bailey!" Ivory cried – but then the deathcharger was beside the open door, her long, silken mane flying in a wind of her own making, legs powering as she galloped. Bailey screamed, a sound of fearsome challenge that could never be mistaken for a neigh, and Devlin launched his body out the door without the slightest hesitation.

"You forgot your head!" Ivory gasped.

"Too annoying. I want both my hands," Devlin's head replied. "This will work just as well."

Bailey, who'd barely broken stride as she dipped her body to catch his, picked up speed as Devlin wrapped the fingers of one hand in her mane and bent low over her neck. He drew his sword as Bailey passed the front of the RV, and Ivory took a moment to admire the black hilt and curving crimson blade splashed with demonic runes.

She flicked a look at the speedometer and blinked. "Just how fast can Bailey go?"

"Faster than this."

True to his declaration, the deathcharger began to close on the nearest magebike. The Hunter on board glanced over his shoulder and startled as he spotted her – and the headless body on her back – but it was already too late. As Ivory watched, Bailey bit at the back tyre while Devlin swung his sword in a wide, flat arc, taking the Hunter's head from his body.

Devoid of a rider, the bike began to wobble. With a giant heave, Bailey tossed both bike and corpse aside, leaving behind a splatter of gore and a lone head, which bounced off the RV's front bumper and then rolled underneath.

Ivory laughed. "One down, two to go!"

Devlin grimaced. "Having been decapitated myself, I feel somewhat guilty."

"I don't see why – he's dead. He didn't feel me running his head over."

"You ... are a very unusual person." Devlin's eyes narrowed as Bailey swung closer to the other magebike. As she did, the Hunter raised his arm, a laser pistol extruding from his sleeve via the convenience of a mechanical holster. Devlin's scimitar flashed but the bike swerved aside and the laser levelled straight at Bailey's chest.

"Tell her to go faster," Ivory urged, planting her foot back on the RV's accelerator. The road curved ahead, and she cut through the inside of the corner to gain ground as Devlin's heels dug into Bailey's ribs.

Ivory could hear the Hunter laughing as he tracked the demonic horse with his laser. Echoing his laughter, she slammed the RV into the back wheel of his bike. It flipped up into the air, narrowly missing the top of the RV as it did so. The Hunter's laser discharged, the blue beam going wide as his arms and legs windmilled uselessly before he slammed into the trunk of a tree and slid to the ground.

With a grunt of effort, Ivory transferred her weight from accelerator to brake, bracing herself as the RV's wheels locked and it skidded across the asphalt in a giant cloud of smoke.

"Stay here," Ivory said, pulling on the handbrake.

"Not like I have much choice at the moment," Devlin muttered. "My body's still outside."

Ivory popped open the door and pulled herself onto the roof. Using the smoke as cover, she scuttled down the length of the vehicle, pausing at the end to peer over the lip. The Hunters' car had swerved to avoid a head-on collision and now rested flush against the back of the RV. As the passenger door cracked open, Ivory dropped onto the sedan's roof and lashed out with her claws. The Hunter who leapt from the vehicle shouted in surprise, two long, thin slices appearing along the side of his face as he sailed by. Pain contorted his features and he slapped both hands to his cheek, collapsing to the ground to scream and thrash as Ivory's poison ate steadily away at flesh and bone. Satisfied that he was no longer a problem, Ivory stuck her head and shoulders into the cabin of the car – where the driver had a crossbow levelled at the open door.

"I wouldn't," Ivory growled, her tongue thick in her mouth as her teeth and horns began to lengthen.

The woman's lips trembled but her grip on the crossbow firmed. "I have to."

"Why?" Digging her toe-claws into the roof, Ivory manoeuvred further inside. Upside down as she was, her dreadlocks draped over the car's gearshift and when she offered the Hunter a smile full of overly long, pointed teeth, the woman flinched. "I have no problem with you. Put the crossbow down, swear off, and I'll let you walk away."

"It's a Hunter's duty to cleanse the world of demonic filth," the woman whispered, her fingers tightening on the stock of her weapon. "To keep people safe."

"The people *you* decide are worth protecting, you mean?" Ivory flexed one hand, showing off her claws, and watched the Hunter swallow. "If you'd met me twenty years ago, you'd think I was human. *I* thought I was human. I lived a normal life, in a normal house, with parents and friends and all that other crap. Then one day the worlds merged and magic remade us into ... whatever we are now." She smiled again, this time more a baring of demonic fangs. "The funny thing is, I didn't feel any different on the inside until people like you became a problem."

"I'm not the problem." The woman's voice firmed. "I'm the solution."

Ivory slapped the nose of the crossbow as it fired, the bolt whizzing past one ear. Wrapping her free hand around the Hunter's throat, she shoved her back in her seat, claws digging deep enough to draw blood.

"I'm not a disease to be cured," Ivory hissed, as the colour began to drain from the Hunter's face. "I may not be perfect – but unlike you, I offered the chance to walk away."

Withdrawing her hand, Ivory plucked the crossbow from the Hunter's nerveless fingers and dismantled it with quick, practised movements. Dropping the pieces onto the floor of the car, she searched the woman's pockets as her eyes slid shut for the final time. With only lint and lip gloss to show for her efforts and the car so clean it might as well have been new, Ivory pulled herself back onto the roof to discover Devlin standing by the open door, head in one hand and sword in the other.

"Are you all right?" His pale eyes flicked down her body and back up again, and a kernel of warmth kindled in Ivory's chest when he didn't flinch at the sight of her altered features.

"I'm fine." Raising up to her knees, she craned her head to look over his shoulder at the Hunter on the ground. "Dead?"

"Dead," Devlin confirmed. "As is the one who collided with the tree."

"Are you sure?"

He hefted his scimitar. "Very."

"Hmm." Ivory bit her lip and brandished the purloined lip gloss. "We need to check for—"

"I did," he cut her off, brows drawn tight. "Nothing on any of them to say who was the intended target."

Sighing, Ivory shoved her demonic energy as far down as it would go, returning to her almost-human form. Hunters were well known for relying on the wrist devices they all wore, but since they were coded to the owner's energy signature, it would be impossible to get anything out of them.

"They'll keep coming," Devlin said softly. "And no matter who they were originally chasing, they're now aware of all three of us."

"I know." Ivory tugged on one of her dreadlocks and, not for any other reason than to fill the silence, added, "I've been avoiding them on and off for years."

Bailey stuck her head around the back of the RV and whickered softly.

"She's right. We should go." Jamming his sword into the scabbard across his back, Devlin offered his hand. "I know you wish to part company, but truly, we'd be safer if we stuck together. The Hunters will overpower us far too easily if we separate."

Ivory stared at his outstretched fingers as though she'd never seen them before. When was the last time someone had offered her such a common courtesy?

"Why?" she asked, tracing Devlin's sword calluses with the tip of one long claw.

He didn't even pretend to misunderstand. "Because I like you."

"Because you need my help," Ivory corrected, glaring down at him from her perch. "To break your curse."

Devlin's hand didn't waver as he caught her gaze with his. "I do need your help, Ivory. That is correct. But I'm offering my hand because we are the same; two warriors on the run from an evil disguised as a cure." His lips curved in a wicked grin. "And because I want the excuse to feel your skin slide against mine."

Ivory's jaw dropped. Was he ... *flirting* with her?

Warmth bubbled again in her chest and she swallowed, as though that would somehow push the odd sensation back into the abyss where the rest of her feelings languished. It stayed stubbornly put and after a long moment, she shook her head and placed her hand in his.

Devlin's skin was warm and dry, his fingers large and gentle as they curled around her paler ones and when she leaned her weight against him, hopping from the car to the ground, he didn't budge so much as an inch.

They stared at each other a long moment, then Devlin carefully withdrew his hand and made a flourishing gesture in the direction of the RV. "Your chariot, my lady."

More warmth, and gods help her, a smile. Ivory strode towards the RV in the hopes he didn't see it, but the rumbling chuckle behind her said she was far too late. Bailey waited by the RV's open door, ears pricked in their direction and head tilted to the side.

"Okay?" she whuffed.

"Yes." Ivory climbed into the RV, dropping into the driver's seat with a sigh. "I'm going to regret this. I just know it."

5

PENANCE FOR THE OVERZEALOUS

As the day wore on and the RV steadily covered ground, Devlin succeeded in eliciting two more smiles from Ivory and, on one occasion, a sound he suspected might have been a hastily stifled laugh. Each time, he felt like a man who'd been handed the keys to the kingdom and each time, when the burst of warmth in his chest began to cool, he sternly reminded himself that nothing good could come of his increasing attraction to the demon who was his only hope for salvation.

Perhaps that was part of his punishment, to endure so many years wishing for nothing more than a chance to repent and then, standing upon the cusp of such an event, to glimpse a creature rarer and more beautiful than anything he'd come across before.

Devlin studied Ivory's profile as she handled the RV with an expertise he could only dream of. She'd tugged the foremost of her dreadlocks back into a tie, emphasising the clarity of her profile, the curl of her horns and the thick sweep of long, dark lashes. The silver ring in her nostril caught the sunlight when she moved, sparkling as though a thousand tiny diamonds encrusted the surface and bringing light to the shadowed skin around her eyes. He longed to form her curves with his hands, to kiss the lips currently set in a pout whilst she stared at the almost incomprehensible instruments on the RV's dash. Once, her biting personality would have turned him off – along with her obviously demonic features – but now all he saw was fire and life and glorious woman, and though he was damned beyond all measure, Devlin couldn't help the frisson of need that had him adjusting his weight in the passenger seat for the fourth time in as many minutes.

When she glanced his way and raised a brow, he realised he'd been caught staring and cleared his throat. "My apologies. You're the first person other than Bailey I've had a conversation with in ... a long time."

"Hmm." Ivory turned back to the road, drumming her clawed fingertips on the wheel. "If I'm guessing correctly, you're the Headless Horseman from myth and legend: a creature cursed to haunt his forested hollow, who kills anyone foolish enough to enter. Yes?"

Devlin gaped. "There are *stories* about me?"

"You don't know?" This time, both brows went up. "Where have you been these last centuries?"

"Bound to a forested hollow," Devlin grumbled, crossing his arms over his chest. "And it's been millennia, not centuries. I should also like to add that I haven't killed anyone who hasn't tried killing me first." He tsked in the back of his throat. "You are the first being since my beheading who's bothered to enter into an actual conversation."

"Probably because nobody else was fluent in demonic," Ivory mused.

"How was I to know I was speaking demonic? Everyone sounds the same to me."

Her face scrunched into a frown. "Everyone?"

"Yes."

"So you understand this?"

"Of course."

"And this?"

"Indeed."

"How about this?"

"Light save me, woman, yes!" Devlin bared his teeth at her and, for some unknown reason, it made her grin in response. "You're simply repeating yourself."

"Actually, I spoke in three different languages and only one of them was demonic." She pursed her lips. "It appears whoever cursed you had the gift of tongues."

"You know the nature of my curse?"

"No." She turned her head to look him in the eye for a single, shattering second before turning back to the road. "Only the nature of demons – which is that in basic cursing, you transfer at least a little of yourself into the target. The stronger the curse, the more energy is required."

"And if the demon who cast the curse died shortly afterwards?"

Ivory shot him another look, this one through half-shuttered lashes. "How exactly did your curse come about?"

"I thought you weren't interested," Devlin replied, adjusting his head where it rested on his lap.

"In breaking it? Not in the least." She checked the mirror, then the road, then the mirror again. "It's dangerous work and I've no reason to risk my neck for you."

"Not even if it's the right thing to do?"

Ivory snorted. "Nobody does the right thing anymore, Devlin. Honour, decency, morality? They're just words. Shields people use to justify whatever action will get the result they desire, all while crushing those they deem lesser beneath their shiny, self-righteous boots."

Devlin's jaw dropped. "Who wronged you so badly that you'd have such a view of the world?"

"Everyone," she said firmly. "It's easy enough for you – as long as your head's on your shoulders, you still look human. Me? I look like the monster under the bed that everybody loves to hate." Ivory glanced in the mirror and grimaced. "Speaking of monsters, there are Hunters up our ass again. You might want to hold on to something."

Devlin snatched his head against his chest, twining his fingers in his unruly hair for good measure. Ivory spun the steering wheel hard to the left and the RV began to skid, tilting precariously until

Devlin braced one foot against the wall in an effort to stay upright. Bailey shrieked in the back, her hooves thumping against the cupboards as she sought to keep her place on the bed, adding to the cacophony of clattering plates and clanging pots that echoed in the space.

A concussive blast hit the side of the RV and the vehicle shuddered before it launched sideways into the air. For a moment Devlin was weightless, held in place by the seating restraint until gravity reasserted itself and the RV hit the ground roof-first, sliding along the road with a great shriek of metal and a dancing array of bright sparks.

"Move," Ivory shouted, somehow crouched neatly on the roof as if it had always been the floor. "We need to get out of here before they hit us again."

Suiting word to action, she raced on all fours towards the rear of the vehicle, where furious whinnying and thumping heralded Bailey's attempts to free herself from beneath the overturned mattress. After a cursory glance to ensure neither female was seriously injured, Devlin turned his mind to the rather knotty problem of removing his restraint. With his full body weight against the straps, the fastening mechanism was reluctant to release and with his head clasped in only one hand, it was difficult to—

"I said *move*," Ivory growled, appearing at his side.

Claws flashed, the straps went alarmingly slack and Devlin thumped shoulder-first into the ceiling-come-floor, his head clutched protectively against his gut. Something large and cold smacked into his rump and when he finally managed to extricate himself from the trap of his own limbs, Devlin realised it was his sword.

"Are you always this slow?" Ivory's head and shoulders appeared from behind a set of cupboards. Her brow furrowed as she looked beyond him. "Ah, fuck."

Claws flashed again, only this time they wrapped around Devlin's ankle, the curved tips digging into his boots as Ivory yanked him across the floor, sword and all, and then tossed him through a broken window and onto the street. He hit the ground and rolled in a clatter of blade and body parts, and before he'd had quite the chance to work out what was going on, Bailey threw her not inconsiderable weight on top of his.

An enormous explosion rent the air, accompanied by the squeal of twisting metal and the unmistakable *whomph* of an oil fire. Fighting against the warmth of Bailey's undercarriage, Devlin angled his head in time to see an enormous blue fireball arc into the sky.

"Get up!" Ivory's voice faded in and out through the crackle of the flames and the thumping of half-melted debris as it peppered the area. "Run!"

Bailey rolled upright and Devlin succeeded in getting to his feet, slinging his sword harness over one shoulder and hastily buckling it at the waist. The burning wreckage of the RV spilled smoke and fumes into the afternoon sky, but it was the silhouettes of many, *many* figures on the other side of the crackling furnace that had Devlin wrapping his hand in Bailey's mane to vault astride her back. Ivory leapt up behind him, arms wrapping tight around his waist, her body fitting to his like a second skin.

"We need to find somewhere safe," Devlin announced, closing his eyes against the sickening blur of trees and sky as Bailey launched into motion.

Behind him, Ivory's body rippled in a long, gusty sigh. "I know a place – and if we can get there, I can throw the Hunters off our trail."

Though her reluctance was palpable, Devlin's heart stirred hopefully at the offer. Prodding at the opening as one might pick the scab from a forming wound, he said, "I thought you wanted to part ways?"

"I do – but the Hunters are categorised by their magical ability to track a target no matter the distance. If we split up, I can clear my own trail, but they'd still track you – and when they catch you, they'll be able to use their skills to regain *my* trail. I don't have the time or energy to cleanse my magical signature morning and night on the offchance that I'm being pursued, so it makes more sense to cleanse everyone before we part company." Her arms tightened around his waist in warning. "And we *will* be parting company."

"Of course," Devlin said, as mildly as he knew how. "You've made it clear you wish nothing to do with me and my curse. I will not inconvenience you any more than I already have."

Ivory growled deep in her chest, an intriguing sound that caused her entire body to vibrate where it was pressed against Devlin's. He fought not to lean back into her, something dark and feral deep inside urging him to answer the sound in kind – as though they weren't people but beasts, creatures of some unknown shadowy plane who had a connection that went beyond society's decorous norms.

As though they were demons.

Bailey's haunches bunched and she leapt over some small obstacle, jostling Devlin so that he had to steady his head where it rested between his thighs. The action had a dry laugh bubbling in his throat – here he was mooning over a beautiful woman, when his head wasn't even attached to his shoulders. Even were he not a walking debt to be repaid, how could he ever hope to attract the interest of another when his head fell off every time he sneezed?

Fool.

Bailey snorted and began to shorten stride, muscles tensing as though for battle. Devlin opened his eyes to see a man on a white horse standing in their way. The sunlight shone off his white leathers so brightly Devlin had to squint. He caught the impression of blonde hair and broad shoulders before Bailey propped and reared, hundreds of years of training and instinct pulling her up short of the arrow that thunked into the ground in front of her.

Devlin glanced down at the arrow, stomach knotting. That was no crossbow projectile but a proper arrow, the fletchings coloured in a pattern he'd not seen since he was human.

"What's going on?" Ivory began to loosen her grip, but Devlin clamped his free arm over the top of hers to prevent the movement.

"Stay seated," he warned. "I cannot die, but you do not have the same luxury."

Bailey dropped back to all fours, neck arched and lip curled to reveal long, deadly teeth. The man on the opposite side of the clearing urged his horse forward with his knees, all the while raising his longbow and notching another arrow to the string. As he moved from light to shadow, his face came into view; strong jaw, golden beard, blue eyes that had once danced with merriment but were now hard and cold.

"Greetings, Gawain." Devlin angled his sword as Bailey pranced, putting herself – and the blade – between the man and Ivory. "I had not thought we would ever meet again."

For a moment Devlin feared his old friend wouldn't understand demonic, but then Gawain blinked and shook his head. *Devlin? I thought you dead."*

"I should be." Devlin shrugged, the movement drawing attention to his headless shoulders. "Perhaps I am, for I'm certainly not alive."

Ivory's chin dug into one of those headless shoulders as she levered upward. "Who's this guy?"

"Ivory, may I present to you Sir Gawain, High Knight of the Round Table under King Arktur – you would, perhaps, know him as King Arthur – of the fae."

"Fae?" Ivory dug her talons into Devlin's ribs as she shifted for a better view. "I thought Arthur was King of England or something like that."

"The stories of my uncle which circulate this pustule of a realm are little more than hearsay and blasphemy," Gawain snapped. "The Round Table is long sundered and though Arktur still reigns over Camelot, I have not seen it in many a year. These days I am known as Gawain Braybrook, Master of Hunters and Head of the Healing Hall."

"Braybrook." Ivory's voice coiled along the ground, rustled through the leaves of the trees, every syllable dripping dark menace. "I know your people. I know what they do. I've lost family to the Hunters who prowl the night like cowards, stealing children from their parents and knifing innocents in their sleep – all for the supposed crime of their birth."

Gawain's blue eyes narrowed and he nudged his horse a step to the left, trying to get a better view of the woman tucked behind Devlin. "You're a Whitehaven."

The sound Ivory made was not a sound Devlin had ever heard made by anyone in his entire existence. Somewhere between a hiss and a growl, with the odd echo of a snapping fire and the cadence of a gale as it whistled through a lonely canyon – it was all of those things and none of them, and it made the hairs on the back of his neck rise and the infernal thing rooted in his gut blossom like a flower before the morning sun.

"I am no-one and nothing but myself," she breathed, the voice Ivory's and yet not; deeper, more guttural, accented in a way that even Devlin noticed. "You have no right to judge me."

Gawain snorted and drew his bow. "Judgement is unnecessary. You are a monster and I am oath-bound to cleanse this land of your filthy taint."

He let go the string.

Devlin twisted, yanking Ivory behind him a moment before the arrow thudded deep into his chest, shoving them both backwards. He wheezed as the projectile dug deep, the impact not painful so much as inconvenient. Ivory's body braced his and he used her strength to rock back upright, tossing his head at Gawain with a well-practiced flick of his arm.

Acting on instinct, the Hunter dropped his bow to catch the head, and Devlin immediately sank his teeth into the calloused thumb pressed against his lips. Gawain swore and shook his arm as though it were on fire, setting Devlin's eyes rolling inside his skull. Blood coated his tongue, his teeth slipped and quite suddenly his head was flying through the air, a dizzying spectacle of light and shade that was likely to end with a broken nose – until clawed fingers twisted into his hair and his cheek was tucked firmly against a pair of spectacular breasts.

"Can you see?" Ivory demanded. She'd risen to her feet on Bailey's back, braced with one hand planted firmly over the grisly stump of Devlin's neck. Though she cradled his head against her chest, it was only a few inches higher than if it was still attached to his body, giving Devlin not only a clear view of the situation but excellent depth perception to boot.

"Yes," he answered, and swung his sword.

Gawain's horse, nowhere near as skilled as Bailey, was too slow to dodge. Devlin's blade bit high into the stallion's shoulder and he jerked backwards with a scream, spraying blood all over Bailey's face and neck. Gawain swore and snatched at the reins but the moment Devlin pulled his sword free, the horse turned and bolted into the forest.

"Prey?" Bailey asked, eyes narrowed as she licked blood from her lips.

"Not today. We might beat Gawain if we work together, but the other Hunters will find us soon enough." Devlin sheathed his sword down his back, took a firm grip on the arrow buried in his chest and snapped the shaft off close to his body. "Safety is still the better choice – for now."

Shifting her grip on his stump of a neck, Ivory swung a leg over his shoulder and Devlin found himself with a sudden lapful of woman, his head sandwiched between their chests and no amount of clothing in the world capable of mitigating the sudden intimacy of their position.

"East," Ivory said, her tone distracted as she bent to inspect the place where the arrowhead was embedded in Devlin's pectoral. "Go east, Bailey."

With little more than a snort and a tail flick, Bailey moved again, her long, powerful legs and sure stride making for a smooth ride despite the lack of saddle or tack.

"Does it hurt?" Ivory asked, peeling his jacket open.

"Yes," Devlin admitted. With her breasts supporting his cheek, her sleek form draped over the top of his larger one and nowhere remotely appropriate to put his hands, how could he not be in pain? He cleared his throat as best he could and tried to keep a grip on Bailey's mane without accidentally grabbing, touching, brushing or poking anything he hadn't been invited to. "I've been shot through the heart."

"I see that." Ivory shifted Devlin's head to their combined laps so that she could have the use of both hands. "I need to dig this out. You're not going to pass out on me, are you?"

"Will you toss me to the side of the road if I do?"

Ivory chuckled, the first real laugh he'd heard from her throat. "You know I will."

"I hate to disappoint you, then, for I wasn't known to swoon even when I was alive."

She chuckled again, face softening as she probed gently at the raw edges of the wound. Cradled in the valley of their thighs, Devlin was somewhat mortified to discover he sported an increasingly enthusiastic erection that, thanks to the location of his own head, was poking him in the chin. What would Ivory do if she noticed? Castrate him, most likely – and though the notion made Devlin wince, his body steadfastly refused to cease craving her touch. And when she glanced at him from beneath long lashes, dark eyes overly large in the shadowed contours of her finely boned face ... well, it was enough to make a man who'd renounced his faith begin to pray all over again.

HOME IS WHERE THE SPIRITS HAUNT YOU

Twice Ivory decided not to take Devlin to the one place in the world that was sacred to her, but each time she changed her mind, inevitability changed it back again.

It wasn't that she felt obliged to keep her word; honour was no longer a moralistic illusion she bothered with. It wasn't even that Devlin needed her help – that much had been obvious from the minute his head fell off in the middle of Mystic Madhouse. It wasn't even because, though she'd die before she admitted it, she could feel the frayed edges of his demonic energy licking against hers, begging to be fixed.

It was, to her ever-increasing chagrin, because she liked him.

As Bailey approached the final rise before the protective wards, Ivory clenched her teeth against the urge to simply dismount and walk away. Enjoying someone else's company was dangerous. Liking them? Potentially fatal – and Ivory was done, *done*, with having her life threatened by her pathetic heart.

And yet here they were, proving her a liar of the highest calibre.

Bailey drew up short, snorting, and Ivory reached forward to smooth her fingers through the deathcharger's silky black mane.

"What is ..." Behind her, Devlin's voice trailed off and she could almost taste his confusion. They'd ridden most of the way facing one another so that Ivory could dig the Hunter's arrow out of his heart, but once it was done, she'd turned around, nestling her smaller body into the cradle of Devlin's thighs. He was nowhere near as warm as a human man but his bulk was comforting – not that she needed such a thing – and he smelled of cinnamon and sandalwood, two of her favourite spices to throw in the fire when the nights grew icy.

"Wait here," Ivory said, ignoring his question in favour of sliding to the ground. Patting Bailey's jaw on the way past, she moved through the first layer of wards and into the second, where she crouched to dig her claws into the dirt and let her eyes slide shut.

The land whispered, thousands of barely-heard voices melding together into a disjointed whole. Tracing the lines that bordered her small slice of safety, Ivory ensured no-one had tried to gain access before pulling her fingers free and moving back towards Bailey and Devlin. "I need a drop of blood from each of you so that I can attune the wards to let you pass."

"All right." Devlin drew a dagger from his jeans and used it to prick his thumb, dripping dark blood onto Ivory's outstretched palm. The moment the liquid touched her skin, lightning shot through Ivory's veins and she drew a sharp breath. There was so much chaos in Devlin's energy that it took everything to avoid being overcome – how was he still standing, let alone walking around? She blinked in a vain effort to clear her vision, ignoring the slap of demonic power in favour of letting it wash over her like water crashing into a pool far below. By the time she had a handle on the influx of energy, Devlin had used the same dagger to prick Bailey's shoulder and Ivory hurried to catch the welling blood before it dribbled to the earth.

The deathcharger's essence was much calmer, her blood a demonic black with an oily sheen – a mirror image for Ivory's own. She frowned as it mixed with Devlin's, the two energies telling her far more about their curse than Ivory wanted to know. Still, there was no other way to let them through the wards, so she pushed her instinctive understanding away and walked back through the layers of magic, pausing between the first and second barriers to carefully anoint each of her dirt-encrusted claws with a mixture of their essences. That done, Ivory once more buried her fingers in the dirt. The air around her shimmered as the barriers shifted and stretched, settling back into place with a contented hum.

Bailey snorted, ears twitching.

"You feel the change?" Ivory asked. When the deathcharger nodded, she allowed a small smile. "They like to be fed."

Devlin's face twisted but Bailey merely chuckled deep in her chest and stepped forward, the wards sliding over her and Devlin with a welcoming touch. Ivory shook the dirt from her hands and stood, leading them down the rise and past the third and final barrier which protected her home.

She heard Devlin gasp but didn't look back, enjoying instead the sight of her little slice of paradise. A cottage rose from the ground as though it had struggled free from great bonds, the walls and roof bunched and gnarled in a cattywampus collection of wood and stone. Overgrown gardens mingled with the natural growth of the forest, spreading out like the train of an elegant gown, and crawling up the walls and over the cottage roof with the tenacity of a spider's thick silk. The trees inside the wards bore leaves the perpetual colour of autumn, offsetting the dark green moss that blanketed the ground and lower walls of the cottage. A small, sturdy well crouched to one side of the front door, the bucket overturned on the stone lip and the sharply pointed roof as crooked as the cottage's.

"This is my home," Ivory said, filling her tone with warning. "My grandmother left it to me when she died."

"It's lovely," Devlin choked out.

"Your sincerity is overwhelming," Ivory muttered, swinging back to face him. "I realise it's not a castle, but – are you *crying?*"

The headless knight sat astride his demonic horse with his head cradled loosely in both hands, twin streaks of silver making his cheeks shine.

"I'm not sure I can find the words, but—" He sniffled, pale green eyes glassy as they met with hers. "It's been a long time since a place has welcomed me with such open affection. I'm honoured you have brought me to your home, Ivory. This is a truly sacred place and I will be forever grateful to have seen it."

They stared at each other, Ivory's tongue frozen as she tried to decide between softness and scorn. It was dumb, dumb, *dumb* to let down her walls but how could she not, when Devlin's words echoed how she'd felt herself the first time – and every time since – she'd arrived at the cottage? The thrumming energy of the land inside the wards called to her like nothing else and she'd been braced to hate Devlin invading her sanctuary … but he fit. Tall and broad and oh-so-alone on Bailey's midnight back, he was dark and real in a way nothing in her life had been for a long time. His tears were ridiculous and by all rights, she should laugh at him – but she stayed silent as her feet took her forward, as her hands lifted to cup Devlin's jaw. When she tugged, he let go, and she burrowed her clawed fingers into his hair as she raised his face to hers.

Ivory had never been much of a romantic but she did believe in following her instincts and right now, they demanded Devlin. As though in a dream, she let her lashes drift shut as she tilted her head down, brushing her lips over his in a gentle, questioning caress. When he didn't protest, she did it again, delighted when his mouth opened in blatant invitation.

With his head unattached to his body, it was up to Ivory to control their kiss, but as soon as she touched her tongue to Devlin's he more than made up for the passive nature of his state. Her fingers tightened in his hair as they devoured each other, tongues dancing and lips locked in a routine as old as the stars. Heat crawled over Ivory's skin and she pressed her body against Devlin's leg, his large hand gripping tight to her shoulder. It was an odd disconnect, his body on Bailey's back and his head in Ivory's hands, but it was equally as intoxicating to think he trusted her – *her* – enough to surrender his passion into her care. Nobody had ever done that before, and the enormity of it broke something inside her, something squishy and warm and dangerous. Ivory ended the kiss on a growl, her eyes flying open to meet Devlin's equally wide ones. His pupils had expanded until there was only a sliver of bright, infernal green remaining, his sharp cheekbones brushed with a delicate layer of pink.

"Sorry." Ivory cleared her throat. "I ... I shouldn't have done that."

She pushed Devlin's head back into his hands and he fumbled, catching at her wrist instead. "Wait. It's okay; I wanted you. It. That. For us."

"You did?"

"I'd be a liar if I didn't say I've wanted to kiss you since we first met." His smile was tentative, but the fire in his eyes was ferocious. "I just didn't think you'd welcome it, since my head and my body are ... somewhat disconnected."

"Somewhat?" Ivory snorted a laugh, and though the stubborn part of her screamed to wrench free of his grip, she drifted closer to Bailey's side. With the deathcharger's height and Devlin's head on his knee, they were almost eye to eye. "I still should have asked first. I am, after all, a demon."

He cocked an eyebrow. "You think that makes a difference?"

"Of course it does." Ivory dropped her gaze, slamming the door on the unpleasant memories which tried to surface. "We need to go inside so I can clear our magical trail. The wards will throw the Hunters off, but not for long."

She pulled on her arm and Devlin let go, dismounting from Bailey in one swift, smooth motion. As Ivory turned towards the house, he caught her shoulder and stepped around in front, raising his head by the hair until they were face height.

"I'm grateful for your help," he murmured, expression serious, "especially when I know you didn't want to give it. And, for what it's worth, I think you're beautiful."

Ivory grunted and ducked under his arm, hurrying towards the house to hide the way her cheeks heated. She'd kissed him on a whim and it had been wonderful – but looking him in the eye afterwards and hearing him say sweet things? Yeah, not her style. Besides, if what she'd gleaned from the confrontation with Gawain was correct, Devlin had once been a demon hunter in his own right; there was no way any attraction he felt was more than dread curiosity. Bitter resentment curdled her stomach and Ivory flattened a palm over her abdomen as she shouldered the front door open.

The interior of the cottage was warm and homey, with thick, plush carpets, wood-panelled walls and brightly lit rooms that smelled of the autumn forest. Her furniture, too, was hand-made from things the forest provided, the gnarled wood sanded until it was smooth and carved with illustrations and symbols before being polished to a welcoming sheen.

Leaving Devlin to explore on his own, Ivory made straight for the kitchen, her favourite place in all the world. To maximise space, the interior of the cottage was mostly open plan, with the enormous kitchen bench providing the central focus of the room. Made from a fallen tree whose trunk had been sliced to reveal the gorgeous rings inside, it appeared to have grown from the floor and was sealed and varnished with a combination of elbow grease and magic. The tree's trunk extended up one of the kitchen walls, a long branch stretching over the benchtop to provide the perfect place for Ivory to hang her favourite mugs and the smaller pots she used most often. Though the rest of the kitchen was more conventionally made, the cupboards and benches were of the same wood and blended seamlessly with the tree so that it appeared the entire room was inside a hollowed-out trunk.

After taking a moment to run her fingers across the benchtop in silent greeting, Ivory washed the dirt from her hands, unhooked her kettle and set it atop the wood stove. Dropping into a crouch, she tugged open the door to the firebox, licked the pinky finger on her left hand and drew a demonic rune on the large central log. The rune immediately began to glow, then smoulder, then, with a pop, caught alight. Powered by magic, the fire spread swiftly through the box and in a matter of seconds the entire woodpile was ablaze.

Ivory shut the door and straightened to find Devlin on the opposite side of the bench, head cradled in the crook of his elbow and a look of astonishment on his handsome face.

"What?" Ivory snapped, going on tiptoe to unhook two large mugs and a small cast iron pot. "I need tea, and we need to get started on the trail cleanser."

"You ... you just ..." Devlin drew in the air with his free hand. "And then it caught fire."

Ivory opened her pantry, stepping into the cramped space to avoid seeing his expression. "My magic is different from other demons."

"Why?"

"Because *I'm* different from other demons."

"Different how?"

"None of your business." Drawing a deep breath, she focussed on the spell to cleanse their magical trail and let the ingredients whisper to her in response. She'd done this ritual before, of course, but now that Devlin was involved, Ivory suspected some tweaks would need to be made. Ah, yes: the duskshroom was singing over the loamroot, and the carrowshire powder was bowing out in favour of the fickleweed.

The man at her bench was silent as Ivory made several trips to and from the pantry, stacking jars on the bench until she had everything she needed. By that time the kettle whistled, so she poured two mugs of tea and offered one to Devlin.

"I wish I could drink it," he said, looking mournfully into the mug.

"You can't eat or drink?"

He raised an eyebrow. "Whatever I swallow goes down my throat, which isn't connected to the rest of me. It's ... messy."

Ivory blinked. "I didn't think of that."

"Me," whinnied Bailey from the door. "Meeeee."

It seemed impossible that the deathcharger would fit through the doorway but Bailey appeared unconcerned by the laws of physics, her enormous bulk contracting and expanding in a decidedly uncomfortable-looking phenomenon until she stood inside the cottage. While Ivory's mind tried to adjust to what she'd just witnessed, the deathcharger picked her way around the lounge room furniture and then curled up on the rug in front of the fireplace like an enormous, infernal hound.

"Me," she repeated, bright eyes filled with hope as they locked on the spare mug in Ivory's hand. Her black ears flickered. "Pleeeeease?"

There was that word again. Please. Ivory wavered between irritated and charmed, but in the end charmed won. She tipped Devlin's tea into a bowl and rounded the bench, setting it by Bailey's front legs. "Here you go, beautiful."

Bailey whickered in delight, lifting her face to lip affectionately at Ivory's jaw. "Thanks."

"Welcome." Ivory laughed, smoothing the silky black forelock back from Bailey's forehead. "Someone might as well enjoy it with me."

When she returned to the kitchen, Devlin's expression had turned sour, his jaw a hard line. Choosing to ignore him, Ivory took a bracing sip of her own tea – a blend of leaves and spices she'd grown and dried herself – and went to the sink. Instead of rinsing her hands as she'd done before, she drew out a small bristled brush and her home-made, magically enhanced soap, and set to scrubbing. For several minutes she worked in silence, until at long last Devlin moved into the kitchen to stand beside her.

"What are you doing?"

"Washing my hands," Ivory answered, flexing her fingers to better display the rapidly blackening suds. "The ritual won't work if I've got other magic in play."

"Other ..." Devlin trailed off as she turned the tap on and rinsed, black suds disappearing down the drain to reveal her clawed finger-tips in their natural, too-pale-to-be-human shade. "I thought your skin was meant to be that way."

Ivory considered telling him to mind his own business a second time. He was, after all, not her problem. Though as the minutes ticked by, she started to worry that the situation wasn't as simple as she'd hoped. With a sigh, she relented and shook her head. "When I leave the safety of the wards, I go prepared. I can't do magic like other demons can, and for a long time I thought I didn't have any. It was only once I moved here and started going through the library that I came across reference to ... different kinds of demons. I discovered that I could make potions and liniments and the like, and they'd serve as a conduit for my magic when I wasn't in my full demon form."

"A conduit?"

"Yes." When he blinked, she smiled wide enough to show off all her pointed teeth. "Let's say I make a liniment for fire. I coat the tip of one finger, letting it soak into the skin as it dries. It's dormant in that state – until I use my saliva, sweat or blood to activate the magic. Sometimes I draw runes to focus the spell but usually I just lick the finger I need and get on with it."

"Like when you melted the magic shop's door."

"Yes."

"Huh." Devlin stared at her hands for a moment, then smiled. "Clever."

Unsure what to do with the compliment, Ivory shrugged and dried her now clean hands before returning to the bench. The potion for cleansing her magical trail was a familiar one and she barely stopped to think as she portioned ingredients into the small pot, added some water and a generous dash of brandy, then set it on the stove where the kettle had been.

"A demon who makes potions," Devlin muttered to himself. Ivory glanced over her shoulder to find his brow furrowed, gaze distant. "I wonder if that's what she was."

"Who?"

He sighed. "The demon who cursed me. She was picking herbs and mushrooms in the forest when I ..."

"Slaughtered her?"

"Yes." Devlin's lashes drifted shut and he grimaced. "That is as good a term for it as any."

Something shifted in the air, a subtle humming in the atmosphere that had Ivory looking around her in surprise. "She was."

"What?"

"She was like me – her magic, I mean," Ivory amended.

Devlin's eyes flew open, his jaw slack with shock. "You ... how do you know that?"

Ivory set one hand against the cottage wall. "She told me."

"She's *here*?" He spun around, but there was nobody other than Bailey, who'd finished her tea and gone to sleep.

"Not in the sense you're thinking." Ivory picked up a wooden spoon and stirred the mixture on the stove. "This place is sacred to my family; it's been part of our heritage since Mu and Earth first began to merge. When we die, our spirits ... I suppose you might say they leave an echo here. It's not their actual ghost, more a spiritual residue that helps replenish the magic in the land and power the wards. Sometimes the echoes resonate with a certain statement or item, and if I listen hard enough I can glean information from them."

Devlin whistled between his teeth. "Is that the power of ... what did Gawain call you? The Whitehavens?"

Ivory froze, clenching the handle of the spoon so tightly that her claws pierced her palm. She wrenched her hand back lest her blood fall into the mixture and ruin it, moving quickly to the sink to wash until the bleeding stopped.

"I'm not a Whitehaven," she hissed, wiping her hands vigorously on a towel.

"All right," Devlin said, his tone easy. "I apologise. I know nothing of the word, or what it means, only that Gawain called you—"

"The Whitehavens are a family of demons, led by Lord Luthier Whitehaven. He protects demons who wish to live in peace and polices any demons who wish to harm others." Ivory tossed the towel in the sink. "They also rescue – or try to – anyone captured by the Braybrooks."

"Gawain, you mean?"

"Yes and no. The Braybrooks are a family almost as old as the Whitehavens. They purport themselves as healers but only heal those they deem worthy of their services – and the healing always costs more than mere coin. They're the driving force behind the Hunters, who are zealots of the worst kind."

"Gawain ... I knew he hated demons, but to foster such bigotry ..." He clicked his tongue against his teeth. "What happened to him that he would discard all honour and become such a villain?"

"No-one knows and to be frank, nobody cares. You might know Gawain as a knight in shining armour, but these days?" Ivory spat in the sink. "He's laughing as he dirties his hands."

Silence thickened the atmosphere and Ivory cursed herself for speaking so honestly. Stepping around Devlin, she returned to the stove, bending to sniff the mixture before removing it from the heat.

"You know an awful lot about this for someone who lives in a hermit's cottage in the forest," Devlin said at last. His tone was soothing rather than accusatory, the low timbre of his voice vibrating through Ivory's bones until she shut her eyes to soak it in.

"I was human, once, you know." A dry chuckle rattled in her throat. What was that saying in her grandmother's journals? In for a penny, in for a pound? "I was a young girl with hopes and dreams. That all changed when the worlds merged and I suddenly found myself overtaken by demonic blood I never knew I had. My parents did the best they could, but they believed in common decency and the world was in chaos." Ivory curled her lip. "They were killed within a week, and I was left alone at fourteen years old."

"Ivory ..." Devlin took a step towards her, but she held up a hand in warning.

"I learned to fend for myself but after two years, a team of Hunters found me. I thought I was going to die – even when a man and woman showed up to rescue me." She blinked, caught in the memory of that moment, then shrugged. "They were Whitehavens."

"They took you in," Devlin guessed.

"They did." Ivory nodded. "I returned with them to the Whitehaven's estate, and even met the great Lord Luthier. He told me I wasn't just a demon, but one with Whitehaven blood – from my grandmother's side, apparently. He insisted that demons like them could assume a human form as well as their demonic form, and that with training and practice, I'd be able to as well." She barked a harsh laugh. "I trained for five years, worked alongside the people I thought were my new family, but what you see now is as human as I could get. I told myself it didn't matter what I looked like and kept working, focussing every waking moment on becoming one of the fabled Whitehavens who fought for equality for all."

"What happened?" Devlin put out a hand, and this time, Ivory didn't protest when he caught her wrist and gently tugged her closer.

"Others who trained alongside me were sent into the world while I remained in the compound. I waited until Luthier next came to visit and confronted him, demanding to know when I'd get my chance."

Her lips pinched, and resentment burned like acid in her blood. "Lord Whitehaven ever so gently explained that though my fighting skills were exceptional, my appearance frightened people. Without any discernible magic and lacking the ability to transform, he feared I'd do irreparable damage to the Whitehaven name if I were sent into the world."

Devlin rumbled deep in his chest, a thick, menacing sound that set Ivory's heart racing even as she refused to look at him, fearing the pity she'd see on his face.

"I hope you fought," he growled. "I hope you proved how wrong he was."

"Yes ... but not in the way you're assuming."

"Oh?"

"I decided that if people thought me a monster, then I would become one." Ivory glanced at him at last, an evil smile tugging the corners of her lips as she dared Devlin to judge her. "I set fire to the training rooms in the middle of the night and while those goody-two-shoes were running around trying to put it out, I snuck into Luthier's office, stole everything of value that wasn't nailed down, and left."

"And came here?"

"Not straight away." Ivory inspected her now clean claws, her voice soft. "I ran from both the Whitehavens and the Braybrooks for almost a year, pawning items from the loot I'd taken whenever I could find someone whose greed overcame their revulsion at my appearance. Eventually, down near the bottom of the sack, I found a stone talisman wrapped in a pigskin map. The characters were strange but the more I stared at them, the more they became legible – until I realised I held the keystone to the wards for this cottage. It was a long journey, but the moment I crossed the wards and felt the spirits singing to me, I knew I was home."

Devlin frowned. "Nobody followed you?"

"I don't know," Ivory admitted, shrugging. "The cottage was a shambles when I arrived, having had nobody to occupy it for so long. I spent the first night in the library as it was the only protected room, and the spirits guided me to my grandmother's journal, where I found the spell for cleansing my magic trail. This spell," she added, picking up the pot and carefully cupping the outside to see if the mixture had cooled. "It was the first one I ever cast, cobbled together from the few ingredients that remained in the pantry. When it worked, I realised that for all his knowledge, for all his long life, Lord Luthier Whitehaven had been wrong; I had magic, it was just different." Ivory tilted her head to the side. "And if he'd been wrong about that, then maybe he'd been wrong about other things, too."

"My oath as a knight, he was," Devlin growled, baring his teeth. "It's no wonder you renounced your name."

"I'd never officially taken the Whitehaven name, though it was my grandmother's maiden name so I suppose I technically am one. After what I'd been through at the estate, I didn't want to use it – but I'd also long since stopped using my human surname in a bid to hide from the Hunters. I realised that we place so much weight on a name or a set of values that they become prisons, and I was tired of being an inmate. I'd never be human again and I'd never even be the type of demon that Luthier Whitehaven judged socially palatable but, in contrast, by refusing those images? I could be anyone. I could be *me*, and even if that meant spending every day of my life fighting for my next breath, nobody could take it away. So ..." she trailed off and shrugged. "I decided to just be Ivory."

"Ivory," Devlin repeated, and the way he said it sounded like a prayer. He shifted closer, his hand sliding around her waist to tug their bodies together. "I'm honoured to be trusted with your story. You are extraordinary, and if it's not too forward, I would very much like to kiss you now."

7

THE COST OF REDEMPTION

*I*f this was the price he had to pay, Devlin swore he would pay it a thousand times over, just to see the softening in Ivory's features and the way her dark eyes shimmered with warmth. One barrier at a time, she was letting him in, this woman who'd been so terribly treated by life that her only solace was in anger, vengeance and bitterness.

"A kiss, you say?" Her lips tilted up at the corners, the guarded expression she normally wore slipping in favour of something intrinsically feminine.

"Yes," Devlin whispered, spreading the fingers of his free hand along the length of her spine. The loose sweater she wore allowed him to feel every dip and hollow, every vertebrae that was slightly more pronounced than a regular human's would be, and damn if that didn't make him want her even more. "I want to kiss you like you deserve, hot and hard and overwhelming. I want to hold you close while I—"

He broke off, body boiling and cock tight even as his heart sank. What was he saying? In order to get his hands on her, he'd have to put his head down somewhere – and if he did that, he couldn't kiss her. Frustration curdled his ardour and Devlin loosened his grip to step away.

"Wait," Ivory murmured, her voice sultry as sin. Tugging his head out of his hands, she rose on her toes and set it atop the stump of his neck. With her weight braced against his and her arms looped over his shoulders, they could have been two completely normal people sharing an intimate moment. "Now," Ivory said, so softly that he shivered, "I believe you were making some rather bold claims involving hot, hard and overwhelming?"

Unable to believe what he was hearing, Devlin tentatively slid his arms – *both* of them – around Ivory's waist, locking her body against his. When he curved his shoulders, the way she held him meant that his head dipped too, and for that wild, incredible second, he remembered what it was like to be whole.

He kissed her.

Damnation had never been so sweet as the feel of Ivory's surrender. Her lips parted under his, her body melting as his fingers dug into her skin and his tongue swept into her mouth with the fervour of a conquering army. He *needed* her and she responded in kind, lifting her legs to wrap them around his waist and growling as he slid one hand over her butt to pull her against his erection. He turned to brace her against the kitchen wall, his free hand slipping under the hem of her top to find smooth skin underneath. Ivory arched into his touch and Devlin ground against her as he explored the muscles covering her ribs, trailing his fingers upward to brush the underside of one breast.

He broke the kiss to stare down at her, glorying in the way her cheeks were flushed and her breath came in gasps. "May I—"

"You fucking better," Ivory growled, snapping her teeth in front of his nose. When Devlin still hesitated, she wriggled in his arms, somehow managing to keep his head in place and deposit her breast in his hand at the same time. "To think you were doing so well at hot, hard, and overwhelming until now."

Devlin's jaw dropped, his brain scrambled by the feel of her against his palm. "Aggression is one thing but taking liberties is quiet another."

"Taking liberties," Ivory repeated, pitching her voice high and speaking as though she had a plum stuck in her mouth. "Well, honourable knight, since you seem to be concerned: you have my unequivocal consent to do as you please until I say otherwise." Her voice dropped back into sinful territory, her hips rolling against his. "I'm no fainting damsel, Devlin. I want you pushy and wild. I want you to let go and embrace who you really are."

"But I'm a monster," Devlin groaned, resting his forehead against hers.

Ivory raised a challenging brow. "So am I."

Oh, gods, that was it. Completely undone, Devlin took her mouth again in a frenzy of teeth and tongue. Her breast was still in his hand and when he moulded her flesh with his fingers Ivory gasped, trailing kisses along the line of his jaw and down the side of his neck to nip at the edge of his collarbone. He was in the process of formulating a plan to get them both naked without his head becoming too much of a hindrance when the cottage shook, the windows vibrating in their frames and the mugs and pots hanging over the bench clattering against one another.

"The wards," Ivory gasped, levering herself up to look over Devlin's shoulder. "There are Hunters in the forest."

"At the cottage?" Though his blood thrummed with disappointment, Devlin made no protest as Ivory unhooked her legs from his waist and hurried over to the kitchen bench.

"No – I have tripwire wards bordering the edge of the forest." Setting his head down on the polished surface, she gave his nose a tweak and snatched up the pot containing the cleansing potion. "If we get this finished fast enough, we can still throw them off."

With quick, steady movements, Ivory strained the liquid through a fine gauze and tipped the solids into a mortar and pestle. Devlin cleared his throat as she began to crush them with practised movements. "I can do that, if it would speed up the process."

"It would." Flashing him a grateful smile, she pushed the pestle to the edge of the bench and rushed out of the room.

Devlin eyed his body, still facing the wall Ivory had been braced against a bare minute earlier. He'd long grown used to having his senses in two places at once, but he winced as he turned and caught sight of the bulge in the front of his trousers. Denim was certainly a marvellous invention in terms of blending durability and comfort, but it did nothing to disguise how badly he wanted Ivory naked and on top of him.

Naked, because he wanted to appreciate every glorious inch of her, and on top of him, because if he was lying on his back, Devlin was pretty sure he could pull off a reasonable imitation of an entire person while he made love to her – provided they weren't too acrobatic. He winced as he scooped the mortar and pestle against his chest. Pulling off a reasonable imitation of an entire person wasn't what he wanted and it certainly wasn't what Ivory deserved, but what more could he offer? If his curse was broken—

Devlin froze, his mouth going dry.

How could he have forgotten his curse? It was, after all, the entire reason he followed Ivory around in the first place ... and to share her bed without disclosing the true nature of it was a level of dishonour to which he would never sink.

Ivory chose that moment to rush back into the kitchen, dreadlocks wild about her face and clothes still mussed from Devlin's earlier attentions. Oblivious to the way her peeking bra strap distracted him from his task, she set a solid wooden chest on the bench, along with an empty ceramic bowl the size of her palm. Her clawed fingers were deft on the chest's clasp and a moment later she used a crude wooden spoon to scoop fine black powder into the ceramic bowl.

"Charcoal," she said, flicking him a look from beneath her lashes. "It's what I use to make the liniments I coat my fingers in before I leave the house."

"And we need it for this ... why?"

She huffed out a breath as she poured some of the liquid from the pan into the bowl, then added a pinch of the crushed ingredients in Devlin's mortar. "Because I normally drink the solution, and it just occurred to me that you can't do that – so unless you want me to toss you to the Hunters, we'll need to get creative."

"Uh ..." Devlin cleared his throat. "When we first met, you gave the impression you'd rather walk away than help me."

"And yet, here we are." Ivory hunted through the top drawer for a smaller wooden spoon, tapping the top of Devlin's head with the handle before mixing the contents of her ceramic bowl into a sticky looking paste. "Trust me – if I wanted you gone, you'd be gone by now."

"You sound angry about that."

"I am." She laughed, even as she lifted the spoon to check the mixture's consistency. "I'm so fucking angry my teeth hurt. Letting people into my life hasn't worked well in the past, so I make a habit of not doing it in the present. Still, no matter how many times I tell myself it would be safer to kick you to the curb, here I am making you a custom cord-cutting liniment to save our hides from your ancient ex-boss and his horde of slavering zealots. Now, strip."

Devlin blinked. "I beg your pardon?"

"Strip," Ivory repeated, and when he didn't immediately respond, she set her bowl on the bench and began yanking his leather jacket off his shoulders. "I need to paint this on your skin. Bailey!"

A harrumphing snort announced Bailey's return to full wakefulness, the deathcharger crowding the bench a second later. Having successfully liberated Devlin's jacket from his body, Ivory dumped it on the floor, snatched the jug of potion off the counter and poured a generous amount back into the cooking pot.

"Drink this, my lovely." Ivory slid the pot underneath Bailey's nose. "All of it."

Bailey's ears flickered, then she shrugged and stuck her face into the pot, lapping away at the potion within.

Devlin's jaw dropped, his attention torn between the deathcharger and the way Ivory tugged his t-shirt up over his pectorals. "How did you do that?"

"Do what? Fuck's sake, Devlin, help me out here," Ivory growled, poking him sharply in the gut with a claw.

Devlin jumped, but obligingly raised his arms so that she could pull his t-shirt off and toss it across the room.

"How did you get Bailey to drink without protest? She wouldn't do that for me, no matter how nicely I asked."

"I'm prettier than you."

Her fingers tugged at his belt, and it was half undone by the time Devlin caught her wrists. "No."

Ivory glanced over her shoulder to meet his eyes. "Yes. I need to paint this on your skin, Devlin, and we don't have time to worry about that awkward birthmark you'd rather I not see. Now let me take your fucking pants off, or I'll shred them."

"I don't have an awkward birthmark," Devlin muttered, releasing her grip on his wrists.

Watching Ivory unzip his jeans and tug them down his legs, leaving him in nothing but the snug cotton undergarments he'd attained in the clothing store, was nothing short of torture. He tried to imagine how it would look if his head was on top of his body rather than viewing proceedings from the middle of the bench, and couldn't – it had been too long since he'd had that viewpoint on a regular basis. But this way ... he could see every single one of his ridged muscles, marred by the patchwork of scars he'd earned over the course of his life as a knight; and he could see the slim, curvy form of Ivory as she knelt at his feet, her face devastatingly close to the insistent bulge in his underwear.

"Left foot," she commanded, and Devlin braced one hand on her shoulder as she tugged off his boot and sock, then his jeans. "Right foot."

After shoving his clothes and boots aside, Ivory rose onto her knees, fingers trailing up the outside of his thighs. Devlin's breath hitched as she settled her palms on his hipbones and flicked a cheeky look over one shoulder. When their eyes met, she winked. "Come on now, big boy, it's not so bad, is it?"

No. Yes. Noyesno. Devlin opened his mouth to respond when she turned back to face his cock and rubbed her cheek against it like a kitten seeking affection. The contact was akin to being struck by lightning and he clenched his fists lest he make a mess all over the place – only his fists somehow ended up in Ivory's hair, the side of her face pressed firmly to his crotch.

She laughed, the sound vibrating through his body and making him whimper. Gently disentangling his fingers from her hair, she stood, scooping his head up in one hand and the ceramic bowl in the other. With soft words and a gentle push, she coaxed his body into the loungeroom and bade him stretch out on the bare wooden floor behind the couch.

"If you're a good knight, you'll get a treat once this is done," she told him, carefully positioning his head atop his neck where it was, biologically speaking, meant to be. "But for now, we have to keep you safe."

"What about you?" Devlin croaked, so far out of his depth that he gave up trying to swim and just let the current sweep him away. "You need to be safe, too."

"Here," Bailey whickered. Ivory turned to accept the jug clenched carefully in the deathcharger's pointed teeth and smiled.

"Thank you." She patted Bailey's jaw, set the jug to her lips and began to swallow, not bothering to stop for breath until the potion was almost entirely gone. Setting the jug on the floor out of the way, she raised a brow at Devlin. "Satisfied?"

"No," he croaked, and she laughed again.

"Hold tight, now." Ivory dipped her fingers into the ceramic bowl. "This might tickle."

It was very difficult to remember that they were in danger as Ivory began to draw on his chest. Her eyes were only partially focussed, as though she listened to a voice only she could hear while strange characters began to take shape on the surface of Devlin's skin. Once his chest was covered in what he now vaguely recognised as demonic runes, she spread liniment on his cheeks, then his forehead, before returning to his torso and working her way down his abs, then his thighs, shins, and even the tops of his feet. Everywhere she touched was like fire but Devlin couldn't decide if it was the liniment or Ivory herself, and the inherent enchantment engendered by her proximity. When she returned to his shoulders, fingers skimming lightly down his arms to draw on his biceps, Devlin let out an involuntary groan.

"Almost there." Ivory drew the last few runes on the backs of his hands then shot Devlin a hot look from beneath her lashes. "Ready?"

"For wh – aaaah!" Devlin arched off the floor as Ivory leant down and licked his abdomen, her tongue trailing across the leading edge of one of the runes she'd drawn. It immediately began to glow, a tingling heat sweeping across his skin as the rest of the characters activated. Crawling up his body with a sinful grin on her face, Ivory licked one of the characters on his cheek, nipped the tip of his nose and then, laughing when his arms banded tight around her waist, pressed her lips against his. She tasted of charcoal and magic and woman, and Devlin let the kiss carry him away even though he knew he shouldn't.

Ivory drew back with a soft chuckle. "There; all better."

"Are we ..." Devlin cleared his throat, tried again. "Cleansed?"

"Yes." Ivory's eyes unfocussed, her brow furrowing. "They haven't tripped any of the inner forest alarms, so I'd wager that once the cleansing ritual settles, the Hunters will move on fairly quickly. You'll be free to go by nightfall."

Devlin swallowed. "You helped Bailey and I, even when you didn't want to. I'd like to repay your kindness."

Ivory raised an eyebrow, lips twitching into a very naughty smile.

"Not like that," Devlin grumbled, catching her hand when it started to slide south. "I mean, yes, I want to do that, but it's not a form of currency and I wouldn't dream of sharing your bed—"

"Or the lounge room floor?"

"—or the lounge room floor, or anywhere for that matter, without being completely honest with you."

She tilted her head to the side. "Your demonic semen is like acid, and will melt my insides?"

"What?" Devlin spluttered and coughed, releasing his grip on her waist to wave his hands in the negative. "No, no! I mean ..." he sighed. "You have to promise to hear me out."

Ivory's smile faded and her eyes narrowed. "This is about the curse I'm not breaking, isn't it?"

Damn, but he wished he could nod his head. Instead, Devlin settled for chewing on his bottom lip. "Yes."

"For the love of – all right. I'll listen, and we can consider it part of whatever payment you think you owe." Pulling out of his grip, Ivory assumed a cross-legged position by his right shoulder and folded both arms over her chest. "Talk."

"Can I get dressed first?"

"No."

Devlin growled, but in the end, what did it matter? It had taken him all this time to simply get Ivory to listen – he wasn't about to throw that opportunity away for the comfort of a pair of pants.

"All right. My curse needs to be broken on Halloween."

One dark brow shot up. "Cliché. Also, Halloween's in ... what? Two days?"

"It's not meant to be cliché, just the truth. What little I've discovered over the centuries dictates that the curse of a demon who has died is very tricky to break. It requires someone on this side of the veil with the right power – in this case, you – and it requires the spirit of the demon on the other side to give his or her permission. The sort of energy harmonising for that kind of co-operation is only possible on the night when the veil between all the worlds is thinnest."

"Halloween." Ivory nodded, her mouth twisting to the side. "Yes, I suppose that makes sense. Travelling between Earth and Mu is one thing, but you're talking about the afterlife; even I know that calls for more juice." Her eyes narrowed. "I'm not sure what this has to do with me, though."

"When the curse is broken, the demonic power trapped inside me will be transferred to whoever broke it. In this case, you." Devlin brushed a hand over her knee, revelling in the warmth of her skin beneath his touch. "I don't know much about demonic magic but I can tell you this with certainty: the woman I killed was able to assume a human form. If her magic passed to you ..."

Ivory gasped. "I'd be able to assume a human form."

"Yes."

"I ... I'd look normal." Ivory extended her hands, staring down at her too-pale skin and clawed fingers, several of which were stained black with liniment. "I'd be able to walk down the street without people hissing or cursing or throwing things at me. I could visit a park, or open a potion shop, or stop to admire the sunset." She swallowed heavily. "I could hide from the Hunters."

"Yes."

A long, tense minute passed, and then Ivory smacked him in the shoulder. "Why didn't you tell me this to begin with? It changes everything!"

"You said you weren't interested," Devlin replied with a shrug. "I may no longer be a knight by technicality, but I'm not an asshole. When a lady says no, she means no."

"I ..."

"A lady also reserves the right to change her mind," Devlin added, hope swirling in his chest. "I made a terrible mistake a long time ago and I want to pay my debt. I can no longer help the woman whose life I stole, but I can help you." He wiggled sideways, putting his body out of alignment with his head but managing to snare her fingers with his own. "Let me atone for my sins. Let me give you this gift."

Ivory stared down at their joined fingers, her eyes glistening with moisture. She swallowed, shook her head, swallowed again. "I ..."

"Please," Devlin whispered, squeezing her hand.

At long last she looked up, their gazes colliding with enough force that had he been a breather, he'd have stopped in that one moment. Ivory took a breath deep enough for both of them, her fingers so tight around Devlin's that her claws dug into the back of his knuckles – but when she spoke, her voice was steady.

"All right, Devlin. I'll do it. I'll break your curse."

THERE'S ALWAYS A CATCH

*N*ormal. She could be normal.

The word rang in Ivory's head like the reverberation from a gong, echoing inside her skull until she moved as though in a dream. She vaguely remembered clearing away the trail-cleansing potion and gathering Devlin's clothes before showing him to the bathroom where he could safely shower the liniment off his oh-so-lickable skin. He didn't ask her to join him and Ivory didn't so much as glance in the direction of his tight ass as she left him to his ablutions.

Could she go to school? Completing formal schooling had never seemed a priority when it was out of reach but now ...

Ivory shook her head in wonder as she opened the door to the basement. Would she *need* to finish her basic schooling? Or, since she could read and write already, would she be able to take a business management course right off the bat? Throat thickening, she paused at the base of the worn wooden stairs.

She could open a shop. She could sell potions and liniments and poultices and teas and spices and books. She could smile at people with normal teeth, rather than a mouth full of pointed predator chompers. She could wear headbands in her hair, because her horns wouldn't be there to get in the way. She could get a manicure at a human beauty salon because she would *look like a human.* Nobody would scream or swear. Nobody would throw things at her, or hit her, or accuse her of being a foul, pestilential creature intent on sodomising Grandma with her barbed tail.

She didn't even *have* a tail.

Ivory cut off her thoughts with a strangled laugh, shoved open the door to the library and moved inside. Due to a clever arrangement of vents and mirrors, the room was filled with ambient light and in the evening, Lemurian crystals suffused the library in a soft glow so it was never in true darkness. Not like the first night Ivory had spent here, frightened and hungry and alone, so desperate for contact that she imagined the voices of her ancestors – contained in the myriad journals lining the library's crude wooden shelves – were talking to her.

Of course, they *were* talking to her; when Ivory read the books, the echo of the author was a constant whisper in her ear. It had taken a lot of reading, ruminating and several epiphanies to realise that was part of her magic, the wondrous, different, not-at-all-missing magic that had been passed down via generations of women with demonic blood.

A book snagged her attention and she smiled as she drew the slim volume from the shelves. What would Jacinta say when Ivory turned up on her doorstep looking normal? They could have tea by the shop's front desk without worrying about scaring the customers, and they could chat about Ivory's proposal to offer goods at wholesale prices in return for references to her own store.

Grinning in anticipation, Ivory settled into a nearby armchair, allowing the book in her hands to drop open where it willed. Once the pages had settled, she took a deep breath, called her chaotic thoughts to order and began to read.

Mother's soul cries out in torment. My ability to connect across the veil grows weaker every day, no matter the circles I cast nor the symbols I evoke, but I'm certain the transfer was arrested somehow and she cannot cross over. The implication that He Who Was Cursed would be able to disrupt the process is staggering; only an event of catastrophic proportions would be strong enough to halt the transition. And, I cannot help but wonder, to what purpose? In this half form, He will be neither alive nor dead, human nor demon, his soul tied to Mother's in an eternal, soul-wrenching twist. If only Father would tell me where He hides, I would seek him myself and endeavour to break the cycle so Mother could rest – but Father is notoriously tight-lipped on the subject. I wonder, if he could hear her pain, would he still feel the same?

Ivory blinked, frowning, and read the passage again. She was in the midst of her third read-through when someone cleared their throat; she looked up to see Devlin at the end of the aisle.

He really was handsome. The more time Ivory spent with him, the less she noticed that his head was detached from his body and the more she was drawn to the sheer masculinity of his presence; tall and broad and so very delicious. Built like a knight was fabled to be, with muscles earned from swinging his sword and that misguided sense of justice and honour which should have irritated her, but that she somehow found charming. His infernal green eyes glowed faintly, a sure sign of demonic blood – and yet they were not as bright as Bailey's, nor his blood as dark as it should be.

"You never completed the transition to full demon." It wasn't a question, because the clues had been there all along. "You stopped the process somehow."

An odd, not-quite smile tugged at his lips. "Decapitation."

"What?"

Devlin sighed, shoulders sagging as though under a great weight. After a few moments' silence, he crossed to the armchair and sank to the floor beside it, resting his head on one bent knee.

"After I killed your ancestor, I spent several days in the forest with a fever and only Bailey to nurse me. Between the horrid aches and hallucinations, I realised the curse was turning me *into* a demon." Devlin's lips thinned. "Back then, I believed as my knightly brethren did: that demons were an unholy blight to be cleansed from the world. I did not wish to contribute to the number of demons needing to be ... removed, so I decided to remove myself. I returned to Gawain in the dark of night and begged him to help me."

"So he cut off your head?"

Devlin's eyes glinted with macabre amusement. "Different

demons require killing in different ways, but we had yet to come across one who could survive without their head attached to their body – so, yes, we agreed that decapitation was the best way to solve the problem." His lips thinned. "I knelt at Gawain's feet and bent my head. I said my knightly funerary rites and my farewells. Gawain wept, but his hand was firm on his sword, and he promised to remember me when I was gone. Then, as you said, he cut off my head."

Ivory inspected the stump, then lowered her eyes to Devlin's. "He did a neat job."

Laughter echoed through the library and Ivory smiled in spite of herself, disarmed by the easy way he'd shared such a traumatic memory.

"My first inkling that something wasn't right was when I opened my eyes, sat up, and spied a set of headless shoulders. It took me several minutes to work out that I was seeing my own body from the angle of my severed head." His brow furrowed. "There must have been a period of disconnect, because I was no longer in Gawain's room but laid out on a funerary bier in one of our churches. I panicked, snatched up my head and ran into the night – and Bailey was there, only her eyes glowed and she was no longer the Bailey I'd known before but this newer, smarter, demonic Bailey. When she lowered to her knees, I fell across her back in a most un-knightly fashion and dropped my head on the ground." He snorted a dry laugh. "Bailey carried my head in her mouth by clenching her teeth in my hair – and I have never been so grateful to have put off cutting it as I was then, I can assure you."

"Wait. You were decapitated by your friend, woke up in an open casket, your destrier had turned into a deathcharger ... and you were worried about the length of your *hair?*" Ivory shoved a fist into her mouth to contain her laugh. "That's ridiculous."

Devlin grinned. "It's the little things, I suppose, when you're stressed."

She sobered at that and nodded. "It is indeed."

"I don't know why I didn't die," Devlin said quietly. "I've asked that question so many times over the thousands of years that followed, but I have never found the answer."

"A glitch in the magic, perhaps." Ivory drummed her fingers on the book in her lap and then, after a moment's indecision, read out the passage she'd found before his arrival.

Devlin's eyebrows shot up. "You think this pertains to me?"

"Definitely." Ivory gestured at the stone and earth walls. "The library, like the cottage and the grounds, is saturated with the echoes of my ancestors. Whenever I come down here with a question, the shelves give me whatever book I need to find the answer."

Rather than look pleased, Devlin's shoulders hunched. "I stole a mother from her children." His eyes squeezed shut. "I stole a wife from her husband, a woman from her life, all because of my own arrogance and bigotry – and if this passage is correct, she has suffered for every moment I have endured in this wretched half state." Long lashes lifted, green eyes burning bright with determination. "It is well past time I set her free."

Ivory ran a hand over the book's worn cover. It had been years since she'd needed kind words and they came rusty off her tongue, her voice stiff. "We'll find a way. I promise."

As her fingers lifted from the journal, a frisson went through the pages. The slim volume bounced off Ivory's lap and tumbled to the floor, falling open at a short entry towards the back. Rather than pick it up, she slid off the chair and onto her knees, hunching over to read aloud.

"Father has taken the location of He Who Was Cursed to his grave. I have heard rumours, however; a Headless Horseman who haunts his hollow and speaks only in shrieks and grunts. I'm convinced he's the one, yet none can tell me where this cursed hollow lies. I refuse to be deterred, for if I can connect this Headless Horseman with Mother's spirit, together they can untangle this mess – and the Cursed One will either accept her power to become whole, or pass it on to her nearest living descendant and resign himself to his fate. At this point, I care not which, so long as it puts Mother's soul to rest. With Father gone and Dindella happily married, there is nothing to keep me here: tomorrow I will begin the search for this cursed hollow and

the Headless One who resides there, and perhaps, together, we can end this tragedy. I can only pray that he will listen, should I be lucky enough to find him."

She glanced up at Devlin and he shrugged. "Nobody ever came to my hollow claiming to know who I was, or how to end the curse."

"Hmm." Ivory flipped the last few pages, but they were blank. She stopped at the back cover and made a face. "There's a note here, presumably from the sister, that says Gloraya died about a month after the final entry was written."

"She dedicated her life to ending her mother's torment," Devlin said miserably. "If I were able to leave the hollow sooner, perhaps I'd have been able to go to her, rather than have her die trying to find me."

"You couldn't leave the hollow?"

"No." His brow furrowed. "There was a clear demarcation which I could not cross, though others could come in. It disappeared a few years ago when, as far as I've been able to piece together, the two worlds were reunited."

"You mean when they merged."

"No – they were partially merged already," Devlin corrected. "I was human, but I worked often with those who had mixed blood, and full Lemurians too. Gawain, for example, is a full-blooded fae; I have also dealt with angels, vampires, centaurs ... what? Why are you looking at me like that?"

"Because you're talking about a time before written history – a time when Atlantis existed and technology was far more advanced than anything humanity has been able to accomplish thus far." Ivory blew out a sharp breath. "You're ... Devlin, you're talking about ..."

"I suppose I'm older than I care to think," he admitted ruefully. "Yes, I hail from a time so long in the past that it's been buried deep – until the gods returned, of course, and set everything to rights."

Since she was a by-product of that return, Ivory snorted at the word 'rights' – but rather than rail at a fate she couldn't change, she pursed her lips and thought back on Devlin's story. "I think I know what went wrong."

"Oh?"

"If the worlds were partially merged, then there must have been magic back then, right?"

He blinked. "Of course; though on Earth, it was limited to those few sites where the Merge had already taken hold. I served Gawain and the Knights of the Round Table in a small kingdom that was the gateway between Earth and the fae realm of Camelot."

"Camelot," Ivory choked, shaking her head. "Fairytales aside, the first journal entry said that Gloraya's ability to connect across the veil was weakening. We already know, from what the gods have revealed, that there was a barrier erected between the two worlds that cut off magic until the Earth was strong enough to bear the load."

"Was there?" Devlin's eyes rounded in amazement.

"Yes. What if that happened around the time of your cursing and decapitation? A surge in magic like that would be more than enough to interrupt not only the transition process and your death, but it could also bind you and Bailey to the hollow – where I'm assuming there was some sort of magical resonance that remained after the barrier was erected."

"And once the barrier came down and the worlds were truly Merged, that restriction eased and I was able to leave." Devlin whistled between his teeth. "It's possible. It's very, very possible."

"It also means we should have no trouble reaching through the veil once Halloween hits." Ivory frowned. "The only thing I don't understand is the choice that was referenced in the journal."

Devlin shifted against the wall, readjusting his head where it sat on his leg. "It is of little matter. As long as you connect me to your ancestor, I can pass the powers to you and pay my debt."

"Pay your debt," Ivory repeated. Her eyes narrowed, an odd, prickly feeling curdling her stomach. "You've said that a few times now. What does it mean, exactly?"

He chewed on his lower lip and said nothing.

... the Cursed One will either accept her power to become whole, or pass it on to her nearest living descendant and resign himself to his fate ...

"You could choose to keep the power," she whispered, watching

Devlin from beneath her lashes. "The magic would restore your head to your shoulders and complete the transition to full demon."

"I didn't know I could complete the rite and be restored, but that matters little; I promised the power to you, and I keep my word."

"Okay, so let's say you give the power to me, and I gain the ability to assume a human form, like we discussed." Ivory swallowed. "Then what happens?"

"I pay my debt."

"How, Devlin?" Her voice rose, her muscles tightening until it seemed they might snap. "How do you pay?"

Devlin sighed, directing his gaze over her shoulder, and for a moment Ivory thought she would have to beat the answer out of him – until he looked back at her with such intensity in his expression that it felt like a physical blow.

"Passing the power to you would revert me to my original state. I'd become fully human again," he said quietly.

"But ... without your head ..."

"I'd die." Devlin's eyes crinkled slightly at the corners, his smile one of gentle acceptance. It was simultaneously the most hideously pious and heartbreakingly beautiful thing Ivory had ever seen. "A life for a life. That is how I pay my debt."

9

THE ILLUSION OF HONOUR

*I*t had been the right thing to do.

At least, that's what Devlin told himself, curled up that night against Bailey's flank. She slept soundly, her soft breathing comforting as he stared out Ivory's lounge room window at the stars that burned brightly overhead.

It had been the right thing to do.

Even if Ivory's face had twisted in horror at his words; even if she'd thrown him out of the house, screaming obscenities all the while. Even if, when she'd let him back in as the sun set, the passion they'd ignited in the kitchen was nothing but ashes. After all this time, after all the suffering he'd caused, honour was all Devlin had left. He'd pay the debt he owed – to Ivory, to the nameless woman whose life he'd stolen, to her husband and her two daughters – because it was the right thing to do.

It was too bad that pointing that out to Ivory had gotten him stabbed in the thigh with a fork.

Devlin brushed a hand over the site of the wound. The punctures had long since disappeared, but a residual ache lingered – though this one, curiously enough, was in his chest instead of his leg. It pulsed in mockery of the heartbeat he no longer had, every passing moment cementing the impossible wish that he could pay his debts and somehow, some way, still chase the fragile thing which connected him to Ivory.

When the soft breath of dawn began to creep through the cottage and her bedroom door creaked open, the ache intensified to such a degree that Devlin rubbed a hand over his sternum. There wasn't enough light to do more than glimpse a sleepy face surrounded by a thick fall of black dreadlocks, the silver ring in Ivory's nose glinting as she moved to set the kettle on the stove.

Devlin sighed. He'd come here chasing peace and forgiveness, and now he craved another second, another minute, another day – however long he could cajole, just to stay close to the woman in the next room.

Damn.

"Halloween is tomorrow." Ivory began scooping a variety of reagents into a small pot, studiously avoiding Devlin's gaze. "Contrary to popular opinion, we won't need midnight to reach across the veil; any time of the day will do."

"You ... you're still going through with it?"

She paused, knuckles white around a jar of star anise. "I don't want to, Devlin. I don't want your powers at the cost of your life. But ... I also can't leave my ancestor tethered to you indefinitely; not if it's causing her pain. So, yeah, I'm still going through with it." Ivory cleared her throat and went back to scooping, though her hands trembled as she did. "I'll be spending today gathering things for the ritual."

"I'll help you," Devlin said at once, sitting up so quickly his head tumbled off his lap and rolled face down on the rug.

"Yes, you will," Ivory agreed, her wooden spoon clanging against the pot while Devlin patted the area around him in search of his wayward head. "We'll be leaving in an hour ... oh, for fuck's sake."

Skin whispered over hardwood floors and then clawed fingers clenched none too gently in his hair. Devlin had the barest glimpse of tattered sleep pants before his head was dropped unceremoniously into his lap and Ivory stalked back into the kitchen.

"Thanks," Devlin muttered, righting his head on his knee so he could watch her continue to brew the tea. "What do you need?"

A short laugh echoed from the kitchen and she turned away, thumping and crashing things over by the stove. "What do I *need?* I need for people I care about not to leave at the drop of a hat. What I'm getting, however, is a blithering idiot who expects me to help him murder himself and be grateful for it."

Devlin's mouth dropped open, and he could only stare as Ivory stormed around the bench and set a bowl of oatmeal in front of Bailey. The deathcharger whickered and Ivory's face softened momentarily as she brushed Bailey's forelock back from her face.

"It's not like that," Devlin managed. Something in his gut turned cold and slippery, and he swallowed against the lump in his throat when neither horse nor woman answered. "I don't ... I don't want to ..."

Moving in perfect unison, Ivory and Bailey turned their heads, pinning him with matching glares.

"You don't want to die? Really?" Ivory's eyes blazed with fury. "Then why aren't you fighting?"

"Fighting for *what?*" He slapped a hand against his chest. "Have you stopped for a second to think that this might be beyond my control?"

Bailey's brow furrowed, and Ivory blinked. "What do you mean?"

"I'm not the one who laid the curse; I'm not the one who must choose to lift it. Do you honestly think, when I come face to face with your ancestor, that she's going to just *forgive me?*" He let out a brittle laugh. "You're acting as though I'm walking away from a second chance, but Ivory, she might not give me one. She might demand I lay down my life and return your family's power to where it rightfully belongs. Then what?"

The silence crackled with tension, but after a long moment, Bailey sighed and dropped her glare. Ivory tsked in the back of her throat and then she, too, looked away.

Devlin forced his voice to remain even. "If you're asking if I want to leave Bailey to an uncertain fate, to walk away from – light save me – from you, then the answer is no. I don't. But you said it yourself; we can't leave your ancestor tethered to me indefinitely, not if it's causing her pain." He curled his hands to fists. "This is the right thing to do."

"I hate doing the right thing." Ivory bared her teeth at him. "And right now, I hate you too."

Devlin choked, searching desperately for a reasonable response, but Ivory walked into the bathroom and slammed the door behind her.

"Dammit." He looked over at Bailey, who watched him with sad eyes. "What now?"

The deathcharger gave a sad little sigh, rolled her shoulders and began to eat her oats – because at the end of the day, no matter how they all felt, there was no other choice.

It was the right thing to do.

Once Ivory reappeared, she announced their first stop to be a human supermarket. She covered her fingers in liniments from a variety of different jars, issued a clipped warning to be alert for Hunters at all times, then withdrew into the depths of a black coat whose hood was so enormously oversized it not only hid her horns but wreathed her entire face in shadows.

She didn't speak, and neither did Devlin.

Bailey took them into town, waiting outside while Devlin followed Ivory up and down the supermarket's many aisles, dutifully holding the shopping basket and trying not to make any sudden movements that might dislodge his head from his shoulders ... even though Ivory had strapped it in place with several layers of a thick silver tape which was, for some odd reason, named after ducks.

When they reached the register, Ivory unloaded the contents of the basket without so much as glancing in Devlin's direction. She fumbled the tin of pineapple slices and they both bent to catch it, colliding with enough force that the duck tape gave way in a spectacular ripping of adhesive. Devlin's head thunked onto the black conveyor belt, bounced off a bottle of soda water and rolled to a stop face up in front of the clerk.

"Damn," he said.

The elderly woman, wearing a grocer's smock and a name tag that read 'Senior Staff: Una,' stared at him with wide eyes.

"I'm terribly sorry," Devlin said. "I really don't think duck tape was the best choice. Perhaps you can recommend something stronger?"

Una screamed, tripping over her own feet in her haste to back away from the register. Devlin winced as her distress garnered the attention of the other people in the supermarket and one scream became two, then three, then a chorus – until, in less than a minute, the store emptied of everyone save Devlin and Ivory.

"Perhaps you can recommend something stronger?" Ivory repeated. Laughter shook her shoulders, and from his vantage point at her waist height, Devlin could just see her biting her lip to contain her mirth. "You know how to joke after all."

"I wasn't joking," Devlin grumbled, though warmth unfurled in his chest. "This duck tape is worse than the kinesiology tape I had in the RV."

Ivory coughed, the sound dissolving into a hearty laugh. "It's duct tape, you idiot. For fixing ducts. And for the record, the tape worked out exactly as I'd hoped."

"You ..." Devlin gasped. "You *meant* for my head to fall off?"

"How else am I supposed to get the groceries for free?"

"Free? They're not free! You have to pay for them!"

She shrugged and winked. "Bit difficult to pay if there's nobody here."

And before he could protest, Ivory scooped his head into the nearest shopping bag, hung the handles over his outstretched arm and tugged him out of the store. Bailey snorted the moment she saw them, and Devlin didn't need to remove his face from the bag of oranges to know she laughed at him rather than with him. Relief thumped in his blood, demanding he laugh and cry and beg their forgiveness, but since the awful tension that had reigned since dawn was only just beginning to lift, he did his best to look unimpressed instead, muttering under his breath while Ivory removed the failed duck – *duct* – tape, and then resecured his head to his neck with a fresh batch.

"There." Ivory adjusted his scarf and the neck of his leather jacket. "Fixed."

"Thank you." Devlin cleared his throat, trying not to blush. "Though I feel I should point out that my head is a little off-centre."

Ivory raised a brow, lips twitching with the barest hint of a smile. "I wouldn't worry. It's not staying on long."

It didn't. In the homewares store, Ivory let out an enormous fake sneeze, jostling Devlin so that his head toppled into a basket of plastic flowers – and once the customers had fled, she propped his head atop her loot, took his wrist and led him back out to a still-laughing Bailey.

"This is the easiest shopping I've ever done," Ivory said, rearranging the contents of the trolley so that the perishables wouldn't get crushed. "Talk about jumping the queue."

Devlin picked at the tape stuck to his chin. "I'm not sure if I'm supposed to approve of theft, but this is the first time anyone's appreciated the fact that my head falls off so easily."

"You're telling me you've never walked out with free stuff after your head fell off?" Ivory raised both her eyebrows. "Because if you do, I'll call you a liar."

"Oh, no – Bailey and I do that all the time. I mean, I try to pay, but it becomes difficult when everyone runs away." He frowned. "Does this make me a bad person?"

"You're asking *me*?" Ivory tilted her head, eyes dancing. "I'm morally ambiguous, remember?"

"Of course." Devlin huffed a laugh as he pulled out the roll of duct tape. "I'm not sure how this is meant to keep us from being noticed by the Hunters, though."

"It's not." Ivory screwed her face up. "One of those goody-two-shoes we scared off is probably flapping their gums even as we speak."

"But... but... *you* were the one who said we had to watch out for them!"

Ivory took the roll of tape from him with gentle fingers. "Devlin, look at me. I have horns. And claws. How long do you think it would be before someone noticed?" Her smile was soft and sad. "I can tell you – not long. Making a scene means the Hunters will still come, but they'll come where we *want* them to come; and by the time they arrive, we'll be gone."

"Oh." He lifted his hair out of the way as she began winding tape around his neck. "That makes sense, I guess. Where next?"

She grinned, and he felt like the sun had just come out. "The hardware store."

Where Ivory gave up all pretence of an accident and hit him with a thick piece of doweling, punting his head halfway across the shop to land with a splash in the ornamental fish tank behind the front counter. As he sank to rest chin-first on the pink gravel at the bottom of the tank, a miniature shark nipping at his nose, Devlin closed his eyes and let Ivory's water-distorted laughter wash over him.

All his life, he'd clung to the morals and manners that his brethren had taught him. He'd believed in justice, and honour, and honesty. Courage, benevolence, loyalty – all the tenets of a strong, righteous knight. Now, though?

Maybe Ivory was right. Maybe it was all just an illusion, because he didn't want to do what honour demanded. He didn't want to leave.

He didn't want to do the right thing.

Soaking up the odd peace that came from being underwater with one's face pressed against a plastic pirate ship, Devlin sighed. His mission had started simply enough; now it involved a demon caring about a headless ex-knight who carried a sword the colour of old blood and rode a destrier-turned-deathcharger. Just as he cared about her, far more than he should for the short time they'd known one another, far more than was reasonable or logical or ... human.

The little shark had begun to nudge the end of Devlin's left eyebrow by the time Ivory's hand plunged into the tank, streams of darkness trailing from her clawed fingers. She cradled the back of his head and brought him to the surface nose-first, like a sunken wreck being salvaged from the very depths of the ocean.

"I'm sorry," Devlin said, the moment his lips were back in the open air.

Ivory paused, and for a moment, he wondered if she was going to drop him back into the tank. "I know."

"I don't know how to fix this," he admitted. "What I broke."

"You do," she responded, her breath catching unsteadily. "And so do I. It's why we're going through with this, in spite of how we feel about it." Her brows furrowed. "But if you tell anyone I'm doing what might be considered the right thing, I will find a way to end you."

Devlin blinked water from his eyes and offered his most charming smile. "I'll be sure to enjoy every minute."

Ivory's mouth dropped open, revealing every single one of her pointed demonic teeth. She stared at him wide-eyed for almost two entire minutes before she shook her head, yanked him the rest of the way out of the tank, and stalked out of the store with her brows furrowed into a frown.

She drew up on the footpath, shoving his head back against his chest so she could fist both hands on her hips. "What happens to Bailey when you die?"

"What?"

"Assuming it all goes wrong tomorrow, and you don't get a choice. If you die, does Bailey die? Is her demonic state connected to yours?"

"I don't think so." Devlin glanced towards where the deathcharger stood guard a few paces away. "She made the full transition when I did not. If my choice is made for me, and I don't return tomorrow, then ... well, I assumed she would simply stay with whoever had broken my curse. So ... you."

Ivory crinkled her nose. "Leaving me to clean up your mess without even asking first? What a guy."

"It's not like that," Devlin protested, his throat inexplicably thick. "I just ..."

"I know." She closed her eyes, and for a moment the three of them stood in tortured silence. "We better get out of here before the Hunters catch wind of us."

"Yes." Devlin followed as she stalked away, hips swaying and the heels of her boots clicking furiously on the pavement. "How much time do we have?"

"No idea, but it'll happen eventually. It always does." Pulling up in front of a vehicle with a large tub at the back, Ivory licked the tip of one claw and stuck it into the locking mechanism. The metal hissed and sagged, silver alloy dripping onto the road until the vehicle issued a sad beep and the door unlocked.

The clatter of hooves announced the arrival of Bailey, her mouth fastened over the handle of the trolley so that she could drag it along behind her. Balancing his head on the side of the vehicle, Devlin unlatched the back and began transferring the many bags and boxes that Ivory had acquired while Bailey curled up in the tub, her enormous bulk squashed against the vehicle's edges and the suspension groaning in protest.

Devlin shut the tailgate as the engine rumbled to life, the vehicle vibrating beneath him. After a moment's hesitation, he spread his fingers across the deathcharger's shoulder. "Is there not honour in repenting my mistakes?"

Bailey considered him a long moment, pale green eyes flickering with infernal light. "Yes."

"Then why does it hurt more than I ever thought possible?"

Bailey's expression softened. "Heart."

"I suppose you're right. If I didn't care, it wouldn't hurt, and if it didn't hurt, it wouldn't be penance." Devlin blew out a long breath. "I never expected the cost to be so steep."

"Hmph." Bailey tipped her head to the side. "Paid already."

Devlin frowned. "You think the time I spent bound to the hollow is payment enough?"

"Yes."

"All we can do is hope my ancestor agrees." Ivory appeared on the opposite side of the vehicle, where she reached to run her fingers through Bailey's mane. "I hate hope."

"I think, perhaps, that I do, too." Devlin gripped the side of the vehicle so hard the metal groaned in protest. "I don't want to leave Bailey."

I don't want to leave you.

"Sad," Bailey whickered.

"I know, gorgeous. I know. But what other choice do we have?" Ivory spat on the pavement. It sizzled. "It's the right thing to do."

ALL HALLOW'S EVE

*I*vory lay in bed until the morning sun peeked through the gap between her curtains, cutting a ray of brilliance across the heavy gloom. Sleep – or lack thereof – had her eyes full of sand and her brain full of wool, and for reasons she absolutely refused to examine, her breathing was truncated and her heart hurt with every rhythmic beat.

Halloween was here.

Perhaps she should've given in to her cravings the previous night and invited Devlin to bed. She knew he'd have come; his interest in her was no secret, after all. And yet ... it was precisely because she wanted him that she'd left him in the lounge room.

Letting out a heavy sigh, Ivory rubbed both hands over her face. Logically, she hadn't known Devlin long enough to feel the depth of emotion that she did. She wasn't a creature of logic, however, she was a demon, and demons burned hot and bright. Sometimes so bright they were consumed by their passions and turned terribly evil.

Ivory lifted a hand and stared at her pale skin, the long, curved claws that marked her as anything but human. Not so long ago, she'd rejoiced at the idea of assuming a human form but now, knowing it meant Devlin's destruction ... she didn't want to give him up.

For once, just once, she wanted someone to choose *her*. She wanted to be enough to fill someone so full that they overflowed with it, that they'd embrace a culture they'd once sworn to destroy. She wanted to be loved.

No.

She wanted to be loved by *Devlin*.

A soft knock sounded at the bedroom door and Ivory rose, opening it to find not Devlin, as she'd expected, but Bailey. The deathcharger looked ludicrous crammed in the small doorway, her shoulders pushing against the frame and smoke curling from her nostrils but rather than comment, Ivory looped her arms around Bailey's neck and buried her face in lengths of long, silky black mane.

"Where is he?" Ivory whispered.

"Washing."

Ivory focussed her attention on the background noise of the cottage and registered the sound of the shower running. She squeezed Bailey a little tighter. "We'll be okay. If ... if things don't go the way we hope, you can stay with me and we'll spend the rest of our years bitter and jaded together. I promise."

The deathcharger sighed as she tucked her head around Ivory in the equine equivalent of a hug. "Yes."

"Gods and demons, this is stupid," Ivory muttered, her eyes stinging. "So, so stupid."

"Yes," Bailey snorted, her chest rumbling with a laugh. "Stupid."

Ivory laughed too, wobbly though it was, and they stood in silence until the shower cut off and Devlin could be heard grumbling to himself as he tried to manage his head and his towel at the same time.

"Well." Ivory stepped back and wiped her eyes. "I guess that means it's my turn, and then ... we get this done."

Bailey nodded, and by the time Devlin emerged, Ivory had packed everything she was going to need into an old-fashioned picnic basket. After a quick shower, she dressed in comfortable jeans and a long-line sweater that clung to her curves and was, in keeping with her mood, a dark grey.

"Ready?" She flicked Devlin a glance, noting he wore the same outfit he'd had on since they'd met. "No clean clothes?"

"They were in the RV." He shrugged, looking uncomfortable. "I didn't mention anything yesterday because ..."

"Right. Fair enough." Pressing her lips together, Ivory snatched up the basket and made for the door. "Let's go, then."

"Wait." Devlin made as if to reach for her, pulling up short at the last moment. "The Hunters have to have worked out we're in this area by now. Is it safe?"

Ivory blew out a long breath. "The Hunters have been chasing me for years, Devlin. Every time I leave the wards, there's a chance that either they'll find me, or someone will tell them where I am – but I refuse to jump at their shadow for the rest of my life. To answer your question, no, it's not safe. If you haven't worked out by now that you need to keep your eyes open and your blade sharp, then no amount of warning from me will be able to change that."

She stomped out of the cottage, unable to bear his stark expression a moment longer. Bailey waited outside by the well, her gaze fixed off in the middle distance. Tension rode in the line of her shoulders and her muscles quivered as though she'd break into a gallop at the slightest noise.

"What is it?" Devlin drew his sword from the sheath down his back and strode to the deathcharger's side. "What do you sense? Is it the Hunters?"

Bailey's nostrils dilated as she lifted her head, sampling air thick with magic. "No. Strange."

"Strange, there's an enemy but you're not sure who it is? Or strange, it's Halloween and the veil between worlds is the thinnest it will be all year?" Ivory knelt in the leaves beside the front door and closed her eyes, listening to the whispers of her ancestors. "Everything's louder than normal, stronger, but I don't feel anything out of place."

After a long moment, Bailey shook her head.

"All Hallow's Eve is a difficult time for us," Devlin said eventually. "Everything feels ... overwhelming."

Ivory nodded. "Of course. When all the layers of magic come together in chaos, it is demonkind who feel it the strongest."

"I ... really?"

"Yes. That's why people traditionally fear those with demonic blood on Halloween; if ever we're to lose our minds, it's on a day like today." Ivory drew a deep breath, then let it out slowly. "If you can learn to control it however, it makes us infinitely more powerful – which, as far as the ritual is concerned, is a very good thing."

Pushing upright, Ivory dusted her knees, retrieved the picnic basket, and strode off towards the forest. They passed through the innermost wards a minute later, the magic shimmering the air around them. A chill pervaded the air as they walked through the second, and when they came to the final, outermost layer, Devlin stopped.

"I don't like this. Wouldn't we be better off doing the ritual inside, where you're safer?"

"The wards would interfere." Ivory waved a hand through the air, feeling the unusually strong energy slip through her fingers like molasses. "We have to find somewhere neutral – a place where all five elements meet."

"All five?"

"Earth, air, fire, water ... spirit." Ivory smiled at his stunned expression. "Why else do you think a pentagram has five points? Don't worry, I know just the place – it'll take us an hour or so to get there, but it'll be worth it."

"And what if the Hunters turn up?" Devlin waved an arm at the forest, as though he expected a horde of demon hunters to materialise the moment they left the safety of the wards. "You may not fear their shadow, but I do. I know Gawain. He never gives up, and he's dangerous – he wouldn't have been a Knight of the Round Table otherwise. To build an organisation like the Hunters proves his ability to inspire blind loyalty hasn't deteriorated over time. If they find us ..."

"Then we'll deal with it." Ivory glared at him, one fist propped on her hip. "We cleansed our trails again last night after we got home;

we're as safe as we can possibly be. Unless you're procrastinating for another reason?"

Devlin flinched, but after a long moment he sheathed his sword and swung onto Bailey's back with a practised movement. When he extended a hand down to Ivory, she gave him the basket and set off into the forest on foot. A long-suffering sigh echoed behind her before Bailey trotted to catch up, her giant hooves almost silent on the soft earth.

Perhaps it was silly not to ride, but Ivory couldn't bring herself to be so close to Devlin knowing that in little more than an hour she might lose him forever. Even astride Bailey, his cinnamon and sandalwood scent taunted her and she clenched her teeth against the urge to climb up behind him, bury her face in his shoulder for no other reason than to breathe him in and pretend, just for a moment, that she wasn't alone.

The terrain dipped and before long they came to a wide, well-lit gully, where one of the forest's many winding streams burbled happily out of a small cave in the side of the earth. Bailey picked her way in from the shallow end, pausing a moment to sample the stream's fresh water. Devlin dismounted to join Ivory at the mouth of the cave, eyeing the low-roofed entrance and shadowy interior with obvious doubt.

"It's bigger inside," she murmured.

He adjusted his head so that it fit better into the crook of his elbow and frowned. "It looks ..."

"What?"

"Like a tomb."

Ivory took the picnic basket from him with a low laugh. "I prefer to think of it as atmospheric."

She ducked into the cave before he could answer, leaving the sunlight behind. As promised, the interior was larger than the entrance made it appear, the stream bisecting a space large enough for four people to comfortably stretch out in before narrowing to a melon-sized tunnel low in the far wall, from where the water flowed clear and cold. The bank of the stream rose sharply before flattening to soft earth that, though cool to touch, was dry enough to sit on.

Setting her basket by the entrance, Ivory flipped the lid and began to rummage for the things she needed. She was aware of Devlin speaking quietly to Bailey outside, and the deathcharger's gentle, whinnied answer – no words, just a heartbreak so huge it made Ivory's eyes itch. When Devlin ducked through the opening of the cave, Ivory didn't look up. Couldn't, else she might lose the fragile hold she had on herself and expose a level of vulnerability she'd thought long hardened.

"Hey," he said eventually, the word so modern it sounded strange from his lips.

Pick me, her heart whispered. *Please, pick me.*

Ivory cleared her throat and pointed at the dirt covered floor. "Hey. Lie down over there and we'll get started."

"Wait." Devlin fell to his knees at her side, catching her wrist so she couldn't turn away. "I wanted to say—"

"Don't," Ivory hissed, jerking from his grasp. "Don't thank me, don't wish things were different, don't say goodbye. Do. Not."

He pressed his lips together, looking unutterably sad. "I'm sorry."

"Don't do that, either," Ivory whispered, smoothing the hem of her sweater. "You don't owe me anything, least of all an apology."

Silence fell, broken only by the trickle of the stream and the sound of Ivory's breathing – which seemed wobbly and much too fast, even to her. Devlin's hand twitched and for a moment she feared what she would do if he reached for her again, but instead, he moved to lie down where she'd indicated.

Once his body was settled, Ivory took his head and placed it against the stump of his neck, creating the illusion of a whole, and sat back on her heels. "Ready? Because once I begin, you need to lie very still."

This time, when he reached out, Ivory let Devlin capture her hand and bring it to his lips, where he pressed a kiss to her knuckles. "Thank you."

Blinking back tears, Ivory nodded. She extended a clawed finger to draw sigils in the dirt, but it shook so violently the first of the runes had to be smudged out.

Pick me. Please, pick me.

"Hey." Devlin squeezed her fingers, his voice unbearably tender. "It's okay. Whatever happens, I promise I'll set your ancestor free."

Ivory blew out a breath. "I know."

Devlin's fingers slipped from hers, the loss like a physical blow – but this time, her hand was steady when she began to draw. The sigils flowed to a rhythm of their own, a long stream of demonic that formed a circle around Devlin's body. When the last of the runes connected to the first, the circle started to hum, a deep, resonant sound that vibrated through Ivory's bones and made the hairs on her arms stand on end. Guided by both instinct and magic, she pulled ingredients from her basket one by one, popping their lids off to flick pinches of this and that into the circle. For each new reagent she added, the hum changed pitch and one by one, the runes began to glow – a soft, earthy orange that became steadily brighter until it seemed impossible that nothing was on fire. Ivory lifted her thumb to her lips and bit down until blood welled, sharp and metallic on her tongue.

Pick me. Pick me. Pick me.

Ivory held her hand over the top of the circle and locked eyes with Devlin one final time. "Good luck."

Blood dripped from the tip of her thumb to land in the centre of his chest, causing the demonic circle to hiss like an over-boiling pot. Dark smoke billowed from the ground, wrapping Devlin's body until he was obscured from view – but she didn't need to see to know the moment his spirit slipped beyond the veil. She could feel it in the way her chest ached, in the way hot, fat tears spilled down her cheeks and her throat thickened with the urge to scream.

She clenched her hand into a fist and rolled to her feet, leaving the basket where it lay in her haste to exit a cave whose atmosphere had become suddenly stifling. Outside, she gulped great breaths of air, bracing herself against the sturdy wall of the gully until the world stopped spinning. Something moved by the stream and Ivory blinked her eyes until they cleared, drinking in the sight of Bailey with her head lifted to the morning sunlight, coat shining and mane fluttering in the breeze. She looked magnificent and utterly alone, and before Ivory knew what she was doing, she'd crossed the gulf between them to throw her arms around the deathcharger's neck.

"It's done," she said, though they both knew it. "Now, we wait."

"Yes."

"How are you so calm? I feel like I want to murder someone."

Bailey turned, then, lashes lifting on eyes burning with infernal green light. "Love."

"Love?" Ivory cracked a harsh laugh. "You're calm because you love him?"

The deathcharger tipped her head to the side. "Not me."

"Huh?"

"Love," Bailey whickered. "You love."

"*Me?* I'm not in love with Devlin." Ivory bopped Bailey's nose, undeterred when the deathcharger's lip pulled back to reveal a mouth full of fangs several inches long. "I've only known him a couple of days."

Bailey shrugged. "Demon."

"I don't care how different demons are; that's just ludicrous. It's not enough time."

The deathcharger's lips pursed and when she spoke, her words came out slow and measured. "Love doesn't keep time."

Ivory stared.

Love doesn't keep time.

She opened her mouth to deny Bailey again but the words wouldn't come. The deathcharger's expression softened and she nudged at Ivory with her nose until there was little option but to stroke her soft, shiny coat.

"I'm in love with him?" Ivory cleared her throat, but the squeak in her voice remained. "How can you tell?"

"Smell."

"Smell ..."

"Energy." Bailey's ears flickered. "Love smells match."

Ivory frowned. "I ... gross?"

"Love," Bailey insisted. Her brow furrowed and her voice dropped until it was almost a hiss. "Fight?"

"You want me to fight love?" Ivory blinked, realising the atmosphere had stilled as though the wildlife held their breath. "No ... you want to know if I'll fight *for* love."

"Yes." Bailey angled her head towards the forest. "Fight Hunters for love."

Ivory glared into the trees, as though she could see through to the menace beyond. "How many Hunters, Bailey?"

"Many."

"Damn." Ivory let out a long breath, glancing back at the cave where Devlin lay inert. "He might not come back, you know. My ancestor might not set him free."

Bailey shrugged. "Maybe."

Maybe. Maybe. Maybe.

Ivory growled deep in her chest. "You're asking me to risk my life on a chance! The tiniest, slimmest, most ridiculous chance."

This time, Bailey chuckled. "Yes."

Shadows began to form beyond the treeline. The energy of Halloween swirled around her, filling her with the chaos of mingling worlds. It would be easy to corral the energy – she could use it to escape, to disappear without a trace and return to her old life, forgetting that she'd ever met an ex-knight named Devlin whose head wasn't attached to his shoulders. She could abandon him the way the entire world had abandoned her, and once the Hunters were done, there'd be nobody left alive to say that she'd been wrong. Sure, reality would become a more terrible place than it was already ... but Ivory would live.

Alone.

For the rest of her life.

Love doesn't keep time.

"Ah, shit. I'm in love with Devlin," Ivory whispered.

Bailey's tail flicked. "Yes."

The moment hung, refracting in the morning light with the brilliance of a diamond. Ivory wanted to capture the painful beauty of it even as she longed to banish the vulnerability it created – but the moment persisted until she had little choice but to accept the inevitable. She loved Devlin, and if she wanted the chance to see him again, she and Bailey had to buy whatever time he needed to make peace with his sins.

"All right." Ivory lifted her chin, allowing the energy of All Hallow's Eve to wash through her body, forming it as nature had intended from the beginning. "Time to show Gawain what a real demon is made of."

11

A FORK IN THE ROAD

*D*evlin wasn't sure what he'd expected to find beyond the veil, but a cute little cottage in a street paved with well-swept cobblestones wasn't it. One moment, he'd closed his eyes against the billowing rush of smoke that filled Ivory's demonic circle and the next, he opened them to find himself standing, head in hand, beside a white picket fence complete with an ornamental gate and a novelty mailbox in the shape of a birdhouse.

"Well," he said, looking down at the not at all ornamental bird sitting on top of the mailbox. "What now?"

The bird, small enough to fit in the palm of his hand, fluffed up unnaturally blue feathers and cheeped at him. When Devlin didn't immediately respond, it hopped to the edge of the mailbox roof, pecked his nose and flew away.

"Ow," Devlin muttered, shifting his grip so he could rub the tiny ache. He glanced up and down the street, but the collection of eclectic abodes lay silent. The road was so clean it sparkled in the bright sunlight and the scent of flowers hung pleasantly in the air, as though someone had taken a snapshot of the perfect spring morning and imprinted it on the environment for all eternity.

Devlin turned his attention to the cottage in front of him; small, with a vibrant green lawn and bright flowers smiling from equally bright window boxes. The windows were round, the walls rendered in bright violet, the shutters and trim a brilliant white. The route from gate to covered porch was marked by quaint grey stepping stones placed just far enough apart to traverse comfortably and the front door, hung with a wreath of twisted branches, swung open as Devlin watched.

The woman in the doorway was unremarkable with her short brown hair, dark eyes and smattering of freckles – but he'd recognise her anywhere, at any time, for she was indelibly marked upon his stained soul as the woman who'd cursed him as he stole her life with callous hands. They stared at each other for long minutes, and then, to Devlin's utter astonishment, her features crinkled into a welcoming smile.

"Are you going to stand there all day?" she asked, waving a hand in his general direction. "Or are you going to come inside?"

"Uh," Devlin replied.

The woman laughed, stepping back from the doorway. "Come along now, Sir Devlin. My tea's getting cold."

With little other option, Devlin traversed the gently meandering pathway and alighted on the porch. It creaked under his weight and he flinched, wishing abruptly for his sword – which promptly appeared on his back, in the leather scabbard he'd worn for thousands of years.

"You won't need that," his host said cheerfully. "Leave it in the umbrella stand."

"Apologies," Devlin murmured as he stepped across the threshold. "I don't know where it came from."

"It's part of you," she answered, reaching around him to close the door with a click. "You thought you needed it, and so it appeared. In my experience, men tend to be irrationally attached to their swords – but no harm will come to you in this place, I promise." She paused, looking down at his face from eyes so dark a brown they were almost black, and smiled. "My name is Jenniker, but you can call me Jenn."

Jenn. He'd murdered a woman named Jenn, with brown hair,

freckles, and a sweet face that held definite traces of Ivory in it. Devlin swallowed heavily. "I never knew your name."

"No," she said breezily, tugging him into a well-lit lounge with curved walls, a hand-woven rug and several brightly upholstered arm chairs. "It wasn't really necessary in your line of work."

"I'm sorry."

Jenn snorted. "Little late for that now, isn't it? Sit down while I fetch my tea."

Devlin watched her bustle away in her blue homespun dress and then, for lack of anything better to do, perched on the edge of an armchair and balanced his head on his knees. When Jenn returned, she had a cup of tea in one hand and a plate of biscuits in the other. Her smile was still firmly in place as she sat, took up a biscuit and bit into it, watching Devlin as she chewed.

"So," she said, swallowing noisily. "Why are you here?"

"I beg your pardon?"

"Here, in this cottage." Jenn waved her biscuit in emphasis. "Sitting on my chair as though it might swallow you whole at any second?"

"I came to repent." Devlin straightened his spine and looked deep into her eyes. "I took something precious from you and your family. I came to beg forgiveness, and to help sever the ties which have bound us together all these years."

"Hmm." Jenn laid a hand over her ribs, in the exact place Devlin's blade – the blade currently in her umbrella stand – had slid home. She chewed her lower lip a long moment, dark eyes solemn as she looked him up and down in exactly the way Ivory had done when they'd first met. "Are you sure?"

Devlin's jaw dropped. "What? Of course I'm sure."

"Well, then, I suppose I have some things that need to be said." Jenn ate the rest of her biscuit and then picked up another. "I hated you when I first arrived here. I didn't get to see my children grow up, or walk into the twilight at my husband's side. The wound you caused when you drove your sword through my heart never healed, and I have lingered in pain ever since." She dusted biscuit crumbs from her dress, then leaned forward and braced both elbows on her knees. "I transferred my powers to you in anger. I wanted you to know what it was like to become the thing you hunted; to understand the terror demons face when we're persecuted simply for existing – as though we are lesser simply by virtue of the fact that we are different." Her lips twisted. "I will not argue that evil demons do not exist, but nor will you argue, I think, that there is not evil in all beings, no matter their species. Evil is not a birthright; it's a choice, and every individual has an opportunity to make it."

The words hit hard, and Devlin closed his eyes to absorb each blow. Manners dictated he speak, the words ragged as they tore from his deepest self. "I wish I'd made a better choice."

Jenn sipped her tea, lashes lowered.

"Here's the thing, though," she said at last. Setting the cup down, she moved from her chair to kneel at Devlin's feet. "You suffered, too. Tied together as we are, every time I close my eyes, I see through yours. I have witnessed your solitude, your life with Bailey and recently, your search for a way to pay your debt." With gentle fingers, Jenn flipped a lock of Devlin's hair back from his face. "Your attitude change, the way you interact with Ivory, the magnetic pull of your attraction ... You have become more than the sum of your parts, Sir Devlin, and though you came here to restore your honour, I will tell you that you never truly gave it up – you learned your lesson in humility and have grown from it."

"But your husband," Devlin murmured. "Your daughters."

"When they died, they passed through here," Jenn smiled. "They were allowed to visit with me for a while, and once you and I are no longer tethered, I'll be free to join them on the other side. We will be together again."

"That's why I'm here," Devlin choked, daring to grasp her hand with his larger one. "I promised Ivory I would set you free, and I will, no matter what you demand of me."

"Is that what Ivory wants?"

"What?" Devlin blinked. "What do you mean?"

Jenn pursed her lips. "Ivory's been kicked more times than any one creature should have to endure. If I take your soul as payment then she'll gain the power to assume a human form and live a human life, but she'll face that life alone. And that, I think, would be *my* crime." She paused. "Unless you don't want to stay with her?"

"Of course I want to stay with her," Devlin snapped. "She's beautiful and funny and wicked and real. I want her to be happy more than I want my next breath."

"And yet you're willing to give away that next breath."

"If that's what you need to be free, then yes." Devlin swallowed. "I don't *want* to leave her, though; or Bailey. And I don't really know how to be a demon—"

"That's because you've been stuck halfway all this time." Jenn crossed both arms over her chest. "Or are your old prejudices still a problem?"

"No," Devlin growled. "There's nothing wrong with being a demon; I know that now."

"Good." Jenn chewed her lower lip. "Do you love her?"

Devlin froze. "Love?"

"You heard me. Yes or no?"

"Um." Heat crept over his cheeks, and he looked away from her piercing gaze. "I have no idea if Ivory feels—"

"Yes or no?"

"Yes!" he cried, slapping a hand against his thigh. "Yes, I love her – but I cannot, in all good conscience, devote myself to her knowing that my continued existence keeps you tethered to this plane. When I first sought Ivory, I knew only that she was the path to this moment, where I could get down on my knees and beg for absolution. In a short space of time, she became everything – but no matter how much my heart belongs to Ivory, you have a prior claim upon my life. If you demand it, I will give it to you."

"Even if it means leaving Ivory alone? And Bailey, who has followed you so long and loved you so well?"

Devlin let his lashes drift shut, forcing words through the agony in his chest. "Even then."

"Then here is your penance, Sir Devlin." Jenn cleared her throat. "To repay the debt you owe, you will return to the living realm as a demon and dedicate your days to making a better world. You will take your second chance in both hands and you will squeeze every drop of laughter, joy, sadness, fury, passion and *life* out of it, filling your days with such substance that they overflow." She took a step forward, jaw set. "Most of all, you will do that which is a knight's highest sworn duty: you will protect. You will fight for those who cannot fight for themselves. You will stand for the people who do not quite fit; the people who are hunted and beaten and excommunicated for no other reason than that they are different. You will be an avatar for the alternative, and you will demonstrate to the non-believers that honour is a choice that can be made every single day." Jenn jabbed a finger into Devlin's bicep. "You will start your life over again and this time, you'll do it right. *That* is the price I demand of you."

Devlin stared, his stomach flipping with such speed he wondered if it might rebel, despite having had nothing inside it for millenia. "And Ivory?"

"Earn her." Jenn caught hold of Devlin's hair, lifting his face closer to her own. "Teach her happiness and love. Though the mists of time separate us, she is still family, my many-times granddaughter. If you truly cherish her, Sir Devlin, then you may spend the rest of your life proving your worth – and I will forgive you for what you stole."

Tears welled in Devlin's eyes and he made no effort to blink them back. "Thank you."

"Is that a yes?" A soft hand landed on his shoulder. "Please say yes, Devlin. Let this end in peace."

"Yes," Devlin croaked, shaking all over. "I accept the terms of your penance."

"About time," drawled a new voice.

With gentle fingers, Jenn wiped the tears from Devlin's eyes and set his head into his lap. When she leaned away, it was to reveal a man slouched against the far wall, hands stuffed casually into the pockets of his long, black coat. Tall and slender, with an angular face and thick hair the colour of eggplant that stuck out at all manner of angles, he looked young and unassuming – but the energy which crackled off him sent chills over Devlin's skin.

"Who are you?" Devlin asked, climbing slowly to his feet.

"Myself." The man shrugged, his voice both smooth and raspy at the same time, as though he'd drunk warm honey to soothe a sore throat but it hadn't yet taken complete effect. "I suppose you might say that I am ..." his lips twisted into a grin, bringing an unholy light to eyes a darker shade of aubergine than his hair. "I am the Guardian of this place."

Jenn rolled her eyes. "He doesn't understand that joke."

"It wasn't for him," the newcomer said, still grinning. Just as quickly as it had come, his amusement faded and those unusually coloured eyes locked on Devlin. "I'm here to set Jenn free, and send you back where you belong."

"You're ..." Devlin fought the urge to take a step back. "A reaper?"

The man tilted his head to the side, brow furrowed and lips moving as though talking to himself. "No," he said at last. "Not *a* reaper."

Unease trickled through Devlin's veins as he glanced at Jenn, but she only looked annoyed. "Can we get on with this, already? Some of us are in pain, you know."

"Of course." Pushing off the wall, the man removed long, thin hands from his pockets and beckoned with the elegance of a dancer. His black coat billowed over a fitted black t-shirt and tattered black jeans, hinting at a frame that was unnaturally thin – yet when he wrapped his fingers around Devlin's wrist, his grip was like steel. "You'll need this."

Devlin stared down at the crimson sword that had been, up until that very moment, in the umbrella stand. "I will?"

"Oh, yes." Those aubergine eyes unfocussed, the man's papery voice taking on an eerie, singsong cadence. "There's a man who, despite all the evidence placed before him, clings to his own hatred. He rides a wave of destruction as though it were justice and wears a cloak woven from twisted dogma."

"Gawain." Devlin hissed out a breath. "I knew something was out of place when we left the wards." He took his sword, and the man blinked as though surprised to find himself amongst company. "I appreciate the warning."

Another blink, and slowly, the man's face resumed some semblance of animation. "Is that what that was?"

"Yes," Jenn replied, reaching out to prise the man's fingers from Devlin's wrist. They came one at a time, as though breaking the rictus took concerted effort – but then the man shook his hand with the same liquid elegance as before, and the moment was lost. Jenn prodded him gently in the chest. "Come on, now. The sooner the better for everyone, I think."

"Yes, you're right." The man positioned Jenn and Devlin so that they stood facing one another, and waved his long fingers between them. "Head. Heart."

Devlin raised a brow but Jenn seemed to understand, for she took his head and placed it upon the stump of his neck, smoothing her palms over the place where skin and bone had been severed. She lifted her eyes to Devlin's and took a deep breath. "Take care of her."

"I will." After a moment's hesitation, Devlin gingerly laid his hand over her heart – where, so many long years ago, he had driven his sword. "Thank you."

Jenn smiled and the strange man stepped in close, gripping one of their shoulders in each of his hands, long lashes dragging his eyes shut. "You're welcome," he said. "May you both find peace beyond the weave."

Devlin frowned but before he had a chance to consider the odd phrase, scalding heat washed through his body and everything went black.

12

YOU'RE NOT EVIL, I'M EVIL

*I*vory held her place at Bailey's side as the trees rustled, her sharper eyesight picking out more than twenty silhouettes lurking among the trunks.

"You have the high ground and the advantage of numbers, Gawain," she called. "And still you choose to hide like a coward."

A sussurus of whispers licked through the air as Gawain Braybrook stepped out of the trees. He'd muddied his blond hair and pale skin, his clothes a mixture of the browns and greens which comprised the forest – but nothing could disguise the hard light of loathing in blue eyes so bright they almost glowed.

"I didn't want you to flee like the animal you are," he boomed, fisting both hands on his hips. "Do not fear, unholy creatures. We're here to grant you the mercy of the light."

Ivory raised an eyebrow as Gawain lifted his face to the sun, showing off the strong column of his dirt-smudged throat. "Ego, much?"

Bailey snorted, her great shoulders shaking with mirth.

"Do you know what you have walked into, Master Hunter?" Ivory brandished her elongated claws. She'd had to forgo her liniments in order to properly cast Devlin's circle but in her true form, that was of little matter. "Do you understand what Halloween is?"

Gawain's eyes blinked open. "Halloween is the one day of the year where the veil between worlds is thinnest, and demonic power rises to new heights. I've fought – and killed – enough of your kind to know that not even a day like today can save you."

A chorus of clicks echoed through the clearing and Ivory chuckled, locking each of the locations into the vast stillness at the centre of her mind. "I suppose we'll see, won't we?"

Ivory took two running steps forward and launched herself at Gawain amidst a chorus of firing crossbows. His lips spread in a victorious smile as the projectiles whizzed through the air – and then Ivory was gone, reappearing behind the first of the Hunters who'd been stupid enough to cock his weapon where she could hear it. He hadn't even registered her presence before she wrapped her clawed hands around his head and jerked, breaking his spine with an audible snap. His crossbow tumbled to the ground and Ivory scooped it up, stepping through space to the second location in her mind. This time, she appeared in front of her wide-eyed opponent – a woman whose astonishment remained even as Ivory put a crossbow bolt right between her eyes. Rather than bother to reload, Ivory snapped the crossbow in two and discarded the pieces, collecting the next one.

"Where is she?" Gawain roared. "Find her!"

Ivory's lips quirked as she made the short teleport to the third archer on her mental map. He went down as silently as his companions. As she destroyed the old crossbow and exchanged it for a fresh one, she caught a hint of elderoot and arkhberry on his clothing.

"Carrying poison, little Hunter?" Ivory leaned over the body, following her nose to the small vial tucked in his top pocket. "Tsk, tsk."

Ivory popped the lid and swallowed the contents. The raspy elderoot tingled through her veins, dragging with it the slower, if more deadly, syrupy arkhberry. She shivered as the energy whispered against her own, flowing down to turn the tips of her fingers a deep plum colour. When she flexed her hands, poison dripped from the end of her claws. She smiled.

A ringing neigh broke through the cacophony of combat and Ivory turned to see Bailey standing on her hind legs, hooves flashing in the sunlight as she fought off two Hunters who stabbed at her with long, wicked knives. The deathcharger dipped and struck, the crack of bone loud as she landed a blow – and then she screamed as a crossbow bolt sank deep into her hindquarters.

"No," Ivory whispered. "I don't think so."

She teleported out to the sound of Bailey's rage. The Hunter who'd shot already had his bow lifted and loaded, and Ivory shunted the muzzle of the weapon aside as she raked her poisoned claws across his face. He dropped to the ground screaming, body convulsing, eyes rolling back in his head.

In the gully, Bailey's opponents pushed in close, seeking to take advantage of her wounds. She let out a shrieking roar as she slashed open the chest of one Hunter and tore out the throat of another – but one hind leg dragged on the ground, the wound in her haunches oozing black blood.

"I'm coming," Ivory whispered, focussing on the final spot marked on her mental map. "Hold on, Bailey."

She teleported again.

The last Hunter was prepared, pulling the trigger on her bow as soon as Ivory appeared. The bolt bit into her side and she hissed as she grabbed at the weapon, yanking it out of the woman's hands and then clobbering her with it. The Hunter's skull crushed with a pulpy sound, and that was that.

Perhaps a better person would have been more remorseful – but as Ivory teleported to Bailey's side, kicking away a short sword that glowed with enchantments, she was glad she lacked a conscience. If this was evil, this great pounding drum in her chest that demanded she *fight*, then she'd embrace it.

"I'm here," she gasped, pulling the crossbow bolt from her side and driving it into the throat of a Hunter with a machete. "I'm here, Bailey."

"Me," Bailey huffed, pivoting so that Ivory could pull the bolt from her hindquarters. She grunted, nostrils flaring, and then ducked the whistling swing of an axe. Ivory stepped beneath the guard of the man who'd swung it and jammed the crossbow bolt up under his ribs. He groaned as he fell, axe clattering to the ground at her feet.

"What does this buy you?" Ivory called, scooping the weapon up in both hands. She glared up at where Gawain lounged against the side of the gully. "Watching your people die? What's the point?"

The Master Hunter tipped his head to one side as the remaining Hunters closed in. "There's honour in dying for your cause. I stand witness to their sacrifice."

"Sacrifice?" Ivory spat on one of the corpses. Her saliva hissed, and the scent of burning flesh filled the air. "This isn't sacrifice, Gawain. This is a slaughter. Honour is nothing but an illusion, and you might be the greatest charlatan I've ever met."

"I am no more and no less than what you see before you." Gawain's smile faded as he took a step forward. "I am the Master of Hunters, and you're nothing but a beast."

Ivory raised an eyebrow. "You think you're so great, why don't you come down here and prove it?"

"No," Bailey huffed, shaking her head. "Bad."

"I don't care. I'm sick and tired of this pompous asshole." Flipping the axe in her hands, Ivory flung it in Gawain's direction.

The Master Hunter caught the weapon with a slapping sound that echoed through the clearing. He dropped the axe to the ground, uncurling his fingers to reveal a bloodied stripe across one palm. "Do you know what I am, demon?"

"Clumsy?" Ivory suggested, wiping the back of her mouth with one wrist. "Conceited? Crazy? Oh!" She snapped her fingers. "I know. How about a royal cu—"

"A healer," Gawain cut in. He wiggled his fingers and the cut on his palm began to glow with soft golden light. When it faded, his skin was smooth and whole. "All true Braybrooks are."

"Are you planning to heal the demon out of me?" Ivory spat on the ground at her feet. The earth sizzled. "I'm terrified."

"It means," Gawain continued as though she'd never spoken, "that I know an awful lot of ways to ensure you don't die. Painful ways."

"Seems counterproductive, since you've been trying to kill us this whole time."

"Have I?" Gawain smiled then, broad and icy. "You'll die, never fear – it'll just be on my terms. You see, unlike other Braybrooks, I have a rather nifty little trick up my sleeve. Want to know what it is?"

"You're going to tell me anyway," Ivory muttered. "That's how this works."

"Indeed. Here's the secret, then – the last one you'll ever hear." Gawain lowered his voice to conspirational whisper. "I can heal from a distance."

The Master Hunter clenched his fist and agony shot through Ivory's bones, arching her back and drawing a scream from her lips. Every injury she'd sustained during the battle flared to life, burning as though someone had poured hot acid onto her flesh. Beside her, Bailey groaned and dropped to her knees, eyes squeezing shut.

"Shit," Ivory gasped. The same golden glow that had emanated from Gawain's hand began to shine through her skin, burning with the fire of a thousand suns.

"Shit," Bailey agreed, shuddering as golden light spilled from her wounds. "So shit."

Gawain opened his hand and the pain subsided. Ivory's wounds were healed, but she felt as though she'd gone head-to-head with a mountain. She forced her head up, glaring from beneath heavy brows. "I'm going to kill you."

"I don't think so," Gawain chuckled. His face turned hard, eyes flicking to the left. "Again."

The nearest Hunter stepped forward and Ivory couldn't even begin to lift her limbs as he rammed his sword deep into her gut. She groaned, vision swimming.

"Will you die this time?" Gawain wondered, tapping his chin in thought. "I wonder."

The Hunter pulled his sword out and Ivory flopped onto her belly as the horrible, healing agony tore through her system. It was like reliving the original wound all over again, along with the burning aches and itches one normally associated with recovery – except instead of over several days or weeks, she endured it in moments, with the wattage dialled up to maximum. When the pain passed, she lay panting in the dirt, bile scratching at the back of her throat.

"No," Gawain chuckled. "No, I don't think you'll die this time – but the next? Or the one after that? Who knows?"

Laughter bubbled up in Ivory's chest. She giggled as the Hunter drove his sword through her spine, and then presumably into Bailey, judging by the way the deathcharger screamed. When the hideous burn of Gawain's magic swept through her once more, her giggles evolved into cackles, tears streaming down her cheeks. She laughed as the magic faded, pressing her face hard against the earth. It whispered to her in demonic, a soft, barely there sound that grew and grew until the ground began to rumble, the trees creaking and rustling as they swayed in time to an ancient song.

"What's that?" Gawain demanded, bracing one arm against the earthen wall of the gully. "What's happening?"

Ivory flipped onto her back, laughter echoing in the air as she caught hold of the Hunter who'd tortured her and severed the tendons in his ankle. He crumpled with a shriek, poison surging through his veins, and Ivory grabbed onto the sword he'd conveniently driven into the ground and hauled herself to her feet.

"That? It's what I was waiting for." Ivory snorted another laugh, looping an arm around Bailey's neck as the deathcharger struggled upright at her side. "This is where it really begins, Gawain. Listen to the wind, to the earth, to the trees. Can you hear it? Can you feel it?"

"What?" Gawain growled, eyes darting all around. "*What?*"

Ivory grinned. "Your old friend Sir Devlin is awake."

13

THE DEMON WITHIN

Energy bubbled and seethed and within it, Devlin's blood. Heat like he'd never known surged through his soul, melting down what had once been a man and forging something new in its place. It was overwhelming in such a way that he couldn't think, couldn't flinch, couldn't do anything other than endure, clinging to the threads of his sanity until even that was swept away by an endless vortex of sensation.

Through the mist and fire and howling wind came a sound; soft and stuttering at first, then gaining in intensity until the furious thumping drowned out everything around it, filling Devlin's mind with the steady, pulsing thunder of a bass drum. It wasn't until his eyes flew open and his lungs drew a sharp, painful breath that he realised the incessant sound was his heart, beating for the first time in thousands upon thousands of years.

And if his heart beat ...

The atmosphere was full of thick, grey smoke, but Devlin didn't need to see to lift his hands to his throat. To start at the base with trembling fingers and feel slowly upwards, along the column of his neck, over the thin ridge of scarring, to his head.

His head, which was attached to his neck.

His head, attached to *his* neck, on a body that was very much *alive*.

Emotion swept through Devlin in a tide, and for a moment he lingered on the precipice of both laughter and tears. He spent several long, distracted moments simply breathing, hands moving up and down his neck to be sure the moment was real. When he felt brave enough, Devlin turned his head to one side and then the other, glorying in the simple bunch and release of muscles that hadn't been connected for millenia.

The smoke began to thin and Devlin sat up, grinning as his head came along for the ride. He hunched his shoulders, leaning forward to brace against his knees; his head behaved as if it had always been attached, his neck arching and his chin tucking down against his chest.

He'd never have to pick his head up off the floor again.

Never have to tuck it under his arm, or set it down nearby in order to perform a two-handed task.

Most of all, he'd be able to kiss Ivory the way she deserved.

... a man who, despite all the evidence placed before him, clings to his own hatred. He rides a wave of destruction as though it were justice and wears a cloak woven from twisted dogma ...

Devlin blinked as the words came rushing back, euphoria turning to dread. Rolling to his knees, he waved away the last of the smoke to see the cave where Ivory had pushed him beyond the veil. He was alone, demonic runes still glowing in the dirt while Ivory's reagents littered the area around the picnic basket.

"Ivory?" He pushed to his knees and froze, arrested by the sight of long fingers that ended in wicked looking claws. Lifting first one hand and then the other, Devlin stared. He had the same skin tone as always, along with the tiny scars from his many years using a sword – but his skeletal structure was slightly different, the bones longer, the claws vicious and sharp.

He flexed his fingers in astonishment, then opened his mouth to discover his teeth were no longer blunt, human teeth but pointed like a proper predator's. Swallowing heavily, Devlin lifted his hands to his head. There, sweeping back from his temples in a deadly curl ... horns.

He had *horns*.

Heart thumping madly, Devlin looked down to discover his t-shirt in shreds. He tore off the remains of the shirt, taking in hard packed muscle that, whilst familiar, was wrapped tighter to his bones somehow, giving him a sturdier presence than he'd had before and emphasising the line of his abdominals as they tracked down to the waistband of his jeans – which clung to his buttocks and thighs as though they'd been painted on.

Demon.

He was a demon.

He'd known it was going to happen, of course, but now it was *real*, and for a wrenching moment the idea of a head on his shoulders, air in his lungs and horns on his head was too much. Then he remembered Ivory, and Jenn, and the promises he'd made, and everything settled into place with an almost audible snap.

Devlin crawled to the edge of the circle and there was a soft popping sound as the glowing characters winked out. All at once the cave filled with sound; screaming and groaning and the unmistakable thump of bodies hitting the dirt.

A growl vibrated in Devlin's throat and he pushed to his feet, swaying a moment as he rediscovered his centre of balance. He clenched his fist, wishing he had his sword – and it was suddenly there, materialising the same way it had done in Jenn's hallway. The crimson blade began to glow, steadily increasing in brightness until scarlet fire licked down the sharpened edge.

Whole. Demon. Whole. Demon. *Whole.*

The words pounded in his blood but it wasn't shame he felt, only fierce elation. This, here, was where he was meant to be. It was *what* he was meant to be.

He ducked through the cave's entrance to find the gully transformed from idyllic picnic spot to grisly nightmare. Dead Hunters littered the ground like macabre river stones and beyond, Bailey spun and ducked and twisted as she battled those who remained standing, her greater bulk preventing them from slipping down the sides of the gully to reach the entrance of the cave.

Devlin strode forward, a growl building deep in his chest as he reached Bailey's side. His sword flashed in a wide arc and two Hunters lost limbs to the blade; a third caught fire as the scarlet flames licked over the sleeve of her jacket.

"You're here," Bailey whickered, arching her neck. Pivoting in place, she delivered a swift kick to her closest opponent, knocking him back into his comrades.

"I'm here." Devlin bumped his shoulder against hers. "Where's Ivory?"

Bailey tossed her head, mane flying. "Gawain."

Devlin inspected their remaining enemies, no more than fifteen in total, then raised his gaze to the treeline at the far end of the gully. He couldn't see or hear anything beyond what was happening in front of him, but instinct said Ivory was in that direction – battling a fae knight who had thousands of years more experience than she did.

"I'll give you one chance to lay down your arms and surrender," Devlin called, directing his attention back to the Hunters in front of him. "Go, now, and live to fight another day."

Several of the Hunters faltered, but one raised her chin. "Demonic filth! So long as righteousness guides us, we will never be vanquished by one such as you!"

Devlin snorted. How similar the words were to the dogma he'd once inhaled – dogma which had led him to slaughter demons without first stopping to check if they were deserving of such a fate.

"So be it," he said, lifting his sword. The flames which licked along the blade began to intensify, crawling up Devlin's arm and leaving a scrolling crimson design in their wake.

Driven by an energy he didn't understand, Devlin twisted his sword in a preparatory movement he'd learned as a boy. The fire which had gathered up his arm surged down the blade and outward, passing through the assembled Hunters in a single, thin arc of flame. Astonishment twisted the features of every single opponent – until their bodies began to drop, cleft in half by the sizzling wave of demonic magic.

"Uh ..." Devlin stared down at his sword, where the flames had reduced until they licked along the bladed edge once more. The swirling crimson design remained etched into his skin, covering his entire arm, spreading over his shoulder and chest. "Oops."

Bailey snorted a laugh and bumped him with her shoulder. "Come."

Devlin mounted in a daze, curling the fingers of one hand through her mane as she plunged up the gully. Barely had they reached the trees when the unmistakable retort of a gun split the air, quickly followed by a second and then a third.

Bailey tore through the forest as fast as she could go, forcing Devlin to lean over her neck or risk losing his seat. They erupted into a small clearing, her hooves skidding on the forest floor as she drew up short in front of Gawain. He held a bulky looking pistol, eyes narrowed as he sighted Devlin down the barrel.

"I don't know what you thought to gain by running into the forest, little demon." The Master Hunter's voice was calm as he cocked the weapon. "If I can't kill you, I'll kill these abominations instead."

"If you don't know a distraction when you see it, you're dumber than I thought." Ivory materialised at Gawain's side, blocking his arm even as she delivered a ringing blow to the side of his head. Just as quickly as she'd appeared she was gone, winking out of existence with a speed that had Devlin's jaw on his chest. She could *teleport?*

Gawain cursed, aiming the weapon in Devlin's direction a second time. Ivory blinked back into existence less than an inch from the Hunter's face, placing her body directly in the line of fire. The gun went off and she grunted as she thrust her elbow into Gawain's throat, ripping the weapon from his hands. Devlin leapt off Bailey's back, intending to catch Ivory as she fell – but she swept Gawain's feet from under him and dropped to one knee on the Hunter's chest, the gun pointed at his head and her finger curved over the trigger.

"Call her off!" Gawain cried, eyes wide with horror. "Call her *off!*"

Blood covered Ivory's skin and clothes, oozing from the gunshot wounds in her ribs. Black dreadlocks hung wild about her face, lips pulled back from pointed teeth, ebony eyes glittering. The horns which curled from her head were larger than Devlin had ever seen them and judging by the gore coating the tips, Ivory knew full well how to put them to use. Her clothes, slicked to her body, highlighted the way her vertebrae were too prominent, the lines of her skeleton sleek and fluid.

She was anything but human, and she was the most beautiful thing Devlin had ever seen.

"Ivory," he murmured, lowering his sword to his side. "Are you all right?"

"I shot her," Gawain shouted. "Twice! With salt bullets! Why isn't she dead?"

"Because I'm not like most demons," Ivory purred, her voice low and deadly. She shifted her grip on the gun, laughter belling from her throat when Gawain flinched. "More interestingly, why haven't you tried your little pain-by-healing trick? Could it be that your powers don't work around salt? Why would that be, I wonder?"

"Shut up," Gawain hissed, his skin turning pale. "*Shut up.*"

Ivory turned her head ever so slightly and though her eyes never left Gawain, her voice softened. "She set you free."

"Yes," Devlin answered. "She did."

"How do you feel?"

"I feel ..." Something took flight in his chest. "I feel like I'm in love with you."

Ivory choked. "*That's* how you decide to tell me? While we're standing over an asshole?"

"Uh." Heat crept into Devlin's cheeks. "It just sort of came out."

She laughed, the sound edged in sin. "Tell me again once I've shot your ex-friend in the head."

"Wait." Devlin held up a hand and, to his surprise, Ivory's finger froze on the trigger. He took a step forward and crouched, remaining just out of Gawain's reach. "Why doesn't your magic work around salt?"

Gawain spat on the ground at his feet. "As if I'd answer that."

"Salt is demonsbane – in most cases, anyway." Ivory tilted her head in consideration. "Are you part demon?"

"Never!" Gawain bared his teeth as though their blunt, human appearance were somehow proof.

"Sounds like too strong a protest to me." Shifting the gun to one hand, Ivory wiped her fingers across a bloodied gash by Gawain's elbow. "Why don't we find out?"

"Stop that," Gawain hissed, jerking his arm away. "I'll kill you; I swear it."

"Uh huh." Ivory lifted her bloodied fingers and sniffed. "Odd."

"What?" Devlin asked.

"It's …" she frowned, licking the pad of one finger. "He's not a demon, but …"

"But?"

Ivory licked again, and blinked. Comprehension dawned on her face and she stared down at Gawain with a mixture of pity and amusement. "You were possessed at some point in your life. The demon's essence lingers in your system, tainting your blood – it's why salt negates your magic." She clicked her tongue against the roof of her mouth. "You know … if the demon who possesses you ever returns, you won't be able to stop it taking you over like a puppet."

"It cannot return," Gawain hissed. "I killed it, just like I swore to kill every other demon I ever came across."

"You do realise that not every demon is capable of possession? That's a rare skill belonging to an equally rare creature." Ivory shrugged. "Whatever that demon made you do probably sucked, but genocide isn't the answer – nor will it erase the touch of a demon from your system."

"You know nothing." Gawain's hiss became a growl, and he lifted his head to press it against the muzzle of the gun. "If you're going to shoot me, then do it now – unless you're a coward?"

"No." Devlin laid one of his fingers over Ivory's wrist. "That isn't the answer."

"Why not? He'd have killed you while you lay helpless in that cave," Ivory whispered, her eyes narrowed.

"I'm not like him," Devlin retorted. "To kill someone in battle is one thing. To murder them in cold blood is another entirely."

"You think to act with honour?" Gawain barked a sharp, incredulous laugh. "You forsook everything I ever taught you. You betrayed a friendship I treasured and turned willingly into the very creature you swore to exterminate."

"That's true," Devlin agreed. "But I still owe you a debt. One of mercy, I believe."

"What?" Gawain and Ivory spluttered in unison.

"Mercy," Devlin answered. "You cut off my head with the noblest intentions, though it cost you dearly. You sacrificed your needs for mine. Now, I will do the same."

"*My* needs?" Gawain flinched back from the gun, his head thumping into the forest floor. "What could I possibly need from you?"

"Something you cannot give to yourself." With careful fingers, Devlin prised the gun from Ivory's grip. He wasn't as familiar with the weapons as many modern warriors were, but he'd picked up enough to know which end was which, and how to put it to deadly effect. "Forgiveness."

"Forgiveness?" Gawain froze for a moment, then began to thrash about, forcing Ivory to readjust her weight in order to hold him pinned. "No. You wouldn't dare."

Devlin sheathed his sword and checked the ammunition in the gun. Salt bullets, as promised. They glittered in the sun, a soft peach hue providing testament to the quality of the materials. He cocked the weapon and fired into Gawain's left shoulder.

"I forgive you for your hatred," Devlin began, raising his voice to be heard over Gawain's scream. The gun clicked a new round into the chamber, and he fired a shot into the Master Hunter's other shoulder. "I forgive you for your fear."

"I'm not afraid!" Gawain shrieked, cords bulging in his neck. "I'm not af—"

Devlin fired a round into Gawain's thigh. "I forgive you for hunting me. I forgive you for hating me. And most of all ..."

"No." Tears trickled down Gawain's face as Devlin aimed at his other leg. "Don't take this from me. You *can't*."

Devlin cocked the gun and looked his old friend in the eye. "I forgive you, Sir Gawain, once of the Round Table, for all you have done in these long, cold centuries. I, Sir Devlin, also once of the Round Table, absolve you of your sins. May you walk forever in the light."

Gawain's voice rose in an agonised wail as Devlin fired the final shot, the bullet burying deep into the flesh of Gawain's thigh. The ex-knight sobbed as he struggled against Ivory's restraining hands but the salt was already taking effect, spreading through his bloodstream and rendering the enormous warrior unconscious in a matter of moments.

"What," Ivory said, pushing away from the limp fae, "the actual fuck did I just witness?"

"An ancient knightly ritual," Devlin murmured, tossing the now-empty gun on the ground. "It is a spell of sorts, I suppose, though not in the way you'd know it. Facing your sins is painful, and takes courage, honesty and sacrifice. Four wounds, one each for those particular knightly pillars. As we heal, we remember the words that were spoken over us, and meditate to achieve peace and purity."

"You used to *shoot* each other?"

"Not specifically. The gun was an improvisation."

"Knights are stupid. Crazy and stupid." Ivory snorted and pushed to her feet. "With that much salt he'll be unconscious for a couple of days, and the wounds will take months to completely heal – if they ever do."

"Such is the price of mercy." Devlin scooped Gawain's larger body up in his arms and slung him across Bailey's back. "Will you return us to Ivory's, my friend? And then, perhaps, deposit Gawain somewhere his allies might find him when they come looking?"

Bailey inclined her head. "Yes."

"It'd be safer to kill him," Ivory pointed out. "When he's recovered, he'll hunt you again."

"Then we will meet free of debt and let fate decide the rest."

"And what of the other demons he could hurt in that time?"

"The Hunters are an organisation led by Gawain, but not personified by him." Devlin shook his head. "Regardless of whether he lives or dies, they will hunt us. Hurt us. *All of us.* But if he lives ... if he's wounded ..."

"They'll be distracted trying to help him." Ivory's lips pinched. "They might even start to wonder why he was so badly affected by salt, too. It'll buy us time to prepare that we wouldn't have had otherwise."

"Yes." Devlin pulled himself up behind Gawain, but when he extended a hand to Ivory, she frowned. "What?"

"Gawain managed to track us somehow." She motioned between them. "If we don't find the item he used, then no amount of trail cleansing will work – not long term, anyway."

"Ah. That problem, also, I can solve." Devlin reached into Gawain's shirt and drew out a heavy chain from which hung a pendant in the shape of a sword. "He didn't track us, specifically; he tracked me. With this."

Ivory eyed the necklace for a long moment. "It was yours?"

"Once, long ago. It is the sigil of a Knight of the Round Table – I gave it to Gawain before he cut off my head, both as a token of my friendship and because I felt I no longer deserved to wear it." Devlin rubbed a thumb over the pendant and sighed. "Aside from my sword, it's the only remaining memento of the life I left behind."

Ivory laid her hand over the top of Devlin's with the pendant sandwiched between them and closed her eyes. "You're a demon now and your essence has changed. This can't be used to track you any more."

"I assumed as much."

She pursed her lips. "I think you should keep it."

"Really? Why?"

"Because it's yours." Ivory undid the chain with a deft flick of her wrist, puddling it in Devlin's palm. "It deserves better than to be left with this asshole."

Devlin chuckled, slipping the pendant into the pocket of his jeans.

"That's true enough, I suppose ... but it'll need a lot of cleansing before I'm ready to wear it again."

"I can cleanse it when we get home." Ivory watched him from beneath her lashes, eyes dark. "If you want."

Devlin smiled and this time, when he offered his hand, she took it. "I should like nothing more."

14

LOVE IS ALL WE NEED

Ivory watched Bailey disappear into the forest and sighed. "Are you sure she'll be all right on her own?"

"Of course." Devlin paused in the act of toeing off his boots, one hand braced against the front wall of her cottage. "We killed all the Hunters and Gawain won't wake from the salt poisoning for days. Besides, Bailey can take care of herself."

Judging by the wink Bailey sent Ivory's way before she cantered off, the deathcharger wasn't worried about taking care of herself in the slightest.

"You still look worried." Warm fingers brushed her dreadlocks over one shoulder, and Ivory shivered.

"I don't know what to do now," she admitted, turning her face into his open palm. The movement was instinctive and mortifying but when she made to step back, Devlin's free arm snaked around her waist.

"I do," he said, voice low and soft as he turned her to face him. "I stare deep into your eyes, just like this, and I say, 'Ivory, I love you,' and you say ..."

Ivory set her palms against Devlin's bare pectorals and let the corner of her mouth tip up. "I say, 'Devlin, you stink like dead people.'"

He laughed, the sound bright and big and beautiful. Now that his head was attached to his body, he was well over six feet and Ivory had to arch her back to meet his eyes, the infernal green colour now tinted with faint streaks of orange.

"You're a fire demon," she whispered, tracing her clawed fingers gently over one cheekbone.

"It seems that way." He shrugged. "I assumed I'd be like you, though."

"Your magic may have originated with my ancestor, but you're also a person in your own right. Your genetics will lend themselves to demonology in their own way."

"That makes sense." His gaze travelled lazily down her body, snagging on the holes in her sweater. "Do I need to dig salt bullets out of you?"

Ivory shook her head. "I've absorbed them by now."

"Really?" He lifted a brow. "I've never met a demon who could do that."

"I found mention of the talent in my family's journals, but it – like my unusual style of magic – are very rare." Ivory chewed on her lower lip a moment, weighing up best how to explain. "I'm a spirit demon. I can sense the spirits of the things around me – people, plants, the earth, and so on. In some cases, I can even manipulate them."

Devlin's eyes widened in comprehension. "The way you make liniments and potions and poultices ... you have an intrinsic understanding of which ingredients to use and your magic blends them together. That's why they're so effective."

"Yes. And in my full demon form, I can absorb elements into my body and use them to alter my genetic makeup – for example, I drank a vial of poison I found on one of the Hunters but rather than kill me, I was able to direct it to my claws." She flexed her hand in front of his face. "My ability to teleport is similar, too; I use spirits as a reference to move to that location."

"And the salt?"

"A cleanser." She smiled. "When Gawain shot me, my body

absorbed the salt – it removed the poison I ingested, but that's it. I cannot use the salt, per se, but neither can it weaken or kill me."

"You should still have a hole, though." Devlin took half a step back, using his claws to shred the side of Ivory's sweater so he could inspect the bullet wound underneath. Ivory couldn't help but flinch as he brushed the back of his knuckles over her puckered flesh. "Sorry."

"You didn't hurt me. We heal fast, and I ..." she cleared her throat. "I like you touching me."

The look he gave her was full of blazing intensity. "Oh?"

Three little words hovered on the tip of Ivory's tongue, but no matter how she wished it, they wouldn't tumble out. Being alone had been difficult, but in other ways it had also been easy; nobody could abandon her if she had nobody close, after all. Now, Devlin was here, and unlike the acquaintances she'd done her best to keep at arm's length, he was inside her armour. He could tear her apart as easily as complete her, leaving her nothing but an empty shell. She couldn't go through that again. Couldn't lose again. There wasn't enough of her left to survive it.

Hysteria bubbled in her chest. Had she lost her mind? She'd wished so deeply for Devlin's love and now, here he was offering it – all she had to do was say the words.

Three. Little. Words.

Instead, she shot Devlin a coy look from beneath her lashes. "If it's all the same to you, I'd rather not trek this gore inside the house. I've a pond around the back we can scrub off in – if you're game."

Before Devlin could open his mouth to respond, she teleported the short distance to the back of the house where the pond was tucked beneath the branches of several over-arching fruit trees. Stripping down to her bra and underwear, she waded into the chest-deep water and sank beneath the surface, closing her eyes as the chill liquid slipped over her face.

Ivory hung suspended, trying to calm her racing heart. There had to be a way around this, some solution that would allow her to keep Devlin without becoming vulnerable ... but dammit, he *deserved* those words, and she wanted desperately to give them to him.

The pond water lurched. Ivory's eyes flipped open as clawed fingers curled into her hair and yanked her above the surface.

"Got you," Devlin growled, lifting her until they were eye to eye. "Don't think I didn't see you trying to avoid this."

"I told you," she panted, hanging limp in his grasp. "I don't know what to do now."

"And I told you that I do." He tipped his head to one side, eyes bright with challenge. "I've never thought you a coward, Ivory, so we're going to face this head on. Are you ready?"

"No."

"Too bad, because I'm going to keep saying this until you listen. I want you. I need you. *I love you.*"

Ivory's breath caught in her throat, and she told herself the moisture on her cheeks was only pond water. She opened her mouth to deliver a scathing retort but instead, what came out was, "I love you, too."

Triumph flashed across Devlin's features and then he crushed her close, the heat of his skin a furnace as he dragged her head back and kissed her like the demon he was. Passion negated tenderness. Lips and teeth and tongues clashed in a fury of elemental need that was everything Ivory had ever wanted. She looped her arms around Devlin's neck and yanked, toppling them both backwards into the water. He didn't break the kiss as they sank, his forearms bracing them against the pebbled bottom of the pond – a pond whose water temperature rapidly changed from chill to tepid to warm as Devlin's innate fire magic responded to the desire in his blood. When the need for air became urgent, he shoved upward, hauling them both onto the soft grass at the pond's edge. Ivory let him roll her over, his eyes blazing a hot path over her soggy underwear and then back up to her face.

"I'm only going to ask once," Devlin growled, setting the tip of one claw at the top of her sternum. "After that, if I do something you don't like, it's up to you to say so."

Ivory placed her hand over his and dragged downwards, using Devlin's claw to slice through her bra so that it twanged aside in a ridiculous display of elastic enthusiasm. "You're still nicer than me," she purred. "I wouldn't have asked at all."

He lowered his head, breath teasing over her damp skin. "Yes, then?"

"Yes."

With a rumbling growl, Devlin fastened his mouth over her breast and suckled hard. The sensation went straight to Ivory's core and she gasped, arching up against the hot, hard planes of his body. While his tongue worked, Devlin shredded the remains of her bra and tossed it aside, a process he repeated with her underpants. Sharp teeth grazed her skin as he nipped his way to her other breast, nuzzling the underside before licking a path up to tease her swollen nipple with his lips.

Ivory slid her hands over his shoulders, glorying in the strength and breadth of him, the way his vertebrae were just a little too prominent – like her own. Devlin had made no attempt to assume a human appearance and the knowledge that they came together in their true forms ratcheted Ivory's need into the stratosphere. She caught at the waistband of his jeans and pulled with all her might. The denim gave way with a satisfying ripping sound and quite suddenly there was nothing between her and Devlin at all.

He groaned as he pressed against her, his erection thick and hard where it lay sandwiched between them. Ivory wriggled in a desperate attempt to get that weapon where she wanted it, but Devlin's groan turned to a chuckle and he skimmed down her body, slipping partially back into the pond as he shoved her knees up and outward.

"Devlin," Ivory made a grab for him but though she got her fingers in his hair and tugged, the damned man didn't budge an inch.

"Ivory," he purred, biting her thigh just enough for his teeth to pinch the skin. The sharp edge of pain shot through her, followed quickly by a desperate, burning heat as Devlin licked across the bite mark. "Are you in a rush?"

"Yes!"

His laughter brushed across her most sensitive flesh, and he watched her squirm over the curves and hollows of her abdomen. "Good."

The first lick of his tongue was a revelation. The next, a wicked delight. The third ... Ivory lost the ability to think of adjectives, surrendering to Devlin's caresses as she'd never surrendered to anyone or anything before in her entire life. With one hand under her lower back to lift her hips, Devlin used his other hand to tease her, his fingers gentle in contrast to the demands of his tongue and his mouth.

Ivory tried desperately to hold on but he was relentless. Her legs began to quiver and her body bucked against his face, demanding a release that only Devlin could give. She yanked at his hair and he growled against her skin, adding a level of sensation that proved too much. Her body exploded, pleasure scouring her veins, drawing a scream of ecstasy from a throat gone raw. Still Devlin gave no quarter, wringing wave after wave of pleasure from her until she thought she'd pass out – and then his mouth and hands were gone, leaving her limp and panting as he crawled up her body like a conqueror.

Knowing Devlin as she did, Ivory expected him to pause for sweet words and gentle caresses. Instead, he braced one forearm beside her head and kissed her as he thrust his cock inside her body in one long, smooth movement.

The friction was incredible. Ivory whimpered into Devlin's mouth as he drew out and snapped back in, setting her nerve endings on fire. This was no polite knight; here was a demon who knew she was his to take, just as he was hers. With every thrust, Devlin's movements grew wilder, the sounds he made desperate and raw. Ivory met him stroke for stroke, needing to stake her claim even as he branded his name on her soul.

They sought infinity in the slick glide of skin on skin, gripping so tight it was impossible to tell where one left off and the other began. They kissed and nipped and licked and gasped, words impossible while passion reigned; a furious, flickering flame that consumed Ivory until all she knew, all she was, belonged to Devlin. It was both terrifying and dizzying to look into his eyes and see the same burning emotion that dwelled in her own, to know that he wanted *her* and no-one else.

Ivory's body tightened as Devlin's movements shifted from

rhythmic to desperate, a growl building in his chest as he sought to push them both ever higher. He tore his mouth from hers. Their gazes collided for a single, electric moment – then Devlin's spine locked and Ivory shattered, tumbling them over the precipice and into paradise together.

When Ivory could next think, she registered that Devlin had collapsed atop her, his face buried in her neck. His breath was hot against her skin and he rumbled in contentment, the vibration sending delicious aftershocks through Ivory's body.

"I want to do that again," he whispered, lips tickling against the skin of her throat. "And again, and again ... and again."

Ivory's heart swelled and though she knew she should answer, all she could do was cling tighter, lost in the storm of emotion created by their lovemaking.

Devlin lifted his head, his lazy, sated expression sharpening as he took in her face. "What's wrong?"

"How do we ... how do I ..." To Ivory's horror, tears welled in her eyes and she swallowed, turning her face away.

"Hey." Devlin rolled over and sat up, arranging Ivory so that she straddled his lap. He cupped her face in both hands and kissed her softly. "I have no idea what I'm doing, either. I never expected to feel such a depth of emotion so quickly – but lack of time shouldn't make this less real, or important." Ducking his head so they were on a level, Devlin offered a wicked smile. "We'll figure out how this works."

Ivory wrapped her fingers around his wrists and let her lashes flutter shut. "It's been a long time since I've had something to lose, Devlin. If I lost you, I... I don't think I'd come back from that."

"I know." Devlin's grip tightened, his claws pricking the sides of her face. "I'm not a seer but I am – I was – a knight. Do you doubt my word?"

"You're still a knight," Ivory muttered, slumping in his grip. "Becoming a demon doesn't erase who you are; it just changes your physical makeup."

"Well, then, I'm the first Demonic Knight," Devlin announced. "And as a Demonic Knight to his Demonic Enchantress, I give you my word: whatever the future holds for us, I will not leave you. I swear it, Ivory. I am yours for as long as you wish it."

Ivory forced her eyes open, hope battling the fear that threatened to choke her. His expression was sincere, those infernal eyes brilliant.

"I'm not perfect," she said, even as she kicked herself for admitting it. "I'm morally grey at the best of times and I have a definite tendency towards bitter and jaded."

Devlin chuckled. "I know."

"And?"

"And I love you exactly as you are. Shall I list my most pressing imperfections to make you feel better?"

Ivory blushed and dropped her gaze. "No."

"I'm fairly certain Bailey has a list somewhere, should you ever care to have them officially noted." His voice was cheerful and when she looked up, it was to find him grinning like an idiot. She scowled, but that grin only widened, becoming so infectious that Ivory couldn't help but splutter a laugh. Devlin wrapped his arms around her and she set her head against his shoulder, feeling raw and vulnerable and oh-so-incredibly complete.

His embrace fell away and Ivory leaned back, brow furrowing. "What's wrong?"

"Nothing. I just had an idea." Devlin held out one hand, palm up, and then curled his fingers into a fist. Magic and heat surged around them, and he opened his fingers with a triumphant grin. "There."

In the middle of his palm, glowing red hot as though it had just come from a forge, was Devlin's pendant. The sword hung straight and true and the chain was thick and heavy – but unlike when Ivory had last seen it, tiny runes were etched down the centre of the blade. Tiny *demonic* runes which darkened as the metal cooled, and said ...

Ivory snickered. "Donut and Ivory?"

Devlin sighed. "I'm not very good at demonic, I'm afraid."

"Like this," Ivory laughed, leaning back to dip her finger in the pond and trace the correct rune on the stones beside them. "See?"

Grumbling under his breath, Devlin closed his fingers over the pendant and screwed up his face. There was a second wave of heat, less intense than the first, and when he opened his fist, the metal was once again glowing – but the runes were now correct.

Once the pendant was silver again, Devlin leaned forward and fastened the chain around Ivory's neck. The necklace was pleasantly heavy, the sword hanging point down between her breasts.

"It's Lemurian silver," she whispered, touching the intricately wrought hilt.

Devlin nodded. "We called it Fae silver back then, but it's the same thing. It was enchanted for protection once upon a time."

Ivory shifted to cover the pendant with her whole palm, brow furrowing as she listened to the soft whispers in her mind.

"It still is," she said at last, "but it's faint. I don't think Gawain was recharging it." She offered a tentative smile. "Nothing a little moonlight won't fix."

Ivory lifted her hand and together they stared down at the pendant where it hung against her chest as though it had been made to rest there. Devlin bent to kiss the hollow of her throat, his hands warm where they circled her ribs.

"Do you believe me now?" He looked up from beneath thick lashes, the afternoon sun gilding the planes of his face in gold and bringing the touches of orange in his eyes to burning life. "Do you trust me enough to see where this goes ... together?"

Biting her lip to hide how it trembled, Ivory followed the surge of emotion in her chest. "Yes. To both."

Devlin kissed her, pulling her tight against his chest as he flopped back onto the grass.

"Good," he said when they came up for air. "Because by my reckoning, we've about an hour before Bailey returns home. I say we use it wisely."

"You don't think she'd fancy the show?"

"I know she wouldn't."

"Well then, Sir Devlin," Ivory purred, kneading his chest with her claws. "You'd best put your back into it."

He did.

THE END

♥

～

THANKS SO MUCH FOR READING!

I hope you enjoyed Devlin and Ivory's story. It was a joy to write, and I'm crossing my fingers that you adored it as much as I did.

So … do I write other stuff? You bet I do! Keep up to date with all the latest shenanigans at:

www.sliceofsammy.com

With fire raging all around, Noah races into the bush to find the wolfkin he loves. To survive, Deanna and Noah must confront not only the fury of Mother Nature... but the ghost whose memory tore them apart.

ALSO BY SAMANTHA MARSHALL

The Weaver's War series:

- Sorcery and Stardust
- Sorcery and Subterfuge
- Sorcery and Sandstorms

The Kin Chronicles series:

- Aislinn's Shadow
- Tobias' Spark
- Deanna's Ghost

The Merged Worlds series:

- The Heart of a Shadow
- Catnip
- Headless (that's this one!)
- Foiled

COMING SOON:

- Sorcery and Sacrilege (Book four in the Weaver's War series)

To find out more about these awesome tales, check out my website:

www.sliceofsammy.com

ABOUT SAMANTHA

Hi, I'm Sam!

I've been writing my whole life, scribbling stories on anything close to hand – from the shopping list to napkins to post-it notes (don't mention post-its to hubby haha).

I grew up reading fantasy of the likes of Anne McCaffrey, Terry Pratchett, and their peers. I'm also a lifelong vampire fan, along with all things spooky. In my late teens I was introduced to paranormal romance and discovered a whole new layer of storytelling with a bit of a spicy edge! Taking what I learnt from all of the above, I devoted myself to creating full-bodied characters, meaty plots, epic adventure, and a little bit of naughty sauce on the side.

I completed a Diploma of Professional Writing and Editing after high school and spent the next several years in my writing cave, working on a novel that is now in a drawer somewhere, followed by a couple of others who shared the same fate. (What can I say? I'm a recovering perfectionist.)

I came close to debuting my novel career in 2009, then ended up pregnant and took some time off to have kids. I debuted for real in 2019 with *Sorcery and Stardust* and won ARRA's Favourite Debut Romance Author for 2019, which was extremely cool!

I write speculative fiction that is a fusion of multiple sub-genres and therefore doesn't fit particularly well into any of them, but after many years and a lot of angst, I'm okay with that. I love all my characters and their stories for different reasons, but have a soft spot for an excellent villain and a tortured protagonist.

I currently live in south east Melbourne, Victoria, with my hubby, two kids, a Golden Retriever and a turtle. I volunteer with the Romance Writers of Australia, and I'm passionate about great writing, interesting characters, chai tea and happily ever afters.

And if you want to get to know the Perfectly Paranormal Anthology authors a bit more, get sneak peeks of what's coming up for the APP Anthologies, as well as giveaways, special offers and just some PNR fun, then join our Perfectly Paranormal Paramours Facebook Group.

Find us here:

https://www.facebook.com/groups/251663560162131

ACKNOWLEDGMENTS

From the moment we decided we were doing a Halloween anthology, I knew I wanted to write about the headless horseman. Little did I realise, writing a character whose head isn't attached to his body is more than a little challenging!

The biggest thank you has to go to Mum, who on top of writing her own story was constantly on hand to workshop exactly how Devlin would be able to do things without his head, and who laughed with me every time we tried to act out how a potential situation might look with one's head held in a hand, or tucked under one arm, or balanced in the crook of an elbow, or set down on the bench.

Following on from that, I'm forever grateful to Leisl and Marnie who got behind my idea and didn't once question the insanity of it; trusting without a doubt that I'd find a way to pull this off and even laughing at my bad jokes.

Massive special mention to Bron, who did an amazing beta read and performed such duties as counting salt bullets and listening to me recount with big enthusiasm and excruciating detail on how my mythological research resulted in Sir Gawain of the Round Table becoming the villain of this story. You are most awesome, I love you, thank you.

As always, thanks to my ARC team for your dedication and excitement – I am ever grateful for your efforts and hope these stories continue to make you smile for a long time to come.

To the readers; I wouldn't be half the author I am if not for you, so thank you for reading this book and I hope it brought a little spooky light into your life.

ANCESTORS AND EXPECTATIONS

HELLUCY HOWE

ANCESTORS AND EXPECTATIONS

Tales from the Fae Court
Book Two

~

Hellucy Howe

🌼 Created with Vellum

ABOUT ANCESTORS AND EXPECTATIONS

What if the truth doesn't set you free?

As eldest child, Seelie Lord DeMaksim Aphiski is expected to be the Papillion Duchy's heir. Until the day he breathes fire. Blue blazes, is the rumour of a Dracon in the family actually true? Needing answers, DeMaksim pursues a report of a draconian family connection into the threatening Dark Reaches, and suddenly his life takes wing.

Unseelie Undine-Eldwytch crossbreed, Cherith Beriaden has the soft core of a plant nurturer but the appearance of a soul-sucking killer. Wrenched away from her water-roses just to tail a spy, Cherith is even more annoyed when the dolt turns out to be gorgeous. River Goddess! Who knew she had a weakness for vazel eyes?

Unexpectedly bound together by a warped Unseelie monster, Cherith and DeMaksim are forced into an awkward partnership. If the monster still lived, she could snap the connection in seconds, but now they have to seek answers elsewhere. Hopefully by All Hallows' Eve. Forced to cuddle together at every rest period, freedom is top priority for both of them ... isn't it?

To Family, Friends, Fellow Authors and Folks who love Fairy tales.

Thank you.

1

DEMAKSIM

$\mathcal{A}$ massive elderoak dominated the clearing, its characteristically drooping branches reaching for the sky, the thick, age-whorled bark a rough brown cloak. The sign – Elderoak Tavern – hung from one branch, squawking in every wind gust. Straightening his leather jacket, DeMaksim thrust the door open and strode inside. Conversation ceased. The curious stares of patrons elicited a crawl of goosebumps as he threaded his way to the bar encircling the tree's heartwood. Rolling his shoulders, he wished he could scrub his spine against bark to ease both the goosebumps and his aching wing muscles.

"Whaddya drinking?" A grey leathery-skinned monolith with a rock-solid build and a voice which rumbled like a grating slide of scree, shuffled from the shadows of the trunk's core.

DeMaksim cleared his throat. "Flamuisge, neat."

The flicker of the Rock-troll's beetling brows dislodged a sliver of crumbling shale to the counter top. "Hope yer gut's strong."

DeMaksim chuckled. "What food's on offer?"

One square thumb elevated. "Squirrel stew." A finger joined the thumb. "Two hunks of toasted rye-bread with berries." The second finger. "Vegies with green dip." A third finger. "Powdered limestone on gemstone chunks." Fourth finger. "Dwarf bread."

"Hmm." DeMaksim rubbed his chin. "The stew, thanks."

"Five coppers the lot."

Reaching into his waist pouch, DeMaksim eased the metal chips free, pushing them across the polished surface. He was impressed how quickly the troll's blunt, stony digits nimbly palmed the coins.

Stubby granite teeth glistening, the craggy behemoth filled a beaker from a keg, then plunked it in front of DeMaksim. "Grab a pew."

Holding his mug, DeMaksim crossed to an empty window booth; his moulded leather trousers slid easily along the wooden pew. Studying the panes of glass beside him, he decided the name 'window' was a misnomer – years of dripping sap covered any possible glass. Fortunately, the gloom was lightened by glow-bug wall sconces.

"May I sit with you, Sir Fae? I dislike drinking alone." A woman approached his table, her red-lipped smile afire with invitation. Coppery hair rustled as she swept it artfully behind her.

"Not buying." Set on his mission, DeMaksim was in no mood for pick-ups.

"I already have a drink." Her wide-lipped smile failed to reach her eyes as she produced a flask from her shoulder-bag and sat. "Are you from around here?"

"Thereabouts."

"Got any kinfolk?" She fingered the design etched on her flask.

"Why?" Her questions, especially to a Seelie this deep into Unseelie territory, raised hackles.

A hiss of laughter. "Just small talk."

The troll appeared, placing a wooden trencher in front of DeMaksim and a second, larger beaker of liquid. "Water's free."

"Thanks." The delicious aroma of the stew was its own advertisement. Fisting the spoon, DeMaksim dug in. Despite his hunger, he remained uncomfortably aware of the fidgeting woman across the table; of her intent gaze, the fingering of her flask, the rearrangement of the burgundy flower nestled in her hair, the trailing of her fingers down her neck, across her throat and down her right breast.

DeMaksim chewed, swallowed. "Not interested."

She frowned. "I'm trying to get to know you."

"I don't want you getting to know me." He spooned up more of the delicious stew.

Pouting, she tapped a finger on the wooden surface. "Just trying to be friendly."

He grimaced. "Take a hint lady – leave."

"Thraxarkzal!" Two dwarves lurched against the table; one with fists in his opponent's beard, jerking the long fibres. DeMaksim flinched as Mr Trapped Beard bit his antagonist's nose and yanked an ear.

"Bezeknazonite!"

"Durkitz!"

Rock-like grey arms yanked hoods tight around dwarfish throats as the Rock-troll bartender – ignoring choked cries – dragged the pair of brawlers to the door and ejected them.

DeMaksim spooned the last few bites of stew, chomping hard on something tough. Rewarded when it popped, he swallowed, grabbing a chunk of bread to drag through the gravy.

A sly smile widened the face opposite. "Good stew?" Lamplight glinted off small, curved fangs. "I thought Fae were herbivores?"

"Look for prey elsewhere."

Her purr was throaty. "I like you."

He tensed. "Go away." Something unpleasant roiled in his stomach; it heaved. Bile threatened. Recalling the tough thing that'd squelched in his mouth, DeMaksim's gaze narrowed on the smiling, over-friendly female fiddling with her hair blossom … again. His lips tightened. "You seeded me."

Hasty fingers dragged red tendrils from her flower – the further her hand stretched, the longer the strands became. Grinning, she cast the threads.

Snarling viciously, he flexed his dagger from its forearm sheath, slicing through the airborne strings. Shrieking pieces plummeted to the table, the strands writhing, blackened where he'd cut them.

"No!" Delicate, curving fangs morphed into vicious, hooked needles.

"Nageen!" DeMaksim vomited, continuing until a coiled pile of snake fell to the table-top. It raised a scaly, hissing head, but DeMaksim called forth a sheeting whoosh of flame, searing the rejected invader and the extra red tendril chunks he'd slashed. Those would've sealed a lesser Fae's fate.

Hissing like steam from a covered billy-tin, the Nageen's eyes slitted, barbed fangs protruding from her suddenly reptilian mouth. Her forked tongue flickered. "But you're just a Fae! Fire isn't possible!"

"Damnation take you!" Slamming fists on the table, DeMaksim spurt-flamed the seeding pod disguised under burgundy hair blossoms. It shrivelled to a blackened wisp.

Screaming, the Nageen abandoned all pretence. It transformed into a large, thick serpent and slithered hastily for the door. The door-bell clanged repeatedly, forced to open and shut for each coil of the reptilian body as she fought to escape. The repetitious sound echoed through the suddenly empty tavern.

DeMaksim retched again.

The Rock-troll appeared, carrying a wooden bucket and a fresh beaker of water which he shoved at DeMaksim. "Good job, Dracon." Using a cleaning cloth he swiped the table several times, rinsing and wringing the cloth between wipes. "She won't be back."

"You could've warned me." Scowling, DeMaksim dragged the back of his hand over his mouth.

The Rock-troll shrugged. "Mate, get real. Ye're in the Dark Reaches. Wasn't sure what she was until she started her play, anyway." His chuckle grated like stones. "Yer handled the rest right fine."

DeMaksim peered around. "Where'd everyone go?"

"Out the back door as soon as yer started flaming." The bartender considered him. "She's right, ye look Fae."

"I *am* Fae." DeMaksim snatched the water beaker, gargled and spat the befouled liquid onto the buckled curl of his plate, all the while holding the Rock-troll's wary gaze.

The bartender raised his hands, the cloth dripping down his upraised arm. "I offer no harm, I'm ..."

"A united Queens' man. Their symbol's etched into your arm."

"Damn." The Rock-troll dropped his arms. "Shouldn't have rolled my sleeves up. Yer got a problem with it?"

"Blue blazing hells, no." DeMaksim's smile was wry. "I'm one too." He flipped the collar of his sleeveless jerkin aside, revealing the united Queen's symbol tattooed under his right collarbone.

"Okay then." The bartender nodded.

DeMaksim held his gaze. "Not that it matters, but I *am* Fae; with a few inherited extras."

"Ah, draconic bloodlines." The Rock-troll nodded sagely. "Hard to dilute traces of ordinary Dracons, never mind Primordial Elementals. Gotta name?"

"I'm Mak."

"Good to know, Mak, but I meant the Dracon. Do ye know which of them is yer ancestor?" One lichen brow raised waiting for an answer.

DeMaksim scratched his head. "How would I know if it was one of the Primordials?"

"How long ago was it?"

"Three centuries, give or take a few years."

"Oh?" The bartender resumed wiping the table. "And yer can still flame? Impressive." His hand swept away ash and molten shrapnel. "Need more clues. What'd yer say its name was?"

"I didn't."

"Do yer know?"

"If I did, how would *you* know whether it was a Primordial Elemental?"

The Rock-troll laughed, a rocky booming sound. "It's all in the name, Mak Fae-Dracon. Names are power and there weren't many Primordial Elementals. They came into being when the world was born, are made of the same stuff and will probably be here until the world ends. Or maybe they'll survive. If yer got one of those in yer ancestral line, I'm staying on yer good side. Ye get me?"

DeMaksim huffed a laugh. "Yeah."

"Mind if I ask what ye're doing in the Dark Reaches? Many of the wilder Unseelie Fae and malcontents from the Fae Wars skulk out here."

"Any Draconfolk?"

The monolith's brows arched. More shale shards crumbled down his body. "So! Ye're hunting?"

"Just information." DeMaksim shrugged. "I want to know who bequeathed us the draconic traits; some family members claim it a myth."

The Rock-troll's guffaw shook the table. "Yer flaming ability's no myth."

"Exactly." DeMaksim drank some water. "The idea consumes me; my evolving abilities have created a personal imperative. Queens Dianathke and Maerovana granted me rights to search the royal archives. That's where I found clues suggesting the Dark Reaches as a good place to seek answers."

Dropping the cleaning rag into the bucket, the bartender braced fists on hips. "It's also a good place to find trouble, young Fae lordling, serious trouble."

"Fae lordling?" DeMaksim frowned. "That's a huge assumption."

"Nah, yer dropped the royal names like rain on daisies." The Rock-troll rolled his eyes. "Dead giveaway. Ye're a Fae lordling alright. Out here, yer gotta watch yerself. Letting on yer know either queen can get yer killed."

"Look around you." Lifting the water beaker, DeMaksim saluted the bartender. "I reckon I'm looking after myself right fine, Sir Troll who knows the Queens right well."

The Rock-troll's laughter rattled the sapped-in windows.

2

CHERITH

Sparkling in the afternoon sunlight, the series of interconnected lagoons in a bend of the Mirkdowd River rippled where the willow branches ran twiggy fingers through the tranquil pools.

"You're not wearing weed, Cherith!" Her aunt glowered as she appeared in front of Cherith, her tangled Undine locks, festooned with algae and duckweed, had her niece shuddering.

Cherith Beriaden glided deeper into the largest of the Mirkdowd Pools. "Weed's slimy, messy and makes my hair hard to keep clean. It's not happening, Aunt Brooke."

"Gah!" Brooke pointed to a second Undine just entering the lagoon. "Cascade, you're weedless too!" She snarled, fangs agleam. "You should wear sedge or watercress, not water hyacinth."

"Hi Aunt Brooke." Cascade grinned. "Flowers are so much prettier since Cherry's been working her green powers on them." A third Undine trailed her, webbed fingers swishing through the water in idle circles.

Brooke glared. "Delta, make your daughters toe the line!"

Delta yawned. "Hi sister. Ranting again? We all know there's no line to toe, so back off."

Brooke smacked the water. "We're Undines! We lure travellers to their doom. I lay the disrespect of Undine ways at your door, Delta! You should've drowned the Eldwytch instead of true-mating him and bearing children. Triplets and one male! Whoever heard of Undines producing male offspring? Be glad the Eldwytch claimed the boy. I would've—"

Shooting through the water, Delta erupted in a geyser, digging claws into Brooke's throat. "The boy, Beckett, is my son and Istondir my mate! Do *not* threaten them, Brooke! My choices are none of your business. You don't run this Undine Swirl; we answer to the River King and last time I checked, you lacked the equipment!"

Trickles of pearlescent fluid oozed around Delta's claw-tips, trailing down Brooke's neck and shoulders. Eyes bulging, Brooke raised her hands, the low slanting sunrays glinting off the water droplets dripping down her arms. "Truce sister." Her voice whispered around the chokehold. Hissing, Delta shoved her away, turning to her daughters.

"Cherith, how are you?" Her loving gaze caressed like finest silk. "What have you been doing today?"

Hugging her mother and sister, Cherith grinned. "I've been cultivating the burgundy night-glowing water roses so they'll bloom early."

Delta's eyes swept over her. "I gather the roses aren't out?"

Cherith shrugged. "They're close. I'll go back that way in a day or two."

"Ooh, the water roses." Cascade clasped her hands. "You've such a green thumb, Cherry. May I go too?"

"Of course." Cherith smiled, fingered a strand of duckweed. "I've been working with plants in several backwater lagoons; we can check them all. But first, do you know why we've been called here?"

Brooke waded nearer. "I cry peace sister-kin." Her weed-draped scowl swept them. "I mightn't be the River King but he sent a message – the reason for this meeting. His emissary advises of a Fae-male searching the River Rubiconia on our side, plus all the tributary creeks, streams, lagoons and water glades that combine the Wetland Demesne under the River King's governance."

"That'll take him a lifetime." Delta finger-combed her hair. "Searching for what?"

"The Nixie didn't say."

Cascade tickled the throat of a tiny ruby-spotted frog on a nearby lily pad. "Why'd King Eskavon send us a message? Is there some sort of danger?"

"From a Fae-male? Doubtful. He's in the Dark Reaches, sometimes walking, sometimes flying; we've been tasked with observing him." Brooke's grimace revealed jagged fangs. "It'd be far easier to feed on his magical essence then drown him, but no – we're only to watch and report his actions." She spat. "We're to take turns, a different one of us each day."

Delta rolled her eyes. "Why'd you agree to this, Brooke?" She palm-smacked the water. "Istondir and I planned a few days in the Eldwytch Demesne – we've no time for such nonsense."

Snarling, Brooke flung some weed at the cluster of lily-pads. "If you think I want to spend precious time spying, Delta, your brains are made of fish scales!"

Ribbit, ribbit!

Rescuing the frog from the sudden curtain of weed, Cascade stroked its head, before easing it into the water to swim away. "Maman, you go home; Cherry and I will stay and cover your turn." She looked at her aunt. "Where is the Fae-male?"

"The Nixie shadowed him to that Rock-troll's tavern in the hollow elderoak. He sent a watcher to search for Undines." Brooke grimaced. "He found me."

Cherith sighed. "Damn." She wasn't the least bit interested in spying on some random Fae-male who had little brain – and no sense if he was sneaking around the Dark Reaches – but she'd do what she had to. "Cassie's right, Maman. You go back to Papan and get ready for the trip."

Delta shook her head. "I can't leave you girls to do my share of the work."

"You can." Cascade hugged her. "We're not babies."

Cherith curved arms around her mother and sister. "We're happy to do an extra half shift each, Maman. You go on."

"Alright. We can leave tomorrow." Delta cast sly eyes at her sister. "There'll be no weeds in my luggage."

Brooke glared. "The water weeds disguise us to our prey!"

Delta laughed. "We're Undines with the power to make ourselves blend into the water, Brooke. Weeds are unnecessary. You've never bothered with them before, why now?"

"They add to our mystique!"

"Mystique?" Delta's brows arched. "Are you crazed? Or trying to dazzle a male?"

"Don't be ridiculous." Brooke's lips tightened, but she looked away.

"Aha!" Delta pointed. "That's it! But who would be impressed by weed, I wonder?"

"Just leave it!"

Delta clapped her hands. "I know!"

Brooke swept a wave of water at her sister. "Shut up! Just shut up."

Dodging, Delta grabbed a floating trail of weed and advanced on Brooke. "The Belkaban Bridge Water-troll!" Delta hooted. "That's who. C'mere sis, let me pretty you up with more of this watercress …"

Brooke back-finned to stay out of reach, but Delta thrust out, her leg-fins flashing through the water as she gave chase.

"I think Aunt Brooke's in heat." Cascade giggled.

Cherith grinned. "Maybe." She cupped a handful of river water, watching as it overflowed around her finger webbing. "Let me know how this ends. I'll go see if this interloper is as stupid as his actions indicate."

Cascade waved. "Okay, I'll see you at shift change tomorrow morning."

~

MOONBEAMS LIT a path across the tree sheltered lagoon where Cherith had made her nest for the night. As comfortable as she could be in a niche at the base of a sweeping water willow, she idled in the water, keeping watch on the Elderoak Inn. The rasp of crickets sounded on the evening air.

Cora-wit, cora-wit, churrr, churrr. The call of a nightjunket carried across the clear flowing stream. A second nightjunket joined in. Calmed by the familiar sounds, Cherith recalled the words of the Nixie whose shift she'd relieved.

The mark's not nocturnal; likely he'll be staying at the inn overnight. There was a dust-up earlier. Roaring and fiery light. All sorts of creatures fled like they'd a ghoul on their tails, including a Nageen in her natural form. Aquinal the Nixie had laughed. *Kind of weird watching her trying to writhe and roil out through the door which kept swinging shut on her.* Aquinal was certain the Seelie Fae-male was still within. *Everyone I spoke to said he hadn't left and I haven't seen him come out.*

Best to make sure. Hoisting herself from the water, Cherith padded alongside one of the well-trodden paths between riverbank and tavern. Slipping from one tree bole to the next, she avoided crackly forest undergrowth, while maintaining a clear view of the elderoak's massive girth. From on high, its glorious canopy swept down in a giant's leafy skirt, while between the leaves, fiery light twinkled through the multitude of windows set into the outer trunk. The welcoming glow gleamed through the gaps around the aged bark of the double doored entry, calling the weary traveller to come inside, rest their aching feet and share a beverage by the warmth of the cheery hearth fire. Cherith wished she could push through those inviting doors in response to the silent invitation, but, ignoring it, she slipped around to the servant's entrance, glancing in every window as she drifted past. To her disgust, ages of dripping sap had glommed-up the windows so all she could see was the warm, but frustrating, internal glow.

Easing down the rear steps into the cellar at the base of one of the gnarled roots, Cherith wondered why she'd heard nothing and seen no-one. Was the place deserted? Aquinal hadn't reported the Rock-troll fleeing, so surely the inn's burly bartender-manager was still here. She crept between two rows of shelves in a room illuminated by glow-bug wall sconces. Shadows reared up over the walls, menacing monoliths of doom. *Quiet, quiet, quiet.* Climbing the two steps to the main level, Cherith's bare feet whispered along the hall until the elderoak's internal trunk – the heartwood – loomed over her. At that central column, she'd a choice of left to the main bar, or right to the stairs winding up to the next level of rooms. The bar door was ajar, the sound of voices drifting from within.

Edging nearer, Cherith was rewarded by the side view of a large Rock-troll. He sat in a pew, feet on a stool as he conversed with someone. Her gaze shifted to a straight-nosed Fae-male with piercing midnight eyes and pointed ears revealed by swept back, shoulder length hair. *Dark hair, nice.* Cherith's anxiety faded. Her target was here and didn't look to be leaving any time soon. She watched for a few minutes, her curiosity roused by the reports, interest piqued by her brief glimpse of the attractive male. What was he searching for? Or who?

Shaking her head, Cherith eventually fell back from her vantage point, retraced her steps, and exited the inn. Once outside, she returned to the stream and her nest between the willow roots where she settled in for the night, her thoughts full of a dusky-haired male with penetrating eyes.

DEMAKSIM

Chewing on teeth-cleansing mint leaves extracted from his travel pouch, DeMaksim walked the well-beaten track to the nearby stream. He refilled his flask with pristine water from the Mirkdowd. Granite, the Rock-troll, had assured him it was: "clean and then some, because it was birthed in the Mountains of Frashdew and that river's where all my water comes from. Ye've already drunk it." Did his survival thus denote a quality product? DeMaksim chuckled, darkly amused.

Morning light bathed the river bank. He relaxed, basking in the sunrays shining through the undergrowth and beneath the forest eaves, highlighting the leaf-strewn path. It was beautiful, quiet. No bird calls, just the breeze sighing through the trees. Too quiet? DeMaksim frowned. Was he the cause of the lack of animal and bird noise? Wary, he checked under the low hanging branches of the large water willow next to the stream, but saw nothing alarming. Ducking beneath the low, sheltering canopy, he used its skirts to scan outside the tree's leafy domain.

His foray into Unseelie territory might be sanctioned by the Queens, but this wasn't a tame land and possessing a royal pass was of little use if he was foolish enough to get himself killed. Some of the local denizens would probably kill him *because* he had a royal pass. His search had brought him to the little-known Dark Reaches; the Unseelie gravitating to its depths were often lawless, had something to hide or nowhere else to go. Some were whole clans, like the murdering Redcaps – others were relics and rebels left from the Fae Wars of 50 years ago, in which his father Yanvian, Duke Papillion, had fought. He'd warned DeMaksim: *there are some very bitter and nasty Unseelie with long memories. You can't relax for an instant unless certain of the safety of your environment.* But, DeMaksim's quarry might also be in the Dark Reaches if court archives and Old Venny's translation were accurate.

Stray leaves dropped. Brushing them away, DeMaksim was about to look up when something fluttered in his peripheral vision. Turning towards the movement, he spied a low hanging withy moving like someone had flicked past. Easing forward, he heard a splash as he rounded the bole of the tree – something had been here if he read the flurry of disturbed leaves correctly. At the stream's edge, DeMaksim peered at the water's reflective surface. *X-ray vision would be helpful. Is that a flash? A fish, maybe.* Dropping to his knees, he leaned over the stream, frowning. *Nothing. Did I imagine it?* Further out a waterlily trembled, the pad dipping. He spied a frog and smiled, before refocusing on the wavelets beneath. *There!*

A blurry face surged upwards.

DeMaksim reared back, hands shooting out reflexively.

Hands breached the water – webbed with claw-bedecked fingers – followed by the head of a snarling, green haired, aqua-eyed female. She swiped at him. "Stalker!"

"Not!"

She lunged again; he countered, the fingers of one hand clenched with hers as if they'd agreed to a strength challenge, the other gripping her waist. Her other hand dug talons into his shoulder. She fought to drag him into the water as hard as he struggled to spin her from it. As they wrestled, a ridiculous thought crossed DeMaksim's mind – *classic dance position!* Their bodies whirled, dipping in a frantic frenzy of heat, rhythm and fury.

"No!" The scream shrilled from above. "I saw him first!" The water willow shook as something sizeable thumped through the branches. A Nageen blasted into view, landing at the base of the tree in a violent hiss of slithery coils.

"Blue blazes!" DeMaksim's fight with the slippery, clawing Water Nymph left no time for the Nageen. His startled pause gave advantage to his watery assailant but she also hesitated. *Can I reason with her?"*

"Shtop!" He gasped into the adorable, bat-wing shaped ear. Lisping around his own distended fangs, he inadvertently nicked her lobe, instinctively licking the tiny wound. "I don't wish you any hurt, but the Nageen ..."

The snake woman lunged, knocking them backwards. Her menacing, flared head reared over them, eyes a hellish scarlet. Holding tight to his partner, DeMaksim danced avoidance, while the Nageen whipped cord after cord from a new hair blossom, flinging them in a continuing barrage of scoring red thread.

His water beauty screamed as one slashed her in passing.

That's not happening again! DeMaksim spun, still gripping, and being gripped by, the Water Nymph. Losing balance, they fell, clasped hands swinging high to swipe at a descending red string. Thin scarlet lashed around their close-set arms at wrist height, glowing with feral brilliance as two ends snapped together. Pain sizzled, brief but razor sharp. But they were rolling, the red dazzle fading as the enclosed strands vanished beneath the skin of both he and his river lady. *Shite! Bugger! Demonhells! What's that going to do to us?* DeMaksim's thoughts fizzled as their revolving momentum dropped them into the stream. A colossal geyser of weed and water erupted as they sank in a weird ballet of thrashing, pointed limbs and arched spines.

Wild with panic, DeMaksim surged to his feet, gasped deeply and spat a roaring sheet of red-gold flame at the Nageen, then a second spout of fire and a third. She dodged it.

Unable to ignore the dragging summons of their new wrist-link, his water maiden surfaced beside him, snatched both hands to her chest and splashed some water towards the snake woman. DeMaksim's hand jerked in and out, alongside hers. His mouth fell open as the small amount of liquid the water maiden had pushed, became a mini-tsunami streaking towards the Nageen. *Nifty magic. Is that normal mermaid power?* He spat another fire-blast, only to have it overtaken by the mer-woman's next sheet of water. A powerful ignition occurred, a whoosh of red sparks and green water droplets.

Expecting the liquid to cancel his flame, DeMaksim gaped as the flames strengthened, shimmering from red to icy pale aqua. The watery aqua completely swallowed his burning red flare before continuing to race towards the Nageen with the momentum of a toppling forest monarch.

"He's mine!" The Nageen waved her arms, hissing and shrieking. Her coils undulated, scales glistening oily-olive in the bright sunlight. "I won't let you steal him, you soul sucking Undine!"

"I'm my own!" His voice emerged an indignant gurgle, just as their combined flaming wave crashed down upon the Nageen, engulfing her in a deluge of sizzling, arctic foam. The Nageen's screams were ear-piercing, but she finally subsided, collapsing in crumpled spirals on the river bank.

His jaw sagged. "What the ever-loving shite?"

A violent push came from his right. "Get away from me!"

DeMaksim staggered. "Take it easy!"

The water maiden pulled her left arm in, dragging DeMaksim's right arm along. "Let go!" Their combined hands reached her well-endowed chest.

His gaze dropped and he licked his lips. *What a time to admire a fabulous set of boobs!*

Those aqua-coloured eyes widened. "Don't you try to grope me, you land locked scum!" She batted at his hand. He obligingly yanked it away – her hand followed his. "We're still ..."

He flattened his hand against his collar bone – which brought hers along for the ride. Her finger, two, touched the skin of his upper chest beneath his torn linen shirt. *That's nice – better than nice, actually.* DeMaksim forced a frown. "Now you're touching me, river-maid."

She jerked their hands away.

He pulled them back.

Lips pressed into thin lines, she heaved to one side.

Mouth quirking, he tugged the opposite way.

She paused, brows knit in the cutest scowl, delightful chest heaving under some sort of fine brown cloth. "How and why did this happen?" Pretty bat-ears twitched amidst long green locks. "I won't stay like this!"

DeMaksim attempted to ignore the delicious breasts outlined by the drape of her snug, wet gown. *Is it made of some type of weed? Or fabric constructed to look like weed?*

Fingers clicked under his nose. "My face is up here, Fae-male."

Cheeks burning, he met her eyes and recalled the Nageen's red strings of entrapment, one of which had curled around both of their wrists. "I think I know what she did to us."

"She? It is you to whom I'm connected, Fae-male." The Water Nymph – or whatever she was – fronted him, green hair curling as it dried in the breeze, ears tautly upright, voice low. "Release me, now."

"Please, wait." DeMaksim held up his free hand, palm out.

"Grrr!" Mouth stretching to reveal fangs, she darted her head forward, those needles piercing the palm of his hand. She retreated, blood on her smirking lips.

"Ow!" He dragged their linked hands up to his mouth to lick-heal her bite mark. *What's that sizzle?* "Listen, I want to be free too, but the Nageen—"

"Oh, fish dung! She threw those bloody mating strings of hers." Bat-wing ears flickered as she twisted to stare at the river bank. Following her lead, DeMaksim also faced the fallen lump of snake woman. The river girl cupped her free hand around her mouth. "Hey, you! Snake bitch in heat! Free me and you can take him!"

"Thanks for nothing!" DeMaksim growled. "I don't want her, nor am I on the market, or free to a good home. I told her last night when she attacked."

The stream maiden hissed at him. "Not content with spying? Leading women on, too?"

"What?" DeMaksim recoiled. "The hell I'm spying – or hunting females! I'm researching family history."

"Whatever!" She tugged her arm; his moved too. "Come on, if we want freedom, we'll have to get closer to the damned Nageen – and she'd better cooperate."

"Or else?" Despite himself, DeMaksim grinned.

"Else she'll regret it. I have powerful kin." Using both hands, the water maiden hoisted herself up the bank, jerking DeMaksim off balance. They toppled back into the water.

Struggling to stand, DeMaksim felt small, strong arms around his midriff helping him up. *This little dynamo doesn't need kin helping her.* He spat a mouthful of water.

"Sorry, Fae-male. I forgot our link."

He wiped clinging weed from his cheek. "We have to work together, Water-Nymph."

"I'm an Undine, not a Water-Nymph."

"Fine. My apologies Lady Undine." DeMaksim shook water from his hair. "Let's try again. It'll be like a three-legged race, but with arms."

"Three-legged race?" Her lips twisted. "A strange concept, but I think I understand. Wait, what about your wings?" She frowned. "Forget I said that – if you flew, so would I and that's a hard no."

He grimaced. "Doesn't matter. They're soaked through, anyway. Too fragile to lift us."

It still took three more tries before DeMaksim dragged both of them from the water, the Undine sprawled across his back and neck in an ungainly fashion, the arm linked to his stretched to her limit. He lay flat on his stomach; her weight disappearing as she slid off to lie beside him on the bed of old willow leaves under the ancient tree.

Recovering his breath, DeMaksim curled his legs beneath him and twisted to sit, then assisted his Undine. Carefully helping each other, they managed to stand, then approached the Nageen. She lay in an icy, slimy blue-green circle, mouth agape, eyes staring.

The Undine hesitated. "Did we knock her out?"

A sense of foreboding invaded DeMaksim. He prodded her with the toe of his soggy boot – there was no give.

He swallowed, voice emerging a papery whisper. "She's solid!"

"Solid?" The Undine blinked. "How can that be? She doesn't look well, but—"

"Because she's dead." His eyes met the Undine's wide aqua orbs.

"What?"

"We killed her."

4

CHERITH

Staring in horror at the lifeless serpentine body, Cherith shuddered. "How could we have killed her?"

Her hawk featured Fae-male companion studied the body. "Some sort of wave swamped her, something I've never seen before." He swallowed. "I spat flame, but she's not burned; that leaves your water …"

"Don't gaslight me! She's a solid block of ice, not water! Smoking ice!"

"You can't do ice?"

"No!"

He pursed his lips. "And ice is usually cold, but she isn't."

Bending, Cherith peered at the ground. "Nor is the sun melting her."

"So she's hot but frozen." Green eyes with violet striations met hers. "That's a contradiction, even though I saw your water and my flame merge."

"And?" She studied him. *Vazel eyes! Violet and green is rare and gorgeous. And his hair! The darkness of black lagoon water highlighted by kingfisher blue and wild violets ...* The distant slamming of a door jerked her from foolish thoughts. The Rock-troll was shuffling towards them.

"Lady Undine?" Her towering, lick-able, Fae-male companion frowned. "Surely you noticed our separate powers linking?"

Cherith swallowed. *Oops! Caught mooning.* She jerked the strand of hair wound around her finger. *Ouch! Never mind wanting to drape yourself over him like the water weed Aunt Brooke always harps about. What'd he say?* She searched her memory. *Something about our powers clinking ... No! Linking, that was it, linking.* "Our powers combined. Right! Yes, they did. How? We're strangers – you spat fire and I splashed water."

"That ..." He frowned, delicious vazel eyes pinning her. "Something wrong Lady Undine? Are you wounded? In pain?"

"A few bruises, why?"

"Your expression – such a pain-filled grimace. I thought ..."

"Oh!" *Massive fail in my interested expression, I'll have to practice in a clear pool of still-water.* She stretched her lips into a smile. "No, no, I'm fine."

"Hm." His gaze flashed over her.

Is that a lick of flame in his eyes?

"I'll have to take your word for it." He cleared his throat. "Well, anyway." His focus returned to the dead Nageen. "Your water should've doused my fire."

No, must have been annoyance. I doubt a Lepidopter-fae-male – highborn with that plummy speech – would find a halfling river Undine attractive. But look at those biteable muscles ...

"Are ye both lack-witted?" Granite the Rock-troll stomped through seasons of leaf litter, a sack in one mammoth grey paw. "It's because she bound ye together!" Approaching the body, he sidestepped to see the face. A quick touch to the inert Nageen had him jerking back, shaking his fingers violently, then sticking them into his mouth for a few seconds. Eyes round and wide, he blew on the digits, flexing them. "Well, I'll be! Nasty way to go, but she made her play and lost." From under beetling brows, his stare pinned the Fae-male. "The Undine's power iced yer fire, Mak, or ..." he paused, bowing to Cherith, "... from yer angle, fired yer ice, river maid. Whichever way it happened, the pair of ye look to have turned that Nageen into a block of hot, dry ice."

The Fae-male scratched his head. "But, how does that make sense, scientifically speaking?

"How the scheelite would I know?" Granite glared. "I'm not skilled in sciences, Mak. Are you?"

"Nothing relevant."

"Never mind that!" Cherith hissed. "She bound us with her mating strings. Shouldn't they have disintegrated upon her death?"

Granite's lips twisted. "Yes, but she usually binds a male to her; instead, she bound her male of choice to another female." He plucked at a trail of lichen hanging from his ear. "It's outside my understanding." He frowned from Cherith to Mak.

Mak barked a laugh. "So, none of us has a clue what in demon-hells actually happened? The Undine and I should've negated one another! I'm fire, she's water …"

"And I'm rock!" Granite hooted. "Was the Nageen paper or scissors?"

Mak threw his hands high, perforce dragging Cherith's left one with it. "Frigging demon-hells, Granite! This isn't a game!"

"No, it isn't! And you're going round in circles." Cherith jerked her arm down and flicked all her fingers, spraying the stupid-arse males with water. "The Nageen's dead! Her damned entrapment strings should've disintegrated with her. Now we'll have to break the threads ourselves. Pull your arm back in opposition to mine Fae-male!"

He did, but the invisible cords stayed firm, allowing no leeway. "It's not working."

She bared fangs. "How very observant!" *River Goddess! We've pulled and twisted and wrenched and wrestled – do NOT think about the wrestling with his hot body, Cherith!*

With his left hand, Mak reached to his hip, producing a dagger. "This will work."

"Be careful!" Cherith screeched. "You can't see—"

"Now who's being obvious?" He glared. "Of course I can't see, but

I've other senses. I can *feel* what I'm doing." Easing the blade between their snug wrists until he met resistance, he sawed back and forth.

"Is yer dagger blunt then, Mak?" Granite's brows drew together. "Nought looks to be happening."

Mak grunted. "It's bouncing off." He pressed harder, but only succeeded in forcing their united wrists downward. Frowning, he sheathed his blade and checked the strings. "Blue blazes, they're not even damaged."

Cherith ground her teeth. "So you and I are stuck together, Sir Fancy Pants Fae?" *What in the black lagoons is going on?* She rounded on the Rock-troll. "Granite, any thoughts, or answers, would be acceptable, about now!"

"I'm not a freaking Oracle, river maid." Arms akimbo, the Rock-troll glared; shale chips trickling down his face. "Why don't ye find one and ask them? Better yet, ask yer King!"

She glared back. "How would King Eskavon know?"

"Well, he's older than you, for a start. Older than me. And, he's *yer* King, not mine."

"Quit arguing!" Mak considered the Rock-troll, cocked his head. "Granite? Those little bits of rock that keep falling off? In the interests of science, do Rock-trolls ever flake away to nothing?"

"Holy River Goddess!" Cherith flicked more water at the dolt. "You're both idiots! Rock for brains and a pretty spy who should still be wearing a swaddling cloth!"

"I'm not a blasted spy! I—"

"You've been seen poking around stream banks and traipsing through backwaters." Cherith glowered. "You're looking for something, or someone, and my king knows about you."

"Wow! I've been observed and reported to your king?" He snorted. "Tell me who's spying now?"

"Don't try your pathetic reverse psychology on me!" She bared her fangs. "I'm not the invader."

"Nor am I." He opened his mouth, closed it and scrubbed his scalp. "I'm simply a traveller touring the complete Fae demesnes and I enjoy exploring waterways."

"Scheelite." Granite turned away, shoulders shaking.

A hoot of laughter burst from Cherith. "That's frog shite! Nobody comes to the Dark Reaches on a scummy holiday." She shook her head. "That's a one-way ticket to hell. Try again pretty fae."

"Why?" He thrust his face towards hers. "It's my business, back off."

"Linked remember? Now it's my business too." Cherith snapped her teeth at his hawkish looming nose.

"Don't you dare!" Mak reared back.

Lurching forward, Cherith fell against him. "I'm over this!"

"On that we agree." His other arm wrapped loosely about her, firming around her waist, his balance steadying, holding them upright.

She held his frustrated gaze. "Let's both stop waving our arms, call truce and work together to break the Nageen's magic."

His fingers gripped her hip, flexed. "A truce is an excellent idea. So is breaking her magic – I agree."

She nodded. "On that note, I'm Cherith – you're Mak?"

He smiled. "Yes …"

An explosive snort burst from Granite. "By the Rock of Ages, ye're a hard-headed pair. About time ye realised ye'll work better as a team."

Mak's mouth bared, revealing even white teeth, the small fangs of the Fae-kind indenting his lips. "You're so helpful, Granite. We wouldn't have coped without you."

Cherith laughed.

"I might be a Rock-troll, but sarcasm ain't lost on me, Mak." Granite hefted the sack he'd brought. "Ye left yer pack behind and I lugged it out, but I can throw it in the river."

"Okay, sorry." Mak's scent was redolent of pine mixed with the delicious tang of bark leather; Cherith couldn't grasp why she wanted to bathe in it. "We need to find someone who understands what's happened."

"Another Nageen would know." Granite shuffled closer.

"We'd have to reveal we killed this one." Cherith shuddered. "I doubt they'd be happy, so – no, not happening."

The Rock-troll shrugged. "Just listing options." He tapped Mak's shoulder, raising the pack by its strap. "Stop cuddling and lift your arm, Mak."

River Goddess! We are *cuddling!* Cherith took a hasty step away.

Mak grimaced, but extended his arm, allowed Granite to position the strap over his head and across his body. His gaze rose to meet hers. "I meant neither harm nor insult."

Cherith rolled her bottom lip between her teeth. "Okay." She smiled weakly. "Supporting each other is a good idea, and not just physically. We need to be fully cooperative to sort this out."

"Agreed." Mak's brows tightened. "So, let's compare suggestions on what to do next."

"Or where to go from here." The rumble of Granite's voice was lost in a loud splash. Water cascaded over all three of them.

"Unhand my sister, Seelie monster! We've been warned about your kind!"

Oh fish crap! Cassie's here for her observation shift.

5

―――――

DEMAKSIM

*D*eMaksim stiffened as a second surge of liquid hit, cold after the sun's warmth. The water became steaming foam as it crashed over the solid statue of the dry-iced Nageen and sizzled on its return path to the stream.

"Cascade Lystreniel Beriaden! Stop that at once." Cherith glared over DeMaksim's shoulder. The rain of water ceased.

"My full name?" Cascade whistled. "You must be okay. Why are you and the spy hugging, Cherry? What's with the dead Nageen? Aquinal said nothing about a body."

"Well, the body's a bit recent-ish." Cherith grimaced. "And we're not hugging. The Nageen tied us together. We were discussing our next course of action when you arrived."

Eyes like saucers, Cascade straightened. "Hopping toad's freckles, Cherry! This was supposed to be simple; watch the spy and see where he goes …"

Turning himself and Cherith, DeMaksim bared his fangs. "I'm damned tired of being called a spy! Sounds like you lot are spying on me!" *Shite! My fangs are larger than usual. What's caused that?* He glowered at the females. "You lot need to butt out of my business." *What's that tingling in my fingertips?* Lifting his free hand, he saw a scaly paw

446

with deadly hooked claws at the tips. *Blue blazes, that's new! And pale blue-green scales instead of mid-brown. Am I evolving?*

Cascade slammed hands to her hips. "What in the name of the River Goddess and all her fishy offspring are you?"

Tongue lolling thickly, DeMaksim hissed. "I'm Fae!" Smoke curled from his nostrils.

"And a whole lot more, Sir Fae-not-Fae."

"Cassie, you're not helping." The shake of Cherith's head dragged silky green locks over DeMaksim's scaly skin. The strands snagged before sliding away.

Arousal twined through him.

"I'm trying to protect you, Cherry!"

"Well back off. I'm a perfectly capable adult."

"I'm older than you—"

"By two minutes! You're being ridiculous."

"Give it a rest!" Granite held both huge hands up. "We just finished arguing and now ye've started again. Nought will get done at this rate."

Cascade folded her arms. "I'm simply trying to understand the situation."

"Well, the Nageen bound these two together with her mating threads. The strands should've disintegrated upon her death, but—"

"You're mated to this creature, Cherry?" Cassie's mouth rounded to an 'o' of horror as she stared at DeMaksim's pale turquoise scales and claws. "Why, he looks draconic, not Fae! I thought Dracons were extinct?"

Cherith glared. "He's not a creature; his name is Mak and we appear to be linked. We're trying to work out how to break the binding."

Granite guffawed. "Ye can't believe everything ye hear, Undine."

Cascade's mouth thinned. "I think I can help." She waded to the bank. "If you'll allow it?"

Cherith relaxed. "Of course, Cassie."

"Your help is appreciated." DeMaksim rumbled. He watched Cherith's sister exit the water and approach. Cascade smoothed both hands down her hips; one vanished within the folds of her skirt and reappeared clutching a strange looking, conical blade. He stared in disbelief as her fist reared. Cherith screamed as the point descended towards his chest. Then his wits returned and he dodged, roaring as anger swamped him. A ball of flame rose in his gullet.

"No!" Cherith surged forward, swinging between her sister and himself.

Cascade shrieked as Cherith plunged into the path of the swiftly falling blade, trying to pull back.

Fire bubbled in the back of DeMaksim's throat … *Too close! I cannot hurt Cherith.* Head aimed high, he belched his gout of flame skyward, tilting off balance as Cherith's momentum tugged him inexorably in her wake. They crashed into the retreating Cascade, tumbling into the river in a thrashing, contorting, intertwined threesome. Light faded as water closed over his head and he sank. A foot to the kidneys, hair in his eyes, fingers jabbing the back of his knee, the sharp sensation forcing him into a spasmodic lunge upward. Sunlight leered tauntingly through filters of liquid, gyrating bodies and waving weed.

Surfacing, DeMaksim gulped breath, then was rolled under the water again. His Undine-tethered wrist wrenched him deeper; he came face to bulging eyes with a balloon-fish. The creature shot away between some reeds as he flailed, wallowed, was jerked over and around, saw the flash of a finned leg and tried to hold his breath. His mind kicked into gear. With his free hand he felt along the arm connected to his until he rubbed against a female form. *Cherith!* Firming his grip, he kicked hard to bring both their faces into the air. A dripping Cascade bobbed up nearby, spluttering and wailing. He glared, but she was no longer intent on him.

"My Narwhal blade! I've dropped it." She dove under the water.

Karack, karack, karack. The grinding clatter of rasping rock assaulted DeMaksim's ears, a continuous stone-on-stone grating. *Is that an earthquake? The ground's not shaking.* Seeking the source of the rasping discord, he swept water from his eyes and identified Granite howling with laughter on the riverbank.

The Rock-troll pointed. "That was the best thing I've seen in a shale's age! Yer faces! The lot of ye writhing like a slither of eels!" Another burst of crushed pebble-mirth erupted from his craggy mouth. "Life was boring before ye came to the Dark Reaches, Mak. How long can ye stay?"

"Shut it, Granite." DeMaksim massaged his forehead. Ignoring another burst of ear jarring rumbles, he focused on the weight sagging against him. Cherith's eyes were wet with tears, her chest heaving. He forced himself to avert his gaze from temptation. "Cherith? You alright?" Her scent was unfamiliar to him, but delicious all the same.

"S-she m-meant to k-kill you! I'm so-sorry. I-I didn't know."

He rocked her. "It's fine. Her blade missed me when you—" He tensed. "Cherry? Did the knife connect? Are you hurt?"

"A scratch." She wrinkled her nose. "Nothing to worry about."

But he did. Turning her, he searched until he located the scratch beneath her unfettered forearm. Swallowing, he stared at the wound she'd taken protecting him; a cut leaking pearlescent fluid in a filmy trail along her delicate flesh. Hand shaking, he raised her arm gently to his mouth and licked the wound clean, tasting her skin, her blood, the essence of her being. The sweetness of tending to her felt satisfying. *Because of the Nageen binding?*

"Stop!" Cherith's mouth trembled. Her entire body shook as she pulled her arm away from him. "I'm alright. Y-you shouldn't do that, but thank you."

Blinking dazedly, DeMaksim cleared his throat. "Right." His gaze returned to the river. "What the blue-blazes ails your sister? She crazy?"

"I don't think she properly understood." Cherith tongued her bottom lip, staring at the violent eddying where Cascade searched for her precious blade. "She's not usually violent, but she likely thought she was rescuing me from an untenable situation."

"Not violent?" His laugh held no mirth. "She's wielding a dagger."

"I know, but ..."

Cascade's upper body appeared; she was brandishing her blade. "I found it!" She arrowed closer, stopping when DeMaksim flung up his left hand.

"No nearer. This isn't my day to die and you've already slashed your sister."

"Oh no, Cherry, I cut you?" Cassie's ears drooped. "I'm so sorry."

"What in blazes were you thinking, Cassie?" Cherith's voice shook.

"To free you from the Nageen's binding!"

"By killing Mak?"

"Well," Cascade reasoned. "He *is* holding you prisoner."

"He's not, we're trapped together!"

"Oh!" Cascade bobbed her head. "My apologies, Mak."

Growling, Cherith pointed. "And just where did you get a Narwhal tusk blade? Why in surging whirlpools do you need it?"

"I got it from Old Venny, the tinker trader, last time he came through." Cascade shrugged. "It called to me, I couldn't stop stroking it and I couldn't leave it there. So I traded for it."

"Traded what, exactly?"

"It must have been something good. Old Venny drives a hard bargain." De Maksim remembered past bargains.

Cassie's head dropped. "The hairpiece of grime-roses you made me."

"What? Cassie how could you? Do you know how much time it took me to cultivate those grime-roses, harvest them at the perfect moment and make that hairpiece?"

Cassie pouted. "I'm sorry. I really am, but I had to have this tusk."

"Fine." Cherith sighed. "May I see it, rather than feel it's edge?"

"As long as you keep your hands away." Cascade gripped the conical blade and clutched it to her bosom. DeMaksim couldn't help where his thoughts went. *Pretty, but from what I've seen so far, Cherith has nicer handfuls.*

Cherith frowned. "You know the Narwhal must be dead for you to have that tusk, don't you?"

Cuddling the knife like a lover, Cascade rolled her lower lip between her teeth. "I don't sense violent death on this blade – nor any death actually."

"That can't be right." Cherith peered at the gleaming spiral shape. "What Narwhal would give away its horn voluntarily?"

"I know it sounds crazy, but there's no death link. There's emotion of course; the love for family, the sensations of everyday life, the bravery of defending oneself. But the strongest is a deep sense of longing. For what, I can't sense, but," Cascade shook her head, "feelings of dying are just not here."

"A puzzle for another time." DeMaksim massaged his temple. "You mentioned Old Venny, the tinker trader – he gets around further than I knew."

"Yeah." Granite smiled, revealing nubby grey teeth shaped like square blocks. "He carries an amazing variety of goods. Always has the right thing, sometimes it's something ye never knew ye needed until he shows ye."

"Goods and information." *Lucky for me he was visiting Queen Dianathke's castle and was able to help me decipher the archaic Eldwytch writing in that old scroll which contained accounts of Dracons.* DeMaksim pursed his lips. "When did you see him, Cascade?"

"A few days ago."

"Hmm." *After he left the castle then. I spent ages searching for the easiest way to get through the tightly tangled scrub bordering the Dark Reaches and he probably knew a way – should've asked him when I had the chance.* DeMaksim rubbed his chin. "Which way did he go? He mightn't be too far away; his advice might help us get free."

"Oh, yeah." Cascade gestured in a southerly direction. "He went upstream. Oh wait! Cherry, that flower which counteracts Nageen venom, maybe it'll work on those entrapment cords?"

Cherith's brow cleared. "That's a great idea."

DeMaksim focused on her. "Where do we find this flower?"

Cherith sighed. "We'd need an Eldwytch mage, like my Papan, to create a potion from them, but it grows a fair way upstream."

"You mentioned King Eskavon might be able to assist – where's he live?"

"Upstream." Cherith and Cascade spoke simultaneously.

"And the deeps of the Dark Reaches?"

"Give ye one guess." Granite winked.

DeMaksim winced. "Right." Dragging his free hand through his hair, he tilted his head towards Cherith. "I've a suggestion then – what say we head upstream?"

"That's brilliant Mak!" The grate of Granite's laughter assaulted their ears. "I knew as soon as I saw ye, last night, that yer pretty head housed useful grey matter."

DeMaksim flipped him off.

6

———

CHERITH

"You'll need help collecting the anti-venom flowers." Cassie's fingers flexed on the hilt of the Narwhal blade, her expression hopeful. "I'm free to join you."

Cherith shook her head. "No you're not. You need to tell Aquinal to cancel the watch rotation and bring Papan up to date so he'll be ready to prepare the potion we need when we return with the blossoms."

"Oh, yes! I can do that." Cassie grinned. "I'll go right now." She waved and dived into the river, surfacing a fair way out to wave again before she swam away.

"Thank you." Mak stared after Cassie until she was out of sight. "That saves me from having to watch my back."

Cherith huffed out a breath, not certain whether she was more annoyed with Cassie or with Mak. "I did it for me, not for you. Cassie has a way of finding trouble and we've got enough already. Shall we get going?"

"Absolutely." Mak turned to Granite. "Thanks for your help. I'll not forget."

The Rock-troll nodded. "Happy to be able to assist. Drop in any time ye're back this way." He turned towards the inn, stumping briskly, and was soon out of view.

"This way." Refusing to look at Mak, Cherith tugged on their link, her brows drawn down. *He'd better not be difficult.* Without a word, he fell into step beside her and they set off upstream.

～

FLANKED by the old-world guardian forest, the river rippled and basked in the afternoon sunlight. Cherith was not in a mood to appreciate the lovely vista. She usually swam her way along the river, but being tied to Mak forced her to walk. *Damn land-dwellers!* A couple of hours of blasted foot slogging and her feet were paying the price. She sighed, bending to massage her right foot and flip away a pointy pebble. "I'm not used to all this land walking. The ground's so hard."

"Should have considered your bare feet sooner." Mak frowned. "We'll get into the water."

"That'll be harder for you."

"I can wade, or swim, as needs be."

"Swimming will wet your wings again." Cherith rolled her top lip. *His wings are so beautiful; the lilac, blue and green splotches glow against their sooty backdrop and are petal soft under my fingertips.*

"Wet wings aren't painful – your feet are." His gaze warmed. "I could fly us both?"

"Oh, no, no, no. You'd be carrying me." Her ears wiggled as she looked up at the sky, eyes huge. "That'd strain your arms or your wings."

"Strain me?" Eyebrows skyrocketing, he stared. His lips formed an 'o'. "You've never flown! Of course – you're nervous?"

She swallowed. "Sorry."

"It's okay." A calm smile. "What if we walk on the softer ground at water's edge?"

Hunched shoulders relaxing, her head tilted. "For me to be on the water side of our pairing, we'd have to cross to the other bank."

454

"Yep. We'll get wet again no matter what." He shrugged. "I'm guessing you need water to survive?"

"Yes, but not as much as true Undines – my father is Eldwytch. An Eldwytch green mage to be precise."

"Ah." Mak nodded. "Must be where your growing thumb comes from." He indicated a water willow stretching long branches low over the river. "We could sit on that branch, have a snack, and bathe our feet before we cross."

"Thanks."

His look turned serious. "Before we let this flying idea go, Cherith, I'm advising you I'll take us both to the air if I deem it necessary."

"It will be unnecessary." *The Mirkdowd river territory is home – what could possibly make it dangerous enough for flight? He needs to see the niche I've carved for myself – despite my differences, I fit in.* "I'm going to share something." Leading him to the willow's trunk, Cherith laid palms on the ancient bark. "Copy me." He frowned but capitulated, twisting his linked hand. "Now close your eyes and focus on the tree. See inside to the heart where time and sap flow slowly." Verbalizing for Mak's sake, she eased her essence along the tree's veins, gradually forming a connection with the water-willow. "Oh mighty willow, greenly growing, your branches, leaves and roots sweeping the water, the ground, the sky, I offer you a heart check in return for permission, for my companion and I, to sit on one of your branches and rest weary feet." The tree responded with a golden surge of warmth. Broadening the channel, Cherith drew on her green power, encouraging the flow through the tree, from trunk to root, then branch, node, leaf and bud. Near the base were signs of a grub infestation, which Cherith scorched with an intense burst of vibrant emerald; her power had never come so easy or been as clear. The willow shivered, then bathed them in golden radiance. "You're most welcome, lovely willow." She patted the bark affectionately and eased free.

"I felt that!" Mak was wide-eyed. "All of it!"

"I wasn't sure whether you would, but the Nageen's link seems to have opened a few doors between us." Cherith smiled. "It's such a beautiful feeling helping plants be healthy."

"You're more Eldwytch than Undine?"

"By nature." Her smile was rueful. "In looks I'm Undine, in skills I lean to Eldwytch green magery like Papan. It's Beckett who looks truly Eldwytch – whereas, Cassie and I don't. We lack Undine natures though. Our parents say looks mean nothing, but most people judge by appearance, expecting us to behave true to our appearance."

"Looks like one, must be one." He rubbed his jaw. "Do Undines really drain souls?"

"They can. Some of the nastiest do." Cherith wrinkled her nose. "I literally can't – I physically lack something, for which I'm grateful. The idea of draining souls sickens me." She shuddered. "My power promotes growth, life and strength." She shook her head. "The opposite to what Undines do."

"What you showed me with the willow indicates a healer. Is it just plants, or can you heal people?"

Her brows shot high. "I've never thought along those lines, I only work with flora. What if I can help people?"

"You were the green flow?"

"Yes! And the willow gave back golden warmth – did you feel it?"

"I did." Smoothing a lock of hair back, his gaze was thoughtful. "You could try healing your injured arm. It's not bleeding, but there's still a wound."

"My arm!" Excitedly, Cherith sourced her power, the swirling green pool of magic she'd always shared with plants, maximizing their health and growing abilities, then thought about her arm healing. Her fingertips did their familiar tingle, but the cut remained a cut. "Oh! It didn't work." She looked at Mak, disappointment choking her.

"Hmm." Mak frowned. "How do you normally make it happen?"

"I usually draw it up in ribbons until my heart is full, then aim my hands at the plant – it flows down my arms and out through my fingertips."

He cocked his head. "Wouldn't you need to send it around your body instead?"

Cherith curled fingers into her palms. "Of course! I don't want it exiting; something needs to push or pump it through me ... Wait, my heart!" Excitement rising, Cherith visualised her power as a green ribbon linking with her blood, flowing out from her heart, circulating through arteries to her extremities and returning through her veins. The sensation was a warm spreading glow. When it reached the area of her slashed arm, the warmth intensified to nearly a burn, fizzed for a few seconds, then faded and continued on.

"It worked!" Mak held her arm, lifted to expose the slash site. Barely a line remained where the wound had been, fading even as they watched.

"River Goddess." Cherith shook her head, eyes riveted to the now unblemished skin. "This is amazing. I've always been a plant nurturer. As a toddler, I'd stroke them and talk to them – afterwards the plants would be better, stronger, grow larger than usual, provide more beautiful blossoms. Everyone said I was a natural with plants, a glorified gardener I suppose. There was never any idea my magic could work on people too."

"Restricted by expectation." Mak's mouth twisted. "I know what that's like."

"You do?"

"Part of the reason I'm here. I've lived my life dancing to the expectations of others; I decided to find out whether that shape really embodies me or whether I've blighted myself by trying to be what everybody wanted." He glanced around. "Come on, let's settle onto the willow branch and talk about it over food and foot soaking."

"That sounds great. Who's going onto the branch first?"

"Well, we're traveling upstream." Mak gestured. "With my right wrist bound to your left, I have to lead with my left side and we must be on the far bank for you to be in water."

"True." Cherith nodded. "You'd better lead."

"Okay." Climbing to the low hanging branch of the willow, left arm spread for balance, Mak stepped carefully onto the branch road. His linked hand stretched back, fingers clasping Cherith's, as she eased along behind him. Jacket riding higher with his outstretched arms, he kept his Lepidopter-fae wings tightly furled. Underneath, the terrain changed from grass to sandy bank, reeds, then the clear swirling water of the river, deepening as they progressed.

Keeping her eyes on Mak's moving form, Cherith stepped instinctively, her feet feeling the branch. *Looky, looky at that nice tight butt in those cuddly leather pants, Cherry. Uh-mmm.*

Mak's voice reached her. "There's a nice shaped part of the branch ahead, that'll make a good seat."

There sure is.

He looked back, smiling encouragement as he continued stepping. Suddenly, the smile vanished, his eyes went impossibly wide, his mouth opened. "Aargh!" He toppled backwards, one arm windmilling, the other attempting to, except she was attached to it.

"Mak!" Jerked from her feet, Cherith fell to the branch, encircling it with her free arm, grasping as tightly as possible. Mak disappeared into the river beneath her. Their arm-link dragged, her hand tickling the water's surface, but she dropped no further. *Thank the River Goddess! We're holding. He'll be able to use me as an anchor to climb out. I hope he's okay – the Mirkdowd is so muddy on the bottom here.* The water roiled. What was going on? *Maybe I'd better go in and ...*

The agitated water parted. Glistening in the sunlight, a huge winged creature erupted skywards, bellowing as it soared. The roar blasted through the atmosphere, deafening Cherith. Quivering, she closed her eyes and tightened her grip, but it wasn't enough. She was wrenched screaming from the branch and dragged into the sky. Wind whistled around her lower limbs as she hung limply, secured only by the tenuous threads binding her wrist to that of ... Mak?

DEMAKSIM

*D*eMaksim choked on a mouthful of water and weeds for the third time that day and was completely unprepared as deep inside, his alter ego snarled, ripped open a previously unknown internal door and bucked into the driver's seat. *Wh-at's this?* His bewilderment allowed the other him to settle; his body jerked, expanded, changed and arrowed for the surface.

Bursting from the water, DeMaksim shot skywards; an exploding supernova with outspread wings, head and limbs thrust out like the arms of a five-pointed star. His bowed back forced his chest forward, his face aimed high and jaws agape for the release of an outraged roar. A gout of icy-green flame sheeted to the heavens; huge curls of fire accompanied a second roar. The world went silent, the forest hushed … until far away, from the depths of the Dark Reaches, a fainter ululating bellow was heard.

An echo? No, a challenger! Hovering above the water, DeMaksim craned his neck, switched his scaly tail, and opened his jaws to answer.

"Mak! Mak is that you? Oh, River Goddess, it must be – the wrist link still holds." The voice distracted him.

I hear a female. His head spun. *I smell a female – my female! Where?*

"Mak!"

A tugging on his right front leg. Before he could look, something shrilled and spat in his face. Jerking back, he fought to focus in close. Clinging to the sparkling curved horn on top of his long snout was a catfish. "Mrrrow!" It shrilled again, head butting his horn – *I have a horn?* A light thwack-thwack-thwack across his snout; the catfish assaulted him with tiny clawed fins. "Mrrrowww!" The catfish glared. DeMaksim glowered back, hissed, tilted his snout and flicked. "Mrrrooowwwwww …" The catfish sailed off, tumbling towards the river, squalling as it fell. He hissed; why hadn't he eaten it? Maybe he would. There was time—

"Ma-a-k." A soft shaking voice, more tugging, weight on his leg. His gaze ran down the scales of his right foreleg.

"Erp?"

"Mak!" A green haired female clung to him, limbs wrapped around his thick foreleg. Gorgeous aqua eyes huge in her sweet, golden skinned face, she was tied to him with red cord around the lower joint of his foreleg. He stared.

There is a female on my foreleg. Foreleg? Shouldn't that be my wrist? And why do I have a snout, a horn and scales? His huge scaly tail with its fan-shaped end lashed as he tried to get a grip on reality. *Tail! I have a tail? Am I dreaming?* His brain reeled, mind working furiously. Facts, he needed them.

"Mak?"

Yes! Mak. No, not Mak, DeMaksim. That was it – he was Heir-Lord DeMaksim Yanvian Aphiski, a Fae-male, eldest child of the Duke and Duchesse of Papillion. His soot-black wings and hair, splashed with lilac, soft blue and grass green, identified him as being of the Swallowtail line of the Lepidopter-fae. His life, his circumstances, rushed back to him, a tornado of thoughts and images swamping his mind.

"Dracon – Mak, please focus."

Blinking, he recognised the little aqua-eyed, golden skinned darling with pert lips and ears mimicking the shape of bat wings as Cherith Beriaden, his—

"Mate?" The word lisped from a mouth that felt strange. He worked his jaw, tried again. "We're mates?"

She grimaced. "Yes, well, the Nageen force-mated us. Remember?" She shook their combined wrists. "It's false, even if all the mate stuff is happening to us, any changes will disappear when her cord does, right? We can't see it now, but it's—"

"Red." Drawing his Cherith decorated foreleg close to his chest, he cupped the claws of his other foreleg around her.

Her brilliant smile returned. "You remember! Thank the River Goddess, I thought you lost to the Dracon body-snatcher."

"Remember? No, I see the string." Wrinkling his snout, he struggled to form words through elongated jaws. "And there's no Dracon body-snatcher, just me. I'm DeMaksim, as I've always been. Though never quite like this." His tongue poked out, testing fangs, sweeping across lips that were not familiar. "What in blue blazes is going on?"

Cherith tilted her head. "Are you alright?"

He shook himself. Water droplets flew. "I think so; maybe." He eyed the sky in which they hovered. "Let's land and talk." Snapping his wings, he took them higher, twisting and banking without conscious thought, performed a wobbly glide towards the further river bank and back-winged to an awkward landing. *Shite! I flew. Without even thinking about it.* Unused to the centre of gravity in his current body, plus female leg decoration, he stumbled a few steps. *Erk! This body is so ungainly.* Recovering, he glanced around at the sandy river bank; it ended in a low bluff which looked to be a few steps away. But when he moved his new larger body reached it in one stride. Freaked out, he tried not to think about how different he was, tried to ignore the inner voice yelling in alarm … Who was he?

Settling onto his haunches, body upright but leaning against the bluff, he brought his cupped and linked fore-legs, cradling Cherith, to one huge knee so that she faced him. Lowering his head, DeMaksim studied her intently, curled his new, powerful wings with their trailing edges of feathery fronds into a protective curtain and created a private niche. Sun bathed the leathery skin; it glistened in a pearly opalescence of aqua, blue and green.

"Look at you!" With her free hand, Cherith stroked down his gleaming foreleg to a three-digited paw, tested the sharp claws, then found their connecting rope. "Why isn't the Nageen's cord hurting, despite your arm's increased size?"

"I really don't want to look at me, right now. This is crazy." DeMaksim shivered. "As for the cord, it must have stretched?"

"Gah! It doesn't stretch – we tried that." She stared at him.

"Well, it has. Why are you staring like that?"

"You're so beautiful!" Her gaze drifted over him.

"I am?"

She nodded. "Your eyes are still vazel, but the rest of you is aqua and green and blue. Your head is scaled and feathered, you've got twin green, spiral horns between simply gorgeous feather-tufted ears, a curving crystalline horn on top of your snout and look how big your nostrils are!" She twisted, looking further. "Then your jaw arches back to your neck in such an elegant way …" She touched a fingertip to one of two large fangs curving down from his top lip, drew her finger over the lower lip, then stretched up and kissed the side of his snout. Staring at the place she'd smooched, she kissed the same spot again.

"Err." He drew his head back, inexplicable warmth flooding him. "What's that for?"

Cherith giggled. "That catfish was funny – your eyes criss-crossed looking at it."

He huffed. "Fierce little thing; but how did that lead to kisses?"

"It cut your nose." She folded her lips, looking sideways at him. "I made it better. Kissed the boo-boo."

"Boo-boo?" A laugh jerked from him. "Haven't heard that term for years. Brave of you to kiss this fierce hulking creature." His eyes widened. "Blue blazes! I'm a creature! A Dracon! What am I going to do?"

"You're not a creature!" She glared. "You're Mak. And you need to calm down."

"How do you suggest I do that?" Nothing in him felt calm.

"How about we talk this through?"

He shuddered. "Don't know how talking is going to help."

"It's a distraction. Think of it like a story."

"This isn't a faery tale."

"No. But you already know a lot about me, so it's time to reciprocate."

She peered up at him, such expectation on her face he couldn't disappoint her. "I suppose it's worth a try." He let out a gusty sigh, his breath blowing fronds of hair back from her lovely face. "Okay. I'm DeMaksim Aphiski, heir to the Seelie-Fae Duchy of Papillion."

"Ha!" Cherith prodded his broad scaly chest. "Seelie-Fae; we were right."

He glared. "But not a spy." Flexing a claw, he stared at it wildly, then averted his gaze. "Although I *am* a Queens' agent, I'm also really here on a personal mission. All our lives …"

"Our?"

"Oh, I'm the eldest of seven. After me come three sisters. Lyssica, Janeska and her twin Tindresse, then my brother Treymeron and my two youngest sisters, Armelle and Zhulija."

"Wow, your parents are prolific."

He snorted, then froze as steam issued from his nostrils. "Shite! I'm, I'm—"

"You're fine, Mak." Cherith's smile was soothing. "We were talking about your parents, yes?"

He nodded. "Oh, that's right. They say we're delightful expressions of their love."

"How sweet."

"Sweet, right – if Maman could just see – no. Better that she can't see me – It'd be better if I couldn't see—"

Cherith grabbed his foreleg. "Stop, Mak, it's okay."

He rolled his eyes, gulped. "Anyway, Maman says we've draconic blood from her family line and, sometimes, the talents of family members reflect that."

"Tell me more." Cherith tilted her head. "How does it show up?"

DeMaksim swallowed. "Okay. Um, usually, Fae exhibit basic magic abilities until puberty arrives and that's when our main gifts start to develop. There can be physical idiosyncrasies because of mixed bloodlines ..."

"What do you mean?"

"Well, I've sensed something extra inside me, because when I became emotional – angry or upset – I showed some scales. That's classed as a mixed bloodline physical idiosyncrasy; a small thing with no real use." DeMaksim frowned. "I've always been able to produce scaled sections of skin at will, emit bursts of flame and my fangs could enlarge. Since meeting and being linked to you this morning, it's more. Suddenly I'm breathing out steam or smoke, or something and my hands turn into clawed paws."

Cherith rested her chin on a fist. "And this afternoon you changed – hmm, let's not go there again." She frowned. "What is this 'basic magic' you spoke of? It's not a term we use."

His eyebrows rose. "Basic magic's part of our genetic make-up; the innate ability to be graceful, to connect to the world of which we are a part, harnessing the natural energy that flows through and around us, to manipulate it in small ways – depending on our personal strength and even our imagination. It stems from our querencia."

Cherith tilted her head. "Querencia?"

"The internal place from which our strength is drawn, where we feel most at home, most our truest self. It manifests differently in everyone – I'm excellent at organising, strategising and sometimes being able to subtly influence things. Perfect skills for being the heir to a Duchy with lands and people relying on continued prosperity. I was always expected to be heir, not because I'm the eldest, but because of those qualities." It had always made him wonder if anybody saw the real him.

Cherith pursed her lips. "So, for me, such skills would naturally be water and nature-linked, based on both my Eldwytch and Undine heritage?"

"Without the Undine soul-sucking ability."

She shuddered. "As I said earlier, I'm so glad I wasn't in that queue. It's a curse, not a skill. The very idea revolts me."

He shrugged, immense shoulders rippling, scales flashing sunlight. "We are what we are."

"I guess so." Cherith sighed.

He eyed her morosely. "Until we're something more."

"And a very handsome more, too." She winked. "Now, what's this 'personal mission' you mentioned?"

"Oh, that." He followed her lead. "For All Hallows' Eve, everyone in our family gains a closer connection, to tradition and our forebears, by researching an ancestor. When the All Hallows' Eve ritual takes place, we each tell the family about our choice of ancestor and light a candle for them. The candles burn all night – the time when the veil between worlds is thinner and spirits may visit. The candle is to light their way home."

"What a lovely tradition." Cherith smiled as if entranced. "I'd like to do that if I ever have children."

He smiled. "It's nice. Last year, Zhulija asked Maman questions about the draconic link." Grimacing, DeMaksim tilted his huge head. "Zhu can magically alter temperature and uses heat in her artwork without being heat-affected, making glass and sculpting metal. She asked if Maman knew who the draconic connection was and where they fitted into the family tree."

"Did she?"

"Maman said not, but that seeded in me a want, a need, to know what truth the rumours held and I began investigating."

"A subtle push from your inner self?"

"Maybe." DeMaksim shrugged again. "I started the next day, investigating all our records, before I visited Maman's parents, Grandmaman and Grandpapan Neptulidae, and scoured their library. Clues pointed me to Elrodel, the palace of Queen Dianathke and then to Queen Maerovana's Castle Synternesse. Both of those castles originally belonged to old King Oberon and I obtained permission to search the archives for draconic references and any information on the Neptulidae line – Maman's family." He tapped a claw on his bottom lip, remembering the rooms and rooms of old books and scrolls in both castles.

"Keep going." Cherith swirled her hand. "What'd you find?"

"Initially, fleeting references to Dracons, similar to things Maman mentioned. Grandmaman spoke of a cousin named Mel, who'd gone to be a royal attendant to one of the older queens, that's how I ended up at the royal residences." He shook his head. "There's so much stuff in those archives; I spent lots of time there. Nothing about anyone named Mel Neptulidae – that dead-ended – but the Mel part could've been a pet name, I suppose. I found a scroll written in old Eldwytch which Old Venny helped me translate."

"Old Venny the tinker trader was there?" Cherith arched her brows. "I wonder how he came to be fluent in old Eldwytch."

DeMaksim chuckled, amazed to discover that her plan had worked – he had calmed and a sense of rightness settled over him. "I asked him that. He said he'd been snowed in, up in the high country one frost season many years ago with an Eldwytch elder who had some old scrolls and he'd little better to do than learn."

"What was in the scroll you found?"

"It listed and described Primordial Elemental Dracons."

"Primordial Elemental Dracons?" Cherith's brows knitted. "What are they?"

"Old Venny called them the Elder Dracons." DeMaksim grinned. "In the wise words of Granite: 'there are a limited number of Primordial Elementals. They came into being when the world was born, are made of the same materials and will probably be here until the world ends. Or maybe they'll survive.' Quote unquote."

"Wow, I wonder how many exist?" Cherith nibbled her bottom lip. "And why that sent you into the Dark Reaches? I don't see the connection."

"The scroll mentioned that Draconfolk had withdrawn from the known world, and had last been heard of migrating into the deeps of the Dark Reaches."

As if on cue, a faraway bellowing rose and fell and rose again, before descending and trailing off in a drawn-out moan. The nearby forest noises hushed.

Cherith's eyes rounded. "What was that?"

8

CHERITH

"Could've been anything. Maybe even one of those lost Draconfolk." Mak shrugged, the motion causing feathery face-fronds to fluff about. He stared upstream from whence the moaning roar had originated. "Maybe we'll find out; we're going that way."

"It was definitely something and I'm not certain it sounded happy. In a fight? Issuing a challenge?" Cherith shook her head. "Probably better if we can avoid whatever it was. There are lots of very nasty Unseelie-Fae; I'm normally not a target, but you're an interloper in Mirkdowd territory and that changes things. We need to be wary."

Mak continued watching upriver. "No argument from me."

Brushing at the filaments tickling her cheek as his jaw worked in speech, Cherith caught a soft strand around her fingers. Pausing, she studied the pale aqua length in arrested surprise. "I thought these were fine feathers, but now I see they actually resemble a water fern which grows in some of the backwaters. What kind of Dracon are you, Mak? If you don't mind discussing it now?"

His faraway gaze refocused, those gorgeous vazel orbs intent. "Er, yeah, I'm okay, I think; but how would I know what sort I am?"

"Oh, I thought your scroll might have described some Dracons."

Tilting her head, Cherith twisted and stretched to study him. "You said you've manifested scales in the past?"

"Yes." He eyed the paw curled around Cherith, deadly claws pointing. "They were brown."

Her eyebrows rose. "Yet now you're this pearlescent greenish blue colour with gold-edged fronds looking like trailing weed, have rippling ferny fins, a spiny tail and you belch green flame."

His jaw worked. "Last night, defending myself at the inn, it was red flame."

Cherith's right hand fisted. "That means the changes have happened today." She swallowed. "Since the Nageen bonded us."

He huffed, producing steam? Fog? Smoke? "In comparison: you have aqua hair, gold skin with a smattering of freckles, green eyes, fern-like fins on the backs of your forearms and lower legs, webbed ears, fingers and toes."

She felt the blood drain from her face. "So you're developing watery characteristics in my colours because of our forced link?" *This can't be happening – surely we're not mated for real?*

Mak swept a forked tongue over his lower lip. "If that's the case, wouldn't you be taking on some of my features?"

"Oh, good point." Cherith looked down at herself. "Nothing's changed."

"Apart from your wave of water turning into ice."

"It was your draconic heat that turned it into hot-ice."

"Just as your water changed my red flame to green." One claw scratched his head. "How can hot, dry-ice exist? And how can water and flame combine?"

Her hands turned palm upwards. "No idea. Didn't we cover this earlier?"

"Yeah, so if we're going round in circles, it's a good time to move on. Thanks for helping me calm down." Stretching, Mak stood; continuing to cradle her.

Looking down, Cherith gulped. "Um, Mak? I believe it's time to change back to your Fae-male self, especially if I'm to walk in the water."

"Ah, about that." His mouth thinned and he looked to be fighting down panic. "I can't shift."

"What?"

"I've never been full Dracon before today, so I'm not certain how it works." He grimaced. "I've been trying to change back while we talked. It's not working."

She stared. "But you said you bring on scales at will – how do you, ah, get rid of them at those times?"

His lips twisted. "I withdraw my will and they fade."

"Try that then."

"I have." He looked away, embarrassment darkening his aqua cheeks. "Only, this time wasn't my choice to change – I didn't even know I could – I think withdrawing my will is failing because—"

"Oh, you didn't will it in the first place." Cherith grimaced. "Okay, walking won't work if you can't shift. I'm already smaller than your person shape, but even tinier compared to your Dracon."

"Exactly." The stretch of his mouth revealed sharp teeth. "There's no choice, we'll have to fly."

"Fly?" Her voice was a screech of horror. "No!" *Goddess-goddess-goddess!*

"Come on Cherith, it'll be fine." Tilting his head, Mak batted dark lashes over his beautiful eyes. *Not noticing those eyes. How come I never knew how much I love eyes that colour? Didn't see how long his freaking eyelashes are, either. Nope.*

"I flew us to the riverbank safely, didn't I?"

"Because I wasn't expecting it! And flying means we'd be in the sky!"

"Well, yes. We can't fly if we're not in the sky."

"Stop sounding so reasonable!" *There's nothing up there. No support. Not like when I'm surrounded and supported by the river.*

Mak huffed, feathery weed-fronds swirling. "You cannot seriously expect me to shuffle along the riverbank at an excruciatingly weird angle, just so you can wade or swim in the water!"

Cherith glared, then pictured what he'd said and dissolved into giggles. "That'd be so funny!"

"You think?" He glowered. "These wings differ from the swallow-tail ones of my Fae-form, but they're still wings and I've been flying all my life."

"But it's air! There's nothing to hold you up!"

"My wings do that. I work them, use the wind and air currents, the same way you do with your arms, legs and fins when you're in water."

Fish poopers. That makes sense. She noticed him grinning. "What?"

"Your ears were wiggling madly, but now they've kind of drooped – you've given in."

"Oh, really?" Cherith reacted instinctively, surging to her feet. She tried clapping palms to hips and glaring, but her bound left wrist twisted against Mak's foreleg, refusing to cooperate. "Dammit!" She bared teeth, attacked where the cord felt firm around their limbs. She couldn't see the string, but it's rubbery texture in her mouth was foul when she fought to grip it in her tiny fangs. *It keeps sliding free. Does the bloody stuff have a mind of its own?*

"By the Queens!" Mak's body shook with laughter. "You know that isn't going to work, Cherith. We couldn't separate the strands earlier no matter how hard we tried and now they're visible, they don't look at all damaged."

She stilled, her mouth releasing their wrists; her eyebrows shot up. "You can see them? It must be because you're in Dracon form."

He nodded. "Yes, as soon as I morphed to Dracon they became visible."

"It doesn't help, though." Cherith dropped her head into her free hand. "What's it going to take?"

"We've got a plan, Cherith. Don't give up." Mak's scaly but soft cheek rubbed comfortingly against hers. "We're going to harvest the antidote flowers and ask your father to brew a potion."

"You're right." She sighed, soaking up the support. *He feels so good.*

"But to do that, we've got to find the plants."

"We're back to flying again."

"Yep."

"But have you flown with a passenger? Me as extra baggage could, um, you know, put you off."

"I just flew with you, so your arguments are pointless." He arched a brow. "You fit cupped in one of my paws or, if you prefer, you could straddle my fore leg – your size isn't a significant factor here."

"I might fall."

"Now you're being ridiculous." Lifting his right front leg had her dangling in the air, before he lowered her back to his propped knee.

Her head sagged. "Damn. I *am* being ridiculous. Sorry."

"Flying will save us lots of time." Mak tipped his head. "Plus, the quicker we harvest the anti-Nageen plant, the sooner we can ask your father to make a potion to break this forced mating, yes?"

"Absolutely. Yes. You're right, of course." Sucking her bottom lip between her teeth, Cherith worried at it. *He wants to be rid of me. I can't blame him. We're not mates – and yet, something about our connection feels right. I want to keep him. Is the Nageen's magic affecting me?* She shuddered in confusion, then shook her head. "Yes, well we're not mates so we deserve to be free of each other."

"Agreed."

"To get on with our lives."

"Yes, so flying?"

Cherith blinked, swallowing hard. "Okay, but hold tight, please."

"Always."

Did that sound like a vow? Filing it away for later consideration, Cherith began wriggling into a position she hoped was safe, wrapping herself around Mak's foreleg, facing forward. "I'm ready."

"Okay." There was a lurch as Mak's heavily muscled back legs bunched and launched them. His wings beat strongly as they ascended. Cherith's stomach was pleased that he didn't go high. Levelling out several feet above the treetops, he followed the line of the Mirkdowd's channel. His voice rumbled, somehow still audible to her despite the wind of their flight. "I thought if I stayed low, you'd find it easier to guide us."

"Good idea." Her breath sawed in her throat, threatening to choke her, but Mak kept his wing-flaps even, their speed moderate as they swept upriver, avoiding the banks and the bluffs, plus any looming trees or growths of reeds and bulrushes. After a while, Cherith relaxed, feeling safe enough to enjoy the experience. When the river angled left and they winged around the bend, her stomach didn't lurch even once. *Yes! I've got this!* In this section, trees crowded closer to the water's edge and Cherith admired how the surface glowed in the late afternoon sunlight.

Mak bent his head towards her. "We need to stop for the night. Know anywhere close suitable for both of us?"

"If you don't mind roughing it."

He snorted. "Done that many a time – as long as it's safe, it'll be fine."

"Just ahead on the right there's a wide lagoon with an island in the middle."

Following Cherith's directions, Mak found the island, located a clearing amidst the tall, dense shrubbery and back-winged to land. Folding his wings he glanced around, noting the stand of trees overhanging one side of the clearing. "Now what?"

"There's a shallow cave with an overhang in amongst those trees. You won't manage the cave, but you'll fit under the overhang."

"Okay." Shambling forward, he made his way between tree trunks and strange shaped boulders until the cave and the overhang came into view. He settled onto his haunches with his right side next to the cave and lowered his right front leg for Cherith to slide off. The surrounding trees obscured the westering sun; the light was dim. "I did have some food in my backpack, too bad I've lost it somewhere"

"We could fish; the river's on our doorstep. Come on, I'll show you the most likely places. The fish love to hide under snags in deepish pools near the bank."

"In that case …" His hunger persuaded him and by the time they'd finished fishing, it was fully dark. Mak charred the fish with his new green flame, and they ate on the riverbank before returning to their campsite.

"Have you wondered why the Dracons came to the Dark Reaches?" Cherith asked as she finished her fish, settling deeper into his cupped paw.

"Ever since I understood the scroll's information."

"And you're looking for them? What do you hope to find out?"

"The name of my draconic ancestor for one. Maybe the reason why, after all this time, I'm who and what I am. Why did the Draconfolk come into the Dark Reaches and withdraw from the known world? The Fae demesnes are home to many and various creatures and species, so what's the problem with Dracons being in the mix? Were they diseased? Maybe there's no problem and they just prefer to be hermits, but they've left behind offspring who need help and answers. I believe there's a duty of care, but maybe being primordially immortal implies that caring is beyond them. Only, where does that leave me? Should I vanish somewhere too, now that I can become a Dracon? If there was a disease, maybe I have it or can contract it." His pause was filled by the whirr of crickets and the sough of the breeze as it danced among the leaves of the trees outside the overhang. "I'm hoping those answers might help me discover I'm not just the child who is expected to take over the Papillion Duchy after my father and whether I still can."

"You're looking for a sense of self, then." Her breath warmed his skin. "Me, too. I've struggled with looking Undine but having an Eldwytch nature. I've learned to accept who I am – a nurturer of plants, the environment and life in general; none of that is Undine."

"You don't hide yourself; that's what I've got to stop doing."

"Why did you? Isn't your family loving and caring?"

"Yes, they are." He sighed. "As my draconic traits emerged, I worried that I was too different, too volatile to be an acceptable next Duke of Papillion. Seelie Fae society has certain expectations of their nobility, so I hid those differences as best I could and forced myself into an imitation of my wonderfully successful father. Until I felt like an impostor in my own skin, someone I didn't even recognise. That's when I knew I had to do something and the All Hallows' Eve ancestor research gave me the excuse I needed." He wrinkled his nose. "This is really weird – I've told you stuff even my family doesn't know. Was there more to the Nageen's bewitchment than her tying us together and instigating the changes we've both had?"

A look of horror crossed Cherith's face. "By the River Goddess, I never thought of anything like that. What if you're right?"

"Then our problems just got bigger." He sighed. "Also, I promised my family I'd be back to participate in this year's All Hallows' Eve celebrations."

"Oh, but, isn't that in two more days?"

"Yes."

"So what will happen if you fail to keep your promise, Mak?"

He blew out a breath. "They'll assume I didn't show because something's wrong and send out search parties."

9

DEMAKSIM

Waking to find someone sprawled atop him, DeMaksim blinked into a sleeping face he'd decided was unfairly adorable. Cherith's lips were slightly parted, one cheek squashed the fastenings of his leather jacket into his chest, her other cheek rosy in the dawn's light. Tousled strands of hair feathered around her ear. Her left arm hung to the ground over his right side, dragged by their link, while her right arm stretched down his other side. Elegant fingers grazed the indentation to the left side of his stomach, just above the waistband of his pants. He swallowed, hardening against her hip despite trying to ignore the scorching heat of her fingertips through the linen of his shirt. He cleared his throat, chest vibrating.

Cherith murmured, rubbing her cheek against him, her face scrunched sleepily. Reaching to shake gently, he stilled, staring at familiar sinewy, long-fingers. *Blue blazes! I'm no longer Dracon! How in demon hells? And I still have my clothes – that must be part of the morph-magic, otherwise I don't understand.* His attention was snagged by Cherith yawning, her mouth a shapely curve of enticement. Stiffening everywhere, he forced himself to relax, body part by body part. He was almost done when Cherith wriggled and his relaxation technique failed him … *morning wood, it's just morning wood. Will you get a frickin' grip! OMG! Grip?* He palm-heeled his forehead, thrusting away the image his thoughts had engendered. Huffing, he rubbed his face, fingers digging into the sinuses above his brows and thumb punishing his cheek. Pretty green eyes opened a slit, met his, then widened.

"Mak! Look at you – you're a person again!"

"A-huh, just realised that myself." His voice was a croak.

Cherith reared up onto her knees, sliding between his rapidly spread thighs, to inspect him with smiling delight. "That's great!" She faltered as she noticed the unmistakeable long thick bar near her knees and blushed. "Oh! Um, how did you do it?" Her blush deepened. "Er, change shape I mean." She clapped a hand to her forehead. "River Goddess! From Dracon to Fae-male – how did you do that?"

He grimaced, choking on his amusement. "Er, I slept?"

"Right!" She nodded vigorously, looking anywhere but at his groin. "That makes sense."

His eyebrows arched. "It does?"

"Yes! You became Dracon under emotional stress, but when you slept, you relaxed and – snap! Things happened." Cherith's thumb and mid-finger clicked together.

"Yeah, snap. Makes a crazy kind of sense. So does returning to my Fae-male shape."

Cherith clenched her eyelids shut. "Duckweed! I don't think I'll ever speak again."

He laughed. "Sorry. It's too easy to tease you. I guess feeling normal again has lightened my spirits."

Her eyes opened and she grinned. "That's good, Mak. Really good."

Deliberately, DeMaksim drew his legs in, moving to his haunches; it reduced the distance between them but eased the strain on their linked wrists. He looked away from her happy smile; it still smacked his chest and soaked through his skin. *What is she doing to me? I need to protect her, want to kiss her and have the strongest urge to keep her.* The reason washed over him. "Ah, it must be the Nageen's binding."

"What?" Cherith cocked her head, looking doubtful. "I doubt the binding has anything to do with your overnight return to being a person, but I could be wrong. And you still have your clothes. Shouldn't they have been torn to pieces or something? I know that happens to other were-animals." She frowned. "So many questions. We need to find a Dracon so that you can get the answers."

Taking advantage of her misconception, DeMaksim sighed. "We can't blame her for everything, I suppose. Too bad." He massaged his chin. "Locating a Dracon would be perfect, but our chances are slim."

"Why? They were here once; we just have to find out where they went."

"My grand plan in a nutshell." DeMaksim nodded. "But they disappeared for a reason and mightn't wish to be found. Plus, right now it's more important to sort out the mess the Nageen created. My Dracon hunt will have to wait." His belly rumbled. "Did we eat all the fish last night?"

"Yes."

"Okay then, food on the run. How far are we from the flower field?"

"The antigeens are in a meadow only a few more hours upriver." Cherith scanned the sky beyond the overhang. "We should start; there's cloud building and we have to walk now."

Standing, they selected the path between the trees used the previous night and arrived on the island's narrow beach within a few minutes. DeMaksim checked the remains of the picnic they'd shared, but now, not even the fish heads remained.

"Do I want to know what the local scavengers might be?"

Cherith shrugged. "Probably crabs. C'mon, let's walk to the tip where the lagoon branches away from the main river." Keeping to the firmer sand just above the water's edge, they began walking. DeMaksim's calf-high leather boots scuffed heel and toe marks in the sand, but Cherith's bare feet left barely a mark. DeMaksim wasn't happy leaving a trail, especially with all the unknown dangers being this far into Unseelie territory brought – besides, it went against all his training – but there was little he could do. Dragging a branch through wet sand would be just as obvious.

The beach ended at a stretch of rocks which they picked their way through to reach the point. Although the Mirkdowd was still wide here, DeMaksim's keen eyes noted a narrowing of the riverbed further upstream. The current was gentle, the water diverging around the small island sprawled across the lake's entrance, bifurcating the river. Either side of the island were narrow channels, the river's entrance to the wider, shallow lagoon.

"Do you still want to do the walking-wading thing?" DeMaksim peered at Cherith. "I have wings in my Fae form too." He spread the black appendages with their cream, lavender, blue and green markings.

"Oh, they're so pretty!" A soft breeze stirred her hair as she twisted to see them. "I'd heard most Seelie Fae and some Unseelie have lepidopter wings, but yours are the first I've seen. Swallowtail butterfly?"

"Correct."

Her eyes took on a faraway dreamy look. "Cassie once saw the Unseelie Beast, Lord Dario Eribifax. He swept through here, hard on the heels of a tribe of murderous Redcaps. He has wings of the Dark Crimson Underwing moth in crimson, black, silvery-grey and cream – Cassie said he was absolutely delicious. I was sorry I missed it, despite the threat of those vampiric Redcap parasites." She sighed, returning to the moment, but her pleasure faded as she met his gaze. "What? Something wrong?"

He rolled his eyes. "Dario Eribifax just true-mated and married my youngest sister."

Her eyes widened. "Lord Dario? And um, Zhulija, I think you said?"

"All the way out in the boonies of the Dark Reaches and still touched by family." He shook his head, forcing a chuckle while choking down the useless feeling of wanting to punch out his brother-in-law because Cherith was drooling over him. *I'm pathetic. Even worse, I know my feelings are all a false construct brought about by the frickin' Nageen and yet I still can't help it.*

"Wow!" Cherith's face glowed. "He found his true-mate, that's so romantic."

"Yes, it is." His voice emerged deep and gruff. "They're beautiful together."

Her eyes rounded. "But he's Unseelie and she's Seelie!"

"Yep, but they definitely true-mated and the union was embraced and blessed by both the Fae Queens."

"How wonderful." Cherith's grin lit a fire in the centre of his chest.

"I agree." He rubbed his burning sternum. *Thank the goddess. She's genuinely happy for Zhu and Dario.* Seeing it helped him overcome his unwanted filthy jealousy of the new brother-in-law he truly liked. "Back to where we are, however. Will you fly with me?" *Demonhells, it sounds like I'm asking her on a date.* Heat flashed up his neck and face.

She tapped her lip with one finger. "Just to the other bank? Because, I really need a soak in the water – I'm not usually out of it for as long as I have been."

"Oh, of course!" DeMaksim smacked his forehead. "Do you feel okay? We'll hurry across, then wade and walk as we originally planned, before my draconic change."

"Thanks." Her smile warmed him. "It's really not far to the antigeen flower field. It won't take us long."

"Let's go then." DeMaksim spread his Fae wings, put both arms around Cherith – which hobbled her, but she hugged him around the neck with her free arm – and flew them across the river. Hunger had them stopping to nibble on berries and some kithgreens they found and Cherith managed to catch an inquisitive fish.

DeMaksim considered the medium-sized fish. "I wonder if I can flame-cook it without changing shape?" He laid the fish on a nearby rock. "Previously, my skills weren't that good." Pursing his lips, he blew a stream of fire, pausing at one point to turn the fish over and blow some fire at the raw side. He gestured between Cherith and the cooked fish. "I did it! Dinner is served Milady."

Cherith laughed. "Breakfast, more like, but I'm happy either way." They shared the hot sweet meat as they continued traveling. When the riverbank ascended to a higher bluff, one of them had to give way on their preference. DeMaksim, thoughts of his mother's glaring lecture on manners surfacing, joined Cherith in the water, despite her protestations.

"Your boots!"

"They'll dry. Really, they're fine. They've been dunked in water several times since we met and still function, whereas your feet are bare and there could be rough ground or prickles up there."

Despite his words, DeMaksim was secretly pleased that the water remained shallow enough to only cover the heels and soles of his boots. He was more than happy to keep his leather pants, leather jacket and linen shirt dry also, and crossed his fingers in the hope they would remain that way.

Part way through the afternoon, Cherith indicated a side tributary on their left; a small rill burbling down a narrow rocky staircase in an area of extended high bluffs. "We have to go this way."

"Up the stairs?" DeMaksim eyed the pathway between the broken cliff edges.

"Yes, then backtrack along the water course."

"How in the Queens' name did you find this place?"

Cherith grinned. "Curiosity. The idea of stairs intrigued me enough to investigate. I've been up and down this river, explored all the banks and tributaries, checking out the plants, cultivating them. I know it fairly well."

"That helps."

"For instance, there's an unusual paved area in a hollow up there. It's on the opposite side of the streamlet, across the antigeen meadow. It looks like an entry, or a gateway, with paving between two garden beds leading to some steps."

"Where do the steps go?"

"Nowhere. They culminate in a small grassy plateau which runs into a cliff after a few seconds and that's all."

"Huh." DeMaksim scratched his jaw. "That is weird."

Cherith nodded. "The entire meadow is a bowl, a valley surrounded by cliffs. It's like someone planned to build a home there, but the paving and the steps is as far as they got. You'll see." She turned to lead him up the rocky flight of stairs, their feet shushing through the shallow water to one side, but avoided the splashing of the main water supply.

DeMaksim shook his head. "It would've been easier to fly."

"But not half as much fun." Cherith smiled over her shoulder.

1 0

———

CHERITH

$\mathcal{M}$ ak shaded his eyes against the sun lowering in the sky. At the top of the streaming stairs was a narrow canyon between higher cliffs, bisected by the little creek's flow. Although the channel gradually widened, the cliff on their left side curved away from the stream-bed to frame a small bowl-shaped pasture. It continued to circle behind the meadow in a continuous wall and became the backdrop to a large stand of trees. On the right side of the stream, a wall of cliff climbed in a series of ascending ledges.

"A beautiful but out of the way place. We getting out of the water here?"

"We are."

"Great." He took a step towards the open field. Grinning, Cherith pulled on their linked arms.

"Not that way." She pointed up. "We're climbing."

"Isn't the meadow easier?"

"Yes." Cherith turned towards the cliff. "But I've been growing increasingly concerned with your safety. I know I said we'd have nothing to worry about, but I've decided to be extra careful anyway. This valley is very open and I'm not the only Unseelie to know about

482

it. I travel a lot and most places are fine, but there's something about this out of the way mountain meadow that always makes me uneasy. I'm not foolish enough to think everybody is friendly – this way I can check the lay of the land without being seen." A cleft in the rock provided footholds to a narrow ledge which widened as they traversed it, snaking at an angle up the cliff wall to a wider crevice. The larger gap was an entrance into an enclosed rocky channel with stone walls rising up each side, much like that of the stream bed.

"At least it's dry underfoot."

Cherith giggled. "You and your boots."

Mak winked. "I have wings – my boots aren't used to rough treatment."

"What are they made of? Reeds and mud?" A reverberating blurt from behind had Cherith whirling. "Did you just blow rude air at me?"

Mak's eyes were wide and innocent. "Me? Why ever would I do that?"

"Because I called you out on your unnatural fixation with a pair of boots, maybe?"

"Unnatural fixation!" He clapped a hand to his chest as if he'd been stabbed. "Harsh."

Cherith's laugh was cut off by a distant roar. She frowned, looking up towards the rocky peak they aimed for. "Come on."

Mak's voice was a low murmur. "Was that from the meadow?"

"Maybe. I need to see." She jogged, Mak keeping pace. The path turned a corner, opening out to a wide ledge with a clear view of the bowl-shaped valley. "Stay low." Cherith went to her knees, Mak quickly hunkering down beside her. She scanned the meadow, the whole of it a panorama beneath them, some areas more shadowed in the lateness of the day.

Warm deep breath tickled her ear. "I can't see anything – you?"

She shivered. "No." Her gaze swept back and forth. "Those trees are the usual place people go and the only real concealment."

As they watched, a hare shot out of the undergrowth beneath the tree line, darting to open ground; a squash-faced Goblin chased it. Cherith gasped, Mak tensing beside her. The creature's strands of grey hair wisped out from under a red hat, fangs protruded from both upper and lower jaws as it leapt after the hare with a four-footed crabby gait. Eagle-taloned hands ripped and tore at the ground, sending clods of turf up in gouts as it galloped in pursuit. Howling, the goblin dived, digging its claws into the hide of the fleeing animal. Snatching the squealing hare close to its chest, the creature lifted its face to the sky and howled in bestial glee before falling, fangs distended on the hapless hare. The animal's blood-curdling scream was drowned out by harsh laughter as another goblin cleared the trees. Slurping noises followed.

"Redcaps!" Shuddering, Cherith dropped flat to the ground, Mak beside her.

A grating voice drifted to them, adding to the ruckus made by the feeding Redcap. "Hare, Malkurx – want some."

"Hunt own, Grisbore!"

"Why no share?"

"Lazy scuz, Grisbore!" a third voice hissed. "I hunt, you watch for Fae-male and water girl."

"Idiot, Vantark! They no come, Malkurx too noisy." In the fading light, the two goblins faced off as they argued.

They're looking for us? Mind whirling, Cherith nudged Mak, voice a whisper. "Go back the way we came."

"Sun's almost set." Mak breathed in her ear. "I don't fancy a downwards climb without light. Is there anywhere to hide near the paved area you've mentioned?"

"No."

"We're better off staying here, then."

Cherith's hand clasped his in a quick tighten and release. They stayed low, watching the Redcaps.

"Alright Grisbore." Vantark made a slashing motion with his claws. "Snack here, go back down river and search. They near." The goblin snorted. "Seelie Fae stupid not to use wings and she just half-breed Undine – no threat. Easy as Snortgrub's sister. We have soon. Tastier than rabbit. We give to River King, then he let us eat." They both sniggered.

"They're leaving." Cherith crossed her fingers, watched the shadows darkening more every second until the sun disappeared below the horizon and night moved in. The darkness veiled the goblins' antics, but there was still lots of slurping, yelling and braying laughter interspersed with arguments. She winced as a tearing noise ended one pain-filled squeal and pitied the small warren of hares destroyed by the three vampiric Redcaps in their orgy of blood and body parts.

Mak shifted beside her in the gathering gloom. "They always like this?"

Cherith shuddered. "Yes. They're bloodthirsty, cunning and vicious and they'll attack without provocation."

"Vantark! Malkurk! Going!" A snarly response, the sound of swishing meadow grass, then feet slapping on rock.

Mak stirred. "They're on their way."

"To hunt for a Seelie Fae and a water girl."

A deep breath. "You know Cherith, that sounds an awful lot like *us*."

She swallowed. "Yes, they must've seen us."

"They referred to a River King. Exactly how many are there?"

"Every major river has one, b-but I thought there was only one in these parts, because there's only the Mirkdowd."

"So, you're working for the Mirkdowd River King – watching me – and they're hunting both of us. How's that make sense?"

"By the River Goddess, Mak, I don't know! Something weird is going on. We've never been asked to spy on anyone before you." She jerked their linked wrists. "What are you involved in?"

"Me? You think this is my fault?" Mak returned the yank. "I was simply looking for information about my ancestry. Then that thrice-damned Nageen wrecked everything."

"What's happening, then?"

"Better to ask why your River King's consorting with Redcaps – that normal?"

"Quicksand no! Redcaps have no allies!"

"That's not what it sounds like."

Cherith threw up her hands, dragging Mak's with it. "I don't understand!"

Mak yanked their joined arms down. "Can you not do that? It's distracting and annoying."

She pinched the bridge of her nose. "Sorry."

He sighed. "Me too. Neither of us has the answer, plus it's dark and we're up on a cliff."

"Oh for Goddess' sake, just fly us down to the meadow!"

"My pleasure!"

Mak's boots scraped on rock, his free arm encircling her, grip firm. "Mmff!" When he leapt from the clifftop, Cherith turned her face into his shoulder, stifling her scream of surprise, before hastily winding her free arm around his strong neck. She barely had time to enjoy the musky male scent of him before they landed.

"Not keen to go near the trees after the Redcap massacre, plus the quicker we get what we came for and leave, the better." Mak grimaced. "This hidden valley is a trap. How soon can we can look for the flowers – are they hard to find?"

Cherith laughed. "This whole place is a mass of them. See those tiny white star-shaped blossoms? They're glowing, even hidden amongst all of the grass." She poked at the grass with her toes, her foot separating blades to expose a glowing flower. "See?" Little white dots glimmered in the gathering dusk.

"Huh. How many do we need?"

"I'm not sure." Cherith sighed. "Just pick some."

"A pity we don't have my backpack to hold them in."

"Well, we don't. Pockets will have to do."

Kneeling, Cherith parted more grass to show Mak the bountiful presence of the star-shaped blooms. His every movement disturbed the grass, revealing more flowers, releasing a delicate perfume.

"I love the scent." Cherith drew deep breaths, noticing Mak's glance straying to her chest before he guiltily averted his eyes. *Damn it. He looks just as attracted to me as I am to him, or maybe I'm just the nearest female. I must remember this is a temporary glitch in our lives, not a permanent mating.*

"I SMELL THEM! THEY UP CLIFF!"

Cherith froze. Beside her, Mak jerked his head to look through the darkness towards the distant shout.

"River Goddess! I didn't think of scent!" Cherith scrambled to her feet and shrank into Mak. Drawing her close, he dropped a fast kiss on her cheek before releasing her. "We got this, Cherith. Remember the Nageen?"

Cheek tingling, she swallowed. "Can you fly us out of here?"

"It's too dark – I'd need moonlight at least; the area is unfamiliar."

"Okay. Let's go closer to the paving. Maybe we can get that cliff behind us?"

"Show me."

"This way!" Cherith lurched into a run, Mak sprinting beside her.

"THERE!"

"SEE THEM!"

The noise of talons tearing the sod was loud behind them. "Stop." Mak pulled up, forcing Cherith to comply. "There's not enough time to reach the cliff. We've got to face them."

Turning, Cherith stood tall beside Mak, bringing her hands up in readiness. Mak roared, spitting flame. The night lit up, blue-green phosphorescence soaring high to reveal three Redcaps galloping closer, their gait a peculiar sideways crablike stance, chunks of dirt flying out behind them as they ran. Fangs and jaw-tusks gleaming in the glow of the rising firebolt, the creatures jerked to a startled halt, milling uncertainly.

"Dracon!" A furious but fearful hiss. The light winked out.

"Fire gone now."

"Yay but where is it, eh? Dracon?"

"See only water girl and Seelie male."

"You! Water girl! Where Dracon?"

Cherith panted. "How badly do you wish to know, Redcap? Want an introduction?"

The only response to her taunt was some muttering. "If Dracon, we burn, Vantark."

"Bah! There no Dracons! She whelped by Eldwytch mage, Malkurx- she have evil fire potion."

"May have more fire potion … careful."

The creatures bounded forward again.

"Now!" Mak barked.

"On it!" Instinctively, Cherith magically pushed water at the attacking goblins while Mak's new burst of flame coloured the night. She had no time to wallow in relief as their powers combined, the flame shading from jade green into aqua, then seafoam.

"Again! Keep going!"

Cherith kept pushing water in partnership to Mak's fiery blasts until her arms ached and her breath shuddered and gasped. Finally, Mak folded his fingers around hers and squeezed.

"Okay, we can stop." The night became dark and silent.

"They're done for?" Cherith sagged.

"NOT!" The guttural snarl came from behind them. A sudden heavy weight knocked them sprawling. Cherith hit the ground on her side, the impact making her dizzy. Beside her, Mak swore viciously. He reared to his knees but a blow flattened him again. "Down Seelie! River King say 'alive' but you let go Malkurx and Vantark or I—"

A brilliant golden firestorm blazed through the ether, cutting off the Redcap's growl. It left behind the nasty smell of burnt flesh. "You'll do nothing, Redcap scum."

At the sound of that voice, Mak stiffened, then grabbed Cherith tight, rolling as if the pair of them were a single entity.

"Old Venny?"

"You have a death wish, youngling? Letting the enemy outflank you?"

Cherith's mouth dropped open as she stared up into the black eyes of Old Venny the tinker trader, balancing a curl of golden flame on the palm of his hand.

11

———

DEMAKSIM

"The Redcaps have night vision, Venny." Recovering from the attack, DeMaksim raised himself to a sitting position and helped Cherith up. "I don't. What in hell are you doing here? Not that I'm ungrateful, but there can't be much call for a tinker trader up here … unless you trade with the Redcaps?"

"I'm passing through; luckily, for the pair of you." Old Venny sighed. "I'm guessing you've basic warrior training but no field experience?"

DeMaksim nodded. "Correct, the Fae Wars were well over before my coming of age." Drawing his legs up, he wrapped his free arm around his shins. "Once we realised the Redcaps were attacking, we made for the cliff, thinking to have it at our backs, but their speed forced us to make a stand. How'd you produce the flame?" The yellow fire was gone now.

"A new gadget I'm trying out." Venny looked away, rubbing his brow. "Those Redcaps are wily devils, for sure." He cocked his head. "Greetings Cherith Beriaden, it's been a while. What brought the pair of you here?"

"Hi Venny." Cherith waved. "We're harvesting antigeen flowers for a potion."

489

He grunted. "Plenty of those here. Which one of you crafts potions?" Old Venny's eyes flickered between them.

"Neither of us." DeMaksim grimaced. "We planned on asking Cherith's father to make the brew."

Old Venny raised an eyebrow. "Correct me if I'm wrong, but when we met up at Castle Synternesse, I understood you intended being home for All Hallows' Eve? That's one day away. If you're going to visit Cherith's father at the Beriaden home, you won't make your family's celebration."

DeMaksim frowned. "Things have changed."

"What things?"

"This, for one." DeMaksim raised his right hand, linked to Cherith's left.

Old Venny stepped closer. "A Nageen mating string?" He scratched his head. "How in the name of prime darkness did you manage to be trapped by that?"

DeMaksim flipped a hand. "I rejected her overtures, but she wouldn't accept that and—"

"Who, Cherith?" Old Venny's head tilted.

DeMaksim glowered. "No, the Nageen!"

"So how did Cherith become part of the scenario?"

"When I discovered her spying on me, we ended up in a struggle. The Nageen dropped from a tree and threw these red ropes at us—"

"I was not spying, Mak!"

"You're the one who answered your River King's call to watch me – that's spying isn't it?"

"No! That's doing my duty. But it's gone sour because now he's chasing both of us!"

Old Venny laughed. "Oh you younglings. Whilst your antics are extremely entertaining, can we stick to the tale? What about the Nageen?"

Cherith and DeMaksim exchanged glances. Cherith swallowed. "Ah, we sort of, um …"

"We killed her." DeMaksim's voice was flat.

Old Venny stared, his gaze shifting from one to the other. "Hmm." One eyebrow rose. "How?"

DeMaksim jerked a thumb over his shoulder. "Like that."

Raising his head, Old Venny eyed the looming lumps of Redcap stillness and pursed his lips. "I think I'd like a closer look." He sauntered off, returning a few minutes later. "Did you have to fight on my doorstep? Now I've got two solid green Redcap statues in my garden. Cyn will not be happy."

As Cherith and DeMaksim stared at him with equally puzzled looks, a female voice spoke.

"What won't I like, Ven, sweetie?"

"Our new lawn ornaments, Cyn darling." Old Venny kissed the lovely Lepidopter-fae female firmly. "Cyn, let me introduce you to DeMaksim Aphiski, and his partner, Cherith Beriaden. DeMaksim, Cherith, meet my mate Cynamelle."

Old Venny's mate was tall and slender with plum-coloured curls, blue eyes, Swallowtail butterfly wings and a wide smile. She wore a fitted violet tunic over black trousers with ankle boots of a deeper purple. "Pleased to meet you both." Cynamelle's voice was a pleasant contralto.

Old Venny grimaced. "You might change your mind when you see the gift they've provided."

"Gift?"

He pointed at the new statues. "Take a look, my dear." Cynamelle walked towards the Redcaps, a light blooming as she approached them.

"That's odd." Cherith frowned. "Did she have a candle or something, with her?"

"Or something."

The dryness of his tone drew DeMaksim's gaze. Old Venny stared back, eyes glimmering, taking DeMaksim's captive. He spun into dizzy blackness, adrift in bottomless wells of intense, expanding dark liquid, swirling down to a sea of darkness that went on and on, like a night without end. *Got to break his hold!* Lips firming, DeMaksim wrenched his gaze away, found himself panting. *Were those stars in his gaze?* Cautiously he checked. Old Venny grinned, his expression innocent, harmless; simply the old tinker trader DeMaksim had always known. *Did I imagine that?*

"Well, frozen green goblins certainly make a fancy decoration in our meadow." Cynamelle strolled up to her mate and drew his arm around her middle. "How did they end up like that?"

Old Venny snugged her tight, kissing her cheek. "My very next question. You read my mind, darling."

DeMaksim exchanged glances with Cherith.

"Which of you is responsible?" The tinker rubbed his chin. "Neither the Cherith nor DeMaksim I've visited over the years had that kind of power. Where'd it come from?"

DeMaksim wondered if he knew Old Venny the tinker trader as well as he'd thought. The whirlpool eyes had shaken him. He focused on Cherith. "What do you think?"

She gulped, grasping his fingers. "We're in over our heads, Mak – we need help and we'd be idiots to trust River King Eskavon now. Just tell them."

"Okay." DeMaksim shrugged. "Truth is, Cherith and I are both culpable."

"Hmm." Old Venny considered them. "Would you like to expand on that?"

"I told you I was searching for links to ancestors when we met at Castle Synternesse."

"For your family's All Hallows Eve ritual." Old Venny nodded.

"Well, there's more to the story. I'm actually looking for possible draconic ancestry."

Old Venny's eyebrows rose. "Which explains why you wanted the old scroll about Dracons translated. But what makes you think your family has draconic ancestry?"

"Maman." DeMaksim revealed. "She's a Neptulidae and because some of us manifested a power or ability appearing to have a draconic link, she believes someone in her family mated a Dracon. For instance, Zhulija can manifest heat and use it to power the forge in her art studio without being heat-affected in any way. She blows glass and works in metal."

"So, you're doing this research on her behalf?"

"No. I'm doing it for me." DeMaksim explained how his ability to bring on a few scales had, over the years, grown into producing a set of claws, some smoke from his nostrils, a lick of fire, then bursts of flame. "I felt out of control, needed answers, that's how it began. The translated scroll mentioned the Dark Reaches, so when we parted company, I headed here. Unfortunately, between swamp and thorny thickets, it's hard to find ground level entries. I flew some of the time, but once I'd entered the region, I wasn't sure where to go and didn't want to miss any clues; there's more people to talk to at ground level."

Cherith's fingers twitched in his. "Which is how you drew the attention of the River King and I was recruited by Aquinal the Nixie."

"And because of that, you're tied to me." DeMaksim snorted. "How's that for irony? Anyway, my first night I went to The Elderoak Inn."

"A pleasant hostelry." Old Venny stroked his chin again.

"That's where I met the Nageen." DeMaksim detailed the encounter, moved on to his morning introduction to Cherith and the Nageen's subsequent intrusive attack, causing DeMaksim and Cherith to defend themselves, culminating in the serpent-woman's death.

"Your flame altered from red to green and your powers combined with Cherith's to become hot frozen ice?" Old Venny frowned.

"Yes. After the Nageen wrapped us together in her mating string, those things changed."

The tinker's gimlet gaze pinned him. "That all?"

"No-o." DeMaksim spoke about their quest to come harvest the antigeens for a potion, Cherith's power taking on a new healing aspect, his fall into the river and inadvertent change into a Dracon with water characteristics. "From which I couldn't change back to a person."

"Fascinating." Cynamelle tapped her lip. "So, you're thinking a potion designed to combat Nageen venom will work on the binding?"

"Yes." Cherith sighed. "We're not really mates; all the changes come back to the Nageen linking cord. When that's gone, things will revert to normal."

"Hmm." Old Venny turned to look at them squarely. "Did either of you, at any stage since being bound together by the Nageen, exchange blood?"

"Ah, yes, we both did." DeMaksim glanced at Cherith, who nodded. "Is that why my draconic abilities surged and changed colour?"

"Partly." Old Venny's smile was mirthless. "This is where I need to remind you, that of the several events involved in a mating, one of the most important is a blood exchange."

DeMaksim choked.

Cherith's voice was a whisper. "W-what are you saying?"

Old Venny's mouth pursed. "I don't think the Nageen's binding matters."

"We're mated?" DeMaksim and Cherith were a single voice.

"Yes."

CHERITH AND DEMAKSIM

"That's ridiculous!" Cherith wasn't sure whether she felt elated, terrified or both. *How can Mak and I possibly be mated? Why did we exchange blood? So stupid, when we both know what it can do. Now, we might be stuck with each other.* She checked herself. *'Stuck' with him? Is that what I think?* A surge of emotion flooded her body; a definitive 'no'. *She might have known Mak for only a couple of days, but he'd shown himself to be everything she desired in a mate.* Suddenly, she wanted Old Venny to be right: she wanted to be Mak's mate. *But was that fair to him? Would he feel trapped? I couldn't deal with that, so when the time comes, I'll have to let him go.* Cherith tightened her lips, overwhelming sadness pushing out every other thought.

"Why is it ridiculous?" The tinker cocked his head, watching her.

She swallowed. "Blood is important, but it's not the only thing. People choose each other." She glanced from Old Venny to Cyn, on to Mak, found them all staring at her. Old Venny and Cyn shook their heads.

"Not in a true mating." Cyn's voice gentled. "That's a Goddess planned pairing. No rhyme, no reason and no returns."

"Ggllk?" Mak coughed. "You mean … you're saying … we … this is a true mating?"

Old Venny nodded. "People can fall in love and choose to be mates, of course. They go through the same set of rituals as true mates, but without the same results. The easiest way to confirm true matings are by the changes the couple undergo. Only true mates take on new characteristics, develop new powers after their mating."

"But I already had draconic traits!"

"Which changed and increased."

"Well, what about Cherith? Nothing's changed for her." Mak's vazel eyes impaled her. "Has it?"

Throat dry, Cherith stared back, uncertain what answer he wanted. "Um."

"You said Cherith's green powers developed a new healing aspect. Your powers combined and changed to kill the Nageen." The tinker was relentless. "A Nageen's mating string binds a mate to *her*. The fact that she miscalculated and bound the two of you *together* has no relevance to the changes you've both experienced; they'd have happened anyway."

Cyn stirred. "Cherith, may I ask when you were last immersed in water?"

"Immersed?" Cherith struggled to think. "Well, we walked in the river, but full immersion hasn't happened since … since Mak and I wrestled, then fought with the Nageen." Her hands flew to her cheeks. "Oh! Two days – I must be a wrinkled old hag!"

"Your skin looks as fresh and dewy as if you'd just left the water." Old Venny smiled. "Isn't that interesting?"

Cherith sagged. Mak's fingers tightened around hers. She winced at his frown; her voice emerged a whisper. "I'm sorry, I know you don't want this."

His frown deepened. "Don't be upset, we'll work it out."

She fought back tears. "What now?"

Cyn held out a hand, her smile inviting. "Now, I think you should both come home with Venny and I. We'll have hot drinks and a meal, yeah?"

Mak nodded. "Okay, although I'm not sure where you're hiding your home. This place is all meadow, cliffs and trees." Standing, he held his other hand out to assist Cherith. She accepted the offer, making it a double handed effort. Pulling her close, Mak hugged Cherith with his free arm and rocked her gently.

"What happened to 'passing through'?" Mak's glare was dagger sharp.

"Well, we are. We're passing through our home, resting between trips; still counts as passing through." Old Venny grinned. "Watch your step, the paving is our front path."

Cherith hesitated. "But, there's only grass and a rock wall after the paving."

"Been up here before, have you?"

"Yes. I explore everywhere along the river looking for plants. It's how I knew where to find antigeen blossoms."

He chortled. "Appearances can be deceiving."

"If you say so." Following Cyn and Old Venny, Cherith wondered if the elderly male was losing his wits. She heard him mutter something as he and Cyn stepped off the paving stones, then, between one step and the next, disappeared.

Mak halted abruptly. "Blue blazes! Where'd they go?" Cherith hovered uncertainly beside him, but as they goggled, the tinker's head reappeared.

"Come on! What's taking so long?"

"Um, I don't think—"

"Good. Don't think, just follow." Old Venny winked, vanishing again.

Cherith shook her head. "Who, or what, is he?"

"Only one way to find out." Mak stepped forward determinedly, Cherith alongside.

～

DeMaksim stumbled into a foggy bottomless whirlpool with no up or down, left or right. He rotated in a disorienting haze with flickers and gouts of incandescent flame bursting spasmodically through the heavy mist. It reminded him of his fall from the willow's branch into the river. No breath, a huge weighted band constricting his lungs. Was he drowning? But there was no water; only vapour and fire.

The fog thinned. Flames surged around him, a writhing mass of colour, fluctuating back and forth across the spectrum. Gut churning, DeMaksim's dread escalated as the curling licks of fire crept closer, bursts of flame reaching amorphous fingers until the enormous conflagration engulfed him in a whoosh of heat and sensation. Someone screamed into the roar of the firestorm. He was burning, his whole body flaring like a torch. His vision tunnelled to a pinpoint of scorching red, then exploded into an inferno of green and blue. He spun in a sense-deprived, flaming mass of bewildered panic and breathlessness, wondering how a quest for an ancestor had become a monstrous nightmare certain to take his life.

Gasping and struggling, his thoughts flew to Cherith. Her hand had been tucked into his; she was tied to him and in equal danger. *I've got to save her!* Concentrating hard, forcing himself to ignore the holocaust, DeMaksim sought the internal link he'd forged with Cherith when she treated the willow.

It wasn't there. For a moment, he doubted, then his resolve firmed.

If we linked like that once, we can do it again! He redoubled his efforts, ignoring the spasming of his muscles, enduring the fiery external hell. His reward was the sound of his own heartbeat, beating in a crazy rhythm. The beats needed to be smoother, more regulated. As he thought it, imagining the beats as they should be, so they were.

His confidence rose. *I can do this! I know she's next to me.* Pushing seeking energy out from his heart, across his chest, down his right arm and through to his fingers, he found other fingers grasped within them. *Cherith!* Carefully, he threaded his awareness into her body, determined she'd not be sacrificed along with him. She must live.

Now that he knew the way of it, he forged a link with Cherith's mind in next to no time. *Cherith!*

Mak?

Yes, I've got to save you!

You must control the fire, Mak! Control the fire!

What?

But that reminder of the external blaze snapped his concentration and he lost his link to her. Around him, flames of red and aqua fought for supremacy, a wicked inferno. *Control this? How? I know I control flame as a Dracon, but this is ...* Awareness bloomed. His draconic flame had been red until he and Cherith combined. After that it had become greenish blue. He was surrounded by his own flame?

Opening his mouth, he roared, sucking in air. The flames wavered slightly, surging as he paused. *Oh no, you don't!* Rounding his lips, he inhaled, then inhaled again, siphoning the flame. It eased towards him, drawn into his mouth on the next inhale. He swallowed it, drew more inside, kept swallowing, grabbed handfuls of the stuff and fed it to himself, swallowing until the last lick of aqua fire disappeared inside his mouth. Sealing his lips, throat working, he massaged his stomach, burped massively. Gravity surged into him and he fell, landing supine on a fluffy surface.

Daze receding, DeMaksim became aware of weight on his chest. Opening one eye, he peered down – met Cherith's anxious gaze as she lay half on and half off him. He conjured a weak smile. Another figure loomed. Squinting, he identified Old Venny.

Voice croaking, he addressed the elderly tinker trader. "What in blue blazes happened?"

"Well done, youngling." Old Venny smiled. "Welcome to our home. Cyn's getting you a cool drink."

"But, that fire? That's your normal doorway?" DeMaksim's bewildered gaze moved to Cherith. "You survived it too?"

"I didn't experience the same thing." Cherith's usual soft apricot complexion looked pale. "It was terrifying seeing you as a ball of flame, but Old Venny said you had to merge your two personalities and gain control of them."

"Wait a minute." DeMaksim glared at Old Venny, hands curling into fists. "You knew that would happen?"

The older man nodded, his expression wary. "Yes, I bespelled the portal."

Cherith tilted her head. "Why do you need a portal into your home?"

"Our home is on a separate plane of reality. The portal is how Cyn and I access it. We—"

"You magicked the portal against us and didn't give any warning?" Cherith's shaking fingers wormed their way inside his fist.

Old Venny ran a hand through his mane of silvery black hair. "Warning you would reduce the effectiveness; you had to work out the answers and find the control."

"You know that, how?" A growl edged DeMaksim's voice.

"You're not the first draconic fledgling I've dealt with." Old Venny's eyes were fathomless.

"Draconic fledgling? I worked through something completely outside the realms of probability and understanding, putting Cherith at risk and you not only *knew*, you set it up?" DeMaksim crouched, eyeballing Old Venny.

The older male tensed. "The magic was specific. Cherith was never in danger."

Roaring, an explosion of rage eclipsing reason, DeMaksim hissed a gout of aqua flame at Old Venny. Eyes flashing, the tinker's return blast of golden flame met the aqua head on; a flaring wall of power. The clash burst in a spiralling wheel of gold and aqua sparks, before the gold swallowed the aqua and the fire vanished in a thunderous shock-wave that swept the room.

Mouth dry, DeMaksim stared. "Wha—?"

Cherith simply gaped.

Luckily the room they occupied was large, because, crouched in front of them, head snaked forward, was a large black Dracon, bared fangs glistening. His smouldering voice rang with warning. "Pull yourself together youngling, I've no wish to hurt you. Don't force it on me."

DeMaksim's mouth dropped; his rage died as he stared at the looming figure. "You? You're a Dracon! How's that possible?"

A hooting buzz of laughter answered. "Haven't figured it out yet, youngling? *I'm* your draconic ancestor. Say hello to Great Grandpa Venstilarquon."

13

CHERITH

"*N*ow that the theatrics are over, here's the promised drink. It's hot chocolate." Cyn's tray held four steaming mugs. "Venny darling, give him a chance to find calm."

Cherith clasped her mug firmly, observing the two males. Old Venny, having shrugged off his draconic form, had assisted a shell shocked Mak to a large cushion-strewn, wooden pew. Cherith plopped beside him, equally grateful to sit. Their transition from the meadow into grey foggy nothingness before exiting the portal into Cyn and Venny's home, had sent her nerves into quivering overdrive. Seeing Mak beside her as a flaming torch, one which ceased at their link, had left her speechless with terror. She still wasn't certain she could speak.

Mak massaged his forehead. "Could you please explain what you meant when you told Cherith I had two selves?"

"Sure." Old Venny sipped from his mug, sparing his mate a glance. "Thanks, Cyn. This is perfect." He eyed Cherith and Mak. "Your description of a full draconic change after the river dunking, your inability to make the change back and the fact the necessary change happened by accident while you slept, told me your two inner entities weren't melded."

Mak frowned. "You mean I'm a split personality?"

"In a way." Old Venny licked chocolate from his lip. "A shapeshifter is one person with two aspects, but they're still, essentially, one being. Whilst some fledglings develop the skill of unification instinctively, others require instruction – which isn't a problem if you grow up within a family of shapeshifters."

"But I didn't." Mak crossed his legs at the ankle. "So how do I combine the two parts of myself?"

Old Venny waved a hand. "You've done it; that's what the spell was about. I rigged the entry portal to force the issue."

Mak shook his head. "You realise that Cherith and I could have been burned or worse with all of that fire contained in the portal?"

The older Dracon snorted. "Hardly. It was your flame, which can't harm either you, or your mate." Old Venny raised his hand, forestalling Mak's next heated outburst. "Enough – we've covered this. You mastered the flame wearing your Fae-male body as you had to; that's sufficient to trigger the changes to align both your aspects."

Mak glared. "Fine. Thanks, I think." He cocked his head. "Except, it's not fine. Why, if you suspected all this, didn't you say something when I saw you at Castle Synternesse? Why put me through all this? I thought something was truly wrong with me."

"I'm sorry for that, but Dracons retreated from sight for a reason. Usually interlopers are discouraged and I couldn't be certain how much of the Dracon existed in your line even though I knew you to be a descendant." Old Venny took another mouthful from his mug. "That's why I dropped clues to bring you to the Dark Reaches without straightforward directions. If you were determined enough to find your way into the territory and subsequently, to me, I'd discover why. Which I have. Although, if I'd known it was because you were developing draconically, I'd have been more forthcoming. I watch for that trait in our descendants; I've never seen it in you during any of my visits. How long has it been occurring?"

Mak cradled his mug. "Years. When flame happened, there were times it scared the Fae-lights out of me and I knew I needed help." He sighed. "Turning full Dracon has only eventuated since meeting

Cherith." He sipped his drink, gaze going to Cyn. "So, Old Venny is related to me, but how are you connected to all this?"

Cyn's spoon clinked in her mug. "Here's where I confess that I'm Cynamelle Neptulidae." Her expression challenged as she met Mak's blank stare, but she smiled as he clicked his fingers.

"The 'Mel' family connection I was looking for!"

"Yes." Her smile morphed into a laugh. "Venny and I confused the records on purpose, to disguise my identity and make it harder to locate anyone draconic, or draconically connected. Secrecy is as much a part of my life as it is my mate's when it comes to safeguarding Draconfolk. Good to know we were so successful."

Cherith propped her elbow on the arm of their seat, resting her chin on her hand. "May I ask why?"

"A number of reasons." Replacing his mug on the tray, the elder Dracon laced his fingers together. "Some personal, some draconic – most I'm not at liberty to share. Suffice to say, we Dracons deemed it wise; many of us don't play well with others. However, I'm not the only one with descendants – we watch for those who need help. It's one of the reasons I travel as a tinker trader, as do a few others of my kind."

"You're sure I'm okay? That I'll be able to manage my draconic nature? How much experience have you had?" Mak leaned forward. "I mean—" He stared. The Dracon and his mate were laughing uproariously. "What's the joke?"

Old Venny gasped, wiping his eyes. "The joke's more on me, young Mak. You need to consult your copy of the old scroll and study the names on it. Then ask me how much experience I've had."

"Er, you knew I made a copy?"

A wry twist wrinkled Old Venny's lips. "It's what I'd have done."

Mak closed his eyes briefly. "A-and you're on it?"

A nod as Old Venny leaned back and crossed his hands behind his head. "Oh, yes."

"Then you're a Primordial."

"So, how old am I, youngling?"

Mak swallowed. "A-as old as the world."

"Older. I saw this world birthed." Old Venny's voice softened. "I watched the other Dracon Primordials coalesce from the magical ether of creation. As for me, I'm a breath of space dust, a child of the stars, I'm *The* Primordial."

"By the Great Goddess." Cherith whispered incredulously. "You've probably forgotten more than we'll ever know."

Galaxies wheeled and burned in the fathomless black eyes focused on Cherith. She shivered. He wasn't simply Old Venny or Venstilarquon; he was *the* Venstilarquon, the ultimate Primordial. "I forget nothing."

Mak's expression was awestruck. "Blue blazes, your brain must be a seething morass!"

A dry chuckle heralded Old Venny's return. "Nah. I've just got amazing storage capacity up here." Tapping his skull, he drew laughter and eased tension. He speared Mak with a look. "You and I need to spend time together, grandson. There are things you must learn. First we'll need to free the pair of you from the clutches of a failed Nageen mating." His gaze shifted to Cherith. "We'll collect the antigeen blossoms and be on our way at dawn. Will Istondir be at home?"

Cherith tongued chocolate on her mug's rim. "Yes. Cassie has gone home to make sure."

Old Venny pursed his mouth. "We'll save time and fly."

"Flying?" Cherith winced.

Amusement curled the corners of the Dracon's lips. "That *is* what wings do."

"I'm not keen." Cherith bit her lip. "Apart from when he was stuck as a Dracon, Mak and I mostly walked."

"Walking from here to your family cottage?" Old Venny studied her. "I thought you wanted to be free of the Nageen's binding?"

"I do." Cherith rolled her bottom lip between her teeth.

"I don't blame you for drawing the captivity out; Mak is rather gorgeous." Cyn winked. "Reminds me of Old Venny when he chooses not to show his age."

"No! That's not ... I mean ..."

Cyn's eyebrows rose. "You don't think Mak is handsome?"

"Yes, of course he is. Oh, gah!" Cheeks burning, Cherith subsided against the cushions. The sofa padding depressed as Mak leaned in.

"Cyn's teasing, but it *would* save lots of time if you agreed to fly. I kept you safe last time, remember?" Cherith did. She'd enjoyed it too, but was still having qualms over thoughts of repeating the experience.

She peeped at him. "Can we re-visit the idea in the morning?"

Mak nodded. "If that's what you need."

Muttering, Old Venny rolled his eyes. Cyn pointed a stern finger at him, but her lips quivered.

He threw up his hands. "Fine, we'll sleep on it."

"Come along Cherith, Mak." Cyn stood. "I'll show you to your bedroom."

Old Venny's grumbling was low-voiced but audible. "Afraid to fly? I don't understand. It's not like she's a fish out of water, or anything. Why, flying is as natural as breathing!"

"Sarcasm is the lowest form of wit." Cherith glowered as she sidled past him. "Try repeating your comment when Maman can hear you."

"Or not." Old Venny grimaced. "Your mother's never afraid to fight." He eyed her. "You're clearly not a chip off the maternal block where that's concerned."

"Venny!" Cyn's hands were on her hips.

Stopping so suddenly that Mak crashed into her, Cherith shook her head. "You misunderstand, *Gramps*. I'm refraining in consideration to your extreme age – I wouldn't want to hurt a doddering old person. Maman won't give two hoots for any of that. Can't wait to see you get your comeuppance at the hands of a fish-lady."

Mak's arm encircled her waist as he laughed in open delight. "Oh, good one Cherith."

"Why you cheeky youngster!"

Cherith echoed Cyn's earlier action, pointing at Old Venny. "And that's another thing – you need an attitude adjustment. Calling Mak a youngling, or a fledgling and labelling me a youngster, is demeaning. We may have plenty to learn and be a lot younger than you, but we're still adults. We deserve to be treated as such, so sleep on that too, Gramps."

DEMAKSIM

$\mathcal{M}$orning sun peeped around the curtains, birds twittering as they went about their business. DeMaksim wondered at the reality of those things; his observations the previous evening made him think the home of Cyn and Old Venny was a massive, made-over cave, its high ceilings catering for a Fae-male who was sometimes a Dracon. Or was that a Dracon who masqueraded as a Fae-male? Old Venny said the home was not on a normal plane of reality, so where'd the windows with sunlight and birds come from?

He could slide out of bed and open the curtains to see, but DeMaksim was loath to move. Cherith was snuggled up, half on and half off his body as she'd been when they camped on the river islet, and he was enjoying her proximity. Unable, and unwilling, to sleep, he pondered their last few days. Here in the Dark Reaches, he'd become Mak: adventurer, historian, Dracon … mate. It felt real, not as if he was hanging around to fill a father-shaped hole if Yanvian Aphiski, the current Duke of Papillion, should die—immortality didn't guarantee you couldn't be killed after all. The Fae Wars 50 years ago were the most recent proof of that. Seelie versus Unseelie. Something he'd never understood. They were all Fae, both variants of the same magical race. His side, the Seelie, were supposed to be honourable, moral and good; on the side of Light. Did it follow then that the Unseelie were dishonourable, immoral, bad and on the side of Dark?

What did that even mean? He'd met Seelie Fae whose honour and morals were heavily tarnished. His youngest sister, Zhulija had met, been courted by, and was now mated to, Dario Eribifax, known as The Unseelie Beast. Dario had shown them strong morals and a high degree of honour – nothing about him was remotely 'bad'. Not in the terms DeMaksim knew.

Now DeMaksim's mate was an Unseelie Undine-Eldwytch – and she was wonderful. Recalling events since meeting Cherith, he agreed with his multitude of greats-Grandpa. Looking down at Cherith's sweet face filled him with a feeling of home; she'd very quickly become his centre, his life goal, his reason for being. Yep, the adorable female in his arms was is true mate. All their physical changes proved it – despite Cherith being Unseelie Fae. Another who didn't fit the immoral, dishonourable and/or bad label. Conclusion? The definition he'd learned and believed in his entire life was wrong. So, what was the real meaning of the gulf between the Seelie and the Unseelie? They were definitely a sundered race. Why? Did Old Venny know?

Ignoring that, he and Cherith were physically tied together in a connection which should've disintegrated when the Nageen died. The search to break the link between Cherith and himself had caused him to stray from his goals of finding answers to his personal physical changes and his draconic ancestry. Yet, the answers he'd been seeking had come to him anyway. He'd discovered who and what he was and he'd stumbled upon Old Venny – ancestors and expectations, who knew?

Head tucked under his chin, Cherith stirred, mumbling incoherently. He swallowed, waited as she sighed and squirmed. Her face scrunched, her head turned a fraction and she rubbed that cute nose against his chest. He'd be lying if he said he didn't enjoy every second of her wake-up; the action in his groin was a giveaway.

Cherith's eyelids lifted; aqua eyes regarded him, deep pools in a river of mystery. Who knew what was beneath the surface until they dived down and became hooked on snags concealed in the depths? All of the best catches lurked in the deeps; anyone who fished could tell you that. *I've been snared and I never knew how wonderful it would be.* The thought came out of nowhere, seizing him. He couldn't take his eyes off her. Not just his mate; he was in love.

"Mak." A tiny smile curled her mouth.

"Good morning, Cherith." He smiled back. They had the rest of their lives together – as soon as they rid themselves of the Nageen's binding. "We've got to get moving. Convey the antigeen blossoms to your father as quickly as possible. The tie is a complete nuisance we've got to dispose of so we can be free to live our lives."

Rubbing her eyes, Cherith ducked her head. When she raised it again, the smile was gone. "Freedom. Yes, absolutely. No time to waste. Today – no, tonight is All Hallows' Eve and you planned to be with your family. Let's get moving and give you a chance to get there – you could still make it if you fly in your Dracon form." She sounded cheerful.

As they eased from the bed, poured water from the ewer into the basin and took turns washing, she continued to sound joyful. DeMaksim stood with his back to her, giving her privacy to wash as she chattered. She shared information about the plants and blossoms she nurtured, both up and down the river. She hummed. When it was his turn to wash and clean his clothes with a whisper of magic, she politely turned her back to him, her talk returning to his family and how he must miss them. DeMaksim couldn't get a word in, never mind talk about a shared future. She appeared driven, determined, unapproachable. He was left scratching his head.

Over pancakes with hot syrup and fresh berries, Cyn brought up the concept of flying again. "It'd be much easier descending to river level, save a lot of time, Cherith. Would you reconsider? Tied to Mak as you are, you can't possibly fall."

Swallowing a mouthful, Cherith laid her spoon down. "I know I'm being squeamish, especially with Mak on a time-line."

Cyn wrinkled her nose. "Time-line?"

"He told his folks he'd return for their All Hallows' Eve celebrations." Old Venny spoke around a mouthful of pancake, his eyes flicking from Cherith to DeMaksim. "That won't happen."

Cherith glared. "It will if he flies. So I will fly."

"Excellent. But you'd have to go too." Another mouthful of syrupy pancake filled Old Venny's mouth.

"Not if we meet Papan and get the potion to rid us of these bonds." Cherith's hands covered her hips. "Anyway, Mak should take you, not me – you're the draconic ancestor."

DeMaksim, hand dragged along, prodded her hip, his voice crisp. "I'm not going home, so this argument is pointless."

Cherith's glare deepened. "My thoughts are not pointless!"

"No, they're not. I apologise." DeMaksim watched her. "If I was to take anyone, my choice would be *you*, okay? Now, are the flowers we picked last night still okay? Or do we need fresher blossoms?"

Mouth open, Cherith stared at him.

"Take both old and new." Cyn drew everyone's attention as she pointed from plate to plate and gestured; the plates stacked themselves. More gesturing moved the stack across the room to a distant workbench. "Some potions need fresh stuff and others are fine with dry."

"True." Cherith grinned. "Levitating dishes away – I like it." DeMaksim relaxed, pleased her ire had vanished.

Cyn laughed. "It's always been a good party trick." She beckoned her mate, who was rolling another pancake ready to eat. "Come on darling, eat that and let's get moving. I'd like to inspect my new lawn ornaments in daylight."

Everyone laughed. Old Venny chomped the pancake, swallowed and wiped his mouth with his napkin as he led the way across the room to the large rug below a niche in the cave wall.

DeMaksim frowned. "You're sure it's safe?"

Old Venny grinned. "Don't worry, the experience will be nothing like last time. Just follow Cyn and I. Here's a pack to put the fresh antigeens in. I've put last night's crop inside already, along with some food." Brows knitting, staring as if he could see right through the rock, Old Venny finally nodded. "It's safe outside. Let's go." Seconds later, he and Cyn vanished.

Despite feeling dubious, DeMaksim clasped Cherith's hand, grabbed the new pack and took the first step. They were immediately surrounded by white fog, but a pace later the sunny meadow materialized. DeMaksim squeezed Cherith's fingers gently. "Let's grab some fresher antigeens." As they picked the white blossoms, Cyn wandered over to the large frozen Redcap statues. She gave them a thorough inspection, her expression oddly delighted.

Old Venny approached as they finished. "Got the flowers? Good. Morph and let's get down to the river. Cherith can immerse herself as her Undine side needs." Cocking his head, he studied her. "Although, you still look as fresh as if you'd just left the water."

Cyn sauntered up, peering at Cherith. "How do you feel?"

"Fine." Cherith pursed her lips. "It's weird, but I feel as if I've recently been in water."

DeMaksim shrugged. "We'll play safe and stick to the plan. Stand back while I see if I can shift." Reconstructing his Dracon in his mind, he thought about becoming it. A tingle chased over him, the world blurred in sparkly mist and he was Dracon standing in the sunshine. Noticing Cherith dangling from his foreleg, he hastily cupped her in his other paw and helped her scoot astride his forearm.

She clutched him tightly. "Thanks."

"Good job." Old Venny's voice issued from the large draconic form taking up space nearby. He wore iridescent black scales, bat-like wings and, like DeMaksim, had three horns on his skull. "Told you things'd be fine."

Smoke plumed from DeMaksim's nostrils. "As long as I can change back."

Old Venny rolled his eyes. "Come on, Cyn." He crouched, extended a forepaw and helped her climb into place astride his neck.

"Hey." DeMaksim eyed Cyn. "You're Lepidopter-Fae – you're not using your wings?"

"My little ones against draconic wings?" She hooted. "You're crazy to think that'd work." Old Venny shook his head.

DeMaksim sighed. "Of course, never thought of that." Old Venny spread his wings, crouched low and launched into the air. DeMaksim dropped his gaze to Cherith. "You still okay with this?" She nodded, so he opened his wings and leapt skyward in pursuit of the black Dracon.

Gaining some height, he flew across the meadow, cleared the cliff and circled above the Mirkdowd River. Lower down, Old Venny and Cyn landed on the far bank. DeMaksim spiralled down to join them, touching down gently on the sandy shore.

Cherith peered at him. "Can you take me to the water?"

"Right." DeMaksim strode to the river, waded in, then sat, moving his foreleg closer to the water.

"Thanks, that's perfect." Cherith slid sideways into the current until she was submerged before floating to the surface. She scrunched water from her hair.

"With the mating changes, does it feel as good as it usually does … being in the water?"

"Yes." She sighed. "Even though I don't seem to need it as much as before, it's still nice. It's where I belong." She looked away, bit her lip, staring downstream. He wished he knew what she was thinking when she looked like that. He was about to ask when her gaze sharpened.

"What's that?"

"Company." Old Venny moved closer. "Saw them a few moments ago."

"Them, who?"

"Cascade and Beckett."

"What? Why?"

The elder Dracon raised eyebrows. "Looking for you, perhaps? They're your siblings. Unless you think they've ventured this far on a casual swimming expedition?"

DeMaksim fought to restrain laughter, but when Cyn chuckled, a snort of mirth escaped.

"Yeah, yeah, very funny." Cherith curled her lip. "But if Cassie and Becks are looking for me, it's because something's wrong."

15

CHERITH

"Your brother and sister only speak to you when something's wrong?" Surprise permeated Mak's voice.

Cherith huffed a laugh. "No, I should have said important, not wrong."

Mak flexed his claws as Cherith's siblings approached. "What are they doing?"

Cassie and Becks had stopped a good distance away, Becks scowling, while Cassie hugged her Narwhal tusk dagger.

"Hmm." Cherith frowned. "I have no idea."

"It's the company you're keeping." Old Venny sat back on his haunches. "How harmless do you think we look, Mak?"

"Oh, yes, of course." Cherith nodded. Dracons were considered a myth and yet, here were two; no wonder Cassie and Becks maintained distance.

Becks cupped hands around his mouth and called, "Cherry? Everything okay?"

Cherith waved. "Yes, I'm with friends; it's safe to join us." Becks and Cassie swam slowly toward them, their eyes flickering to each person waiting in the shallows. Cherith surged forward as far as their linked limbs allowed. Mak, for his part, lowered his bulk in the water trying to appear smaller, less threatening.

Cherith and her siblings hugged, their smiles huge. "It's so good to see you both. But Cassie, weren't you supposed to be with Papan helping him prepare to make the potion?"

Cassie's smile dropped away like falling leaves. "Oh, Cherry! I didn't even get to tell Papan about the potion because River King Eskavon arrived and took Maman and Papan hostage. He wants to exchange them for you and Mak!" Her gold skin was cream-pale, her hands twisting constantly around the handle of her Narwhal tusk. "He said you're a traitor and you ran off with Mak. I told him about the crazy Nageen linking you together, but the only proof is a frozen statue, so he didn't believe me. He said he's never heard of anyone with power like that and—" Cassie tossed up her hands. "He's just crazy!"

"Becks?" Bewilderment rang in Cherith's voice.

"It's true." His lips firmed. "He arrived accompanied by a squad of Nixies."

"Headed by Aquinal." Cassie grimaced. "I can't imagine why that Nixie got mixed up in this."

Cherith glanced at her sister. "He's probably following orders, but that's irrelevant, right now."

Becks shot Cherith a grateful glance. "We left right away to find you and Mak."

"But Cherry!" Cassie clutched Cherith's arm. "Where *is* Mak? If we're to save Maman and Papan, we need him! Where is he? How did you get free? Are these Dracons? Is that Cyn, Old Venny the tinker trader's mate? Did the Dracons eat Old Venny and Mak?"

Rolling his eyes, Becks splashed his sister with water. "By Eletherion and the River Goddess, Cassie! Stop panicking and let these people speak. It's obvious that Cherry and Lady Cyn are completely unharmed and, by the way the black Dracon is laughing, I think it's safe to say you've invented a load of quicksand."

Cassie burst into tears. "I'm sorry!"

"Shh." Cherith hugged her as best she could with one arm and saw

Becks staring over her shoulder. He studied the binding at her wrist, followed the link to Mak, his gaze rising up Mak's gleaming foreleg to the scaled and feathered head.

He stared hard at their wrist-foreleg proximity, then cocked an eyebrow. "Since you're attached to Cherry, I'm going to take a wild guess that you're Mak?"

"Correct." Mak extended his other foreleg. "Heir-Lord DeMaksim Yanvian Aphiski at your service, although, you can just call me Mak."

Becks tried to clasp Mak's paw in his hand, but could only manage a single claw. "A pleasure to meet you. I'm Junior Mage Beckett Mornenion Beriaden, known hereabouts as Becks." Eyes gleaming, Becks switched his gaze between Mak and Old Venny. "You two are really something amazing. Clearly, the report of the demise of Dracons is completely fabricated."

"Well, now that the secret's out …" Old Venny waded forward, Cyn still perched around his neck. "I'm Venstilarquon. You already know my mate Cynamelle." Becks stiffened, peering at him, then up at Cyn and back. He did a double take, his mouth falling open.

"Old Venny?"

Behind Becks, Cassie choked, her hands flying to her cheeks. "You're *Old Venny*?"

"Been a while, Becks." The black Dracon winked.

"All this time …" Becks shook his head. "By Eletherion, you *do* know how to keep a secret."

Old Venny's eyes rolled. "As you say. Now what's this nonsense about Eskavon?"

"Nonsense?"

Venstilarquon the Black snorted. "When you've been around as long as I have, you've seen a lot of supposedly intelligent people do some damned stupid things. Apparently Eskavon is proving my point."

"Well, this time his 'nonsense' involves my family." Becks looked towards Cherith and Mak.

Mak nodded. "Since the Seelie and Unseelie Fae are currently at peace under the combined rule of Queens Dianathke and Maerovana, this is senseless."

Cherith could only shake her head. "River King Eskavon, as Unseelie Fae, is subject to the joint Queens' rule – so what wasp's gotten into his trousers?"

"He's calling Mak a Queens' spy." Becks frowned.

Old Venny wrinkled his snout. "My hunch? He's not happy about Fae unity."

"Blue blazes." Mak swiped claws through the water, the corners of his mouth pinched. "Either he's gone mad or he's a rebel. Dario needs to know – keeping the Fae peace and locating rebels are within his jurisdiction."

"Dario?" Cassie licked her lips. "Are you referring to dreamy Lord Dario Eribifax, The Unseelie Beast?"

Mak's stare drilled into her. "I'm talking about Duke Dario Eribifax Garadenya, true mate to my sister, Zhulija."

"Oh, sorry, I meant no offense." Cassie's chagrin flushed her cheeks. "Sometimes news is slow to spread through the Dark Reaches." She smiled nervously. "A true mating, how lovely, and he's your brother-in-law? You must be thrilled."

Cherith sighed, ignoring Mak's chuckle. "Alright Cassie, stop now before plunging any deeper into the foot-in-mouth whirlpool you've created."

"There are bigger problems." Becks frowned at Cassie.

Cassie tucked hair behind an ear. "I know. We've got to free Maman and Papan without giving over Mak and Cherry. Not to mention that Papan can't make a potion from the antigeen flowers while he's a prisoner and if we trade Mak and Cherry to free Papan to make the potion, they won't be able to use the potion because they'll be prisoners instead. We don't want that to happen, because neither Cherry nor Mak have done anything wrong and, anyway, who'd want to be at the mercy of someone who's a madman or a criminal?" She flung her arms wide, smiling hopefully. "Right?" Her smile faltered when she caught everyone staring.

Becks shook his head. "Cassie, sometimes I really … never mind. You're mostly right despite that confused rambling."

Old Venny tapped a claw against his jaw. "A paradox. We need to decide what we're going to do. Anyone got any ideas?"

Mak eyed Becks. "When the River King attended the arrest of your parents, did he give terms or instructions?"

Becks' mouth twisted. "His instructions were to meet at the Whortlebog, at dawn tomorrow for an exchange. If we don't comply within an hour of dawn, he said he'd kill Maman. If we haven't arrived by noon, he'll kill Papan too."

Cherith gasped.

A cloud of smoke issued from Old Venny's nostrils. "He's definitely crazy if he plans to kill both hostages when doing that will not only alienate his own people, but start a war with the Eldwytch."

"So, we've got about 18 hours." Mak hummed, thoughts churning. "How fast can we fly, Gramps?"

"Hmm." Old Venny's eyes narrowed. "It's only a couple of hours to reach Whortlebog, but that's not what you're asking, is it?"

"No. Is there enough time for you to reach Castle Synternesse, alert Queen Maerovana and maybe bring her and a couple of warriors back, while I fly home to collect Dario and Papan?"

Old Venny squinted. "That'd work."

Cassie glared, smacking the surface of the river with her palms. "What good will that do? You'll just be bringing a whole lot of important people here to watch my family die!"

Becks reached for her arm. "Think Cassie. They're also some of the most powerful people amongst the Fae and we'll have the element of surprise. Eskavon won't be expecting to confront Queen Maerovana or the Unseelie Beast – we might have a chance."

"Might?" Cassie flung her hands high.

Cherith scowled. "Do you have another plan, Cassie? Because, right now, nobody else does." Cassie covered her face with her hands, shaking her head.

Frown easing, Old Venny turned back to Mak. "If we leave straight away, we'll give our reinforcements time to make whatever preparations they require. It'll also give us a few hours to rest up before flying back." Old Venny squinted. "If you begin the return journey in the early hours of tomorrow morning, you'll be here early enough to further throw Eskavon off-balance by setting up at the Whortlebog first."

Cyn cleared her throat. "Venny, we should take Cassie and Becks back to our place for the tonight. There's no point us going to the Whortlebog early, and you'll be better able to concentrate if you know I'm safe."

"Excellent idea." Old Venny nodded. "Come on, you two, climb up behind Cyn and I'll drop the three of you off outside our door. Mak, you and Cherith get going."

"Wait, where will we meet?"

"Look for a draconically shaped rock in the forest not far from the Whortlebog. Be there at least an hour before dawn."

"Okay." Mak grinned. "Hey Becks, Cassie, watch out for that first step across the portal at Cyn and Venny's – it's nasty!"

Cyn gurgled a laugh.

Old Venny's mouth twisted. "Smart arse!"

16

DEMAKSIM

*H*ours later, DeMaksim spied the Rubiconia River, worked out exactly where he was along its meandering length and swung south to fly past Garadenya Island, now the Duchy of Garadenya. Banking to the right, he glanced down at Cherith. She was supine on his foreleg, arms and legs wrapped around him. Every time he'd checked, she was intent on the panorama below. He smiled wryly; huge progress from her previous fear of flying.

"You doing okay, Cherith?"

"Yes! Is that Garadenya Island? I thought that's where The Beast lived now." They'd not flown far when she'd astonished him by communicating with him via their minds, explaining that she'd followed the trail he'd blazed during his portal fight. It was the best way to talk when atmospheric winds, combined with flight speed, made verbal speech impossible. Another mating perk.

"It is, but we're going to the Papillion Duchy — I've realized they'll all be there preparing for tonight's All Hallows' Eve celebration and bonfire."

For the first time since their departure, she twisted her head to stare at him, eyes huge. *"Your home. With all your family."*

"That's right."

518

"But – all your family! And you're stuck to me! We've been forced into mating and—"

"I don't think that matters right now, does it?" It certainly didn't matter to him. Especially not since finding out they were true mates. Although, if he was truthful with himself, he hadn't even minded it before that either. But did Cherith? She seemed so focused on them being separated. In her mind were they simply tragically tied together by the mating strings of a now dead Nageen? His heart sank. Maybe she didn't want to accept the true mating.

Her head dropped to his paw. *"What will your family think of me?"*

"You're adorable – they'll love you." Just like he did. There wasn't any aspect of Cherith he didn't delight in. Considering there'd been no choice but to live in each other's pockets, that was saying something. He hoped she felt affection for him, at least.

The Papillion Estate hove into view. *"There! That place with all the gardens, the fences and gates stretching along the river. The one with the huge house – that's the part of the estate we've cultivated to live on."*

"River Goddess! That's your home? It's amazing. And massive. No wonder your Papan requires help to manage it."

"Estate management is the last thing on my mind right now." The wind whipped her laugh back to him as he dropped height and crossed the boundary.

BOOM!

Powerful force-waves catapulted them backwards across the sky. Cherith screamed as her body was tossed outward in a wide arc around their link point. Wings stretched agonisingly, DeMaksim bunched his muscles and fought his way out of a somersault to level out, heart in mouth as he saw Cherith dangling. *"Cherith!"*

Swinging her left leg over his foreleg, Cherith began climbing. DeMaksim reached with his other paw to help her. *"I'm sorry, I forgot the make-up of the protective field. I thought it'd still know me, but it mustn't have recognised my draconic form."* He banked to avoid the still looming boundary.

Her grip firmed. *"Or me at all."*

"I thought it'd be okay because you're with me – I'll land and change shape."

By the time he touched down outside the gates and morphed back to his Fae-male form, the entrance was swamped by a crowd, with the guards trying to organise some semblance of control.

"They probably heard the explosion leagues away." DeMaksim ran fingers through his hair, sifting and settling the unruly mass. "Papan will have visitors for days wanting to know what the ruckus was."

"Something to talk about." Cherith grinned, fluffing her hair. "I believe it's called a nine-day wonder."

He swallowed. "You're taking the explosion calmly."

Cherith straightened her dress. "I knew you'd save us." Her eyes met his, staggering him with the trust and acceptance in their depths. Gulping, DeMaksim closed his eyes, re-opening them to find her on tiptoe, mouth puckered as she aimed a kiss for his cheek. He twisted, ensuring her lips landed firmly on his, savouring the delicious contact until she dropped back to even footing, staring up at him with soft, doe-like eyes. When her fingers rose to caress her mouth, he reached for her, unable to resist the lure of more, but she swallowed, glanced over his shoulder and shook her head. "Company coming."

Turning, he beheld his father striding towards them. Next to him was Dario, a phalanx of guards close behind.

"DeMaksim!" His father hugged him, then turned to survey Cherith with combined curiosity and fascination. "I'm so very pleased you're here. We were getting worried. We'd heard nothing since you left Castle Synternesse."

"You made it!" Dario smiled, extending his arm for a clasped forearm greeting. "I'm glad you're home today, because Zhu said if you weren't, she was off searching tomorrow."

"There was no way to send messages." DeMaksim drew Cherith nearer. "This is Lady Cherith Beriaden – we've shared adventures which are still ongoing. Cherith, my father Duke Yanvian Aphiski of Papillion and Duke Dario Eribifax of Garadenya."

"A pleasure, Lady Cherith." Duke Yanvian bowed over her hand.

"Likewise." Dario grinned as he welcomed her.

Cherith blushed. "Thank you both."

Duke Papillion's eyes narrowed. "Was that boundary explosion connected to you? Or should we look further afield?"

"Something chasing you?" Dario's expression was wicked. "I'll save you."

"Perhaps I need saving from myself." DeMaksim's laugh was hollow. "No, I caused the explosion." Dario's brows winged up.

"You?" His father frowned. "But the wards are set to recognise family."

DeMaksim shook his head. "Unless family doesn't look like they're expected to."

"Hmm." Duke Papillion rubbed his chin. "I think we'd better go inside for this story. Besides, your mother and your siblings want to see you."

"Good idea. It's a lengthy tale; easier if I only have to tell it once, especially given time is of the essence. And I'd like to introduce Cherith."

DeMaksim was effusively welcomed by the gathered crowd as they entered the Duchy's gates. Eyes wide, he waved, gripping Cherith's hand supportively as they moved towards the house. Stepping into the foyer, DeMaksim laughed as a new, smaller crowd – comprised of all his sisters and his brother – encircled him and Cherith, all talking at once.

A small bell rang, crystal clear tones transcending the din. At once, the hubbub ceased; the siblings fell back to make a path for their mother. Duchesse Azura's broad smile revealed even white teeth and dimpled cheeks. "DeMaksim! I'm so pleased you're home safely." She drew him in for a hug, pulled his head down and kissed his cheek. Hugging her in return, he noticed when she turned her head to smile at Cherith. "Hello, my dear. Welcome to our home." DeMaksim eased up on the hug, but kept his mother in the circle of his left arm.

"Maman, everyone, this is Lady Cherith Beriaden." His lips turned up warmly as he gazed at his companion. "Cherith, meet my mother: Duchesse Azura, my sisters: Duchesse Zhulija, then Lyssica, Janeska, Tindresse, Armelle and my brother Treymeron."

"Lovely to meet you all." Cherith's smile faltered as everyone spoke at once, creating a cacophony of sound in which nobody could be heard, let alone understood.

To DeMaksim's relief, his mother chimed her crystal bell again. "That's enough. We'll adjourn to the large parlour where everyone will please remember their manners and take turns speaking. Poor Lady Cherith is probably ready to flee." As the foyer emptied, DeMaksim caught sight of Dario, arms crossed.

The Unseelie Beast smirked. "Lots of emotion – last chance to escape."

"Only if Cherith wants to."

"What? Joined at the hip already?"

Cherith raised her hand, drawing DeMaksim's along with it. "No Duke Beastly, just at the wrist." She started down the hall with DeMaksim, who chuckled at Dario's astonished expression. "This I've got to hear!" Dario's hasty footsteps echoed behind them as DeMaksim guided Cherith to the large sitting room.

Once everybody had seated themselves, DeMaksim related his adventures, encouraging Cherith to join in and tell her side of the story. They omitted some private parts but his family listened wide-eyed, fully attentive to every word. When he finished, everyone stared at him in amazement.

Duchesse Azura spoke first. "You can turn into a Dracon? The family rumour is true then!"

"Forget that," Lyssica blurted. "You're mated?"

He nodded. "By the Nageen."

"At least you killed her." Dario nodded. "Good job. She was off her rocker."

"I don't think that's the truly important bit," Zhulija said. "What about Lady Cherith's parents?"

Duke Yanvian cleared his throat. "Zhulija is right. Even if you didn't need Lady Cherith's father to make a potion to break the Nageen's spell, I would wish to come and help rescue her parents. This business with River King Eskavon cannot be allowed to continue. We sacrificed too many lives in the Fae Wars to have the still fragile peace destroyed."

"Absolutely right." Dario frowned. "If he's not a major player among the malcontents, I'd be very surprised. How long did it take you and Lady Cherith to get here, DeMaksim?"

"Four hours, give or take."

Dario's eyebrows rose. "That's good going. Without draconic wings, your father and I won't be as fast on the return."

"That's why I'll carry you both on my back."

Duke Yanvian looked doubtful. "It won't be too much for you?"

DeMaksim chuckled. "No. You'll understand when I change forms."

Duchesse Azura clapped her hands. "Good. I know you'll want to talk and plan, but there's no reason why we still can't continue with tonight's All Hallows bonfire ritual – especially now everyone is home." She looked hopefully at his father. "It's important."

Yanvian smiled softly at her. "Of course my dear. In times of trouble, our traditions are what give us comfort and strength."

His mother clapped her hands together and stood. "Wonderful. You can spend the afternoon planning and then still have time to prepare for tonight."

They spent the afternoon going over the plans with his father and Dario, finessing everyone's role and utilising Dario's expertise in war-strategising. DeMaksim kept squeezing Cherith's hand every time it found its way into his, her worry a rasping in his heart. He understood. He was worried too and they weren't his parents.

They had a subdued dinner with the family and then everyone helped complete the decorations for the All Hallows' Eve celebration before heading out to the specially crafted area where the bonfire was held and where they would share their ancestor stories.

DeMaksim found himself seated, with Cherith and the rest of his family, facing a specially created bonfire in one of the gardens. Hung from poles around the bonfire were hand-carved lanterns containing beeswax candles. He was home for All Hallows' Eve – something he hadn't expected but found himself pleased about. Especially now he had Cherith with him. Each member of the family took turns discussing the ancestor they'd chosen to study from their extensive family tree. The ancestor's name was aired, their life expanded upon, then toasted with a sip of whisky-nectar. When DeMaksim rose to speak, he couldn't help smiling.

"On this All Hallows' Eve, more than any other, I give thanks for my family members, Venstilarquon the Black and his mate Cynamelle Neptulidae, for creating offspring. From their union came our own lives. Long live all family and may our lanterns light their way home!" He raised his glass of whisky-nectar in salute, waited as each member of his family did the same, took a sip, then tossed the rest of the drink on the bonfire. His actions were echoed by everyone, in the ritual they'd created to honour their family members, past and present.

"May our lanterns light their way home!"

17

CHERITH

Cherith enjoyed sharing the bonfire ritual with Mak's family; they were friendly and welcoming. The title of 'Lady,' with which they'd all addressed her had been dispensed with as quickly as she could say: 'call me Cherith or Cherry.' Eventually the fun wound down and the others began to wander back to their rooms hoping to get some sleep before it was time to depart.

"Cherith, it's bedtime."

Mak's soft voice had her straightening and nodding. "Good idea." Not that she thought she could sleep, even though she was exhausted. Too much had happened, and her mind was too full of everything that could go wrong. Mak clasped her free hand in his, long enough to pull her to her feet and turn them towards the house. As they walked, Duchesse Azura joined them, tucking her arm through Cherith's, snugly supportive.

"Thank you for a lovely evening, Ma'am."

"You're very welcome, Cherith." The Duchesse smiled. "I'd like to offer you the choice of sleeping in the guest room."

Mak sighed. "Maman, I've already explained about the binding. Did you forget?"

"No dear, I just thought Cherith might prefer something prettier than your male kitted out room. You'd have to endure the change, for the sake of Cherith's comfort."

"Oh, never thought of that. Where would you like to sleep?" he asked Cherith.

She shook her head. "I've no wish to be any trouble, just somewhere neat and clean."

"My room's not clean, Maman?"

Duchesse Azura stiffened. "DeMaksim Yanvian Aphiski! Of course your room's clean and fresh! What sort of housekeepers do you think we have here?"

"Sorry, Maman. I meant no insult ..." When Cherith squeezed Mak's fingers, he trailed off.

"I appreciate the kind thought, Ma'am, but I don't mind staying in Mak's room."

"Are you certain, dear?"

"Yes, thank you." Cherith stifled a laugh at Mak's huffed out breath. "I'm sure I'll be very comfortable."

Duchesse Azura stopped at the foot of a set of stairs. "Very well, I'll say goodnight. Sleep well." She hugged Cherith, then Mak. "I'm thrilled to see you safe, son; and your lady is lovely."

Mak returned the hug, kissing his mother's cheek. "Thanks, Maman. See you in the morning."

Echoing Mak's words, Cherith climbed the circular stairs by his side. The carpeted marble stairwell led to a suite of three rooms in one of the turrets built into the large, rambling, multi storey home. They entered a sitting room, which opened into a bedroom. Off that was a bathing room. The suite was decorated in shades of cream, old gold, rust and jade green; it was welcoming and restful. She bee-lined for the bed, crawled in and made room for Mak as he slid in beside her. "I'm so glad we can magically clean our clothing, otherwise they'd be filthy and reeking by now."

Mak sighed. "They're clean, but I'm mighty sick of them. I've thought about cutting my jacket and shirt off, but I couldn't get anything on over our wrists to replace them. Damn Nageen and her binding."

Cherith nodded, looking away. "Not long before we'll be free of her."

"Yes." Mak stroked her hair. "Try to rest." He continued his soothing motion, but Cherith was too wrought up to relax properly and it was revealed by the tension in her body. He sighed again. "It's not working, is it?"

Wincing, she cracked an eye open. Her face cuddled into Mak's neck; their linked arms were underneath, along with at least half of Mak's body. She mentally face-palmed; she'd ended up sleeping on top of Mak every sleep period since the Nageen had bound them. He must be heartily sick of being squashed. She started to ease away. Mak's hand, the one beneath her, squeezed her leg. Cherith propped herself onto her elbow and peered down. Mak's gorgeous vazel eyes gleamed back at her.

"I know, I'm crushing you again. Sorry."

Mak grinned. "Actually, it's delightful. You're soft in all the right places."

Blushing, Cherith made to pull away, but Mak's other hand cupped her cheek.

"Don't go, please."

She swallowed. "Mak, I know the Nageen messed our lives up but I – I …" She firmed her mouth, gulped, knew this was the moment to tell Mak she wouldn't – couldn't force him to stay with her. "After we save my parents, Papan will make our potion, the link will be nullified and you'll be free again."

He shook his head, one finger stroking the side of her face. "I don't wish to be free of you, Cherith."

She bit her lip. "I – we – you – I understand you think we're mates because, well because Old Venny said so. But really, it's likely just something caused by the Nageen's mating strings."

"I don't agree – is that really what you think?" He shook his head. "After pondering Old Venny's words and carefully considering all of the changes we've gone through, I know we're mates. The signs are unmistakable but you're in denial for some reason." He tilted his head. "If you don't want to be mated to me, I'd be horribly disappointed, because you're amazing, adorable and wonderful. I've fallen in love with everything about you."

"What?"

"I love you, Cherith."

She stared, lips trembling. "You … you love me?" Her voice cracked.

"With all that I am." He watched her, a slight smile curling his lips, eyes aglow with tenderness.

"Oh, Mak." Happiness washed over her. "I do want to be your mate! I love you too. I just didn't want you feeling trapped and I thought, I thought it was too good to be true. So strange that we're accidentally tied together and we turn out to be true mates."

He laughed, his eyes searching hers. "We're meant to be. You, my gorgeous Undine-Eldwytch, are forever stuck with this Seelie Fae-male Dracon."

"Best deal ever."

They reached for each other at the same moment, their lips meeting with time-stopping intensity. Cherith wound her free arm around Mak's neck, finding his kisses hot, tender; his taste addictive; his scent mesmerising. His free arm encircled her waist, hand moving down to her hip and back to her waist before sliding up her rib cage. Their linked hands were in a constant battle as they fought to touch each other.

Cherith swept her tongue out, licking Mak's lower lip. Mouth opening, his tongue flicked to meet hers in a tangling, taste-teasing duel. She thrilled to the feel of his sex lengthening and hardening against her leg and hip. His free hand left her ribs to pull the shoulder of her dress aside and down, exposing one breast. Cupping it, his fingers rubbed a circle around the tip, then flicked the nipple. Cherith flung her head back, gasping as delightful sensations zinged through her. His head dropped, teeth grazing the tingling peak before his warm, wet mouth nibbled and kissed and licked its way from one breast, nuzzling under fabric to find and tend to her other breast, his hand plumping and stroking and shaping as he went.

The sweet, plundering kisses left her senses spinning and her breasts delightfully sensitive. Desire was a burning ember, coiling low in her belly and sparking up her spine. Cherith wriggled until she straddled Mak fully, then tilted her hips to rub herself against the fullness of his groin. His choked exclamation was music to her ears as she fisted her free hand in his leather jacket and slid against his heavily swollen sex again and again. When his wet inferno of a mouth resumed adoring her breasts, his hand slipped between her legs and pushed aside her underwear, his fingers tickling through her damp curls. He circled the sensitive nub gently but firmly, rubbing and stroking the slick bud, building the intensity, twisting his fingers to find her sweet centre, repeating the actions over and over until she splintered into a million shards of shining glory. Cherith mewed when the fiery pleasure shot through her, whimpered, shivered and shook, before finally sagging in Mak's arms, limp and overcome.

With a throaty sound of approval, Mak raised his head, dragged Cherith close and kissed her again. A series of fierce, open-mouthed kisses across her flesh; tasting and teasing, his lips nibbling and savouring, licking and sucking. Senses sparkling with love and pleasure, she met him kiss for kiss, releasing her grasp on his jacket to slide her hand down to his groin and pluck at his trousers.

"Off." As the intense longing and the electric aching renewed, Cherith's voice was a frantic mumble between the searing tangling of their lips and tongues. "I want to touch you, Mak! I need all of you." She stroked his length; his hips bucked and frustrated annoyance flooded her. "Clothes off!" The command accompanied a burst of her fiery will and to the astonishment of both of them, they were instantly nude.

The passion in Mak's eyes intensified as he savoured her nakedness, his roving gaze almost as physical as his available hand. "You're so gorgeous, my darling, so adorably, unbelievably gorgeous." His fingers returned to her centre, their movement re-igniting sensations of pleasurable intensity. Cherith lunged towards him, kissing and nipping his jaw, his chin, his neck; inhaling the delicious scent that she would always identify as Mak's. Her hand between them, gripped his erection, stroking the rigidity, caressing the soft tip. He moaned, thrusting upwards in her clasp. Propelling her hips forward, Cherith surged along the heated length of him, then back, raising herself so that she could guide him into her desperate, aching core. Mak grasped her hips, helping her seat herself.

They gasped in unison as she flexed around his shaft, sliding down, accepting him into her body, lowering herself until she was fully seated and they were groin to groin. She swallowed, eyes closed, feeling wonderfully, deliciously full.

"Oh, blue bla-azes ..." His words trailed off in a gasp.

Cherith's eyelids drifted open again and she stared into the face of her mate. Words taught to her by her Eldwytch sire surged from her memory into her mouth, spilling from her lips. "You, DeMaksim Yanvian Aphiski, are my mate. I see you. I accept you. I take you as mine and give myself unto you. There is no other, there will be no other. I willingly twine my soul to yours and seal our lives together." Her throat rippled. "Will you say those words back to me, Mak?"

"It would be my honour, darling." With a little prompting, he spoke the vows. As he concluded, the tension snapped taut between them, the pleasure in their bodies spiking until they could do nothing but succumb. He drove up, she pushed down, they pulled back, flexing and repeating the mind-numbing, senses stealing, delight of loving each other until Cherith convulsed, again and again, in helpless rapture. As the waves of bliss overtook her, Mak stiffened beneath her. Her pleasure achieved new heights as he climaxed, pulsing hot and hard inside her, his fingers digging into her hip bones like claws.

Following her instincts, Cherith bared her small fangs and dove on Mak, biting into his pectoral muscles until she drew blood. His claw rose from her hip with traces of her blood decorating the tip. Eyes locked on each other, both smiling, she swept her tongue across her fangs while he sucked his claw.

Lightning struck. A sizzling whiplash shot between them, illuminating their bodies in glorious splendour, creating a glowing mate-cord from one to the other.

"What?" Mak's voice emerged as a croak.

Cherith managed to gasp the words, "Eldwytch mating magic."

"Another thing to be thankful for this All Hallows' Eve."

She nodded. He was right. There would never be another All Hallows' Eve like this one. And even though she was still worried about her parents, in this moment, lying quiescent and content in Mak's arms, she allowed herself not only to feel this moment of happiness, but to revel in it.

Kissing her brow, he held her close, murmuring words of love in her ear until they both dozed.

18

DEMAKSIM

They made love again after dozing for an hour, put the wall to good use on their way to the shower and enjoyed a very long, involved shower before towelling each other off. Their drying took even longer than their washing routine, but they finally reached the point of needing clothes.

DeMaksim traced a finger along Cherith's collarbone and down to one breast. "You magicked our old clothes away somewhere – even if we had them, how do we get them on, over and around this infernal linking string?"

"I don't even know how I disposed of them." Cherith sucked her bottom lip between her teeth and rolled it, releasing it with a smacking sound. "But I magicked them off, so it stands to reason I'd be able to magic them back." Cherith frowned. "Clothes return to us." Nothing happened. She tried a second time, and a third, becoming first concerned. "There has to be a way." Then annoyed. "Why the swamp-slush isn't it working?"

"We'll have to try non-magical dressing." DeMaksim pursed his lips, eyeing Cherith's breasts. "Although our chests will be naked – not so bad for me, but I'd rather keep your loveliness private. Perhaps we can rip a shirt open and pin it back together somehow? Or wind bandages around you ..."

"No!" Cherith bared her fangs in a snarl. "No, no, no! I want us properly dressed. I want clothes on both of us and I want that now!" Both suddenly fully clothed, boots and all, they stood gaping at each other.

DeMaksim looked down. "You did it!" He grinned, then kissed her.

They headed downstairs to meet the others and grab something quick to eat.

Once they were done, everyone crowded out through the door to see him change.

Treymeron shrugged as they walked outside together. "He always showed patches of brown scales, so he's probably brown all over."

Duchesse Azura shook her head. "You haven't been listening Trey; lots of things have changed for DeMaksim since he was last here; one of the most wonderful is how he's brought Cherith into the family."

DeMaksim exchanged a glance with Cherith, who was blushing. "I'll lift you up when I change." She nodded; they both grinned and DeMaksim sought his alter ego, becoming enveloped in a swirl of sparkling fog before coalescing into his opalescent blue-green draconic form. Mouths gaped as he towered over the lot of them, his hide a mix of scales and feathery fronds with Cherith perched on his foreleg.

"Not a brown scale on him from this angle. Your memory's gone." Dario chuckled as he ribbed Trey.

Duke Yanvian massaged his jaw. "Parts of you look like you're draped in weeds, yet it's feathery and scaly too. Amazing!"

Armelle came closer to pat his hide, low on one powerful hind leg. "I think you're some sort of water Dracon."

"Because Cherith is part Undine." Janeska's eyes were wide.

Tindresse had circled completely around them. "But also Eldwytch. So fascinating."

"I agree." Lyssica walked to where Cherith sat. "I'm so glad for you both. Welcome sister."

"Wonderful to see DeMaksim in this form, but it's time to go," Duchesse Azura said, gesturing at the moon which had travelled across the sky, telling them her words were true. DeMaksim helped Cherith make herself comfortable, then crouched to allow his father and Dario to climb up after they'd said farewell to their mates and family. With a bit of manoeuvring, they finally settled on the back of his neck. It felt strange having riders, but their weight wasn't an issue. Bunching his haunches, he leaped skywards, wings drumming strongly for altitude, before he levelled off and struck out for the Dark Reaches.

The journey to the Whortlebog seemed to take forever. The tension rising from everyone permeated the air like a black cloud. Wings beating strongly, DeMaksim scanned the shadowed land below. With draconic night vision he had no trouble identifying the landmarks, and when the Mirkdowd River finally appeared beneath them, his internal clock indicated they were well within their time line. *"Cherith, we're near the Whortlebog: do you know where the Dracon stone is Venny spoke of?"*

She pointed. *"To the east, not far from where Whortle Creek spills out into the bog."* Banking right, DeMaksim flew on. When he saw the signs of a swamp in the distance, he began looking for the Dracon-shaped rock. He dropped closer to the forest, seeking to make himself harder to detect, in case there were enemies this close to the rendezvous even though they were a few hours early.

Spying the rock, he circled once, marvelling at how realistically draconic it appeared, before back-winging down to land in the adjacent clearing. An ancient forest towered around them; massive oaks, elms and ash reached for the sky, some of the green leaves interspersed with reds and oranges as autumn moved in.

As planned, nobody moved while they reconnoitred their surroundings; each of them focusing eyes and senses in different directions and calling soft-voiced acknowledgments after completing their check: "Clear."

Dario spoke from his position on DeMaksim's neck. "I'll dismount first, Yanvian will stand guard, then I'll be on alert while he descends." They'd agreed Dario would take charge since, of the two experienced warriors, he was a current Queen's agent while Duke Yanvian was retired. Crouching low, DeMaksim waited as Dario scooted sideways, then slid to the ground; Duke Yanvian followed soon after.

Lowering Cherith to her feet, DeMaksim swirled back to his Fae-form. "Okay?" She nodded.

Dario gestured. "Okay, into the trees." His low-voiced orders continued. "Mak, Cherith, you're watching from here, look for movement, or anything out of place. Yanvian, scout a shallow left circle around the clearing. I'll do a deeper right circle." Duke Yanvian nodded and within seconds the two Fae-males had faded into the bushes.

Not long after, an unusual flapping breeze in the treetops caused DeMaksim to glance up. A familiar black Dracon appeared from the north-west, flying low. It circled as he'd done, then cruised in to land next to the rock before crouching to unload passengers. First down was a tall Fae-male with tawny hair who quickly unsheathed a sword and, balancing on the balls of his feet, spun slowly.

Venstilarquon the Black snorted a smoke trail. "Stand down, Athys. I don't want you skewering any of my family."

The swordsman retained his vigilance. "We can't be too careful, Ancient One."

"Yeah, but the only people I scent are those we came to meet." Old Venny narrowed his eyes, staring straight at Cherith and DeMaksim, despite them being concealed by trees. "Come out, you two. I won't let Athys stab you." He swung his head to the swordsman. "Put your pig-sticker away!"

As DeMaksim and Cherith stepped from their concealment, the regal female still astride Venny spoke. "Oh, do as he says, Athys. I'm certain his sense of smell is superior to ours."

Athys sighed. "Majesty, I can't protect you if I'm not allowed to do my job." Deep brown eyes settled on Cherith and DeMaksim, flickering over them, assessing, the sword weaving a tight pattern.

Old Venny muttered something unintelligible; Athys responded with a sharp look, but he huffed, lowering his sword. Old Venny nodded. "Mak, Cherith, good to see you. Where—"

"Here." His father stepped from the trees to flank Cherith and DeMaksim.

"Good. What about—"

"I'm here also." Dario came from behind Old Venny.

Spinning with a curse, sword rising, Athys halted as he saw Dario. Sheathing the blade, he stepped to meet the warrior's proffered forearm greeting. "Trust you to sneak up behind me, Beast." He raised his voice. "Micron, weren't you on rear watch?"

Dario smiled mirthlessly. "I made myself known to Her Majesty and Micron."

"That he did." Another male voice, rife with amusement, called from high on Old Venny.

Athys rolled his eyes. "I need to be able to rely on you, Micron."

There came a loud female sigh. "Dario, do help me down. These two could be at it for hours."

Dario bowed. "At once, Your Majesty."

"Both unfair and untrue, Your Majesty." Athys moved to join Dario in helping the queen descend from Old Venny's back. Her hair was a continuous, playful pattern of colour and light as it morphed from golden blonde to pale blue, then all shades of blue to midnight and back again. Bright blue eyes brimming with power and charisma flashed over them all.

"My Queen." Cherith dropped into a curtsy, her linked wrist stretching to where DeMaksim bowed, alongside his father.

"Rise." Unseelie Queen Maerovana rubbed her hands briskly. "Thank you and well-met." She cast amused eyes over Duke Yanvian. "I'll have such fun informing Cousin Dia how one of her subjects is mated to one of mine – again – and her subjects both children of yours, Sir Duke."

"I'm glad that you are enjoying the dichotomy, Your Majesty." Duke Yanvian bowed again. "I'm simply a father pleased to have two children achieve true matings, regardless of the origins of their part- ners. I didn't shed blood for Fae unity, only to turn my back on its fulfillment."

"Well spoken, Duke Papillion." Queen Maerovana twitched the

skirts of her long green gown and turned up the collar of her cloak. "Let's move closer to the meeting point." She glanced at Old Venny who had resumed his Fae-shape and was inspecting the draconically shaped stone outcrop. "Your mate, Lady Cynamelle will be there, with the remaining two offspring of the captives, you said, Venny?"

Old Venny patted the rock, then turned away. "Cyn tells me they've already arrived, but haven't yet found any traces of Eskavon." He gestured east. "That way." Arranging themselves with Dario and Yanvian on point, Cherith and DeMaksim followed Athys, Queen Maerovana, and Micron, with Old Venny bringing up the rear. Moving into the trees, DeMaksim paused, looking back at the large rock dominating the clearing.

"Very detailed rock, Gramps. Is it a carving or a natural phenomenon?"

Old Venny glanced at him, mouth turned down at the corners. "That's Kadendall. One of my sons; he offended the wrong entity. I suppose you could call him a natural phenomenon."

19

CHERITH

Cherith was relieved to arrive where Becks and Cassie waited with Cyn. The trio were seated with backs to tree trunks, an array of large shrubs and bushes separating and obscuring their view of the Whortlebog. Cassie leapt to her feet, bolted for Cherith and hugged her fiercely. "Thank the River Goddess you made it safely Cherry! Hi Mak."

Becks followed. "We—" His eyes widened as he identified Unseelie Queen Maerovana. "Your Majesty!" He immediately bowed. Mouth open, Cassie released Cherith and executed a curtsy.

"I beg pardon, Your Majesty." Her throat rippled as she swallowed.

Queen Maerovana gestured. "Please rise. I gather you're Cascade and Beckett Beriaden?"

Becks smiled. "Yes, Your Majesty. Thank you for assisting us."

The Queen's smile was wintry. "I'm not happy with Eskavon's potentially treasonous behaviour, not to mention him kidnapping loyal subjects. He and I will be having *words*."

Old Venny, his arm around Cyn, barked a laugh. "More than words, I'm thinking."

Queen Maerovana glanced his way. "Very perceptive, Ancient One. Greetings Lady Cynamelle, a pleasure to have your company."

Cyn smiled, curtsying. "Lovely to see you, Your Majesty."

"I wish it was under better circumstances." The queen's fists landed on her hips. "Old Venny told me the basics of the plan, but I imagine you've fine tuned it, Dario?"

"You know your subject too well, Your Majesty."

She waved her hand. "Tell me what you've come up with."

Dario swept his hair behind one pointed ear. "Certainly, Your Majesty. We tried to think of as many scenarios as possible. The Whortlebog has only one area of firm ground, a tongue of land extending into the bog. The plan we go with will depend largely on which direction Eskavon comes from and whether he brings the elder Beriadens with him."

The Queen frowned. "Why wouldn't he have his victims with him?"

"No idea." Dario shrugged. "But it's a possibility we can't ignore. As for direction, he may approach from safe ground or from the bog. Lady Delta is water based but Lord Istondir is not, so if Eskavon brings them through the bog, it'll have to be by boat. There's also the issue of how many he'll have in his retinue and whether those Fae are also traitors, or merely led astray by their River King, thinking they're doing the right thing."

Cassie sounded bewildered. "Why would anyone think kidnapping was the right thing?"

"A very good question." The Queen tapped her foot. "Continue, Lord Dario."

"Right." Dario rubbed his jaw. "As far as we know, Eskavon wants DeMaksim because he's decided Mak is a spy for the joint Queendom – that tells us at least two things. Number one: Eskavon has something to hide; number two: he's not a fan of said joint Queendom. He also wants Cherith because he believes she ran off with the supposed spy, instead of watching him as per orders – even though DeMaksim tells me he was made aware of the Nageen roping Cherith and Mak together."

Cyn shook her head. "Eskavon must be insane. It's inconceivable that Cassie and Becks would be willing to swap their sister for their parents, nor would Delta and Istondir want to be freed from captivity in exchange for any of their children."

"Exactly." Dario grinned at her. "Even if he's annoyed at Cherith's alleged behaviour, he may simply want to chastise her. Unfortunately, thanks to the Nageen, if Eskavon insists on taking Mak, he'll get Cherith too."

The queen levelled Dario with a frosty stare. "Eskavon gets no-one."

Grimacing, Dario returned her gaze. "That's the core of the plan, Your Majesty, but there are no guarantees."

The queen's glare intensified. "That was an order, Beast. Make it so."

Dario nodded crisply. "Our best strategy is to take him by surprise and keep him off balance. If we station people in the trees nearest the land-spit, as well as the bog, we should be able to prevent him escaping. He'll be expecting a party of four people: Becks and Cassie with Mak and Cherith. If you're agreeable, my Queen, I suggest that you wear your hooded cloak, pretend to be Cassie and reveal your true self when you consider it appropriate."

Queen Maerovana's smile made Cherith shiver. When the queen spoke, her voice was just as deadly. "Yes, Dario, I like that part of the plan, but one person wearing a hooded cloak will be a bit odd, won't it?"

"Yes, that's why we brought four cloaks, enough for the whole focal party." Dario smirked. "And, that will hopefully be where he loses control of the situation – he won't be expecting Your Majesty's presence. It'll also be when we discover how deep the rot goes. The rest of us will be positioned with regard to our strengths."

"I already have a cloak."

"With all due respect, Your Majesty." Cherith smiled. "Your cloak is of velvet, while the cloaks we brought are every day wear. It would be better if you matched the rest of the party."

"Smart." The queen nodded approvingly at Cherith. "Of course, I will."

Dario turned to Cassie. "Are you willing to be our bog liaison? Not in the mud, but in one of the fresh water flows that bisect it – with Queen Maerovana masquerading as yourself, you'll be the only water-based person not in the focal party and we need all directions guarded."

"Yes, of course." Cassie's eyes were huge. "But what do I do?"

Dario's lips twisted. "Hopefully nothing, but if things fall apart and you find yourself in the thick of the action, you'll have to act as you see fit. With luck, Becks will be able to assist you." He glanced around. "Everybody will need to react to however the confrontation pans out. Eskavon may surrender, or he may seek to escape. Micron, Athys and I will form a loose circle to prevent Eskavon leaving along the land-spit." Dario glanced at Old Venny and Cyn. "I doubt if there'll be sky action, but if there is—"

"Don't fret, we'll be there backing up whoever needs help." Old Venny gestured. "Cyn's a fantastic archer and she brought along her bow and a loaded quiver."

Dario rubbed his hands. "Another unexpected bonus!"

"I'm nervous." Cassie clutched Cherith's arm.

"We all are, but you'll do great." Cherith smiled at her sister.

Mak gave Cassie an encouraging pat on the shoulder. "Your Maman and Papan will be so proud." Cassie's grip eased, she nodded, smiling weakly.

"Time to go." Dario appeared before them. "Cassie, you ready?"

Cassie saluted. "On it!" With a last squeeze of Cherith's arm, she set off.

Frowning, Cherith watched Cassie disappear into the under-growth to make her stealthy way to the bog; she hoped her sister stayed safe. Sighing, she allowed Duke Yanvian to help her don a cloak, while Dario assisted Mak. By the time she and Mak were ready, Queen Maerovana and Becks were cloaked, hooded and waiting.

Dario looked from person to person. "Everyone's ready? Fine, let's do this."

"Wait!" Cherith grasped Dario's arm. "Shouldn't Mak look like a prisoner? Eskavon won't believe he's here willingly."

"Hmm, good point." Dario scratched his head, glancing around.

"I might have something," Duke Yanvian said, digging into his backpack. "Here." He straightened, holding a length of rope. "Never know when a good bit of rope will come in handy."

Dario's brow cleared. "Excellent!" He formed a loop and pushed it onto Mak's linked hand. "Just hold it, nobody will know the difference until it's too late." He linked the rope to Mak's other hand and formed a second loop. Once Mak had hold of it, he trailed the rope end across to Becks and handed it over. "You're the obvious choice for jailer. You and the queen follow Cherith and Mak as if you're herding them. Good luck, everyone."

Conscious of their escorts, Cherith and Mak walked slowly clear of the concealing forest undergrowth. Before them lay the open ground which continued until it became a tiny peninsula pushing into the Whortlebog. The sky was paling as dawn approached.

The smell of the sulphurous and methane gasses produced by decaying plant matter hit them hard. "Oh, River Goddess!" Cherith switched to breathing through her mouth. "I'd forgotten how intensely it stinks."

"Play your parts." The queen murmured. "There may be watchers." They continued walking in silence until they reached the end of the spit, where they clustered, looking down at the swamp. Beneath them, at the base of the rock was a layer of crusty grey mud; a little further out was clear flowing water, then more mud, followed by tussocks of grass and reeds at the feet of some scrubby, windswept bushes. Beyond, the pattern of mud, water channels, tussocks, reeds and scrub continued across the bog like a convoluted maze, with no people in sight.

"Okay, it's showtime." Becks tugged gently on the rope, voice quiet. "Mak, follow my lead, I'll push you down; pretend you don't want to go, then give in and sit, acting like a reluctant prisoner. Cherry you drop and sit next to him, while Her – ah, um, false-Cassie and I stand sentinel over you."

Holding back a grin as the tiny struggle played out, Cherith lowered herself to sit cross-legged on the ground. She watched Mak glaring up at Becks and 'Cassie'. The latter had her arms crossed.

Becks' gaze darted over Cherith's head towards the forest, then lowered to her. He shook his head. "Stop smiling Cherry."

"I'm trying."

He prodded her with the toe of his boot and started shouting. "And as for you Cherry, you've been really stupid!" Cherith was startled; Becks waved his fist in front of her face.

She reared back. "W-what? Why?" Was that squeak her voice?

"Instead of being a loyal Dark Reaches Unseelie Undine, doing the job laid out for you by your River King, you sided with this spy!" He frowned heavily. "What possessed you? Were you bewitched? If so, Papan could break an enchantment by crafting a potion, but your rank idiocy has caused both Maman and Papan to be arrested. I hope you're pleased with yourself. It's no wonder the River King is incensed."

"I couldn't have said it better myself." Their attention jerked up as River King Eskavon strolled across the spit of land towards them. Behind him marched Aquinal, leading a mixed group of Nixies, Water Sprites, Undines, Kelpies and other Water Fae. Eskavon was clothed in trousers of tightly woven brown bulrushes, a jerkin of green weeds and a cloak that looked like rippling water with foam-bedecked edges. Atop his sandy hair, he wore a crown of a green quartz, studded with small nuggets of gold and gemstones. He shook his head. "Such a disappointment, Cherry, both to me and to your parents." Cherith swallowed. "Nothing to say, sweet Cherry? Tsk, tsk."

Becks cleared his throat. "As you see, Your Majesty, Cassie and I have brought the spy to you. Where are our parents? You said they'd be released."

Eskavon studied him. "You look very Eldwytch, just as your sisters look very Undine." His mouth turned down. "I never trusted Delta after she mated an Eldwytch Mage. Unnatural." He hissed the word. "And mixed triplets?" He hawked and spat. "Even more unnatural. Mixed breeds, mixed sexes in one birth – that is not the way of *my* Water Fae – how can I be certain of loyalty?" He shook his head again. "Cherry has proved my point so aptly with her behaviour." He switched his gaze to Mak and his mouth twisted. "This creature beside you must be the spy who's given us so much trouble. Do you spy for the Queens, Seelie filth?"

"Spy? What in blue blazes?" Mak glared at the River King. "As I've explained time and again, I came here on a personal matter, but I'd like to know how I can be a spy with Fae unity in place? The queens rule jointly over a combined Queendom, so what're you talking about?"

"Fae unity!" Eskavon snarled. "We don't honour that sort of pond scum here! None of my people do if they know what's good for them."

"Is that so, Eskavon?" Queen Maerovana threw back the hood of her cloak, her ever-changing hair glinting in the sunlight. "The vow of fealty you swore, to both myself and my cousin, Queen Dianathke, means nothing to you then?"

He gasped, paling. "Your Majesty!" Behind him, more gasps sounded, followed by lots of murmurs. Most of the Water Fae lowered themselves towards the ground in either a bow or curtsy.

Without taking her eyes from Eskavon, the queen called out to the genuflecting Water Fae. "If you are loyal subjects of the Queendom, you may rise and leave. My knights will confirm your faithfulness and allow you passage once you convince them."

He glared. "They're my people!"

She smirked. "Are they, indeed?" He risked a glance behind him, swearing viciously when he saw the stampede of Water Fae aiming for the forest. A line of fire sprang up, preventing a mass exodus. Three tall figures stood in the only clear passage between the flames. The hair of one of the figures roiled with red flame.

"The Unseelie Beast!"

"A very patriotic subject, Eskavon, unlike you."

Eskavon's lip curled. "A fanny-licker!"

Queen Maerovana pursed her lips, her stare arctic. "An interesting idea, but I've missed my chance – his true mate would probably get very unpleasant if I tried to follow up on it." Her eyes narrowed. "Now, tell me where Lord and Lady Beriaden are?"

Eskavon grinned nastily. "Out there." He waved at the Whortlebog.

"In a boat with a hole in it and they're tied together. If they're not found before the boat sinks, they'll die."

Cherith stiffened as her brother shouted, "That wasn't the deal you made."

"What do I care for deals?" The River King's unpleasant grin broadened.

"How a dishonourable piece of shite like you fooled us enough to command our allegiance, I'll never understand." Cherith bristled. "Anyway, Maman is an Undine, she can't drown."

"No, she won't drown, but she'll starve to death." He paused. "Over a number of days and all while she's bound to the body of her mate – who *can* and *will* drown." He smirked. "So very sad."

Becks went for Eskavon's throat, but Queen Maerovana grasped his arm, even while the River King danced aside. His retreat brought him closer to Cherith; grinning nastily he kicked her lower leg.

Cherith cried out.

"Bastard!" Mak grabbed Cherith's hand, pulling her closer to him.

Becks stared at the Queen. "Why'd Your Majesty stop me?"

"He provoked you on purpose. Leave him to me." She returned her attention to Eskavon, just as he lunged after Cherith.

"You've ruined everything, you little half-breed bitch!" He aimed a knee at her face. "I'll destroy you and kill this Seelie scum you ran away with!"

"Mak is mine." Dodging the knee, Cherith drove her fist between Eskavon's legs.

"Aargh!" The River King bellowed, curling over, hands flying to his groin. His crown toppled from his head to roll across the ground. "My crown!" His voice emerged a tortured croak. One hand cupping his groin, the other reaching for the lost diadem, he staggered a step, then dropped to his knees and fell sideways, writhing in pain.

Stooping, Queen Maerovana caught the bejewelled circlet, looping it over her wrist. "It's no longer your crown, Eskavon. For your crimes, I decree you no longer River King of the Mirkdowd River or its tributaries." She made a violent wrenching gesture in the space between the coronet on her arm and where Eskavon lay. There was a sharp crack which reverberated and echoed from one end of the Queendom to the other. It belled across the sky, roared over the land and ripped through the waters; Queen Maerovana's justice a whirlwind that tore at clothing and sent hair flying as she snapped Eskavon's psychic link to the river kingdom. His drawn-out shriek of agony caused those near him to shudder. The Water Fae still in the clearing fell to the ground, their connection with their King abruptly cut. Cherith staggered, kept upright and conscious by her link to Mak, as everyone else – her siblings included – were felled by the blow.

"You may have been born to this crown," the queen said into the sudden quiet. "But it's still a division of the Fae Demesnes as a greater whole – and the Fae Demesnes are united under the combined crowns of Queens Dianathke and Maerovana. Let all who gainsay us remember this day and beware."

Terror trembling inside her as she took in all the unconscious Water Fae, Cherith turned to Mak. "Maman and Papan – what if the breaking of the crown affected Maman too? They'll drown. We have to find them. Now."

Mak caught her close, his mouth in her hair as he rocked her. "We'll find them, darling. Two of us are Dracons, remember? We'll find them, I promise."

2 0

DEMAKSIM

Morphing to Dracon, he waited for Cherith to settle herself, then leaped for the sky with a massive down-stroke of his wings. *"Watch for Gramps, I need to bring him up to date."*

They scanned the sky, looking for a large winged shape. *"Over there!"* Cherith pointed. Following the angle of her finger, DeMaksim saw the unmistakeable draconic shape. Altering direction, he flew to meet the black Dracon, circling to fly alongside.

"What's happening?" Old Venny tilted his scaled head.

"Cherith's parents are tied up in some sort of sinking boat. Not only that – the queen broke the River King's bond to his people and it felled most of them. We don't know how far the shockwave went. If it felled Cherith's mother, she won't be able to keep them afloat when the boat sinks. They'll die if we don't find them quickly. You go the east and I'll take the west." DeMaksim bellowed.

"Got it." Venstilarquon banked and flew east.

"I'll keep watch my side and you watch the other one." Cherith sounded breathless. The trees and shrubs which survived in the slimy morass made searching more difficult, forcing them to fly up and down the water channels in the bog, following the twists and turns in the maze of mud and water. The search took them further and further from

their starting point, and their efforts startled quite a few ducks and other water fowl, who swam or flew away, quacking or peeping in anxiety as a large creature overflew them.

Hours later, Cherith pointed. *"Could that be them?"* They were searching a side channel, the solid ground of the meeting place nowhere nearby. DeMaksim dropped lower, circling for a better look. Beneath them, a decrepit bark canoe sat low in the water. The bodies of the two people inside faced each other, their upturned faces struggling to stay above the water lapping high on their necks. *"Yes!"* Cherith flung a happy grin over her shoulder.

"They need to see you to understand I'm no danger to them." DeMaksim went in low, with Cherith waving and hallooing madly at her parents.

"How are we going to save them?" Cherith twisted her head to stare anxiously at him.

"Hold tight." Circling again, DeMaksim swooped, snatched the rope binding the trapped couple in the claws of his free paw, then beat his wings strongly, rising with his new burden. Fortunately, their movements were minimal, just enough for DeMaksim to see they were alive. As he circled into a rising thermal, the ungainly canoe beneath, buffeted by the downdraught of his wings, capsized and sank leaving only sluggish ripples to mark the place where it had been.

"Oh, my goddess!" Cherith clasped her throat.

"I've got them." With his extra, very awkward burden, DeMaksim was grateful the way back could be flown in a straight line.

"Look." Cherith pointed again. *"There's your Gramps."* The black dragon coasted to join them; they were surprised to see he cupped a bedraggled and muddy Cassie in one claw.

The tongue of firm land came into view, along with the small rise between the water and the forest. Fae-people sat or lay everywhere, either still or barely moving. Sighting them, a figure DeMaksim identified as Dario, ensured an area near the tip of the tiny peninsula was clear enough for he and Old Venny to land.

"Athys, help needed here!" Dario bellowed towards the forest. The Fae-male stood up and sprinted towards them.

Settling slowly, DeMaksim was relieved when Dario and Athys

slid the bundle of Cherith's parents free of his aching foreleg and lowered them to the ground.

"What's all this?" DeMaksim stared around, at what was now a makeshift camp full of moaning Fae, in bewilderment. He reverted to his Fae form, assisting Cherith to gain her balance when she seemed a bit wobbly.

Dario produced a dagger to cut the wet ropes binding the Beri-adens. "Many of the Water Fae have gone into shock since you left." He looked to Cherith. "How are you coping?"

She looked at him doubtfully. "I'm okay. Just a bit unsteady."

Dario frowned. "Could be you're getting energy from your link to DeMaksim." He turned to Venstilarquon who was crouching to allow Cyn to climb down. "Is that Cassie? She's covered in mud."

"Found her mired in the bog, barely noticed her waving." Old Venny, with Cyn's assistance, laid Cassie gently on the ground. "She hasn't moved much, seems dazed."

Cherith gave a tiny laugh. "Poor Cassie; one of the rescue team and she had to be rescued too!" She stared across at her parents, her heart in her eyes. "Maman? Papan?"

Dario met her worried gaze. "They're alive, but weak. Of the two of them, your Papan is in better condition."

DeMaksim felt her fingers grip his tightly. "He wasn't a subject of the River King."

"That helps. Your Maman is in a similar state to the majority of the Water Fae."

Queen Maerovana arrived. "I've started feeding my energy into the Mirkdowd sub-kingdom loop. There have been no fatalities and I want to keep it that way, but we need supplies.

Venny? DeMaksim? Are you willing to fly some in?"

CRANING HER NECK, Cherith peered into the large kettle simmering over the open-air pit. "Is the potion done yet, Papan?" DeMaksim closed his free hand around her shoulder, steadying her as she stood on tiptoe. *Careful, darling.* She flashed him a loving smile.

Grinning, Istondir Beriaden tapped his daughter on the tip of her nose with one of his long, elegant fingers. "So impatient. It'll be ready when it's ready and not before."

Watching them, DeMaksim was pleased to see Cherith had the kind of close relationship with her parents that he had with his. It made him realise anew that the differences between Seelie and Unseelie were not unbridgeable.

"I hope you're not overdoing things, Papan." Cherith wagged her finger. "You didn't have to prepare the anti-Nageen potion today."

Istondir hugged his daughter. "I'm fine, and a night's rest has done wonders for my state of mind. I'm also delighted to discover such a wonderful son-in-law. The least I can do is help break the Nageen's curse." He waved his hands around. "We've fed and helped all the suffering Water Fae, so I've the time, the ingredients and the inclination." He eyed her. "Perhaps you should sit down, too. You're pale; I know the broken bond with Eskavon must be affecting you as much as it has Cassie, Becks and your Maman."

Cherith glanced lovingly at her mate. "I'm not as badly off as most. Mak has been pushing energy through our link."

"As I said, an excellent choice. I was helping your Maman in a similar fashion after she came close to losing consciousness in the boat. A partnership as well as a mating – the best kind." Istondir clapped an approving hand on DeMaksim's shoulder, before returning to the cooking pot and peering in. "Ah, the colour is changing. Almost done." He stirred the brew with a wooden paddle, watching it gently bubbling. Presently, he ladled the syrupy concoction into a bowl. "You both need to drink some, then pour it over the strings. But let it cool first; it'll scald you right now." He prodded around their joined wrists, long fingers searching. "Huh, I can't see the binding, but I can feel it."

DeMaksim nodded. "I can see it when I'm in my draconic form – not that seeing it is much help."

After the brew was sufficiently cool, Istondir held the bowl out to

Cherith. "Two mouthfuls, then pass it to Mak." She did as directed, pulling a face as she swallowed. Then it was Mak's turn. He tried not to gag over the thick, tasteless brew, then returned the bowl to Istondir. Cherith's father ladled more potion into the dish, then began basting it onto the cords, adding more and more as the potion formed a white lather. The outline of the binding ropes became visible under the froth. "Now we'll wash this off and, with luck, the binding will disintegrate." He looked around, caught sight of his son talking with Dario and Old Venny. "Becks, would you bring a bowl of water, please?"

While Becks fetched water, Old Venny and Dario moved closer.

"Here you are, Papan." Becks carried a wide-mouthed jug. "Fresh out of the river."

Istondir nodded. "Thank you. Please hold it under the lathered area." Becks complied and Istondir firmly pushed Cherith and DeMaksim's lathered wrists into the container. The brew foamed violently.

Old Venny rubbed his hands. "Here we go!"

Cherith gasped as the lather seeped away into the surrounding water. "It's working!" But when, at Istondir's urging, they lifted their wrists from the water, the link was intact – the only difference ...

"The binding's red!"

Cherith's pale face flushed. "But, it's still there! Why didn't it work? What'll we do now?"

"Shh, shh, Cherry," Istondir soothed. "The cords are now visible. We'll lather them again and they'll surely disintegrate."

But they didn't and Cherith burst into heart-rending sobs, tears flowing down her face. Her father and DeMaksim both moved to hug her and when neither backed down, the embrace ended up being three-way.

DeMaksim met Istondir's gaze over the top of Cherith's head; Istondir looked as miserable as he felt. Despite their best efforts, the cursed binding of the dead Nageen still existed. *Are we destined to spend the rest of our immortal lives chained together?* Sighing, DeMaksim dropped a kiss on Cherith's hair. Her tears dripped onto his hand.

Water hadn't worked, maybe his flame? He knew he couldn't harm himself with his flame, but what about Cherith? Old Venny would likely know.

"Hey Gramps? Will my flame harm Cherith?"

Old Venny shook his head. "As I said when you went through my portal, neither you nor your mate can harm each other with your powers – you thinking of flaming the strings?"

"Yes." DeMaksim's brow furrowed. "I haven't tried it because I worried I'd hurt Cherith. Let's try. Istondir, could you move back, please?"

When Istondir joined Becks, Dario and Old Venny, DeMaksim directed a fine stream of flame over the cords. They glowed incandescently, but when he ceased blowing flame, the glow faded, leaving the red strings intact. His heart sank, but Cherith, who'd dried her tears to watch, gasped, clutching Mak's fingers.

"Mak! I think I have the answer!" Her eyes brimmed with excitement. "Remember how we vanquished the Nageen!"

DeMaksim stared at her. "You pushed water, I spat fire and they …" A grin split his face. "Together! Our powers combined and we overcame her together. Of course!"

"Ready?" Cherith grinned up at him. "Now!" Cherith flicked her fingers, creating and throwing magical water while DeMaksim breathed fire at it. A sizzling blue-green wave of icy arctic foam hit the Nageen's rubbery mating strings – turning them crystalline and solid.

Dario gaped.

Becks whooped. "You've turned it to ice!"

"Yes!" DeMaksim crowed. "And ice breaks." He urged Cherith closer to the metal cooking pot and smashed their iced wrists against its lip. Shattering, the ice fell away and the strings were gone as if they'd never been, leaving them unrestrained individuals once more.

"We're free!" Cherith squealed. She flung herself at Mak, grabbing him around the neck with both hands. Mak firmed his arms around her waist and danced them in a circle before stopping to take her in a sweeping kiss. Only easing back when they needed to breathe,

DeMaksim became aware of the grinning crowd. Family members and other Fae, including Queen Maerovana, had gathered, drawn by the excitement.

"Congratulations!" The queen smiled.

As the congratulations died down, the queen pulled them aside. "It was serendipitous the Nageen caught you with her mating strings, despite the problems it caused."

"Yes," DeMaksim said, smiling down at his mate. "Although, I still don't understand how her spell lasted so strongly after her death."

"Ah," the queen nodded sagely. "I think I do. It's because they're imbued with a small part of her life essence just before they're cast; only the Nageen can recall her essence, but having died, she couldn't, leaving the life essence to continue carrying out its programme, to the best of its minimal ability. The entrapment of two people was an added complication it was incapable of dealing with."

"Oh!" Cherith shuddered. "Kind of sad in a way, like she was haunting us."

DeMaksim snorted. "A mindless parasite can't become a ghost, All Hallows' Eve or not."

Cherith shrugged. "No matter now. She and her influence are gone, something we achieved as a team."

"You did." The Queen smiled. "You excel together – true mates, I believe?"

"Yes!" They laughed because they'd spoken in unison.

"Excellent." Queen Maerovana nodded. "I recognise and accept your true mating – we'll have a ball in the not-too-distant future so that you can dance the Rhynfallia and seal the deal." She cleared her throat. "Meanwhile, I've decided you two are the perfect replacement for that traitorous fool, Eskavon. I can't waste any time sorting this out, so I hereby pronounce you River Queen Cherith and Dracon River King DeMaksim – joint rulers of the Mirkdowd River and all tributaries from this moment forth." She raised both hands, placing one on Cherith's chest and one on Mak's chest. From that link, power snapped into place, arcing through them and bowing their bodies. It shot from their pores and out in a growing radius to arc over the suffering Water Fae and rain down upon them in a shower of sparks which were thirstily absorbed into their skins. The change was immediate; Fae-folk crying out in joy, hands on their chests, rejoicing over their restored links to the river and their new rulers.

Cherith focused on DeMaksim, her expression creased with worry. "Mak! You're no longer heir of the Papillion duchy – are you okay with that?"

Framing Cherith's face in his, DeMaksim smiled at his gorgeous mate. "It'll take some getting used to, but the position will just have to move on to one of my siblings." He caressed her cheeks. "I love you, Cherith. You're the person I never knew I needed until I found you in the river and I'll spend the rest of our lives proving it, wherever we are. You complete me."

"Oh, Mak." Cherith nuzzled into the hand cupping her cheek. "I love you, too. To think you, my Seelie Spy, turned out to be my true mate. How many times we've cursed the Nageen and yet, the queen is right: if it wasn't for her tying us together, we might never have guessed the truth."

DeMaksim laughed. "Somehow we would've, darling, I'm sure of it." He kissed her briefly. "But I can honestly say, I'll be happy to never see a Nageen again for as long as I live."

Cherith's aqua eyes sparkled at him. "I'll dance to that."

And they did.

The End.

♥

AUTHOR'S NOTE

Dear Reader,

Thank you for reading Cherith and Mak's story. I hope you enjoyed it. If you missed the story of Zhulija and Dario, you'll find it, with three other wonderful stories, in "A Perfectly Paranormal Valentine".

Reader reviews are wonderful, so if you did enjoy the story, please leave a review. It will be gratefully appreciated.

If you wish to know more about me, I have a website:

www.hellucywrites.com

ALSO BY HELLUCY HOWE

Filigree and Fate
Dario and Zhulija's story in:
A Perfectly Paranormal Valentine

Ancestors and Expectations
Cherith and DeMaksim's story in:
A Perfectly Paranormal Halloween

Blizzards and Beginnings
Lyssica and Emryn's story in:
A Perfectly Paranormal Easter

ABOUT HELLUCY

Meet Hellucy Howe, a Book Dragon who teethed on romantic fairy tales and went on to voraciously devour anything paranormal. Writing was also second nature but became something to do in secret when the stories of her young child mind were ridiculed. Homes were populated with books and hidden caches of story notebooks inspired by a fertile brain and a massive creative streak.

She became a Professional Reader and a Closet Scribbler, convinced no one would want to look at the mad ramblings of someone who hates getting dirt under her fingernails and knows ironing was invented as a torture method.

Nowadays, Helen loves inventing paranormal and fantasy romance from the comfort of her cosy study with a hot cup of tea beside her laptop and her little spaniel, Lexie, snoring at her feet. With her anthology contribution of 'Filigree and Fate', Helen was dragged kicking and screaming from her closet, into the deer-in-headlights world of being a Real Author.

And if you want to get to know the Perfectly Paranormal Anthology authors a bit more, get sneak peeks of what's coming up for the APP Anthologies, as well as giveaways, special offers and just some PNR fun, then join our Perfectly Paranormal Paramours Facebook Group.

Find us here:

https://www.facebook.com/groups/251663560162131

ACKNOWLEDGMENTS

This story is loosely based on traditional fairy tales. There are no mistakes, only design changes and my imagination.

I would like to thank:

- Everyone who encouraged me to write this story.
- My fellow Anthology authors: Leisl, Georgia, Marnie and Samantha
- All my readers
- My daughter Samantha for her constant love and assistance
- My puppy-dog Lexie for her continual devotion and her desire to sit in my lap, even when I'm typing
- My kettle for providing numerous cups of tea
- My chocolate stash for its persistent nagging

LOVE PNR? JOIN OUR PERFECTLY PARANORMAL PARAMOURS FACEBOOK GROUP

If you want to get to know the Perfectly Paranormal Anthology authors a bit more, get sneak peeks of what's coming up as well as giveaways, special offers and just some PNR fun, then join our Perfectly Paranormal Paramours Facebook Group.

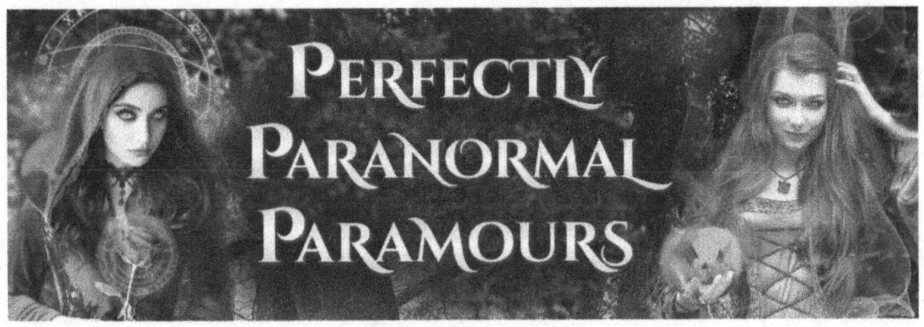

Find us here:

https://www.facebook.com/groups/251663560162131